JOHN GARDNER

GRENDEL

Illustrated by Emil Antonucci

Vintage Books
A Division of Random House, Inc.
New York

Vintage Books Edition, April 1989

Library of Congress Cataloging in Publication Data

Gardner, John, 1933–1982
  Grendel.

  I. Title.
PS3557.A712G7   1985   813'.54   85-40133
ISBN 0-679-72311-0 (pbk.)

Manufactured in the United States of America

73rd Printing

GRENDEL

ALSO BY JOHN GARDNER,
AVAILABLE IN VINTAGE BOOKS

The Art of Fiction
The Art of Living and Other Stories
Gilgamesh
Jason and Medeia
The King's Indian and Other Stories
The Life and Times of Chaucer
Mickelsson's Ghosts
Nickel Mountain
October Light
The Resurrection
The Sunlight Dialogues

For Joel and Lucy

And if the Babe is born a Boy
He's given to a Woman Old,
Who nails him down upon a rock,
Catches his shrieks in cups of gold.

—WILLIAM BLAKE

GRENDEL

I

The old ram stands looking down over rockslides, stupidly triumphant. I blink. I stare in horror. "Scat!" I hiss. "Go back to your cave, go back to your cowshed—whatever." He cocks his head like an elderly, slow-witted king, considers the angles, decides to ignore me. I stamp. I hammer the ground with my fists. I hurl a skull-size stone at him. He will not budge. I shake my two hairy fists at the sky and I let out a howl so unspeakable that the water at my feet turns sudden ice and even I myself am left uneasy. But the ram stays; the season is upon us. And so begins the twelfth year of my idiotic war.

The pain of it! The stupidity!

"Ah, well," I sigh, and shrug, trudge back to the trees.

Do not think my brains are squeezed shut, like the ram's, by the roots of horns. Flanks atremble, eyes like stones, he stares at as much of the world as he can see and feels it surging in him, filling his chest as the melting snow fills dried-out creekbeds, tickling his gross, lopsided balls and charging his brains with the same unrest that made him suffer last year at this time, and the year before, and the year before that. (He's forgotten them all.) His hindparts shiver with the usual joyful, mindless ache to mount whatever happens near—the storm piling up black towers to the west, some rotting, docile stump, some spraddle-legged ewe. I cannot bear to look. "Why can't these creatures discover a little dignity?" I ask the sky. The sky says nothing, predictably. I make a face, uplift a defiant middle finger, and give an obscene little kick. The sky ignores me, forever unimpressed. Him too I hate, the same as I hate these brainless budding trees, these brattling birds.

Not, of course, that I fool myself with thoughts that I'm more noble. Pointless, ridiculous monster crouched in the shadows, stinking of dead men, murdered children, martyred cows. (I am neither proud nor ashamed, understand. One more dull victim, leering at seasons that never were meant to be observed.) "Ah, sad one, poor old freak!" I cry, and hug myself, and laugh, letting out salt tears, he he! till I fall down gasping and sobbing. (It's mostly fake.)

The sun spins mindlessly overhead, the shadows lengthen and shorten as if by plan. Small birds, with a high-pitched yelp, lay eggs. The tender grasses peek up, innocent yellow, through the ground: the children of the dead. (It was just here, this shocking green, that once when the moon was tombed in clouds, I tore off sly old Athelgard's head. Here, where the startling tiny jaws of crocuses snap at the late-winter sun like the heads of baby watersnakes, here I killed the old woman with the irongray hair. She tasted of urine and spleen, which made me spit. Sweet mulch for yellow blooms. Such are the tiresome memories of a shadow-shooter, earth-rim-roamer, walker of the world's weird wall.) "Waaah!" I cry, with another quick, nasty face at the sky, mournfully observing the way it is, bitterly remembering the way it was, and idiotically casting tomorrow's nets. "Aargh! Yaww!" I reel, smash trees. Disfigured son of lunatics. The big-boled oaks gaze down at me yellow with morning, beneath complexity. "No offense," I say, with a terrible, sycophantish smile, and tip an imaginary hat.

It was not always like this, of course. On occasion it's been worse.

No matter, no matter.

The doe in the clearing goes stiff at sight of my horridness, then remembers her legs and is gone. It makes me cross. "Blind prejudice!" I bawl at the splintered sunlight where half a second ago she stood. I wring my fingers, put on a long face. "Ah, the unfairness of everything," I say, and shake my head. It is a matter of fact that I have never killed a deer in all my life, and never will. Cows have more meat and, locked up in pens, are easier to catch. It is true, perhaps, that I feel some trifling dislike of deer, but no more dislike than I feel for other natural things— discounting men. But deer, like rabbits and bears and even men, can make, concerning my race, no delicate distinctions. That is their happiness: they see all life without observing it. They're buried in it like crabs in mud. Except men, of course. I am not in a mood, just yet, to talk of men.

So it goes with me day by day and age by age, I tell myself. Locked in the deadly progression of moon and stars. I shake my head, muttering darkly on shaded paths, holding conversation with the only friend and comfort this world affords, my shadow. Wild pigs clatter away through brush. A baby bird falls feet-up in my path, squeaking. With a crabby laugh, I let him lie, kind heaven's merciful bounty to some sick fox. So it goes with me, age by age. (Talking, talking. Spinning a web of words, pale walls of dreams, between myself and all I see.)

The first grim stirrings of springtime come (as I knew they must, having seen the ram), and even under the ground where I live, where no light breaks but the red of my fires and nothing stirs but the flickering shadows on my wet rock walls, or scampering rats on my piles of bones, or my mother's fat, foul bulk rolling over, restless again— molested by nightmares, old memories—I am aware in my chest of tuberstirrings in the blacksweet duff of the forest overhead. I feel my anger coming back, building up like invisible fire, and at last, when my soul can no longer resist, I go up—as mechanical as anything else—fists clenched against my lack of will, my belly growling, mindless as wind, for blood. I swim up through the firesnakes, hot dark whalecocks prowling the luminous green of the mere, and I surface with a gulp among churning waves and smoke. I crawl up onto the bank and catch my breath.

It's good at first to be out in the night, naked to the cold mechanics of the stars. Space hurls outward, falconswift, mounting like an irreversible injustice, a final disease. The cold night air is reality at last: indifferent to me as a stone face carved on a high cliff wall to show that the world is abandoned. So childhood too feels good at first, before one happens to notice the terrible sameness, age after age. I lie there resting in the steaming grass, the old lake hissing and gurgling behind me, whispering patterns of words my sanity resists. At last, heavy as an ice-capped mountain, I rise and work my way to the inner wall, beginning of wolfslopes, the edge of my realm. I stand in the high wind balanced, blackening the night with my stench, gazing down to cliffs that fall away to cliffs, and once again I am aware of my potential: I could die. I cackle with rage and suck in breath.

"Dark chasms!" I scream from the cliff-edge, "seize me! Seize me to your foul black bowels and crush my bones!" I am terrified at the sound of my own huge voice in the darkness. I stand there shaking from head to foot, moved to the deep-sea depths of my being, like a creature thrown into audience with thunder.

At the same time, I am secretly unfooled. The uproar is only my own shriek, and chasms are, like all things vast, inanimate. They will not snatch me in a thousand years, unless, in a lunatic fit of religion, I jump.

I sigh, depressed, and grind my teeth. I toy with shouting some tidbit more—some terrifying, unthinkable threat, some blackly fuliginous riddling hex—but my heart's not in it. "Missed me!" I say with a coy little jerk and a leer, to keep my spirits up. Then, with a sigh, a kind of moan, I start very carefully down the cliffs that lead to the fens and moors and Hrothgar's hall. Owls cross my path as silently as raiding ships, and at the sound of my foot, lean wolves rise, glance at me awkwardly, and, neat of step as lizards, sneak away. I used to take some pride in that—the caution of owls when my shape looms in, the alarm I stir in these giant northern wolves. I was younger then. Still playing cat and mouse with the universe.

I move down through the darkness, burning with murderous lust, my brains raging at the sickness I can observe in myself as objectively as might a mind ten centuries away. Stars, spattered out through lifeless night from end to end, like jewels scattered in a dead king's grave, tease, torment my wits toward meaningful patterns that do not exist. I can see for miles from these rock walls: thick forest suddenly still at my coming—cowering stags, wolves, hedgehogs, boars, submerged in their stifling, unmemorable fear; mute birds, pulsating, thoughtless clay in hushed old trees, thick limbs interlocked to seal drab secrets in.

I sigh, sink into the silence, and cross it like wind. Behind my back, at the world's end, my pale slightly glowing fat mother sleeps on, old, sick at heart, in our dingy underground room. Life-bloated, baffled, long-suffering hag. Guilty, she imagines, of some unremembered, perhaps ancestral crime. (She must have some human in her.) Not that she thinks. Not that she dissects and ponders the dusty mechanical bits of her miserable life's curse. She clutches at me in her sleep as if to crush me. I break away. "Why are we here?" I used to ask her. "Why do we stand this putrid, stinking hole?" She trembles at my words. Her fat lips shake. "Don't ask!" her wiggling claws implore. (She never speaks.) "Don't ask!" It must be some terrible secret, I used to think. I'd give her a crafty squint. She'll tell me, in time, I thought. But she told me nothing. I waited on. That was before the old dragon, calm as winter, unveiled the truth. He was not a friend.

And so I come through trees and towns to the lights of Hrothgar's meadhall. I am no stranger here. A respected guest. Eleven years now and going on twelve I have come up this clean-mown central hill, dark shadow out of the woods below, and have knocked politely on the high oak door, bursting its hinges and sending the shock of my greeting inward like a cold blast out of a cave. "Grendel!" they squeak, and I smile like exploding spring. The old Shaper, a man I cannot help but admire, goes out the back window with his harp at a single bound, though blind as a bat. The drunkest of Hrothgar's thanes come reeling and clanking down from their wall-hung beds, all shouting their meady, outrageous boasts, their heavy swords aswirl like eagles' wings. "Woe, woe, woe!" cries Hrothgar, hoary with winters, peeking in, wide-eyed, from his bedroom in back. His wife, looking in behind him, makes a scene. The thanes in the meadhall blow out the lights and cover the wide stone fireplace with shields. I laugh, crumple over; I can't help myself. In the darkness, I alone see clear as day. While they squeal and screech and bump into each other, I silently sack up my dead and withdraw to the woods. I eat and laugh and eat until I can barely walk, my chest-hair matted with dribbled blood, and then the roosters on the hill crow, and dawn comes over the roofs of the houses, and all at once I am filled with gloom again.

"This is some punishment sent us," I hear them bawling from the hill.

My head aches. Morning nails my eyes.

"Some god is angry," I hear a woman keen. "The people of Scyld and Herogar and Hrothgar are mired in sin!"

My belly rumbles, sick on their sour meat. I crawl through bloodstained leaves to the eaves of the forest, and there peak out. The dogs fall silent at the edge of my spell, and where the king's hall surmounts the town, the blind old Shaper, harp clutched tight to his fragile chest, stares futilely down, straight at me. Otherwise nothing. Pigs root dully at the posts of a wooden fence. A rumple-horned ox lies chewing in dew and shade. A few men, lean, wearing animal skins, look up at the gables of the king's hall, or at the vultures circling casually beyond. Hrothgar says nothing, hoarfrost-bearded, his features cracked and crazed. Inside, I hear the people praying—whimpering, whining, mumbling, pleading—to their numerous sticks and stones. He doesn't go in. The king has lofty theories of his own.

"Theories," I whisper to the bloodstained ground. So the dragon once spoke. ("They'd map out roads through Hell with their crackpot theories!" I recall his laugh.)

Then the groaning and praying stop, and on the side of the hill the dirge-slow shoveling begins. They throw up a mound for the funeral pyre, for whatever arms or legs or heads my haste has left behind. Meanwhile, up in the shattered hall, the builders are hammering, replacing the door for (it must be) the fiftieth or sixtieth time, industrious and witless as worker ants—except that they make small, foolish changes, adding a few more iron pegs, more iron bands, with tireless dogmatism.

Now fire. A few little lizard tongues, then healthy flames reaching up through the tangled nest of sticks. (A feeble-minded crow could have fashioned a neater nest.) A severed leg swells up and bursts, then an arm, then another, and the red fire turns on the blackening flesh and makes it sizzle, and it reaches higher, up and up into greasy smoke, turning, turning like falcons at warplay, rushing like circling wolves up into the swallowing, indifferent sky. And now, by some lunatic theory, they throw on golden rings, old swords, and braided helmets. They wail, the whole crowd, women and men, a kind of song, like a single quavering voice. The song rings up like the greasy smoke and their faces shine with sweat and something that looks like joy. The song swells, pushes through woods and sky, and they're singing now as if by some lunatic theory they had won. I shake with rage. The red sun blinds me, churns up my belly to nausea, and the heat thrown out of the bone-fire burns my skin. I cringe, clawing my flesh, and flee for home.

2

Talking, talking, spinning a spell, pale skin of words that closes me in like a coffin. Not in a language that anyone any longer understands. Rushing, degenerate mutter of noises I send out before me wherever I creep, like a dragon burning his way through vines and fog.

I used to play games when I was young—it might as well be a thousand years ago. Explored our far-flung underground world in an endless wargame of leaps onto nothing, ingenious twists into freedom or new perplexity, quick whispered plottings with invisible friends, wild cackles when vengeance was mine. I nosed out, in my childish games, every last shark-toothed chamber and hall, every black tentacle of my mother's cave, and so came at last, adventure by adventure, to the pool of firesnakes. I stared, mouth gaping. They were gray as old ashes; faceless, eyeless. They spread the surface of the water with pure green flame. I knew—I seemed to have known all along—that the snakes were there to guard something. Inevitably, after I'd stood there a while, rolling my eyes back along the dark hallway, my ears cocked for my mother's step, I screwed my nerve up and dove. The firesnakes scattered as if my flesh were charmed. And so I discovered the sunken door, and so I came up, for the first time, to moonlight.

I went no farther, that first night. But I came out again, inevitably. I played my way farther out into the world, vast cavern aboveground, cautiously darting from tree to tree challenging the terrible forces of night on tiptoe. At dawn I fled back.

I lived those years, as do all young things, in a spell. Like a puppy nipping, playfully growling preparing for battle with wolves. At times the spell would be broken suddenly: on shelves or in hallways of my mother's cave, large old shapes with smouldering eyes sat watching me. A continuous grumble came out of their mouths; their backs were humped. Then little by little it dawned on me that the eyes that seemed to bore into my body were in fact gazing through it, wearily indifferent to my slight obstruction of the darkness. Of all the creatures I knew, in those days, only my mother really looked at me.—Stared at me as if to consume me, like a troll. She loved me, in some mysterious sense I understood without her speaking it. I was her creation. We were one thing, like the wall and the rock growing out from it.—Or so I ardently, desperately affirmed. When her strange eyes burned into me, it did not seem quite sure. I was intensely aware of where I sat, the volume of darkness I displaced, the shiny-smooth span of packed dirt between us, and the shocking separateness from me in my mama's eyes. I would feel, all at once, alone and ugly, almost—as if I'd dirtied myself—obscene. The cavern river rumbled far below us. Being young, unable to face these things, I would bawl and hurl myself at my mother and she would reach out her claws and seize me, though I could see I alarmed her (I had teeth like a saw), and she would smash me to her fat, limp breast as if to make me a part of her flesh again. After that, comforted, I would gradually ease back out into my games. Crafty-eyed, wicked as an elderly wolf, I would scheme with or stalk my imaginary friends, projecting the self I meant to become into every dark corner of the cave and the woods above.

Then all at once there they'd be again, the indifferent, burning eyes of the strangers. Or my mother's eyes. Again my world would be suddenly transformed, fixed like a rose with a nail through it, space hurtling coldly out from me in all directions. But I didn't understand.

One morning I caught my foot in the crack where two old treetrunks joined. "Owp!" I yelled. "Mama! Waa!" I was out much later than I'd meant to be. As a rule I was back in the cave by dawn, but that day I'd been lured out farther than usual by the heavenly scent of newborn calf —ah, sweeter than flowers, as sweet as my mama's milk. I looked at the foot in anger and disbelief. It was wedged deep, as if the two oak trees were eating it. Black sawdust—squirreldust—was spattered up the leg almost to the thigh. I'm not sure now how the accident happened. I must have pushed the two boles apart as I stepped up into the place where they joined, and then when I stupidly let go again they closed on my foot like a trap. Blood gushed from my ankle and shin, and pain flew up through me like fire up the flue of a mountain. I lost my head. I bellowed for help, so loudly it made the ground shake. "Mama! Waa! Waaa!" I bellowed to the sky, the forest, the cliffs, until I was so weak from loss of blood I could barely wave my arms. "I'm going to die," I wailed. "Poor Grendel! Poor old Mama!" I wept and sobbed. "Poor Grendel will hang here and starve to death," I told myself, "and no one will ever even miss him!" The thought enraged me. I hooted. I thought of my mother's foreign eyes, staring at me from across the room: I thought of the cool, indifferent eyes of the others. I shrieked in fear; still no one came.

The sun was up now, and even filtered as it was through the lacy young leaves, it made my head hurt. I twisted around as far as I could, hunting wildly for her shape on the cliffs, but there was nothing, or, rather, there was everything but my mother. Thing after thing tried, cynical and cruel, to foist itself off as my mama's shape—a black rock balanced at the edge of the cliff, a dead tree casting a long-armed shadow, a running stag, a cave entrance— each thing trying to detach itself, lift itself out of the general meaningless scramble of objects, but falling back, melting to the blank, infuriating clutter of not-my-mother. My heart began to race. I seemed to see the whole universe, even the sun and sky, leaping forward, then sinking away again, decomposing. Everything was wreckage, putrefaction. If she were there, the cliffs, the brightening sky, the trees, the stag, the waterfall would suddenly snap into position around her, sane again, well organized; but she was not, and the morning was crazy. Its green brilliance jabbed at me, live needles.

"Please, Mama!" I sobbed as if heartbroken.

Then, some thirty feet away, there was a bull. He stood looking at me with his head lowered, and the world snapped into position around him, as if in league with him. I must have been closer to the calf than I had guessed, since he'd arrived to protect it. Bulls do such things, though they don't even know that the calves they defend are theirs. He shook his horns at me, as if scornful. I trembled. On the ground, on two good feet, I would have been more than a match for the bull, or if not, I could have outrun him. But I was four or five feet up in the air, trapped and weak. He could slam me right out of the tree with one blow of that boned, square head, maybe tearing the foot off, and then he could gore me to death at his leisure in the grass. He pawed the ground, looking at me up-from-under, murderous. "Go away!" I said. "Hssst!" It had no effect. I bellowed at him. He jerked his head as if the sound were a boulder I'd thrown at him, but then he merely stood considering, and, after a minute, he pawed the ground again. Again I bellowed. This time he hardly noticed it. He snorted through his nose and pawed more deeply, spattering grass and black earth at his sharp rear hooves. As if time had slowed down as it does for the dying, I watched him loll his weight forward, sliding into an easy lope, head tilted, coming toward me in a casual arc. He picked up speed, throwing his weight onto his huge front shoulders, crooked tail lifted behind him like a flag. When I screamed, he didn't even flick an ear but came on, driving like an avalanche now, thunder booming from his hooves across the cliffs. The same instant he struck my tree he jerked his head and flame shot up my leg. The tip of one horn had torn me to the knee.

But that was all. The tree shuddered as he banged it with his skull, and he pivoted around it, stumbling. He gave his head a jerk, as if clearing his brains, then turned and loped back to where he'd charged me from before. He'd struck too low, and even in my terror I understood that he would always strike too low: he fought by instinct, blind mechanism ages old. He'd have fought the same way against an earthquake or an eagle: I had nothing to fear from his wrath but that twisting horn. The next time he charged I kept my eye on it, watched that horn with as much concentration as I'd have watched the rims of a crevasse I was leaping, and at just the right instant I flinched. Nothing touched me but the breeze as the horn flipped past.

I laughed. My ankle was numb now; my leg was on fire to the hip. I twisted to search the cliffwalls again, but still my mother wasn't there, and my laughter grew fierce. All at once, as if by sudden vision, I understood the emptiness in the eyes of those humpbacked shapes back in the cave. (Were they my brothers, my uncles, those creatures shuffling brimstone-eyed from room to room, or sitting separate, isolated, muttering forever like underground rivers, each in his private, inviolable gloom?)

I understood that the world was nothing: a mechanical

chaos of casual, brute enmity on which we stupidly impose our hopes and fears. I understood that, finally and absolutely, I alone exist. All the rest, I saw, is merely what pushes me, or what I push against, blindly—as blindly as all that is not myself pushes back. I create the whole universe, blink by blink.—An ugly god pitifully dying in a tree!

The bull struck again. I flinched from the horntip and bellowed with rage and pain. The limbs overhead, stretching out through the clearing like hungry snakes reaching up from their nest, would be clubs if I had them in my two hands, or barricades, piled between me and my cave, or kindling down in the room where my mother and I slept. Where they were, above me, they were—what? Kind shade? I laughed. A tearful howl.

The bull kept on charging. Sometimes after he hit he'd fall down and lie panting. I grew limp with my anarchistic laughter. I no longer bothered to jerk back my leg. Sometimes the horntip tore it, sometimes not. I clung to the treetrunk that slanted off to my right, and I almost slept. Perhaps I did sleep, I don't know. I must have. Nothing mattered. Sometime in the middle of the afternoon I opened my eyes and discovered that the bull was gone.

I slept again, I think. When I woke up this time and looked up through the leaves overhead, there were vultures. I sighed, indifferent. I was growing used to the pain, or it had lessened. Unimportant. I tried to see myself from the vultures' viewpoint. I saw, instead, my mother's eyes. Consuming. I was suddenly her focus of the general meaninglessness—not for myself, not for any quality of my large, shaggy body or my sly, unnatural mind. I was, in her eyes, some meaning I myself could never know and might not care to know: an alien, the rock broken free of the wall. I slept again.

That night, for the first time, I saw men.

It was dark when I awakened—or when I came to, if it was that. I was aware at once that there was something wrong. There was no sound, not even the honk of a frog or the chirp of a cricket. There was a smell, a fire very different from ours, pungent, painful as thistles to the nose. I opened my eyes and everything was blurry, as though underwater. There were lights all around me, like some weird creature's eyes. They jerked back as I looked. Then voices, speaking words. The sounds were foreign at first, but when I calmed myself, concentrating, I found I understood them: it was my own language, but spoken in a strange way, as if the sounds were made by brittle sticks, dried spindles, flaking bits of shale. My vision cleared and I saw them, mounted on horses, holding torches up. Some of them had shiny domes (as it seemed to me then) with horns coming out, like the bull's. They were small, these creatures, with dead-looking eyes and gray-white faces, and yet in some ways they were like us, except ridiculous and, at the same time, mysteriously irritating, like rats. Their movements were stiff and regular, as if figured by logic. They had skinny, naked hands that moved by clicks. When I first became aware of them, they were all speaking at the same time. I tried to move, but my body was rigid; only one hand gave a jerk. They all stopped speaking at the same instant, like sparrows. We stared at each other.

One of them said—a tall one with a long black beard—"It moves independent of the tree."

They nodded.

The tall one said, "It's a growth of some kind, that's my opinion. Some beastlike fungus."

They all looked up into the branches.

A short, fat one with a tangled white beard pointed up into the tree with an ax. "Those branches on the northern side are all dead there. No doubt the whole tree'll be dead before midsummer. It's always the north side goes first when there ain't enough sap."

They nodded, and another one said, "See there where it grows up out of the trunk? Sap running all over."

They leaned over the sides of their horses to look, pushing the torches toward me. The horses' eyes glittered.

"Have to close that up if we're going to save this tree," the tall one said. The others grunted, and the tall one looked up at my eyes, uneasy. I couldn't move. He stepped down off the horse and came over to me, so close I could have swung my hand and smashed his head if I could make my muscles move. "It's like blood," he said, and made a face.

Two of the others got down and came over to pull at their noses and look.

"I say that tree's a goner," one of them said.

They all nodded, except the tall one. "We can't just leave it rot," he said. "Start letting the place go to ruin and you know what the upshot'll be."

They nodded. The others got down off their horses and came over. The one with the tangled white beard said, "Maybe we could chop the fungus out."

They thought about it. After a while the tall one shook his head. "I don't know. Could be it's some kind of a oak-tree spirit. Better not to mess with it."

They looked uneasy. There was a hairless, skinny one with eyes like two holes. He stood with his arms out, like a challenged bird, and he kept moving around in jerky little circles, bent forward, peering at everything, at the tree, at the woods around, up into my eyes. Now suddenly he nodded. "That's it! King's right! It's a spirit!"

"You think so?" they said. Their heads poked forward.

"Sure of it," he said.

"Is it friendly, you think?" the king said.

The hairless one peered up at me with the fingertips of

one hand in his mouth. The skinny elbow hung straight down, as if he were leaning on an invisible table while he thought the whole thing through. His black little eyes stared straight into mine, as if waiting for me to tell him something. I tried to speak. My mouth moved, but nothing would come out. The little man jerked back. "He's hungry!" he said.

"Hungry!" they all said. "What does he eat?"

He looked at me again. His tiny eyes drilled into me and he was crouched as if he were thinking of trying to jump up into my brains. My heart thudded. I was so hungry I could eat a rock. He smiled suddenly, as if a holy vision had exploded in his head. "He eats *pig!*" he said. He looked doubtful. "Or maybe pigsmoke. He's in a period of transition."

They all looked at me, thinking it over, then nodded.

The king picked out six men. "Go get the thing some pigs," he said. The six men said "Yes sir!" and got on their horses and rode off. It filled me with joy, though it was all crazy, and before I knew I could do it, I laughed. They jerked away and stood shaking, looking up.

"The spirit's angry," one of them whispered.

"It always has been," another one said. "That's why it's killing the tree."

"No, no, you're wrong," the hairless one said. "It's yelling for pig."

"Pig!" I tried to yell. It scared them.

They all began shouting at each other. One of the horses neighed and reared up, and for some crazy reason they took it for a sign. The king snatched an ax from the man beside him and, without any warning, he hurled it at me. I twisted, letting out a howl, and it shot past my shoulder, just barely touching my skin. Blood trickled out.

"You're all crazy," I tried to yell, but it came out a moan. I bellowed for my mother.

"Surround him!" the king yelled, "Save the horses!"—and suddenly I knew I was dealing with no dull mechanical bull but with thinking creatures, pattern makers, the most dangerous things I'd ever met. I shrieked at them, trying to scare them off, but they merely ducked behind bushes and took long sticks from the saddles of their horses, bows and javelins. "You're all crazy," I bellowed, "you're all insane!" I'd never howled more loudly in my life. Darts like hot coals went through my legs and arms and I howled more loudly still. And then, just when I was sure I was finished, a shriek ten times as loud as mine came blaring off the cliff. It was my mother! She came roaring down like thunder, screaming like a thousand hurricanes, eyes as bright as dragonfire, and before she was within a mile of us, the creatures had leaped to their horses and galloped away. Big trees shattered and fell from her path; the earth trembled. Then her smell poured in like blood into a silver cup, filling the moonlit clearing to the brim, and I felt the two trees that held me falling, and I was tumbling, free, into the grass.

I woke up in the cave, warm firelight flickering on walls. My mother lay picking through the bone pile. When she heard me stir, she turned, wrinkling her forehead, and looked at me. There were no other shapes. I think I dimly understood even then that they'd gone deeper into darkness, away from men. I tried to tell her all that had happened, all that I'd come to understand: the meaningless objectness of the world, the universal bruteness. She only stared, troubled at my noise. She'd forgotten all language long ago, or maybe had never known any. I'd never heard her speak to the other shapes. (How I myself learned to speak I can't remember; it was a long, long time ago.) But I talked on, trying to smash through the walls of her unconsciousness. "The world resists me and I resist the world," I said. "That's all there is. The mountains are what I define them as." Ah, monstrous stupidity of childhood, unreasonable hope! I waken with a start and see it over again (in my cave, out walking, or sitting by the mere), the memory rising as if it has been pursuing me. The fire in my mother's eyes brightens and she reaches out as if some current is tearing us apart. "The world is all pointless accident," I say. Shouting now, my fists clenched. "I exist, nothing else." Her face works. She gets up on all fours, brushing dry bits of bone from her path, and, with a look of terror, rising as if by unnatural power, she hurls herself across the void and buries me in her bristly fur and fat. I sicken with fear. "My mother's fur is bristly," I say to myself. "Her flesh is loose." Buried under my mother I cannot see. She smells of wild pig and fish. "My mother smells of wild pig and fish," I say. What I see I inspire with usefulness, I think, trying to suck in breath, and all that I do not see is useless, void. I observe myself observing what I observe. It startles me. "Then I am not that which observes!" I am *lack*. *Alack!* No thread, no frailest hair between myself and the universal clutter! I listen to the underground river. I have never seen it.

Talking, talking, spinning a skin, a skin . . .

I can't breathe, and I claw to get free. She struggles. I smell my mama's blood and, alarmed, I hear from the walls and floor of the cave the booming, booming, of her heart.

3

It wasn't because he threw that battle-ax that I turned on Hrothgar. That was mere midnight foolishness. I dismissed it, thought of it afterward only as you remember a tree that fell on you or an adder you stepped on by accident, except of course that Hrothgar was more to be feared than a tree or snake. It wasn't until later, when I was fullgrown and Hrothgar was an old, old man, that I settled my soul on destroying him—slowly and cruelly. Except for his thanes' occasional stories of seeing my footprints, he'd probably forgotten by then that I existed.

He'd been busy. I'd watched it all from the eaves of the forest, mostly from up off the ground, in the branches.

In the beginning there were various groups of them: ragged little bands that roamed the forest on foot or horse-back, crafty-witted killers that worked in teams, hunting through the summer, shivering in caves or little huts in the winter, occasionally wandering out into the snow to plow through it slowly, clumsily, after more meat. Ice clung to their eyebrows and beards and eyelashes, and I'd hear them whining and groaning as they walked. When two hunters from different bands came together in the woods, they would fight until the snow was slushy with blood, then crawl back, gasping and crying, to their separate camps to tell wild tales of what happened.

As the bands grew larger, they would seize and clear a hill and, with the trees they'd cut, would set up shacks, and on the crown of the hill a large, shaggy house with a steeply pitched roof and a wide stone hearth, where they'd all go at night for protection from other bands of men. The inside walls would be beautifully painted and hung with tapestries, and every cross-timber or falcon's perch was carved and gewgawed with toads, snakes, dragon shapes, deer, cows, pigs, trees, trolls. At the first sign of spring they would set out their shrines and scatter seeds on the sides of the hill, below the shacks, and would put up wooden fences to pen their pigs and cows. The women worked the ground and milked and fed the animals while the men hunted, and when the men came in from the wolf-roads at dusk, the women would cook the game they'd caught while the men went inside and drank mead. Then they'd all eat, the men first, then the women and children, the men still drinking, getting louder and braver, talking about what they were going to do to the bands on the other hills. I would huddle, listening to their noise in the darkness, my eyebrows lifted, my lips pursed, the hair on the back of my neck standing up like pigs' bristles. All the bands did the same thing. In time I began to be more amused than revolted by what they threatened. It didn't matter to me what they did to each other. It was slightly ominous because of its strangeness—no wolf was so vicious to other wolves—but I half believed they weren't serious.

They would listen to each other at the meadhall tables, their pinched, cunning rats' faces picking like needles at the boaster's words, the warfalcons gazing down, black, from the rafters, and when one of them finished his raving threats, another would stand up and lift up his ram's horn, or draw his sword, or sometimes both if he was very drunk, and he'd tell them what *he* planned to do. Now and then some trivial argument would break out, and one of them would kill another one, and all the others would detach themselves from the killer as neatly as blood clotting, and they'd consider the case and they'd either excuse him, for some reason, or else send him out to the forest to live by stealing from their outlying pens like a wounded fox. At times I would try to befriend the exile, at other times I would try to ignore him, but they were treacherous. In the end, I had to eat them. As a rule, though, that wasn't how all their drinking turned out. Normally the men would howl out their daring, and the evening would get merrier, louder and louder, the king praising this one, criticizing that one, no one getting hurt except maybe some female who was asking for it, and eventually they'd all fall asleep on each other like lizards, and I'd steal a cow.

But the threats were serious. Darting unseen from camp to camp, I observed a change come over their drunken boasts. It was late spring. Food was plentiful. Every sheep and goat had its wobbly twins, the forest was teeming, and the first crops of the hillsides were coming into fruit. A man would roar, "I'll steal their gold and burn their mead-hall!" shaking his sword as if the tip were afire, and a man with eyes like two pins would say, "Do it now, Cowface! I think you're not even the man your father was!" The people would laugh. I would back away into the darkness, furious at my stupid need to spy on them, and I would glide to the next camp of men, and I'd hear the same.

Then once, around midnight, I came to a hall in ruins. The cows in their pens lay burbling blood through their nostrils, with javelin holes in their necks. None had been eaten. The watchdogs lay like dark wet stones, with their heads cut off, teeth bared. The fallen hall was a square of flames and acrid smoke, and the people inside (none of them had been eaten either) were burned black, small, like dwarfs turned dark and crisp. The sky opened like a hole where the gables had loomed before, and the wooden benches, the trestle tables, the beds that had hung on the meadhall walls were scattered to the edge of the forest, shining charcoal. There was no sign of the gold they'd kept—not so much as a melted hilt.

Then the wars began, and the war songs, and the weapon making. If the songs were true, as I suppose at least one or two of them were, there had always been wars, and what I'd seen was merely a period of mutual exhaustion.

I'd be watching a meadhall from high in a tree, night-birds singing in the limbs below me, the moon's face hidden in a tower of clouds, and nothing would be stirring except leaves moving in the light spring breeze and, down by the pigpens, two men walking with their battle-axes and their dogs. Inside the hall I would hear the Shaper telling of the glorious deeds of dead kings—how they'd split certain heads, snuck away with certain precious swords and necklaces—his harp mimicking the rush of swords, clanging boldly with the noble speeches, sighing behind the heroes' dying words. Whenever he stopped, thinking up formulas for what to say next, the people would all shout and thump each other and drink to the Shaper's long life. In the shadow of the hall and by the outbuildings, men sat whistling or humming to themselves, repairing weapons: winding bronze bands around gray ashspears, treating their swordblades with snake's venom, watching the goldworker decorate the handles of battle-axes. (The goldworkers had an honored place. I remember one of them especially: a lean, aloof, superior man of middle age. He never spoke to the others except to laugh sometimes— "Nyeh heh heh.")

Then suddenly the birds below me in the tree would fall silent, and beyond the meadhall clearing I'd hear the creak of harness-leather. The watchmen and their dogs would stand stock-still, as if lightning-struck; then the dogs would bark, and the next instant the door would bang open and men would come tumbling, looking crazy, from the meadhall. The enemies' horses would thunder up into the clearing, leaping the pig-fences, sending the cows and the pigs away mooing and squealing, and the two bands of men would charge. Twenty feet apart they would slide to a stop and stand screaming at each other with raised swords. The leaders on both sides held their javelins high in both hands and shook them, howling their lungs out. Terrible threats, from the few words I could catch. Things about their fathers and their fathers' fathers, things about justice and honor and lawful revenge—their throats swollen, their eyes rolling like a newborn colt's, sweat running down their shoulders. Then they would fight. Spears flying, swords whonking, arrows raining from the windows and doors of the meadhall and the edge of the woods. Horses reared and fell over screaming, ravens flew, crazy as bats in a fire, men staggered, gesturing wildly, making speeches, dying or sometimes pretending to be dying, sneaking off. Sometimes the attackers would be driven back, sometimes they'd win and burn the meadhall down, sometimes they'd capture the king of the meadhall and make his people give weapons and gold rings and cows.

It was confusing and frightening, not in a way I could untangle. I was safe in my tree, and the men who fought were nothing to me, except of course that they talked in something akin to my language, which meant that we were, incredibly, related. I was sickened, if only at the waste of it: all they killed—cows, horses, men—they left to rot or burn. I sacked all I could and tried to store it, but my mother would growl and make faces because of the stink.

The fighting went on all that summer and began again the next and again the next. Sometimes when a meadhall burned, the survivors would go to another meadhall and, stretching out their hands, would crawl unarmed up the strangers' hill and would beg to be taken in. They would give the strangers whatever weapons or pigs or cattle they'd saved from destruction, and the strangers would give them an outbuilding, the worst of their food, and some straw. The two groups would fight as allies after that, except that now and then they betrayed each other, one shooting the other from behind for some reason, or stealing the other group's gold, some midnight, or sneaking into bed with the other group's wives and daughters.

I watched it, season after season. Sometimes I watched from the high cliff wall, where I could look out and see all the meadhall lights on the various hills across the countryside, glowing like candles, reflected stars. With luck, I might see, on a soft summer night, as many as three halls burning down at once. That was rare, of course. It grew rarer as the pattern of their warring changed. Hrothgar, who'd begun hardly stronger than the others, began to outstrip the rest. He'd worked out a theory about what fighting was for, and now he no longer fought with his six closest neighbors. He'd shown them the strength of his organization, and now, instead of making war on them, he sent men to them every three months or so, with heavy wagons and back-slings, to gather their tribute to his greatness. They piled his wagons high with gold and leather and weapons, and they kneeled to his messengers and made long speeches and promised to defend him against any foolhardy outlaw that dared to attack him. Hrothgar's messengers answered with friendly words and praise of the man they'd just plundered, as if the whole thing had been his idea, then whipped up the oxen, pulled up their loaded back-slings, and started home. It was a hard trip. The tall, silky grass of the meadows and the paths along the forest would clog the heavy wagon spokes and snarl the oxen's hooves; wagon wheels sunk in the rich black earth that only the wind had ever yet seeded or harvested. The oxen rolled their eyes, floundering, and mooed. Men swore. They pushed at the wheels with long oak poles and slashed at the oxen till their backs were crosshatched with bleeding welts and their noses ran pink foam. Sometimes with one terrific heave, an ox would break free of the traces and plunge into the brush. A man on a horse would go after it, slashed by branches, cutting through tangles of hazel and hawthorn, his horse balking at the pain of thorns, and sometimes when the man found the ox he would fill it with arrows and leave it to the wolves. Sometimes he merely sat, when he found the ox, and met its stupid, gloomy eyes and wept. Sometimes a horse, mired to the waist, would give up and merely stand, head hanging, as if waiting for death, and the men would howl at it and cut it with whips, or throw stones, or club it with heavy limbs, until finally one of them came to his senses and calmed the others, and they would winch out the horse with ropes and wagon wheels, if they could, or else abandon the horse or kill it—first stripping off the saddle and bridle and the handsomely decorated harness. At times, when a wagon was hopelessly mired, the men would walk back to Hrothgar's hall for help. When they returned, the wagon would be emptied of all its gold and burned, sometimes by people of Hrothgar's own tribe, though usually by others, and the oxen and horses would be dead.

Hrothgar met with his council for many nights and days, and they drank and talked and prayed to their curious carved-out creatures and finally came to a decision. They built roads. The kings from whom they'd taken tributes of treasure they now asked for tributes of men. Then Hrothgar and his neighbors, loaded like ants on a long march, pushed foot by foot and day by day around the marshes and over the moors and through the woods, pressing flat rocks into the soft ground and grass, and packing smaller stones around the rocks' sides, until, from my watch on the wall of the cliff, Hrothgar's whole realm was like a wobbly, lopsided wheel with spokes of stone.

And now when enemies from farther out struck at kings who called themselves Hrothgar's friends, a messenger would slip out and ride through the night to the tribute-taker, and in half an hour, while the enemy bands were still shouting at each other, still waving their ashspears and saying what horrible things they would do, the forest would rumble with the sound of Hrothgar's horsemen. He would overcome them: his band had grown large, and for the treasures Hrothgar could afford now to give them in sign of his thanks, his warriors became hornets. New roads snaked out. New meadhalls gave tribute. His treasure-hoard grew till his meadhall was piled to the rafters with brightly painted shields and ornamented swords and boar's-head helmets and coils of gold, and they had to abandon the meadhall and sleep in the outbuildings. Meanwhile, those who paid tribute to him were forced to strike at more distant halls to gather the gold they paid to Hrothgar—and a little on the side for themselves. His power overran the world, from the foot of my cliff to the northern sea to the impenetrable forests south and east. They hacked down trees in widening rings around their central halls and blistered the land with peasant huts and pigpen fences till the forest looked like an old dog dying of mange. They thinned out the game, killed birds for sport, set accidental fires that would burn for days. Their sheep killed hedges, snipped valleys bare, and their pigs nosed up the very roots of what might have grown. Hrothgar's tribe made boats to drive farther north and west. There was nothing to stop the advance of man. Huge boars fled at the click of a harness. Wolves would cower in the glens like foxes when they caught that deadly scent. I was filled with a wordless, obscurely murderous unrest.

One night, inevitably, a blind man turned up at Hroth-gar's temporary meadhall. He was carrying a harp. I watched from the shadow of a cowshed, since on that hill there were no trees. The guards at the door crossed their axes in front of him. He waited, smiling foolishly, while a messenger went inside. A few minutes later the messenger returned, gave the old man a grunt, and—cautiously, feeling ahead of himself with his crooked bare toes like a man engaged in some strange, pious dance, the foolish smile still fixed on his face—the blind old man went in. A boy darted up from the weeds at the foot of the hill, the harper's companion. He too was shown in.

The hall became quiet, and after a moment Hrothgar spoke, tones low and measured—of necessity, from too much shouting on midnight raids. The harper gave him back some answer, and Hrothgar spoke again. I glanced at the watchdogs. They still sat silent as treestumps, locked in my spell. I crept closer to the hall to hear. The people were noisy for a time, yelling to the harper, offering him mead, making jokes, and then again King Hrothgar spoke, white-bearded. The hall became still.

The silence expanded. People coughed. As if all by itself, then, the harp made a curious run of sounds, almost words, and then a moment later, arresting as a voice from a hollow tree, the harper began to chant:

> *Lo, we have heard the honor of the Speardanes,*
> *nation-kings, in days now gone,*
> *how those battle-lords brought themselves glory.*

Oft Scyld Shefing shattered the forces
of kinsman-marauders, dragged away their
meadhall-benches, terrified earls—after first men found him
castaway. (He got recompense for that!)
He grew up under the clouds, won glory of men
till all his enemies sitting around him
heard across the whaleroads his demands and gave
him tribute. That was a good king!

So he sang—or intoned, with the harp behind him—twisting together like sailors' ropes the bits and pieces of the best old songs. The people were hushed. Even the surrounding hills were hushed, as if brought low by language. He knew his art. He was king of the Shapers, harpstring scratchers (oakmoss-bearded, inspired by winds). That was what had brought him over wilderness, down blindman's alleys of time and space, to Hrothgar's famous hall. He would sing the glory of Hrothgar's line and gild his wisdom and stir up his men to more daring deeds, for a price.

He told how Scyld by the cunning of arms had rebuilt the old Danish kingdom from ashes, lordless a long time before he came, and the prey of every passing band, and how Scyld's son by the strength of his wits had increased their power, a man who fully understood men's need, from lust to love, and knew how to use it to fashion a mile-wide fist of chain-locked steel. He sang of battles and

42

marriages, of funerals and hangings, the whimperings of beaten enemies, of splendid hunts and harvests. He sang of Hrothgar, hoarfrost white, magnificent of mind.

When he finished, the hall was as quiet as a mound. I too was silent, my ear pressed tight against the timbers. Even to me, incredibly, he had made it all seem true and very fine. Now a little, now more, a great roar began, an exhalation of breath that swelled to a rumble of voices and then to the howling and clapping and stomping of men gone mad on art. They would seize the oceans, the farthest stars, the deepest secret rivers in Hrothgar's name! Men wept like children: children sat stunned. It went on and on, a fire more dread than any visible fire.

Only one man in the kingdom seemed cast down: the man who'd been Hrothgar's harper before the blind man came to make his bid. The former harper crept out into the darkness, unnoticed by the rest. He slipped away through fields and forests, his precious old instrument under his arm, to seek out refuge in the hall of some lesser marauder. I too crept away, my mind aswim in ringing phrases, magnificent, golden, and all of them, incredibly, lies.

What was he? The man had changed the world, had torn up the past by its thick, gnarled roots and had transmuted it, and they, who knew the truth, remembered it his way—and so did I.

I crossed the moors in a queer panic, like a creature half insane. I knew the truth. *It was late spring. Every sheep and goat had its wobbly twins. A man said, "I'll steal their gold and burn their meadhall!" and another man said, "Do it now!"* I remembered the ragged men fighting each other till the snow was red slush, whining in winter, the shriek of people and animals burning, the whip-slashed oxen in the mire, the scattered battle-leavings: wolf-torn corpses, falcons fat with blood. Yet I also remembered, as if it had happened, great Scyld, of whose kingdom no trace remained, and his farsighted son, of whose greater kingdom no trace remained. And the stars overhead were alive with the promise of Hrothgar's vast power, his universal peace. The moors their axes had stripped of trees glowed silver in the moonlight, and the yellow lights of peasant huts were like scattered jewels on the ravendark cloak of a king. I was so filled with sorrow and tenderness I could hardly have found it in my heart to snatch a pig!

Thus I fled, ridiculous hairy creature torn apart by poetry—crawling, whimpering, streaming tears, across the world like a two-headed beast, like mixed-up lamb and kid at the tail of a baffled, indifferent ewe—and I gnashed my teeth and clutched the sides of my head as if to heal the split, but I couldn't.

There was a Scyld, once, who ruled the Danes; and other men ruled after him, that much was true. And the rest?

At the top of the cliffwall I turned and looked down, and I saw all the lights of Hrothgar's realm and the realms beyond that, that would soon be his, and to clear my mind, I sucked in wind and screamed. The sound went out, violent, to the rims of the world, and after a moment it bounced back up at me—harsh and ungodly against the sigh of the remembered harp—like a thousand tortured rat-squeals crying: *Lost!*

I clamped my palms to my ears and stretched up my lips and shrieked again: a stab at truth, a snatch at apocalyptic glee. Then I ran on all fours, chest pounding, to the smoky mere.

4

He sings to a heavier harpsong now, old heart-string scratcher, memory scraper. Of the richest of kings made sick of soul by the scattered bones of thanes. By late afternoon the fire dies down and the column of smoke is white, no longer greasy. There will be others this year, they know; yet they hang on. The sun backs away from the world like a crab and the days grow shorter, the nights grow longer, more dark and dangerous. I smile, angry in the thickening dusk, and feast my eyes on the greatest of meadhalls, unsatisfied.

His pride. The torch of kingdoms. Hart.

The Shaper remains, though now there are nobler courts where he might sing. The pride of creation. He built this hall by the power of his songs: created with casual words its grave mor(t)ality. The boy observes him, tall and solemn, twelve years older than the night he first crept in with his stone-eyed master. He knows no art but tragedy—a moving singer. The credit is wholly mine.

Inspired by winds (or whatever you please), the old man sang of a glorious meadhall whose light would shine to the ends of the ragged world. The thought took seed in Hrothgar's mind. It grew. He called all his people together and told them his daring scheme. He would build a magnificent meadhall high on a hill, with a view of the western sea, a victory-seat near the giants' work, old ruined fortress from the world's first war, to stand forever as a sign of the glory and justice of Hrothgar's Danes. There he would sit and give treasures out, all wealth but the lives of men and the people's land. And so his sons would do after him, and his sons' sons, to the final generation.

I listened, huddled in the darkness, tormented, mistrustful. I knew them, had watched them; yet the things he said seemed true. He sent to far kingdoms for woodsmen, carpenters, metalsmiths, goldsmiths—also carters, victualers, clothiers to attend to the workmen—and for weeks their uproar filled the days and nights. I watched from the vines and boulders of the giants' ruin, two miles off. Then word went out to the races of men that Hrothgar's hall was finished. He gave it its name. From neighboring realms and from across the sea came men to the great celebration. The harper sang.

I listened, felt myself swept up. I knew very well that all he said was ridiculous, not light for their darkness but flattery, illusion, a vortex pulling them from sunlight to heat, a kind of midsummer burgeoning, waltz to the sickle. Yet I was swept up. "Ridiculous!" I hissed in the black of the forest. I snatched up a snake from beside my foot and whispered to it, "I knew him *when!*" But I couldn't bring out a wicked cackle, as I'd meant to do. My heart was light with Hrothgar's goodness, and leaden with grief at my own bloodthirsty ways. I backed away, crablike, further into darkness—like a crab retreating in pain when you strike two stones at the mouth of his underwater den. I backed away till the honeysweet lure of the harp no longer mocked me. Yet even now my mind was tormented by images. Thanes filled the hall and a great silent crowd of them spilled out over the surrounding hill, smiling, peaceable, hearing the harper as if not a man in all that lot had ever twisted a knife in his neighbor's chest.

"Well then he's changed them," I said, and stumbled and fell on the root of a tree. "Why not?"

Why not? the forest whispered back—yet not the forest, something deeper, an impression from another mind, some live thing old and terrible.

I listened, tensed.

Not a sound.

"He reshapes the world," I whispered, belligerent. "So his name implies. He stares strange-eyed at the mindless world and turns dry sticks to gold."

A little poetic, I would readily admit. His manner of speaking was infecting me, making me pompous. "Nevertheless," I whispered crossly—but I couldn't go on, too conscious all at once of my whispering, my eternal posturing, always transforming the world with words—changing nothing. I still had the snake in my fist. I set it down. It fled.

"He takes what he finds," I said stubbornly, trying again. "And by changing men's minds he makes the best of it. Why not?" But it sounded petulant; and it wasn't true, I knew. He sang for pay, for the praise of women—one in particular—and for the honor of a famous king's hand on his arm. If the ideas of art were beautiful, that was art's fault, not the Shaper's. A blind selector, almost mindless: a bird. Did they murder each other more gently because in the woods sweet songbirds sang?

Yet I wasn't satisfied. His fingers picked infallibly, as if moved by something beyond his power, and the words stitched together out of ancient songs, the scenes interwoven out of dreary tales, made a vision without seams, an image of himself yet not-himself, beyond the need of any shaggy old gold-friend's pay: the projected possible.

"Why not?" I whispered, jerking forward, struggling to make my eyes sear through the dark trunks and vines.

I could feel it all around me, that invisible presence, chilly as the first intimation of death, the dusty unblinking eyes of a thousand snakes. There was no sound. I touched a fat, slick loop of vine, prepared to leap back in horror, but it was only vine, no worse. And still no sound, no movement. I got up on my feet, bent over, squinting, and edged back through the trees toward the town. It followed me—whatever it was. I was as sure of that as I'd ever been of anything. And then, in one instant, as if it had all been my mind, the thing was gone. In the hall they were laughing.

Men and women stood talking in the light of the mead-hall door and on the narrow streets below; on the lower hillside boys and girls played near the sheep pens, shyly holding hands. A few lay touching each other in the forest eaves. I thought how they'd shriek if I suddenly showed my face, and it made me smile, but I held myself back. They talked nothing, stupidities, their soft voices groping like hands. I felt myself tightening, cross, growing restless for no clear reason, and I made myself move more slowly. Then, circling the clearing, I stepped on something fleshy, and jerked away. It was a man. They'd cut his throat. His clothes had been stolen. I stared up at the hall, baffled, beginning to shake. They went on talking softly, touching hands, their hair full of light. I lifted up the body and slung it across my shoulder.

Then the harp began to play. The crowd grew still.

The harp sighed, the old man sang, as sweet-voiced as a child.

He told how the earth was first built, long ago: said that the greatest of gods made the world, every wonder-bright plain and the turning seas, and set out as signs of his victory the sun and moon, great lamps for light to land-dwellers, kingdom torches, and adorned the fields with all colors and shapes, made limbs and leaves and gave life to the every creature that moves on land.

The harp turned solemn. He told of an ancient feud between two brothers which split all the world between darkness and light. And I, Grendel, was the dark side, he said in effect. The terrible race God cursed.

I believed him. Such was the power of the Shaper's harp! Stood wriggling my face, letting tears down my nose, grinding my fists into my streaming eyes, even though to do it I had to squeeze with my elbow the corpse of the proof that both of us were cursed, or neither, that the brothers had never lived, nor the god who judged them. "Waaa!" I bawled.

Oh what a conversion!

I staggered out into the open and up toward the hall with my burden, groaning out, "Mercy! Peace!" The harper broke off, the people screamed. (They have their own versions, but this is the truth.) Drunken men rushed me with battle-axes. I sank to my knees, crying, "Friend! Friend!" They hacked at me, yipping like dogs. I held up the body for protection. Their spears came through it and one of them nicked me, a tiny scratch high on my left breast, but I knew by the sting it had venom on it and I understood, as shocked as I'd been the first time, that they could kill me—eventually *would* if I gave them a chance. I struck at them, holding the body as a shield, and two fell bleeding from my nails at the first little swipe. The others backed off. I crushed the body in my hug, then hurled it in their faces, turned, and fled. They didn't follow.

I ran to the center of the forest and fell down panting. My mind was wild. "Pity," I moaned, "O pity! pity!" I wept—strong monster with teeth like a shark's—and I slammed the earth with such force that a seam split open twelve feet long. "Bastards!" I roared. "Sons of bitches! Fuckers!" Words I'd picked up from men in their rages. I wasn't even sure what they meant, though I had an idea: defiance, rejection of the gods that, for my part, I'd known all along to be lifeless sticks. I roared with laughter, still sobbing. We, the accursed, didn't even have words for swearing in! "*AAARGH!*" I whooped, then covered my ears and hushed. It sounded silly.

My sudden awareness of my foolishness made me calm.

I looked up through the treetops, ludicrously hopeful. I think I was half prepared, in my dark, demented state, to see God, bearded and gray as geometry, scowling down at me, shaking his bloodless finger.

"Why can't I have someone to talk to?" I said. The stars said nothing, but I pretended to ignore the rudeness. "The Shaper has people to talk to," I said. I wrung my fingers. "Hrothgar has people to talk to."

I thought about it.

Perhaps it wasn't true.

As a matter of fact, if the Shaper's vision of goodness and peace was a part of himself, not idle rhymes, then no one understood him at all, not even Hrothgar. And as for Hrothgar, if he was serious about his idea of glory—sons and sons' sons giving out treasure—I had news for him. If he had sons, they wouldn't hear his words. They would weigh his silver and gold in their minds. I've watched the generations. I've seen their weasel eyes.

I fought down my smile.

"That could change," I said, shaking my finger as if at an audience. "The Shaper may yet improve men's minds, bring peace to the miserable Danes."

But they were doomed, I knew, and I was glad. No denying it. Let them wander the fogroads of Hell.

❁ ❁ ❁

Two nights later I went back. I was addicted. The Shaper was singing the glorious deeds of the dead men, praising war. He sang how they'd fought me. It was all lies. The sly harp rasped like snakes in cattails, glorifying death. I snatched a guard and smashed him on a tree, but my stomach turned at the thought of eating him. "Woe to the man," the Shaper sang, "who shall through wicked hostilities shove his soul down into the fire's hug! Let him hope for no change: he can never turn away! But lucky the man who, after his deathday, shall seek the Prince, find peace in his father's embrace!"

"Bullshit!" I whispered through clenched teeth. How was it that he could enrage me so?

Why not? the darkness hissed around me. *Why not? Why not?* Teasing, tormenting, as cold as a dead hand closing on my wrist.

Imagination, I knew. Some evil inside myself pushed out into the trees. I knew what I knew, the mindless, mechanical bruteness of things, and when the harper's lure drew my mind away to hopeful dreams, the dark of what was and always was reached out and snatched my feet.

And yet I'd be surprised, I had to admit, if anything in myself could be as cold, as dark, as centuries old as the presence I felt around me. I touched a vine to reassure myself. It was a snake. I snapped back in terror.

Then I calmed myself again. The fangs hadn't hit. It came to me that the presence was still there, somewhere deeper, much deeper, in the night. I had a feeling that if I let myself I could fall toward it, that it was pulling me, pulling the whole world in like a whirlpool.

Craziness, of course. I got up, though the feeling was as strong as ever, and felt my way back through the forest and over to the cliffwall and back to the mere and to my cave. I lay there listening to the indistinct memory of the Shaper's songs. My mother picked through the bone pile, sullen. I'd brought no food.

"Ridiculous," I whispered.

She looked at me.

It was a cold-blooded lie that a god had lovingly made the world and set out the sun and moon as lights to land-dwellers, that brothers had fought, that one of the races was saved, the other cursed. Yet he, the old Shaper, might make it true, by the sweetness of his harp, his cunning trickery. It came to me with a fierce jolt that I wanted it. As they did too, though vicious animals, cunning, cracked with theories. I wanted it, yes! Even if I must be the outcast, cursed by the rules of his hideous fable.

She whimpered, scratched at the nipple I had not sucked in years. She was pitiful, foul, her smile a jagged white tear in the firelight: waste.

She whimpered one sound: *Dool-dool! dool-dool!*, scratching at her bosom, a ghastly attempt to climb back up to speech.

I clamped my eyes shut, listened to the river, and after a time I slept.

I sat up with a jerk.

The thing was all around me, now, like a thunder charge.

"Who is it?" I said.

No answer. Darkness.

My mother was asleep; she was as deadlooking as a red-gray old sea-elephant stretched on the shore of a summer day.

I got up and silently left the cave. I went to the cliffwall, then down to the moor.

Still nothing.

I made my mind a blank and fell, sank away like a stone through earth and sea, toward the dragon.

5

No use of a growl, a whoop, a roar, in the presence of that beast! Vast, red-golden, huge tail coiled, limbs sprawled over his treasure-hoard, eyes not firey but cold as the memory of family deaths. Vanishing away across invisible floors, there were things of gold, gems, jewels, silver vessels the color of blood in the undulant, dragon-red light. Arching above him the ceiling and upper walls of his cave were alive with bats. The color of his sharp scales darkened and brightened as the dragon inhaled and exhaled slowly, drawing new air across his vast internal furnace; his razorsharp tusks gleamed and glinted as if they too, like the mountain beneath him, were formed of precious stones and metals.

My heart shook. His eyes stared straight at me. My knees and insides were so weak I had to drop down on all fours. His mouth opened slightly. Bits of flame escaped.

"Ah, Grendel!" he said. "You've come." The voice was startling. No rolling boom, as I would have expected, but a voice that might have come from an old, old man. Louder, of course, but not much louder.

"We've been expecting you," he said. He gave a nervous laugh, like a miser caught at his counting. His eyes were heavy-lidded, minutely veined, wrinkled like an elderly mead-drinker's. "Stand around the side, if you don't mind, boy," he said. "I get a cough sometimes, and it's terrible straight out front." The high dead eyelids wrinkled more, the corners of his mouth snaked up as he chuckled, sly, hardly hiding his malice. I quickly ducked around to the side.

"Good boy," he said. He tipped his head, lowering an eye toward me. "*Smart* boy! He he he!" He lifted a wrinkled paw with man-length talons for nails and held it over my head as if to crush me with it, but he merely brought it down lightly, once, twice, three times, patting my head.

"Well, speak, boy," he said. "Say 'Hello there, Mr. Dragon!' " He cackled.

My throat convulsed and I tried to get my breath to speak, but I couldn't.

The dragon smiled. Horrible, debauched, mouth limp and cracked, loose against the teeth as an ancient dog's. "Now you know how *they* feel when they see *you,* eh? Scared enough to pee in their pants! He he!" He looked startled by an unpleasant thought, then cross. "You didn't, did you?"

I shook my head.

"Good," he said. "That's valuable stuff you're standing on. Boobies, hemorrhoids, boils, slaver (nyeh heh heh) . . . *Now.*" He moved his head as if adjusting his flaking neck to a tight metal collar and put on what looked like, for him, a sober expression, like an old drunk preparing a solemn face for court. Then, as if involuntarily, he cackled again. It was horrible, horrible! Obscene! He couldn't stop himself. He cackled so hard a brilliant tear like a giant diamond rolled down his cheek. And still he couldn't stop. He raised up the taloned paw and pointed at me. His head tipped back, laughing, blowing fire out his mouth and nostrils. He tried to say something, but the laughing got worse. He rolled over on his side, stretching up one vast, wrinkled wing for balance, covering his eyes with one claw, still pointing with the other, roaring with laughter and kicking a little with his two back feet. I felt cross all at once, though I didn't dare show it. "Like a rabbit!" he brought out. "Nyee he he he! When you're scared, you look—nyee he he he—exactly . . . (*gasp!*) exactly . . ."

GRENDEL

I scowled and, realizing I had my hands out in front of me like a rabbit sitting up, I jerked them behind my back. My scowl of rage nearly finished him. He hooted, gasped, sobbed, began to choke with laughter. I forgot myself completely. I snatched up an emerald the size of a fist and pulled it back to throw it at him. He was sober instantly. "Put it down!" he said. He drew in breath and turned his huge head straight at me. I dropped it and fought to keep my bowels from moving down.

"Don't touch," he said. The old-man voice was as terrible now as the eyes. It was as if he'd been dead for a thousand years. "Never never *never* touch my things, " he said. Flame came out with the words and singed the hair on my belly and legs. I nodded, trembling all over. "Good," he said. He stared at me a moment longer, then slowly, slowly turned his head away. Then, old womanish, as if he were, though still spiteful, slightly embarrassed, he got back up onto his treasure pile, stretched out his wings, and settled.

He was in the foulest of moods. I doubted that I could learn anything from him now. I'd be lucky to get away alive. I thought all at once about what he'd said: "Now you know how *they* feel when they see *you*." He had a point. From now on I'd stay clear of them. It was one thing to eat one from time to time—that was only natural: kept them from overpopulating, maybe starving to death, come winter—but it was another thing to scare them, give them heart attacks, fill their nights with nightmares, just for sport.

"Fiddlesticks," the dragon said.

I blinked.

"Fiddlesticks, that's what I said," he repeated. "Why *not* frighten them? Creature, I could tell you things . . ." He rolled his eyes up under the heavy lids and made a noise, "*Glaagh.*" He remained that way, breathing hard with peevish anger. "Stupid, stupid, *stupid!*" he hissed. "The whole damned kit and caboodle. Why did you come here? Why do you bother me?—Don't answer!" he added quickly, stopping me. "I know what's in your mind. I know everything. That's what makes me so sick and old and tired."

"I'm sorry," I said.

"Be still!" he screamed. Flame shot clear to the cave-mouth. "I know you're sorry. For right now, that is. For this one frail, foolish flicker-flash in the long dull fall of eternity. I'm unimpressed—No no! Be still!" His eye burst open like a hole, to hush me. I closed my mouth. The eye was terrible, lowering toward me. I felt as if I were tumbling down into it—dropping endlessly down through a soundless void. He let me fall, down and down toward a black sun and spiders, though he knew I was beginning to die. Nothing could have been more disinterested: serpent to the core.

But then he spoke after all, or rather laughed, and reality snapped back. Laughed, spoke, and broke my fall not as a kindness to me but because of his cold pleasure in knowing what he knew. I was in the cave again, and his horrible smile was snaking up his wrinkled cheek and his eye was once more half-closed. "You want the word," he said. "That's what you've come for. My advice is, don't ask! Do as I do! Seek out gold—but not *my* gold—and guard it!"

"Why?" I said.

"BE STILL!" The cave went white with his fire, and the rock walls roared the echo back. Bats flew like dust in a granary, then returned to their places, a few at a time, until all was still again, motionless, as if lifeless. His wings, which had stretched out slightly, relaxed and settled.

I waited for what seemed hours, huddling, my fingers protecting my head.

Then: "You want to know about the Shaper."

I nodded.

"Illusion," he said. He half smiled, then let it go as if infinitely weary, sick of Time. "I know everything, you see," the old voice wheedled. "The beginning, the present, the end. Everything. You now, you see the past and the present, like other low creatures: no higher faculties than memory and perception. But dragons, my boy, have a whole different kind of mind." He stretched his mouth in a kind of smile, no trace of pleasure in it. "We see from the mountaintop: all time, all space. We see in one instant the passionate vision and the blowout. Not that we *cause* things to fail, you understand." He was testy all at once, as if answering an argument that had been put to him so often he was sick of it. "Dragons don't mess with your piddling free will. Pah! Listen to me, boy." The dead eye brightened. "If you with your knowledge of present and past recall that a certain man slipped on, say, a banana peel, or fell off his chair, or drowned in a river, that recollection does not mean that you *caused* him to slip, or fall, or drown. Correct? Of course it's correct! It happened, and you know it, but knowledge is not *cause*. Of course! Anyone who argues otherwise is a stupid ignoramus. Well, so with me. My knowledge of the future does not *cause* the future. It merely *sees* it, exactly as creatures at your low level recall things past. And even if, say, I interfere— burn up somebody's meadhall, for instance, whether because I just feel like it or because some supplicant asked me to—even then I do not change the future, I merely do what I saw from the beginning. That's obvious, surely. Let's say it's settled then. So much for free will and intercession!"

The dragon's eye closed to a slit. "Grendel!"

I jumped.

"Don't look so bored," he said. He scowled, black as midnight. "Think how *I* must feel," he said.

I almost said "I'm sorry," but caught myself.

"Man," he said, then left a long pause, letting scorn build up in the cave like the venom in his breath. "I can see you understand them. Counters, measurers, theory-makers.

> *All pigs eat cheese.*
> *Old Snaggle is a pig.*
> *If Snaggle is sick and refuses to eat, try cheese.*

Games, games, games!" He snorted fire. "They only think they think. No total vision, total system, merely schemes with a vague family resemblance, no more identity than bridges and, say, spiderwebs. But they rush across chasms on spiderwebs, and sometimes they make it, and that, they think, settles that! I could tell you a thousand tiresome stories of their absurdity. They'd map out roads through Hell with their crackpot theories, their here-to-the-moon-and-back lists of paltry facts. Insanity—the simplest insanity ever devised! Simple facts in isolation, and facts to connect them—ands and buts—are the *sine qua non* of all their glorious achievement. But there are no such facts. Connectedness is the essence of everything. It doesn't stop them, of course. They build the whole world out of teeth deprived of bodies to chew or be chewed on.

"They sense that, of course, from time to time; have

uneasy feelings that all they live by is nonsense. They have dim apprehensions that such propositions as 'God does not exist' are somewhat dubious at least in comparison with statements like 'All carnivorous cows eat meat.' That's where the Shaper saves them. Provides an illusion of reality—puts together all their facts with a gluey whine of connectedness. Mere tripe, believe me. Mere sleight-of-wits. He knows no more than they do about total reality—less, if anything: works with the same old clutter of atoms, the givens of his time and place and tongue. But he spins it all together with harp runs and hoots, and they think what they think is alive, think Heaven loves them. It keeps them going—for what that's worth. As for myself, I can hardly bear to look."

"I see," I said. It was to some extent untrue.

The dragon smiled, seemed almost friendly for an instant. "You've been very attentive and thoughtful," he said, "all things considered. So I will tell you about Time and Space."

"Thank you," I said, as heartily as I could manage. I had more than enough to think about, it seemed to me.

He scowled, and I said no more. He took a deep breath, shifted his forelegs to a position more comfortable, and, after a moment's thought, began:

"In all discussions of Nature, we must try to remember the differences of scale, and in particular the differences of time-span. We (by which I mean you, not us) are apt to take modes of observable functioning in our own bodies as setting an absolute scale. But as a matter of fact, it's extremely rash to extend conclusions derived from observation far beyond the scale of magnitude to which the observation was confined. For example, the apparent absence of change within a second of time tells nothing as to the change within a thousand years. Also, no appearance of change within a thousand years tells anything concerning what might happen in, say, a million years; and no apparent change within a million years tells anything about a million million years. We can extend this progression indefinitely; there is no absolute standard of magnitude. Any term in this progression is large compared to its predecessor and small compared to its successor.

"Again, all special studies presuppose certain fundamental types of things. (Here I am using the word 'thing,' notice, in its most general sense, which can include activities, colors, and all other sensa, also values.) As lower minds function, study, or 'science,' is concerned with a limited set of various types of things. There is thus, in the first place, this variety of types. In the second place, there is the determination as to what types are exhibited in any indicated situation. For example, there is the singular proposition—'This is green'—and there is the more general proposition—'All those things are green.' This type of

inquiry is what your usual reasoning takes care of. Undoubtedly such inquiries are essential in the initial stage
of any study, for lower minds. But every such study must
strive to get beyond it. Unfortunately—"

He glanced at me, suspicious. "You're not paying attention."

"I am!" I said, clasping my hands to show my serious-
ness.

But he shook his head slowly. "Nothing interests you
but excitement, violence."

"That's not true!" I said.

His eye opened wider, his body brightened from end
to end. "*You* tell *me* what's true?" he said.

"I'm trying to follow. I do my best," I said. "You
should be reasonable. What do you expect?"

The dragon thought about it, breathing slowly, full of
wrath. At last he closed his eyes. "Let us try starting
somewhere else," he said. "It's damned hard, you understand, confining myself to concepts familiar to a creature
of the Dark Ages. Not that one age is darker than another.
Technical jargon from another dark age." He scowled as
if hardly capable of forcing himself on. Then, after a long
moment: "The essence of life is to be found in the frus-
trations of established order. The universe refuses the
deadening influence of complete conformity. And yet in its
refusal, it passes toward novel order as a primary requisite

for important experience. We have to explain the aim at forms of order, and the aim at novelty of order, and the measure of success, and the measure of failure. Apart from some understanding, however dim-witted, of these characteristics of historic process . . ." His voice trailed off.

After another long pause, he said: "Approach it this way. Let us take this jug." He picked up a golden vessel and held it toward me, not letting me touch it. In spite of himself, as it seemed, he looked hostile and suspicious, as if he thought I might perhaps be so stupid as to snatch the thing and run. "How does this jug differ from something animate?" He drew it back out of reach. "By organization! Exactly! This jug is an absolute democracy of atoms. It has importance, or thereness, so to speak, but no Expression, or, loosely, ah-ha!-ness. Importance is primarily monistic in its reference to the universe. Limited to a finite individual occasion, importance ceases to be important. In some sense or other—we can skip the details—importance is derived from the immanence of infinitude in the finite. Expression, however—listen closely now—expression is founded on the finite occasion. It is the activity of finitude impressing itself on its environment. Importance passes from the world as one to the world as many, whereas expression is the gift from the world as many to the world as one. The laws of nature are large average effects which reign impersonally. But there is nothing average about expression: it is essentially individual. Consider one definite molecule—"

"A what?" I said.

The closed eyes squeezed tight. He let out a long, cross sigh of red-orange fire.

"Put it this way," he said. His voice had grown feeble, as if he were losing hope. "In the case of vegetables, we find expressive bodily organizations which lack any one center of experience with a higher complexity either of expressions received or of inborn data. Another democracy, but with qualifications, as we shall see. An animal, on the other hand, is dominated by one or more centers of experience. If the dominant activity be severed from the rest of the body—if, for example, we cut off the head—the whole coordination collapses, and the animal dies. Whereas in the case of the vegetable, the democracy can be subdivided into minor democracies which easily survive without much apparent loss of functional expression." He paused. "You at *least* follow that?"

"I think so."

He sighed. "Listen. Listen closely! An angry man does not usually shake his fist at the universe in general. He makes a selection and knocks his neighbor down. A piece of rock, on the other hand, impartially attracts the universe according to the law of gravitation. You grant there's a difference?"

He waited, furious with impatience. I met his eye as long as I could, then shook my head. It was unfair. For all I knew he might be telling me gibberish on purpose. I sat down. Let him babble. Let him burn me alive. The hell with it.

After a long, long time, he said, "It was stupid of you to come."

I nodded, sulking.

He stretched his wings—it was like a huge, irascible yawn—then settled again. "Things come and go," he said. "That's the gist of it. In a billion billion billion years, everything will have come and gone several times, in various forms. Even I will be gone. A certain man will absurdly kill me. A terrible pity—loss of a remarkable form of life. Conservationists will howl." He chuckled. "Meaningless, however. These jugs and pebbles, everything, these too will go. Poof! Boobies, hemorrhoids, boils, slaver ..."

"You don't know that!" I said.

He smiled, showing all his teeth, and I knew he knew it.

"A swirl in the stream of time. A temporary gathering of bits, a few random dust specks, so to speak—pure metaphor, you understand—then by chance a vast floating cloud of dustspecks, an expanding universe—" He shrugged. "Complexities: green dust as well as the regular kind. Purple dust. Gold. Additional refinements: sensitive dust, copulating dust, *worshipful dust!*" He laughed, hollow as the cavern around him. "New laws for each new form, of course. New lines of potential. Complexity beyond complexity, accident on accident, until—" His leer was like icy wind.

"Go on," I said.

He closed his eyes, still smiling. "Pick an apocalypse, any apocalypse. A sea of black oil and dead things. No wind. No light. Nothing stirring, not even an ant, a spider. A silent universe. Such is the end of the flicker of time, the brief, hot fuse of events and ideas set off, accidentally, and snuffed out, accidentally, by man. Not a real ending of course, nor even a beginning. Mere ripple in Time's stream."

I squinted. "That really could happen?"

"It has happened," he said—and smiled as if it pleased him—"in the future. I am the witness."

I thought about it for a while, remembering the harp, then shook my head. "I don't believe you."

"It will come."

I went on squinting at him, hand on my mouth. He could lie. He was evil enough.

He shook his ponderous head. "Ah, man's cunning mind!" he said, and cackled. "Merely a new complexity, a new event, new set of nonce-rules generating further nonce-rules, down and down and down. Things lock on, you know. The Devonian fish, the juxtaposed thumb, the fontanel, technology—*click click, click click* ...”

“I think you're lying,” I said, confused again, aswirl in words.

“I noticed that. You'll never know. It must be very frustrating to be caged like a Chinaman's cricket in a limited mind.” His cackle lacked spirit, this time. He was growing very weary of my presence.

“You said ‘Fiddlesticks,’ ” I said. “Why is it fiddlesticks if I stop giving people heart attacks over nothing? Why shouldn't one change one's ways, improve one's character?” I must have been an interesting sight, that instant, big shaggy monster intense and earnest, bent like a priest at his prayers.

He shrugged. “Whatever you like. Do as you think best.”

“But why?”

“ ‘Why? Why?’ Ridiculous question! Why anything? My advice to you—”

I clenched my fists, though it was absurd, of course. One does not swing at dragons. “*No, why?*”

The dragon tipped up his great tusked head, stretched his neck, sighed fire. “Ah, Grendel!” he said. He seemed that instant almost to rise to pity. “You improve them, my boy! Can't you see that yourself? You stimulate them! You make them think and scheme. You drive them to poetry, science, religion, all that makes them what they are for as long as they last. You are, so to speak, the brute existent by which they learn to define themselves. The exile, captivity, death they shrink from—the blunt facts of their mortality, their abandonment—that's what you make them recognize, embrace! You *are* mankind, or man's condition: inseparable as the mountain-climber and the mountain. If you withdraw, you'll instantly be replaced. Brute existents, you know, are a dime a dozen. No sentimental trash, then. If man's the irrelevance that interests you, stick with him! Scare him to glory! It's all the same in the end, matter and motion, simple or complex. No difference, finally. Death, transfiguration. Ashes to ashes and slime to slime, amen."

I was sure he was lying. Or anyway half-sure. Flattering me into tormenting them because he, in his sullen hole, loved viciousness. I said, "Let them find some other 'brute existent,' whatever that is. I refuse."

"Do!" he said leering scornfully. "Do something else, by all means! Alter the future! Make the world a better place in which to live! Help the poor! Feed the hungry. Be kind to idiots! What a challenge!"

He no longer looked at me, no longer made any pretense of telling the truth. "Personally," he said, "my great ambition is to count all this"—he waved vaguely at the treasure around him—"and possibly sort it into piles.

'Know thyself,' that's my dictum. Know how much you've got, and beware of strangers!"

I scraped away rubies and emeralds with the side of my foot. "Let me tell you what the Shaper said."

"Spare me, I beg you!" He covered his ears with his claws, gave a hideous grin.

But I was stubborn. "He said that the greatest of gods made the world, every wonder-bright plain and the turning seas. He said—"

"Ridiculous."

"Why?"

"What god? Where? Life-force, you mean? The principle of process? God as the history of Chance?"

In some way that I couldn't explain, I knew that his scorn of my childish credulity was right.

"Nevertheless, something will come of all this," I said.

"Nothing," he said. "A brief pulsation in the black hole of eternity. My advice to you—"

"Wait and see," I said.

He shook his head. "My advice to you, my violent friend, is to seek out gold and sit on it."

6

Nothing was changed, everything was changed, by my having seen the dragon. It's one thing to listen, full of scorn and doubt, to poets' versions of time past and visions of time to come; it's another to know, as coldly and simply as my mother knows her pile of bones, what is. Whatever I may have understood or misunderstood in the dragon's talk, something much deeper stayed with me, became my aura. Futility, doom, became a smell in the air, pervasive and acrid as the dead smell after a forest fire—my scent and the world's, the scent of trees, rocks, waterways wherever I went.

But there was one thing worse. I discovered that the dragon had put a charm on me: no weapon could cut me.

I could walk up to the meadhall whenever I pleased, and they were powerless. My heart became darker because of that. Though I scorned them, sometimes hated them, there had been something between myself and men when we could fight. Now, invulnerable, I was as solitary as one live tree in a vast landscape of coal.

Needless to say, I misunderstood in the beginning: I thought it an advantage.

It was the height of summer, harvest season in the first year of what I have come to call my war with Hrothgar. The night air was filled with the smell of apples and shocked grain, and I could hear the noise in the meadhall from a mile away. I moved toward it, drawn as always, as if by some kind of curse. I meant not to be seen that night. For all the dragon's talk, I had no intention of terrifying Hrothgar's thanes for nothing. (I had not begun, at that time, my systematic raids. In fact I hadn't yet admitted to myself that it was war. I killed stragglers now and then—with a certain grim pleasure very different from that which I got from cracking a cow's skull—but I'd never yet struck at the hall, hadn't even revealed myself there—except on that one ridiculous night when I walked up and tried to join them.) I hunkered down at the edge of the forest, looking up the long hill at the meadhall lights. I could hear the Shaper's song.

I no longer remember exactly what he sang. I know only that it had a strange effect on me: it no longer filled me with doubt and distress, loneliness, shame. It enraged me. It was their confidence, maybe—their blissful, swinish ignorance, their bumptious self-satisfaction, and, worst of all, their *hope*. I went closer, darting from cowshed to cowshed and finally up to the wall. I found a crack and peeked in. I do remember what he said, now that I think about it. Or some of it. He spoke of how God had been kind to the Scyldings, sending so rich a harvest. The people sat beaming, bleary-eyed and fat, nodding their approval of God. He spoke of God's great generosity in sending them so wise a king. They all raised their cups to God and Hrothgar, and Hrothgar smiled, bits of food in his beard. The Shaper talked of how God had vanquished their enemies and filled up their houses with precious treasure, how they were the richest, most powerful people on earth, how here and here alone in all the world men were free and heroes were brave and virgins were virgins. He ended the song, and people clapped and shouted their praise and filled their golden cups. All around their bubble of stupidity I could feel the brume of the dragon.

Then a stick snapped behind me, and the same instant, a dog barked. A helmeted, chain-mailed guard leaped out at me, sword in two hands above his head, prepared to split me. I jerked back, but there was something in the way, and I fell. I tried to roll, and then, out of the corner of my eye, I saw the sword coming and I knew I couldn't escape it. I went limp, the way animals sometimes do at the moment of the predator's leap. Nothing happened.

I was as surprised as the guard. We both stared, I sprawling helpless on my back, the sword across my belly, the guard leaning forward, still holding the hilt as if afraid to let it go. His beard and nose stuck out through the cheekplates, and his eyes, in the shadowed recess of the helmet, were like two dark holes in a tree. My heart was pounding, filling my chest with pain. Still, neither of us moved. Then, almost the same instant, the guard screamed and I roared like a bull gone mad to drive him off. He let go of the sword and tried to retreat, walking backward, but he tripped on the dog and fell. I laughed, a little wild, and reached out fast as a striking snake for his leg. In a second I was up on my feet again. He screamed, dangling, and then there were others all around me. They threw javelins and axes, and one of the men caught the guard's thrashing arms and tried to yank him free. I held on, but except for that I couldn't act. It was as if I too was drunk on mead. I saw their weapons come flying straight at me, saw them touch my fur and drop quietly in the grass.

Then, little by little, I understood. I felt laughter welling up inside me—at the dragon-charm, at Hrothgar's whispering and trembling by the meadhall door, at everything—

the oblivious trees and sky, the witless moon. I'd meant them no harm, but they'd attacked me again, as always. They were crazy. And now at last the grim laughter came pouring out, as uncontrollable as the dragon's laugh, and I wanted to say, "Lo, God has vanquished mine enemies!" —but that made me laugh harder, though even now my heart raced and, in spite of it all, I was afraid of them. I backed away, still holding the screaming guard. They merely stared, with their useless weapons drawn, their shoulders hunched against my laughter. When I'd reached a safe distance, I held up the guard to taunt them, then held him still higher and leered into his face. He went silent, looking at me upside-down in horror, suddenly knowing what I planned. As if casually, in plain sight of them all, I bit his head off, crunched through the helmet and skull with my teeth and, holding the jerking, blood-slippery body in two hands, sucked the blood that sprayed like a hot, thick geyser from his neck. It got all over me. Women fainted, men backed toward the hall. I fled with the body to the woods, heart churning—boiling like a flooded ditch—with glee.

Some three or four nights later I launched my first raid. I burst in when they were all asleep, snatched seven from their beds, and slit them open and devoured them on the spot. I felt a strange, unearthly joy. It was as if I'd made some incredible discovery, like my discovery long ago of the moonlit world beyond the mere. I was transformed. I was a new focus for the clutter of space I stood in: if the world had once imploded on the tree where I waited, trapped and full of pain, it now blasted outward, away from me, screeching terror. I had become, myself, the mama I'd searched the cliffs for once in vain. But that merely hints at what I mean. I had *become* something, as if born again. I had hung between possibilities before, between the cold truths I knew and the heart-sucking conjuring tricks of the Shaper; now that was passed: I was Grendel, Ruiner of Meadhalls, Wrecker of Kings!

But also, as never before, I was alone.

I do not complain of it (talking talking, complaining complaining, filling the world I walk with words). But I admit it was a jolt. It was a few raids later. The meadhall door burst open at my touch exactly as before, and, for once, that night, I hesitated. Men sat up in their beds, snatched their helmets, swords, and shields from the covers beside them, and, shouting brave words that came out like squeals, they threw their legs over the sides to stumble toward me. Someone yelled, "Remember this hour, ye thanes of Hrothgar, the boasts you made as the meadbowl passed! Remember our good king's gift of rings and pay him with all your might for his many kindnesses!"

Damned pompous fools. I hurled a bench at the closest. They all cowered back. I stood waiting, bent forward with my feet apart, flat-footed, till they ended their interminable orations. I was hunched like a wrestler, moving my head from side to side, making sure no sneak slipped up on me. I was afraid of them from habit, and as the four or five drunkest of the thanes came toward me, shaking their weapons and shouting at me, my idiotic fear of them mounted. But I held my ground. Then, with a howl, one plunged at me, sword above his head in both fists. I let it come. The charm held good. I closed my hand on the blade and snatched it from the drunken thane's hand and hurled it the length of the hall. It clattered on the fireplace stones and fell to the stone floor, ringing. I seized him and crushed him. Another one came at me, gloating in his blear-eyed heroism, maniacally joyful because he had bragged that he would die for his king and he was doing it. He did it. Another one came, reeling and whooping, trying to make his eyes focus.

I laughed. It was outrageous: they came, they fell, howling insanity about brothers, fathers, glorious Hrothgar, and God. But though I laughed, I felt trapped, as hollow as a rotten tree. The meadhall seemed to stretch for miles, out to the edges of time and space, and I saw myself killing them, on and on and on, as if mechanically, without contest. I saw myself swelling like bellows on their blood, a meaningless smudge in a universe dead as old wind over bones, abandoned except for the burnt-blood scent of the dragon. All at once I began to smash things—benches, tables, hanging beds—a rage as meaningless and terrible as everything else.

Then—as a crowning absurdity, my salvation that moment—came the man the thanes called Unferth.

He stood across the hall from me, youthful, intense, cold sober. He was taller than the others; he stood out among his fellow thanes like a horse in a herd of cows. His nose was as porous and dark as volcanic rock. His light beard grew in patches.

"Stand back," he said.

The drunken little men around me backed away. The hallfloor between us, Unferth and myself, lay open.

"Monster, prepare to die!" he said. Very righteous. The wings of his nostrils flared and quivered like an outraged priest's.

I laughed. "Aargh!" I said. I spit bits of bone.

He glanced behind him, making sure he knew exactly where the window was. "Are you right with your god?" he said.

I laughed somewhat more fiercely. He was one of those.

He took a tentative step toward me, then paused, holding his sword out and shaking it. "Tell them in Hell that Unferth, son of Ecglaf sent you, known far and wide in these Scanian lands as a hero among the Scyldings." He took a few sidesteps, like one wrestler circling another, except that he was thirty feet away; the maneuver was ridiculous.

"Come, come," I said. "Let me tell them I was sent by Sideways-Walker."

He frowned, trying to puzzle out my speech. I said it again, louder and slower, and a startled look came over him. Even now he didn't know what I was saying, but it was clear to him, I think, that I was speaking words. He got a cunning look, as if getting ready to offer a deal—the look men have when they fight with men instead of poor stupid animals.

He was shaken, and to get back his nerve he spoke some more. "For many months, unsightly monster, you've murdered men as you pleased in Hrothgar's hall. Unless you can murder me as you've murdered lesser men, I give you my word those days are done forever! The king has given me splendid gifts. He will see tonight that his gifts have not gone for nothing! Prepare to fall, foul thing! This one red hour makes your reputation or mine!"

I shook my head at him, wickedly smiling. "Reputation!" I said, pretending to be much impressed.

His eyebrows shot up. He'd understood me; no doubt of it now. "You can talk!" he said. He backed away a step.

I nodded, moving in on him. Near the center of the room there was a trestle table piled high with glossy apples. An evil idea came over me—so evil it made me shiver as I smiled—and I sidled across to the table. "So you're a hero," I said. He didn't get it, and I said it twice more before I gave up in disgust. I talked on anyway, let him get what he could, come try for reputation when he pleased. "I'm impressed," I said. "I've never seen a live hero before. I thought they were only in poetry. Ah, ah, it must be a terrible burden, though, being a hero—glory reaper, harvester of monsters! Everybody always watching you, weighing you, seeing if you're still heroic. You know how it is—he he! Sooner or later the harvest virgin will make her mistake in the haystack." I laughed.

The dragon-scent in the room grew stronger, as if my teasing were bringing the old beast near. I picked up an apple and polished it lightly and quickly on the hair of my arm. I had my head bowed, smiling, looking at him up through my eyebrows.

"Dread creature—" he said.

I went on polishing the apple, smiling. "And the awful inconvenience," I said. "Always having to stand erect, always having to find noble language! It must wear on a man."

He looked hurt and slightly indignant. He'd understood.

"Wretched shape—" he said.

"But no doubt there are compensations," I said. "The pleasant feeling of vast superiority, the easy success with women—"

"Monster!" he howled.

"And the joy of self-knowledge, that's a great compensation! The easy and absolute certainty that whatever the danger, however terrible the odds, you'll stand firm, behave with the dignity of a hero, yea, even to the grave!"

"No more talk!" he yelled. His voice broke. He lifted his sword to make a run at me, and I laughed—howled—and threw an apple at him. He dodged, and then his mouth dropped open. I laughed harder, threw another. He dodged again.

"Hey!" he yelled. A forgivable lapse.

And now I was raining apples at him and laughing myself weak. He covered his head, roaring at me. He tried to charge through the barrage, but he couldn't make three feet. I slammed one straight into his pock-marked nose, and blood spurted out like joining rivers. It made the floor slippery, and he went down. *Clang!* I bent double with laughter. Poor Jangler—Unferth—tried to take advantage of it, charging at me on all fours, snatching at my ankles, but I jumped back and tipped over the table on him, half burying him in apples as red and innocent as smiles. He screamed and thrashed, trying to get at me and at the same time trying to see if the others were watching. He was crying, only a boy, famous hero or not: a poor miserable virgin.

"Such is life," I said, and mocked a sigh. "Such is dignity!" Then I left him. I got more pleasure from that apple fight than from any other battle in my life.

I was sure, going back to my cave (it was nearly dawn), that he wouldn't follow. They never did. But I was wrong; he was a new kind of Scylding. He must have started tracking me that same morning. A driven man, a maniac. He arrived at the cave three nights later.

I was asleep. I woke up with a start, not sure what it was that had awakened me. I saw my mother moving slowly and silently past me, blue murder in her eyes. I understood instantly, not with my mind but with something quicker, and I darted around in front to block her way. I pushed her back.

There he lay, gasping on his belly like a half drowned rat. His face and throat and arms were a crosshatch of festering cuts, the leavings of the firesnakes. His hair and beard hung straight down like seaweed. He panted for a long time, then rolled his eyes up, vaguely in my direction. In the darkness he couldn't see me, though I could see him. He closed his hand on the sword hilt and jiggled the sword a little, too weak to raise it off the floor.

"Unferth has come!" he said.

I smiled. My mother moved back and forth like a bear behind me, stirred up by the smell.

He crawled toward me, the sword noisily scraping on the cave's rock floor. Then he gave out again. "It will be sung," he whispered, then paused again to get wind. "It will be sung year on year and age on age that Unferth went down through the burning lake—" he paused to pant "—and gave his life in battle with the world-rim monster." He let his cheek fall to the floor and lay panting for a long time, saying nothing. It dawned on me that he was waiting for me to kill him. I did nothing. I sat down and put my elbows on my knees and my chin on my fists and merely watched. He lay with his eyes closed and began to get his breath back. He whispered: "It's all very well to make a fool of me before my fellow thanes. All very well to talk about dignity and noble language and all the rest, as if heroism were a golden trinket, mere outward show, and hollow. But such is not the case, monster. That is to say—" He paused, seemed to grope; he'd lost his train of thought.

I said nothing, merely waited, blocking my mother by stretching out an arm when she came near.

"Even now you mock me," Unferth whispered. I had an uneasy feeling he was close to tears. If he wept, I was not sure I could control myself. His pretensions to uncommon glory were one thing. If for even an instant he pretended to misery like mine . . .

"You think me a witless fool," he whispered. "Oh, I heard what you said. I caught your nasty insinuations. 'I thought heroes were only in poetry,' you said. Implying that what I've made of myself is mere fairytale stuff." He raised his head, trying to glare at me, but his blind stare was in the wrong direction, following my mother's pacing. "Well, it's not, let me tell you." His lips trembled and I was certain he would cry, I would have to destroy him from pure disgust, but he held it. He let his head fall again and sucked for air. A little of his voice came back, so that he no longer had to whisper but could bring out his words in a slightly reedy whine. "Poetry's trash, mere clouds of words, comfort to the hopeless. But this is no cloud, no syl-labled phantom that stands here shaking its sword at you."

I let the slight exaggeration pass.

But Unferth didn't. "Or lies here," he said. "A hero is not afraid to face cruel truth." That reminded him, ap-parently, of what he'd meant to say before. "You talk of heroism as noble language, dignity. It's more than that, as my coming here has proved. No man above us will ever know whether Unferth died here or fled to the hills like a coward. Only you and I and God will know the truth. That's inner heroism."

"Hmm," I said. It was not unusual, of course, to hear them contradict themselves, but I would have liked it if he'd stuck to one single version, either that they would know and sing his tragedy or that they wouldn't. So it would have been in a poem, surely, if Unferth were a character, good or evil, heroic or not. But reality, alas, is essentially shoddy. I let out a sigh.

He jerked his head up, shocked. "Does *nothing* have value in your horrible ruin of a brain?"

I waited. The whole shit-ass scene was his idea, not mine.

I saw the light dawning in his eyes. "I understand," he said. I thought he would laugh at the bottomless stupidity of my cynicism, but while the laugh was still starting at the corners of his eyes, another look came, close to fright. "You think me deluded. Tricked by my own walking fairytale. You think I came without a hope of winning— came to escape indignity by suicide!" He did laugh now, not amused: sorrowful and angry. The laugh died quickly. "I didn't know how deep the pool was," he said. "I had a chance. I knew I had no more than that. It's all a hero asks for."

I sighed. The word "hero" was beginning to grate. He was an idiot. I could crush him like a fly, but I held back.

"Go ahead, scoff," he said, petulant. "Except in the life of a hero, the whole world's meaningless. The hero sees values beyond what's possible. That's the *nature* of a hero. It kills him, of course, ultimately. But it makes the whole struggle of humanity worthwhile."

I nodded in the darkness. "And breaks up the boredom," I said.

He raised up on his elbows, and the effort of it made his shoulders shake. "One of us is going to die tonight. Does *that* break up your boredom?"

"It's not true," I said. "A few minutes from now I'm going to carry you back to Hrothgar, safe and sound. So much for poetry."

"I'll kill myself," he whispered. He shook violently now.

"Up to you," I answered reasonably, "but you'll admit it may seem at least a trifle cowardly to some."

His fists closed and his teeth clenched; then he relaxed and lay flat.

I waited for him to find an answer. Minutes passed. It came to me that he had quit. He had glimpsed a glorious ideal, had struggled toward it and seized it and come to understand it, and was disappointed. One could sympathize.

He was asleep.

I picked him up gently and carried him home. I laid him at the door of Hrothgar's meadhall, still asleep, killed the two guards so I wouldn't be misunderstood, and left.

He lives on, bitter, feebly challenging my midnight raids from time to time (three times this summer), crazy with shame that he alone is always spared, and furiously jealous of the dead. I laugh when I see him. He throws himself at me, or he cunningly sneaks up behind, sometimes in disguise—a goat, a dog, a sickly old woman—and I roll on the floor with laughter. So much for heroism. So much for the harvest-virgin. So much, also, for the alternative visions of blind old poets and dragons.

7

Balance is everything, riding out time like a helmless sheep-boat, keel to hellward, mast upreared to prick out heaven's eye. He he! (Sigh.) My enemies define themselves (as the dragon said) on me. As for myself, I could finish them off in a single night, pull down the great carved beams and crush them in the meadhall, along with their mice, their tankards and potatoes—yet I hold back. I am hardly blind to the absurdity. Form is function. What will we call the Hrothgar-Wrecker when Hrothgar has been wrecked?

(Do a little dance, beast. Shrug it off. This looks like a nice place—oooh, my!—flat rock, moonlight, views of distances! Sing!

Pity poor Hrothgar,
Grendel's foe!
Pity poor Grendel,
O, O, O!

Winter soon.

(whispering, whispering. Grendel, has it occurred to you my dear that you are crazy?)

(He clasps hands delicately over his head, points the toes of one foot—*aaie!* horrible nails!!—takes a step, does a turn:

Grendel is crazy,
O, O, O!
Thinks old Hrothgar
Makes it snow!

Balance is everything, tiding out rhyme . . .

Pity poor Grengar,
Hrothdel's foe!
Down goes the whirlpool:
Eek! No, no!

It will be winter soon.

Midway through the twelfth year of my idiotic war.

Twelve is, I hope, a holy number. Number of escapes from traps.

[*He searches the moonlit world for signs, shading his eyes against the dimness, standing on one shaggy foot, just slightly bloodstained, one toe missing from an old encounter with an ax. Three dead trees on the moor below, burned up alive by lightning, are ominous portents. (Oh man, us portents!) Also trees. On a frostbitten hill in the distance, men on horses. "Over here!" he screams. Waves his arms. They hesitate, feign deafness, ride away north. Shoddy, he observes. The whole chilly universe, shoddy.*]

Enough of that! A night for tearing heads off, bathing in blood! Except, alas, he has killed his quota for the season. Care, take care of the gold-egg-laying goose! There is no limit to desire but desire's needs. (Grendel's law.)

The scent of the dragon. Heavy all around me, almost visible before me, like my breath.

I will count my numberless blessings one by one.

1. My teeth are sound.
1. The roof of my cave is sound.
1. I have not committed the ultimate act of nihilism: I have not killed the queen.
1. Yet.

(*He lies on the cliff-edge, scratching his belly, and thoughtfully watches his thoughtfully watching the queen.*)

Not easy to define. Mathematically, perhaps a torus, loosely cylindrical, with swellings and constrictions at intervals, knobbed—that is to say, a surface generated, more or less, by the revolutions of a conic about an axis lying in its plane, and the solid thus enclosed. It is difficult, of course, to be precise. For one thing, the problem of determining how much is queen and how much queenly radiation.

The monster laughs.

Time-Space cross-section: *Wealtheow.*

Cut *A:*

It was the second year of my raiding. The army of the Scyldings was weakened, decimated. No more the rumble of Hrothgar's horsemen, riding at midnight, chain-mail jangling in the whistling wind, cloaks flying out like wimpling wings, to rescue petty tribute-givers. (O *listen* to me, hills!) He couldn't protect his own hall, much less theirs. I cut down my visits, conserving the game, and watched them. Nature lover. For weeks, all day and far into the night, he met with his counselors, talking, praying, moaning. I became aware, listening to them, that I was not their only threat. Far to the east of Hrothgar's hall there was a new hall a-building, its young king gaining fame. As Hrothgar had done, this younger king was systematically burning and plundering nearby halls, extending the circle of his tribute power. He was striking now at the outer rim of Hrothgar's sphere; it was only a matter of time before he struck Hrothgar. The counselors talked and drank and wept, sometimes Hrothgar's allies among them. The Shaper sang songs. The men stood with their braceleted arms around one another's shoulders—men who not long before had been the bitterest of enemies—and I watched it all, wringing my fingers, smiling rage. The leaves turned red. The purple blooms of thistles became black behind the people's houses, and migrant birds moved through.

Then, from all corners of Hrothgar's sphere of influence and from towns beyond—the vassals' vassals—an army began to form. They came walking or riding, oxen dragging their wagonloads of shields, spears, tents, clothes, food. Every night when I went down to look there were more of them. Cartwheels tall as a man, with rough, square spokes. Big-hoofed gray horses spackled like wolves, that rolled their eyes and whinnied at my footfall, leagued with men as if strapped to their business by harness I could not see. Horns cracked out in the darkening stillness; grindstones screeched. The crisp air reeked with the aftersmell of their cooking.

They made camp in a sloping pasture rimmed by enormous oak trees and pines and nut trees, a stream moving down through the center, over steps of rock. Where the forest began, there was a lake. Every night there were new groups of campfires to push away the frost, and soon there was hardly a place to stand, there were so many men and animals. The grass, the withering leaves were full of whispering, but the campground was hushed, muffled by their presence, as if blighted. I watched from my hiding place. They talked in mumbles or not at all. Message carriers moved from fire to fire, talking softly with the leaders. Their rich furs shone like birds' wings in the firelight. Heavily guarded, the younger soldiers pushed through the crowd and, all night long, washed clothes and cooking ware in the stream until the water was thick with dirt and grease and no longer made a sound as it dropped toward the lake. When they slept, guards and dogs watched over them in herds. Before dawn, men rose to exercise the horses, polish weapons, or move out with bows in search of deer.

Then one night when I went down to spy, they were gone, vanished like starlings from a tree. I followed their trail—footprints, hoofprints, and wagon ruts cutting a wide dirty swath toward the east. When I came in sight of them, I slowed down, laughing and hugging myself; it was going to be a massacre. They marched all night, then scattered into the forest like wolves and slept all day without fires. I snatched an ox and devoured it, leaving no trace. At dusk, they formed again. At midnight the armies arrived at the antlered hall.

Hrothgar called out to him, glorious protector of the Scyldings, hoarfrost bearded: "Hygmod, lord of the Helmings, greet your guests!" Unferth stood beside him, his huge arms folded on his byrnie. He stood with his head bowed, eyes mere slits, clamped mouth hidden where his mustache overlapped his beard. Bitterness went out from him like darkness made visible: Unferth the hero (known far and wide in these Scanian lands), isolated in that huge crowd like a poisonous snake aware of what it was. King Hrothgar called again.

The young king came out, well armed, leading a bear and six retainers. He looked around him, blond and pale, arms ringed with gold, a vague smile hiding his shock. The army of the Scyldings and all their allies stretched off in the darkness as far as the eye could see—down the slopes of the hill, down the stone-paved roadways, away into the trees.

Hrothgar made a speech, lifting his ashspear and shaking it. The young man waited like stone, his gloved right hand grasping the chain that led the bear. He had no chance, and he knew it. Everyone knew it but the bear beside him, standing upright, considering the crowd. I smiled. I could smell the blood that would drench the ground before morning came. There was a light breeze, a scent of winter in it. It stirred the fur on the men's clothes and rattled the leaves around me. The bear dropped down on all fours and grunted. The king jerked the chain. Then an old man came out of the meadhall, went to the young king, just clear of the bear, and spoke to him.

GRENDEL

Hrothgar and all his allies were silent, waiting. The young king and the old man talked. The retainers at the mead-hall door joined in, their voices low. I waited. Hrothgar's whole army was silent. Then the young king moved toward Hrothgar. A rumble went through the crowd, then fell away like a wave retreating, drawing pebbles out from shore. At last, very slowly, the young king drew out his sword, with his left hand—a sign of truce—and dropped it, as if casually, in front of Hrothgar's horse.

"We will give you gifts," the young king said, "splendid tribute in sign of our great respect for the honorable Scyldings." His voice and smile were gracious. His eyes, slanting downward like the eyes of a fish, were expressionless as dried-up wells.

Unferth laughed, all alone in the silence. The sound rolled away to the darkness to die among trees.

Hrothgar, white-haired, white-bearded as the ice-god, shook his head. "There is no gift your people can give the Scyldings," he said. "You think you can buy a little time with gold, and then some night when we're sitting at our mead, you and all your brave allies will come down on us —crash!—as we tonight have come down on you, and no gift we can offer then will turn away your fury." The old man smiled, his eyes wicked. "Do you take us for children that play in the yards with pets? What could we give you that you couldn't take by force, and at that time take from us tenfold?"

Unferth smiled, looking at the bear. The young king showed nothing, accepting the joke and the argument as if he'd been expecting them. He gave the chain another jerk and the bear moved closer to him. When he'd waited long enough, he looked back up at Hrothgar.

"We can give you such piles of treasure," he said, "that I have nothing left to pay an army with. Then you'll be safe."

Hrothgar laughed. "You're crafty, lord of the Helmings. A king shrewd with words can mount a great army on promises. The treasure you'd take by destroying my house could make all your swordsmen rich. Come, come! No more talk! It's a chilly night, and we have cows to milk in the morning. Take up your weapons. We'll give you ground. We haven't come to kill you like foxes in a hole."

But the young king waited on. He was still smiling, though his eyes had no life in them. He had something in reserve, some ingenious product of his counselor's wits that would overwhelm their scheme. He said, speaking more quietly than before, "I will show you a treasure that will change your mind, great Hrothgar." He turned to an attendant and made a sign. The attendant went into the meadhall.

After a long time he returned. He was carrying nothing.

Behind him, men opened the meadhall door wide. Light burst over the hillside and glinted on the weapons and eyes of the Scyldings. The bear stirred, restless, irritable, like the young king's anger removed to the end of a chain. Old Hrothgar waited.

Then at last, moving slowly, as if walking in a dream, a woman in a robe of threaded silver came gliding from the hall. Her smooth long hair was as red as fire and soft as the ruddy sheen on dragon's gold. Her face was gentle, mysteriously calm. The night became more still.

"I offer you my sister," the young king said. "Let her name from now on be Wealtheow, or holy servant of common good."

I leered in the rattling darkness of my tree. The name was ridiculous. "Pompous, pompous ass!" I hissed. But she was beautiful and she surrendered herself with the dignity of a sacrificial virgin. My chest was full of pain, my eyes smarted, and I was afraid—O monstrous trick against reason—I was afraid I was about to sob. I wanted to smash things, bring down the night with my howl of rage. But I kept still. She was beautiful, as innocent as dawn on winter hills. She tore me apart as once the Shaper's song had done. As if for my benefit, as if in vicious scorn of me, children came from the meadhall and ran down to her, weeping, to snatch at her hands and dress.

"Stop it!" I whispered. "Stupid!"

She did not look at them, merely touched their heads. "Be still," she said—hardly more than a whisper, but it carried across the crowd. They were still, as if her voice were magic. I clenched my teeth, tears streaming from my eyes. She was like a child, her sweet face paler than the moon. She looked up at Hrothgar's beard, not his eyes, afraid of him. "My lord," she said.

O woe! O wretched violation of sense!

I could see myself leaping from my high tree and running on all fours through the crowd to her, howling, whimpering, throwing myself down, drooling and groveling at her small, fur-booted feet. "Mercy!" I would howl. "Aargh! Burble!" I clamped my palms over my eyes and struggled not to laugh.

No need to say more. The old king accepted the younger king's gift, along with some other things—swords and cups, some girls and young men, her servants. For several days both sides made speeches, long-winded, tediously poetic, all lies, and then, with much soft weeping and sniffling, the Scyldings loaded up Wealtheow and the lesser beauties, made a few last touching observations, and went home.

A bad winter. I couldn't lay a hand on them, prevented as if by a charm. I huddled in my cave, grinding my teeth, beating my forehead with my fists and cursing nature.

Sometimes I went up to the frozen cliffwall and looked down, down, at where the lights lay blue, like the threads running out from a star, patterning the snow. My fists struck out at the cliff's ice-crusted rock. It was no satisfaction. In the cave again, I listened to my mother move back and forth, a pale shape driven by restlessness and rage at the restlessness and rage she felt in me and could not cure. She would gladly have given her life to end my suffering —horrible, humpbacked, carp-toothed creature, eyes on fire with useless, mindless love. Who could miss the grim parallel? So the lady below would give, had given, her life for those she loved. So would any simpering, eyelash-batting female in her court, given the proper setup, the minimal conditions. The smell of the dragon lay around me like sulphurous smoke. At times I would wake up in panic, unable to breathe.

At times I went down.

She carried the mealbowl from table to table, smiling quietly, as if the people she served, her husband's people, were her own. The old king watched with thoughtful eyes, moved as he'd have been by the Shaper's music, except that it was different: not visions of glorious things that might be or sly revisions of the bloody past but present beauty that made time's flow seem illusory, some lower law that now had been suspended. Meaning as quality. When drunken men argued, pitting theory against theory, bludgeoning each other's absurdities, she came between them, wordless, uncondemning, pouring out mead like a mother's love, and they were softened, reminded of their humanness, exactly as they might have been softened by the cry of a child in danger, or an old man's suffering, or spring. The Shaper sang things that had never crossed his mind before: comfort, beauty, a wisdom softer, more permanent, than Hrothgar's. The old king watched, remote from the queen, though she shared his bed, and he mused.

One night she paused in front of Unferth. He sat hunched, bitterly smiling, as always, his muscles taut as old nautical ropes in a hurricane. He was ugly as a spider.

"My lord?" she said. She often called the thanes "my lord." Servant of even the lowliest among them.

"No thank you," he said. He shot a glance at her, then looked down, smiled fiercely. She waited, expressionless except for perhaps the barest trace of puzzlement. He said, "I've had enough."

Down the table a man made bold by mead said, "Men have been known to kill their brothers when they've too much mead. Har, har."

A few men laughed.

Unferth stiffened. The queen's face paled. Once again Unferth glanced up at the queen, then away. His fists closed tight, resting on the table in front of him, inches from his knife. No one moved. The hall became still. She stood strange-eyed, as if looking out from another world and time. Who can say what she understood? I knew, for one, that the brother-killer had put on the Shaper's idea of the hero like a merry mask, had seen it torn away, and was now reduced to what he was: a thinking animal stripped naked of former illusions, stubbornly living on, ashamed and meaningless, because killing himself would be, like his life, unheroic. It was a paradox nothing could resolve but a murderous snicker. The moment stretched, a snag in time's stream, and still no one moved, no one spoke. As if defiantly, Unferth, murderer of brothers, again raised his eyes to the queen's, and this time didn't look down. Scorn? Shame?

The queen smiled. Impossibly, like roses blooming in the heart of December, she said, "That's past." And it was. The demon was exorcised. I saw his hands unclench, relax, and—torn between tears and a bellow of scorn—I crept back to my cave.

It was not, understand, that she had secret wells of joy that overflowed to them all. She lay beside the sleeping king—I watched wherever she went, a crafty guardian, wealthy in wiles—and her eyes were open, the lashes bright with tears. She was more child, those moments, than woman. Thinking of home, remembering paths in the land of the Helmings where she'd played before she'd lain aside her happiness for theirs. She held the naked, bony king as if he were the child, and nothing between him and the darkness but her white arm. Sometimes she'd slip from the bed while he slept and would cross to the door and go out alone into the night. Alone and never alone. Instantly, guards were all around her, gem-woman priceless among the Scylding treasures. She would stand in the cold wind looking east, one hand clutching her robe to her throat, the silent guards encircling her like trees. Child though she was, she would show no sign of her sorrow in front of them. At last some guard would speak to her, would mention the cold, and Wealtheow would smile and nod her thanks and go back in.

Once that winter her brother came, with his bear and a great troop of followers, to visit. Their talk and laughter rumbled up to the cliffwall. The double band drank, the Shaper sang, and then they drank again. I listened from a distance for as long as I could stand it, clenching my mind on the words of the dragon, then, helpless as always, I went down. The wind howled, piling up snow in drifts and blinding the night with ice-white dust. I walked bent over against the cold, protecting my eyes with my arms. Trees, posts, cowsheds loomed into my vision, then vanished, swallowed in white. When I came near Hart, I could smell the guards of the hall all around me, but I couldn't see them—nor, of course, could they see me. I went straight to the wall, plunging through drifts to my knees, and pressed up against it for its warmth. It trembled and shook from the noise inside. I bent down to the crack I'd used before and watched.

She was brighter than the hearthfire, talking again with her family and friends, observing the antics of the bear. It was the king, old Hrothgar, who carried the meadbowl from table to table tonight. He walked, dignified, from group to group, smiling and filling the drinking cups, and you'd have sworn from his look that never until tonight had the old man been absolutely happy. He would glance at his queen from time to time as he moved among his people and hers, the Danes and Helmings, and with each glance his smile would grow warmer for a moment, and a thoughtful look would come over his eyes. Then it would pass—some gesture or word from a guest or one of his Scylding thanes—and he would be hearty, merry: not false, exactly, but less than what he was at the moment of the glance. As for the queen, she seemed not to know he was there. She sat beside her brother, her hand on his arm, the other hand on the arm of a shriveled old woman, precious relative. The bear sat with his feet stuck out, playing with his penis and surveying the hall with a crotchety look, as if dimly aware that there was something about him that humans could not approve. The Helming guests all talked at once, eagerly, constantly, as if squeezing all their past into an evening. I couldn't hear what they said. The hall was a roar—voices, the clink of cups, the shuffle of feet. Sometimes Wealtheow would tip back her head, letting her copper-red hair fall free, and laugh; sometimes she listened, head cocked, now smiling, now soberly pursing her lips, only offering a nod. Hrothgar went back to his high, carved chair, relinquishing the bowl to the noblest of his thanes, and sat like an old man listening inside his mind to the voices of his childhood. Once, for a long moment, the queen looked at him while listening to her brother, her eyes as thoughtful as Hrothgar's. Then she laughed and talked again, and the king conversed with the man on his left; it was as if their minds had not met.

Later that night they passed a harp—not the old Shaper's instrument, no one touched that—and the queen's brother sang. He was no artist, with either his fingers or his throat, but all the hall was silent, listening. He sang, childlike except for the winter in his gray eyes, of a hero who'd killed a girl's old father out of love of the girl, and how the girl after that had both loved and hated the hero and finally had killed him. Wealtheow smiled, full of sorrow, as she listened. The bear irritably watched the dogs. Then others sang. Old Hrothgar watched and listened, brooding on dangers. (The queen's brother had straw-yellow hair and eyes as gray as slate. Sometimes when he stole a glance at Hrothgar, his face was a knife.)

Toward morning, they all went to bed. Half buried in snow, the deadly cold coming up through my feet, I kept watch. The queen put her hand on Hrothgar's bare shoulder as he slept and looked at him thoughtfully, exactly as Hrothgar had looked at her and at his people. She moved a strand of hair from his face. After a long, long time she closed her eyes, but even now I wasn't sure she was asleep.

And so in my cave, coughing from the smoke and clenching feet on fire with chilblains, I ground my teeth on my own absurdity. Whatever their excuse might be, I had none, I knew: I had seen the dragon. Ashes to ashes. And yet I was teased—tortured by the red of her hair and the set of her chin and the white of her shoulders—teased toward disbelief in the dragon's truths. A glorious moment was coming, my chest insisted, and even the fact that I myself would have no part in it—a member of the race God cursed, according to the Shaper's tale—was trifling. In my mind I watched her freckled hand move on the old man's arm as once I'd listened to the sigh of the Shaper's harp. Ah, woe, woe! How many times must a creature be dragged down the same ridiculous road? The Shaper's lies, the hero's self-delusion, now this: the idea of a queen! My mother, breathing hard, scraping through her hair with her crooked nails, watched me and sometimes moaned.

And so, the next night—it was dark as pitch—I burst the meadhall door, killed men, and stormed directly to the door behind which lay the sleeping queen. Glorious Unferth slept beside it. He rose to fight me. I slapped him aside like a troublesome colt. The queen's brother rose, unleashed the bear. I accepted its hug in my own and broke its back. I slammed into the bedroom. She sat up screaming, and I laughed. I snatched her foot, and now her unqueenly shrieks were deafening, exactly like the squeals of a pig. No one would defend her, not even suicidal Unferth at the door, screaming his rage—self-hatred. Old Hrothgar shook and made lunatic noises and drooled. I could have jerked her from the bed and stove in her golden-haired head against the wall. They watched in horror, Helmings on one side, Scyldings on the other (balance is anything), and I caught the other foot and pulled her naked legs apart as if to split her. "Gods, gods!" she screamed. I waited to see if the gods would come, but not a sign of them. I laughed. She called to her brother, then Unferth. They hung back. I decided to kill her. I firmly committed myself to killing her, slowly, horribly. I would begin by holding her over the fire and cooking the ugly hole between her legs. I laughed harder at that. They were all screaming now, hooting and yawling to their dead-stick gods. I would kill her, yes! I would squeeze out her feces between my fists. So much for meaning as quality of life! I would kill her and teach them reality. Grendel the truth-teacher, phantasm-tester! It was what I would be from this day forward—my commitment, my character as long as I lived—and nothing alive or dead could change my mind!

I changed my mind. It would be meaningless, killing her. As meaningless as letting her live. It would be, for me, mere pointless pleasure, an illusion of order for this one frail, foolish flicker-flash in the long dull fall of eternity. (End quote.)

I let go her feet. The people stared, unbelieving. I had wrecked another theory. I left the hall.

But I'd cured myself. That much, at least, I could say for my behavior. I concentrated on the memory of the ugliness between her legs (bright tears of blood) and laughed as I ran through the heavy snow. The night was still. I could hear their crying in the meadhall. "Ah, Grendel, you sly old devil!" I whispered to the trees. The words rang false. (The east was gray.) I hung balanced, a creature of two minds; and one of them said—unreasonable, stubborn as the mountains—that she was beautiful. I resolved, absolutely and finally, to kill myself, for love of the Baby Grendel that used to be. But the next instant, for no particular reason, I changed my mind.

Balance is everything, sliding down slime. . . .

Cut *B*.

8

After the murder of Halga the Good,
dear younger brother of bold king Hrothgar
(helm of the Scyldings, sword-hilt handler,
bribe-gold bender   who by his wife had
now two sons) came Hrothulf out of
orphan's woe to Hart.

                         (O hear me,
rocks and trees, loud waterfalls! You imagine I tell you
these things just to hear myself speak? A little respect
there, brothers and sisters!

      (Thus poor Grendel,
        anger's child,

red eyes hidden in the dark of verbs,
brachiating with a hoot from rhyme to rhyme.)

SCENE: *The Arrival of Hrothulf at Hart.*

"Hrothulf! Come to Aunt Wealtheow!
You poor, poor dear boy!"
"It is very kind of you, madam, to take me in."
"Nonsense, dearest! You're Hrothgar's flesh and blood!"
"So I'm told." A mumble. Trace of smile.
The old king frowns in his carved chair.
The boy has the manners, he broods, of a half-tamed wolf.
Fourteen years old and already a God-damned pretender?
Age, old chain of victories, where is your comfort?
He clears his throat.
No no; I jump to conclusions.
The boy has been through a bad time,
naturally. Father-funeral and all the rest.
And gifted, of course, with a proud heart,
like all his line. (Oft Scyld Shefing . . .)
(The hawk in the rafters hands down no opinion.)
The Shaper sings—the harp soughing out through the long
    room
like summer wind—"By deeds worth praise
a man can, in any kingdom, prosper!"
So.

The boy sits solemn and hears the harp
behind closed eyes. The October hills in his calm mind
run wolves.
Theorum: Any action (A) of the human heart
must trigger an equal and opposite reaction (A^1).
Such is the golden opinion of the Shaper.
And so—I watch in glee—they take in Hrothulf;
quiet as the moon, sweet scorpion,
he sits between their two and cleans his knife.

SCENE: *Hrothulf in the Yard.*
Hrothulf speaks:

In ratty furs the peasants hoe their fields,
fat with stupidity, if not with flesh. Their foodsmells
foul the doorways, dungeon dark, where cow-eyed girls
give tit to the next generation's mindless hoe. Old men
with ringworm in their beards limp dusty lanes
to gather like bony dogs at the god-lined square
where the king's justice is dispensed; to nod like crows
at slips of the tongue by which a horse is lost, or delicate
    mistakes
of venue through which murderers run free. "Long live
the king!" they squeak, "to whom we owe all joy!"
Obese with imagined freedom if not with fat, great lords
of lords look down with cowdog eyes and smile.

"All's well," they sigh. "Long live the king! All's well!"
Law rules the land. Men's violence is chained
to good (i.e., to the king): legitimate force
that chops the bread-thief's neck and wipes its ax.—Death
by book.
      Think, sweating beast! Look up and think!
Whence came these furs on the backs of your kind
   protectors?
Why does the bread-thief die and the murdering thane
escape by a sleight by the costliest of advocates?
Think! Squeeze up your wrinkled face
and seize the hangnail tip of a searing thought:
Violence hacked this shack-filled hole in the woods where
   you
play freedom games. Violence no more legitimate then
than a wolf's. And now by violence they lock
us in—you and me, old man: subdue our vile
unkingly voilence. Come into the shade.
I would have a word with you and your wart-hog son.

SCENE: *Hrothulf in the Woods.*

The nut tree, wide above my head,
stretching its cool black limbs to take
the sun, sends darkness down my chest.
Its dappled, highcrowned roadways make

safe homes for birds; quick squirrels run
the veins of its treasure-giving hand;
but the ground below is dead.

Strange providence! Shall I call the tree
tyrannical, since where it stands
nothing survives but itself and its high-
borne guests? Condemn it because it sends
down stifling darkness, sucks the life
from grass, and whitens the sapling leaf
for trifling, fluttering friends?

The law of the world is a winter law,
and casual. I too can be grim:
snatch my daylight by violent will
and be glorified for the deed, like him;
drain my soil of Considerations,
grip my desires like underground stones,
let old things sicken and fail.

She touches my hair and smiles, kind,
trusting the rhetoric of love: Give
and get. But the thought flits through my mind,
There have got to be stabler things than love.
The blurred tree towering overhead
consumes the sun; the ground is dead;
I gasp for rain and wind.

SCENE: *The Queen Beside Hrothulf's Bed.*
Wealtheow speaks:

So sad so young? And even in sleep?
Worse times are yet to come, my love.
The babes you comfort when they weep
Will soon by birthright have

All these gold rings! Ah, then, then
Your almost-brother love will cool;
The cousin smile must grind out lean
Where younger cousins rule.

When I was a child I truly loved:
Unthinking love as calm and deep
As the North Sea. But I have lived,
And now I do not sleep.

In short, I watched the idea of violence growing in him, and apprehension in all of them, and I enjoyed myself (old hellroads-runner, earth-rim-roamer), sucking glee from spite,—O sucking to the pits! He hardly spoke when he first came, skinny, pimply, beardless except for the babyhair on his upper lip and chin. At the end of a year he never spoke at all, unless he was forced to it or found himself alone with the foul old old peasant he met in the woods sometimes, his counselor. Hrothulf had hair as black as coal and hazel eyes that never blinked. He stood, always, with his head slung forward and his lips in a pout, like a man straining to remember something. The old man —he was nicknamed Red Horse—had a perpetually startled look, round, red eyes and mouth, white hair that flared around his high, empty dome like the beams of the sun: the look of a man who has suddenly remembered something. I followed the two down shaded paths, skull-lined, since I had used them often (but our travelers did not see the skulls)—Hrothulf stumbling over roots and stones, the old man swinging along on one stiff leg. He spit when he talked, his eyes bugged. He stunk.

"To step out of the region of legality requires an extraordinary push of circumstance," the old man yelled. He was deaf and shouted as if everyone else were too. "The incitement to violence depends upon total transvaluation of the ordinary values. By a single stroke, the most criminal acts must be converted to heroic and meritorious deeds. If the Revolution comes to grief, it will be because you and those you lead have become alarmed at your own brutality."

Hrothulf fell down. The old man went on swinging along the path, oblivious, waving his fists. Hrothluf looked around him in slight surprise, understood that he had fallen, and got up. He almost fell again as he ran to catch his adviser. "Make no mistake, my beloved prince," the old man was yelling. "The total ruin of institutions and morals is an act of creation. A *religious* act. Murder and mayhem are the life and soul of revolution. I imagine you won't laugh when I tell you that. There are plenty of fools who would."

"Oh no, sir," said Hrothulf.

"The very soul! What does a kingdom pretend to do? Save the values of the community—regulate compromise—improve the quality of the commonwealth! In other words, protect the power of the people in power and keep the others down. By common agreement of course, so the fiction goes. And they do pretty well. We'll give them that."

Hrothulf nodded. "We have to give them that."

"Rewards to people who fit the System best, you know. King's immediate thanes, the thanes' top servants, and so on till you come to the people who don't fit at all. No problem. Drive them to the darkest corners of the kingdom, starve them, throw them in jail or put them out to war."

"That's how it works."

"But satisfy the greed of the majority, and the rest will do you no harm. That's it. You've still got your fiction of consent. If the lowest of the workers start grumbling, claim that the power of the state stands above society, regulating it, moderating it, keeping it within the bounds of order—an impersonal and higher authority of justice. And what if the workers are beyond your reconciliation? Cry 'Law!'

Cry 'Common good' and put on the pressure—arrest and execute a few."

"A stinking fraud," Hrothulf said, and bit his lip. There were tears in his eyes. The old serf laughed.

"Exactly, my boy! What is the state in a time of domestic or foreign crisis? What is the state when the chips are down? The answer is obvious and clear! Oh yes! If a few men quit work, the police move in. If the borders are threatened, the army rolls out. Public force is the life and soul of every state: not merely army and police but prisons, judges, tax collectors, every conceivable trick of coercive repression. The state is an organization of violence, a monopoly in what it is pleased to call *legitimate* violence. Revolution, my dear prince, is not the substitution of immoral for moral, or of illegitimate for legitimate violence; it is simply the pitting of power against power, where the issue is freedom for the winners and enslavement of the rest."

Hrothulf stopped. "That's not at all what I intend," he said. "There can be more freedom or less freedom in different states."

The old man stopped too, several steps ahead of him on the forest path, and looked back, polite by an effort. "Well, that may be," he said. He shrugged.

Hrothulf, though clumsy, was no fool. He said angrily (unaware of the irony that he, a prince, had a right to anger, and the old man, a peasant, did not), "Nobody i.. his right mind would praise violence for its own sake, regardless of its ends!"

The old man shrugged and put on a childish smile. "But I'm a simple man, you see," he said, "and that's exactly what I do. All systems are evil. All governments are evil. Not just a trifle evil. *Monstrously* evil." Though he still smiled, he was shaking, only half controlling it. "If you want me to help you destroy a government, I'm here to serve. But as for Universal Justice—" He laughed.

Hrothulf puckered his lips, stared thoughtfully past him.

Hrothgar's nephew was kind, for all that, to the cousins he half intended to displace. He was a moody, lonely young man, after all, afraid of strangers, awkward even with the adults he knew well, and the cousins were plump blond children of three and four. There was one other cousin, Freawaru, Hrothgar's daughter by a woman who'd died. Whenever Freawaru spoke to him, Hrothulf blushed.

He sat between the two boys at the table and helped them with their food, smiling when they talked but rarely answering. The queen would glance at the three now and then. So would others, sometimes. They all knew what was coming, though nobody believed it. Who can look into the wet-mouthed smiles of children and see a meadhall burning, or listen past their musical prattle to the midnight roar of fire?

—Except, of course, old Hrothgar. Violence and shame have lined the old man's face with mysterious calm. I can hardly look at him without a welling of confused, unpleasant emotion. He sits tall and still in his carved chair, stiff arms resting on the chair-sides, his clear eyes trained on the meadhall door where I'll arrive, if I come. When someone speaks to him, he answers politely and gently, his mind far away—on murdered thanes, abandoned hopes. He's a giant. He had in his youth the strength of seven men. Not now. He has nothing left but the power of his mind—and no pleasure there: a case of knives. The civilization he meant to build has transmogrified to a forest thick with traps. Hrothulf, he knows, is a danger to his sons; but he cannot abandon the child of his dead younger brother. Hygmod, his brother-in-law, is biding his time while Hrothgar lives, because of Wealtheow; but Hygmod, he knows, is no friend. And then there is a man named Ingeld, ruler of the Heathobards, as famous for slaughter as was Hrothgar in his day. The old man intends to deal out Freawaru to him; he has no assurance it will work. And then too there's his treasure-hoard. Another trap. A man plunders to build up wealth to pay his men and bring peace to the kingdom, but the hoard he builds for his safety becomes the lure of every marauder that happens to hear of it. Hrothgar, keen of mind, is out of schemes. No fault of his. There are no schemes left. And so he waits like a man chained in a cave, staring at the entrance or, sometimes, gazing with sad, absent-minded eyes at Wealtheow, chained beside him. Who is one more trap, the worst. She's young, could have served a more vigorous man. And beautiful: need not have withered her nights and wasted her body on a bony, shivering wretch. She knows all this, which increases his pain and guilt. She understands the fear for his people that makes a coward of him, so that, that night when I attacked her, he would not lift a finger to preserve her. And his fear is one he cannot even be sure is generous; perhaps mere desire that his name and fame live on. She understands too his bitterness at growing old. She even understands—more terrible, no doubt, than all the rest—old Hrothgar's knowledge that peace must be searched through ordeal upon ordeal, with no final prospect but failure. Lesson on lesson they've suffered through, recognizing, more profoundly each time, their indignity, shame, triviality. It will continue.

How, if I know all this, you may ask, could I hound him—shatter him again and again, drive him deeper and deeper into woe? I have no answer, except perhaps this: why should I *not*? Has he made any move to deserve my kindness? If I give him a truce, will the king invite me in for a kiss on the forehead, a cup of mead? Ha! This nobility of his, this dignity: are they not *my* work? What was he before? Nothing! A swollen-headed raider, full of boasts and stupid jokes and mead. No more noble than Red Horse, Hrothulf's friend. No one would have balked at my persecuting him then! I made him what he is. Have I not a right to test my own creation? Enough! Who says I have to defend myself? I'm a machine, like you. Like all of you. Blood-lust and rage are my character. Why does the lion not wisely settle down and be a horse? In any case, I too am learning, ordeal by ordeal, my indignity. It's all I have, my only weapon for smashing through these stiff coffin-walls of the world. So I dance in the moonlight, make foul jokes, or labor to shake the foundations of night with my heaped-up howls of rage. Something is bound to come of all this. I cannot believe such monstrous energy of grief can lead to nothing!

I have thought up a horrible dream to impute to Hrothgar.

Hrothgar speaks:

I have dreamt it again: standing suddenly still
In a thicket, among wet trees, stunned, minutely
Shuddering, hearing a wooden echo escape.
A mossy floor, almost colorless, disappears

In depths of rain among the tree shapes.
I am straining, tasting that echo a second longer.

If I can hold it ... familiar if I can hold it ...
A black tree with a double trunk—two trees
Grown into one—throws up its blurred branches.

The two trunks in their infinitesimal dance of growth
Have turned completely about one another, their join
A slowly twisted scar ... that I recognize. ...

A quick arc flashes sidewise in the air,
A heavy blade in flight. A wooden stroke:
Iron sinks in the gasping core.
                              I will dream it again.

9

December, approaching the year's darkest night, and the
   only way out of the dream is down and through it.

The trees are dead.

The days are an arrow in a dead man's chest.

Snowlight blinds me, heatless fire; pale, apocalyptic.

The creeks are frozen; the deer show their ribs.

I find dead wolves—a paw, a scraggly tail sticking up
   through snow.

The trees are dead, and only the deepest religion can break
   through time and believe they'll revive. Against the
   snow, black cuts on a white, white hand.

In the town, children go down on their backs in the

drifted snow and move their arms and, when they rise, leave behind them impressions, mysterious and ominous, of winged creatures. I come upon them as I move through sleeping streets to the meadhall, and though I know what they are, I pause and study them, picking at my lip.

I do not pretend to understand these feelings. I record them, check them off one by one for the dead ears of night.

Something is coming, strange as spring.

I am afraid.

Standing on an open hill, I imagine muffled footsteps overhead.

I watch one of Hrothgar's bowmen pursue a hart. The man, furred from his toes to his ears, walks through the moon-and-snowlit woods, silent as an owl, huge bow on his shoulder, his eyes on the dark tracks. He moves up a thickly wooded hill, and at the crest of it, standing as if waiting for him, he finds the hart. The antlers reach out, motionless, as still as the treelimbs overhead or the stars above the trees. They're like wings, filled with otherworldly light. Neither the hart nor the hunter moves. Time is inside them, transferred from chamber to chamber like sand in an hourglass; it can no more get outside than sand in the lower chamber can rise to the upper without a hand to turn stiff nature on its head. They face each other, unmoving as numbers on a stick. And then, incredibly, through the pale, strange light the man's hand moves—click click click click—toward the bow, and grasps it, and draws it down, away from the shoulder and around in front (click click) and transfers the bow to the slowly moving second hand, and the first hand goes back up and (click) over the shoulder and returns with an arrow, threads the bow. Suddenly time is a rush for the hart: his head flicks, he jerks, his front legs buckling, and he's dead. He lies as still as the snow hurtling outward around him to the hushed world's rim.

The image clings to my mind like a growth. I sense some riddle in it.

Near Hrothgar's hall stand the images of the Scyldings' gods, grotesque faces carved out of wood or hacked from stone and set up in a circle, eyes staring inward, gazing thoughtfully at nothing. The priests approach them, carrying torches, their shaggy white heads bent, obsequious. "Great spirit," the chief of the priests wails, "ghostly Destroyer, defend the people of Scyld and kill their enemy, the terrible world-rim-walker!" I smile, arms folded on my chest, and wait, but nobody comes to kill me. They sing, an antique language as ragged and strange as their beards, a language closer to mine than to their own. They march in a circle, from god to god—maybe uncertain which one is the Great Destroyer. "Is it you?" their meek old faces ask, lifting the torch to each monster-shape in turn. "Not I," whispers the head with four eyes. "Not I," whispers sly old dagger-tooth. "Not I," says the wolf-god, the bull-god, the horse-god, the happily smiling god with the nose like a pig's. They stab a calf and burn it, the corpse still jerking. The old peasant, friend of Prince Hrothulf, whispers crossly: "In the old days they used to kill virgins. Religion is sick."

Which is true. There is no conviction in the old priests' songs; there is only showmanship. No one in the kingdom is convinced that the gods have life in them. The weak observe the rituals—take their hats off, put them on again, raise their arms, lower their arms, moan, intone, press their palms together—but no one harbors unreasonable expectations. The strong—old Hrothgar, Unferth—ignore the images. The will to power resides among the stalactites of the heart. (Her-kapf.)

Once, years ago, for no particular reason, I wrecked the place; broke up the wooden gods like kindling and toppled the gods of stone. When they came out in the morning and saw what I'd done, no one was especially bothered except the priests. They lamented and tore their hair, the priests, as fraught and rhetorical as they were when they prayed, and after a few days their outcries made people uneasy. On the chance that there might be something to it all, whatever a reasonable man might think, the people tipped the stone gods up again, with levers and ropes, and began to carve new gods of wood to replace those I'd ruined. It was dull work, you could see by their faces, but it was, for some reason, necessary. When the ring was complete, I considered wrecking it again, but the gods were inoffensive, dull. I decided the hell with it.

I have eaten several priests. They sit on the stomach like duck eggs.

Midnight. I sit in the center of the ring of gods, musing on them, pursuing some thought that I cannot make come clear. They wait, as quiet as upright bones in the softly falling snow. So Hrothgar waits, lying on his back with his eyes open. Wealtheow lies on her back beside him, her eyes open, her hand resting lightly in his. Hrothulf's breathing changes. He is having bad dreams. Unferth sleeps fitfully, guarding the meadhall; and the Shaper, in his big house, tosses and turns. He has a fever. He mumbles a few inchoate phrases to someone who is not there. All the gods have hats of snow and snow-crested noses. In the town below me there are no lights left. Overhead, the stars are blanked out by clouds.

But someone is awake. I hear him coming toward me in the snow, vaguely alarming, approaching like an arrow in a slowed-down universe, and a shudder runs through me. Then I see him, and I laugh at my fear. An old priest, palsied, walking with a cane of ash. He thinks it has magic in it. "Who's there?" he pipes, coming to the edge of the ring. He has a black robe, and his beard, as white as the snow all around us, hangs almost to his knees. "Who's there?" he says again, and pokes himself through between two gods, feeling ahead of himself with the cane. "Is there somebody here?" he whimpers.

"It is I," I say. "The Destroyer."

A violent shock goes through him. He shakes all over, practically falls down. "My lord!" he whimpers. He goes down on his knees. "O blessed, blessed lord!" A look of doubt crosses his face, but he resists it. "I heard someone down here," he says. "I thought it was—" The doubt comes again, mixed with fear this time. He squints, cocks his head, struggling to penetrate his blindness by force of will. "I am Ork," he says uncertainly, "eldest and wisest of the priests." I smile, say nothing. I intend to paint the images with the old man's steaming blood. "I know all mysteries," the priest says. "I am the only man still living who has thought them all out."

"We are pleased with you, Ork," I say, voice very solemn. Then, suddenly impish—at times I cannot resist these things: "Tell us what you know of the King of the Gods."

"The King?" he says.

"The King." I do not giggle.

He rolls his blind eyes, figuring the odds, snatching through his mind for doctrines.

"Speak to us concerning His unspeakable beauty and danger," I say, and wait.

The snow falls softly on the images. The old priest, kneeling, has one knee on his beard and is unable to lift his head. He shakes all over, as if the palsy is something outside him, an element like wind.

"The King of Gods," he whispers, and searches his wits.

At last he folds his arthritic white hands, raises them before him like a nightmare flower, and speaks. "The King of the Gods is the ultimate limitation," he keens, "and His existence is the ultimate irrationality." A tic goes down one cheek; jerks the corner of his mouth. "For no reason can be given for just that limitation which it stands in His nature to impose. The King of the Gods is not concrete, but He is the ground for concrete actuality. No reason can be given for the nature of God, because that nature is the ground of rationality."

He tips his head, waiting for some response from me that will tell him how he's doing. I say nothing. The old man clears his throat, and his face takes on an expression still more holy. The tic comes again.

"The King of the Gods is the actual entity in virtue of which the entire multiplicity of eternal objects obtains its graded relevance to each stage of concrescence. Apart from Him, there can be no relevant novelty."

I notice, with surprise, that the priest's blind eyes are brimming with tears. They seep down his cheeks into his beard. I raise my fingers to my mouth, baffled.

"The Chief God's purpose in the creative advance is the evocation of novel intensities. He is the *lure for our feeling*." Ork is now weeping profusely, so moved that his throat constricts. I observe in wonder. His knotted hands shake and sway.

"He is the eternal urge of desire establishing the purposes of all creatures. He is an infinite patience, a tender care that nothing in the universe be vain."

He begins to moan, shaking violently, and it occurs to me that perhaps he is merely cold. But instead of hugging himself, as I expect him to, he stretches out his arms toward the sky, huge-knuckled fingers gnarled and twisted as if to frighten me. "O the ultimate evil in the temporal world is deeper than any specific evil, such as hatred, or suffering, or death! The ultimate evil is that Time is perpetual perishing, and being actual involves elimination. The nature of evil may be epitomized, therefore, in two simple but horrible and holy propositions: 'Things fade' and 'Alternatives exclude.' Such is His mystery: that beauty requires contrast, and that discord is fundamental to the creation of new intensities of feeling. Ultimate wisdom, I have come to perceive, lies in the perception that the solemnity and grandeur of the universe rise through the slow process of unification in which the diversities of existence are utilized, and nothing, *nothing* is lost." The old man falls forward, arms thrown out in front of him, and weeps with gratitude. I have trouble deciding what to do.

Before I can make up my mind about him, I become aware that there are others moving toward the place, drawn by the old man's keening. So quietly that even old Ork cannot hear me, I tiptoe out of the ring and hide behind a fat stone image of a god with a skull in his lap and a blacksmith's apron. Three of his fellow priests arrive. They gather around him, bend over to look at him. The snow falls on them softly.

FIRST PRIEST: Ork, what are you doing here? It is written that the old shall keep to the comfort of their beds!

SECOND PRIEST: It's a bad habit, beloved friend, this wandering about at night when monsters prowl.

THIRD PRIEST: Senility. I've been telling you the old fool's gone senile.

ORK: Brothers, I've talked with the Great Destroyer!

THIRD PRIEST: Bosh.

FIRST PRIEST: Blasphemy! It is written: "Ye shall not see my face."

SECOND PRIEST: Think what shape you'll be in for your morning devotions!

ORK: He stood as near to me as you are.

FIRST PRIEST: "Worship is the work of priests. What the gods do is the business of the gods." You know the text.

THIRD PRIEST: He's a blamed fool. If a man hankers for visions, he should do it in public, where it does us some good.

SECOND PRIEST: It doesn't look right, beloved friend, wandering around in the middle of the night. A man should try to be more regular.

ORK: Nevertheless, I saw him. My life of study and devotion has been rewarded! I told him my opinion of the King of the Gods, and he didn't deny it. I believe I'm approximately right.

FIRST PRIEST: The theory's ridiculous. Idle speculation. For it is written—

SECOND PRIEST: Please do come in with us, beloved friend. I hate being up after midnight. It ruins me the whole next day. It makes me put my clothes on wrong, and scramble the service, and eat incorrectly—

THIRD PRIEST: Lunatic priests are bad business. They give people the willies. One man like him can turn us all to paupers.

As I listen, shaking my head at the strangeness of the priestly conversation, another priest comes running up, younger than the others, pulling his outer robe on as he comes. They turn their heads, looking at the younger priest in annoyance. It occurs to me that perhaps he has been drinking. "What's this?" he cries. "Precious gods, what's this?" He throws his hands out, delighted by all he sees. Ork tells him what he has seen, and he listens in rapture. Before Ork has finished, the younger priest drops to his knees and throws his hands up, shaggy lips smiling, wild.

FOURTH PRIEST: Blessed! O blessed! (On his knees he goes over to Ork, seizes the old man's head between his hands, and kisses him.) I feared for you, dear blessed Ork—I feared your bloodless rationalism. But now I see, I see! The will of the gods! The rhythm is re-established! Merely rational thought—forgive me for preaching, but I must, I must!—merely rational thought leaves the mind incurably crippled in a closed and ossified system, it can only ex-trapolate from the past. But now at last, sweet fantasy has found root in your blessed soul! The absurd, the in-spiring, the uncanny, the awesome, the terrifying, the ecstatic—none of these had a place, for you, before. But I should have seen it coming. O I *kick* myself for not seeing it coming! A vision of the Destroyer! Of course, of course!

Before we know it, you'll be kissing girls! Can't you grasp it, brothers? Both blood and sperm are explosive, irregular, feeling-pitched, messy—and inexplicably fascinating! They transcend! They leap the gap! O blessed Ork! I believe your vision proves there is hope for us all!

So he raves, overflowing with meadbowl joy, and the older three priests look down at him as they would at a wounded snake. Ork ignores him, sniffling privately. I back away. Even a monster's blood-lust can be stifled by such talk. They remain inside the image ring, snow falling softly on their hair and beards, and except for their forms, their prattle, the town is dead.

Hrothgar is asleep now, resting up for tomorrow's ordeal of waiting. Wealtheow breathes evenly, beside him. Hrothulf and the king's two children are asleep. In the main hall, row on row in their wall-hung beds, the guardians snore, except Unferth. Puffy-eyed, he gets up, and in a kind of stupor goes to the meadhall door to piss. A dog barks—not at me: I have put my spell on them. Unferth hardly hears. He looks out over the snowy rooftops of the town to the snowy moor, the snowy woods, unaware of my presence behind the wall. The snow falls softly through the trees, closing up the foxes' dens, burying the tracks of sleeping deer. A wolf, asleep with his head on his paws, awakens at the sound of my footsteps and opens his eyes but does not lift his head. He watches me pass, his gray eyes hostile, then sleeps again, his cave half hidden by snow.

I do not usually raid in the winter, when the world is a corpse. I would be wiser to be curled up, asleep like a bear, in my cave. My heart moves slowly, like freezing water, and I cannot clearly recall the smell of blood. And yet I am restless. I would fall, if I could, through time and space to the dragon. I cannot. I walk slowly, wiping the snow from my face with the back of my arm. There is no sound on earth but the whispering snowfall. I recall something. A void boundless as a nether sky. I hang by the twisted roots of an oak, looking down into immensity. Vastly far away I see the sun, black but shining, and slowly revolving around it there are spiders. I pause in my tracks, puzzled—though not stirred—by what I see. But then I am in the woods again, and the snow is falling, and everything alive is fast asleep. It is just some dream. I move on, uneasy; waiting.

10

Tedium is the worst pain.

The dull victim, staring, vague-eyed, at seasons that never were meant to be observed.

The sun walks mindlessly overhead, the shadows lengthen and shorten as if by plan.

"The gods made this world for our joy!" the young priest squeals. The people listen to him dutifully, heads bowed. It does not impress them, one way or the other, that he's crazy.

The scent of the dragon is a staleness on the earth.

The Shaper is sick.

I watch a great horned goat ascend the rocks toward my mere. I have half a mind to admire his bottomless stupidity. "Hey, goat!" I yell down. "There's nothing here. Go back." He lifts his head, considers me, then lowers it again to keep an eye on crevasses and seams, icy scree, slick rocky ledges—doggedly continuing. I tip up a boulder and let it fall thundering toward him. His ears flap up in alarm, he stiffens, looks around him in haste, and jumps. The boulder bounds past him. He watches it fall, then turns his head, looks up at me disapprovingly. Then, lowering his head again, he continues. It is the business of goats to climb. He means to climb. "Ah, goat, goat!" I say as if deeply disappointed in him. "Use your reason! There's nothing here!" He keeps on coming. I am suddenly annoyed, no longer amused by his stupidity. The mere belongs to me and the firesnakes. What if everybody should decide the place is public? "Go back down, goat!" I yell at him. He keeps on climbing, mindless, mechanical, because it is the business of goats to climb. "Not here," I yell. "If climbing's your duty to the gods, go climb the meadhall." He keeps on climbing. I run back from the edge to a dead tree, throw myself against it and break it off and drag it back to the cliffwall. "You've had fair warning," I yell at him. I'm enraged now. The words come echoing back to me. I lay the tree sideways, wait for the goat to be in better range, then shove. It drops with a crash and rolls crookedly toward him. He darts left, reverses himself and bounds to the right, and a limb catches him. He bleats, falling, flopping over with a jerk too quick for the eye, and bleats again, scrambling, sliding toward the ledge-side. The tree, slowly rolling, drops out of sight. His sharp front hooves dig in and he jerks onto his feet, but before his balance is sure my stone hits him and falls again. I leap down to make certain he goes over this time. He finds his feet the same instant that my second stone hits. It splits his skull, and blood sprays out past his dangling brains, yet he doesn't fall. He threatens me, blind. It's not easy to kill a mountain goat. He thinks with his spine. A death tremor shakes his flanks, but he picks toward me, jerking his great twisted horns at air. I back off, upward toward the mere the goat will never reach. I smile, threatened by an animal already dead, still climbing. I snatch up a stone and hurl it. It smashes his mouth, spraying out teeth, and penetrates to the jugular. He drops to his knees, gets up again. The air is sweet with the scent of his blood. Death shakes his body the way high wind shakes trees. He climbs toward me. I snatch up a stone.

At dusk I watch men go about their business in the towns of the Scyldings. Boys and dogs drive the horses and oxen to the river and break through the ice to let them drink. Back at the barns, men carry in hay on wooden forks, dump grain in the mangers, and carry out manure. A wheelwright and his helper squat in their dark room hammering spokes into a hub. I listen to the grunt, the blow of the hammer, the grunt, the blow, like the sound of a leaky heart. Smells of cooking. Gray wood-smoke rises slowly toward a lead-gray sky. On the rocky cliffs looking out to sea, Hrothgar's watchmen, each man posted several stone's-throws away from the next, sit huddled in furs, on their horses' backs, or stand in the shelter of an outcropping ledge, rubbing their hands together, stamping their feet. No one will strike at the kingdom from the sea: icebergs drift a mile out, grinding against one another from time to time, letting out a low moan like the sigh of some huge sea-beast. The guards watch anyway, obedient to orders the king has forgotten to cancel.

People eat, leaning over their food together, seldom talking. The lamp at the center of the table lights their eyes. Dogs beside the men's legs wait, looking up from time to time, and the girl who brings the food from the stove stands looking at the wall as she waits for the plates to empty. An old man, finished before the rest, goes out to bring in wood. I spy on an old woman telling lies to children. (Her face is dark with some disease, and the veins on the backs of her hands are ropes. She is too old to sweep or cook.) She tells of a giant across the sea who has the strength of thirty thanes. "Someday he will come here," she tells the children. Their eyes widen. A bald old man looks up from his earthenware plate and laughs. A gray dog pushes against his leg. He kicks it.

The sun stays longer each day now, climbing mechanical as a goat off the leaden horizon. Children slide down the hills on shaped boards, sending their happy cries through drifted stillness. As twilight deepens, their mothers call them in. A few feign deafness. A shadow looms over them (mine) and they're gone forever.

So it goes.

Darkness. At the house of the Shaper, people come and go, solemn faced, treading softly, their heads bowed and their hands folded for fear of sending dreadful apparitions through his dreams. His attendant, the boy who came here with him—a grown man now—sits by the old man's bed and plays pale runs on the old man's harp. The old man turns his blind head, rising from confusion to listen. He asks about a certain woman who does not come. No answer.

But the king comes, with the queen on his arm, young Hrothulf walking four steps behind them, holding the hands of their children. The king sits beside the Shaper's bed as he sits in the hall, motionless, his patient eyes staring. Hrothulf and the children wait out in the entry room. The queen puts her fingertips gently on the old man's forehead.

The Shaper whispers for the lamp. The attendant pretends to bring it, though it stands already on the table beside his bed. "That's better," the queen says dutifully, and the king says, as if he couldn't see well before, "You look healthier today." The Shaper says nothing. Crouched in the bushes beside the path, peeking in like a whiskered old voyeur, wet-lipped, red-eyed, my chest filled with some meaningless anguish, I watch the old man working up the nerve to let his heart stop. "Where are all his fine phrases now?" I whisper to the night. I chuckle. The night, as usual, doesn't comment.

He sits motionless, propped up in bed, deathwhite hands folded on top of the covers: his eyes, once webbed with visions, are shut. The young man, the attendant sitting with the harp, does not play. The king and queen wait, dutiful, probably counting the time off in their heads, and the herbalist—humpbacked, robed in black (a tic screws taut one whole side of his face)—the herbalist, no longer useful to the onetime king of poets, paces back and forth slowly, rubbing his hands. He waits for the soft, dry throat-rattle that will free him to go pace elsewhere.

The Shaper speaks. They bend closer. "I see a time," he says, "when the Danes once again—" His voice trails off; puzzlement crosses his forehead, and one hand reaches up feebly as if to smooth it away but forgets before it can find the forehead, and falls back to the covers. He lifts his head a little, listening for footsteps. There are none. The head drops back weakly. His visitors wait on. They do not seem to realize that he is dead.

In another house, at a large, carved table, a middle-aged woman with hair just slightly less red than the queen's (she has close-together eyes and eyebrows plucked neat as the lines of a knife wound) sits by lamplight listening, as he did, for footsteps. Her nobleman husband lies sleeping in a nearby room, his head on his arm, as if listening to his heartbeat. She is a lady I have watched with the greatest admiration. Soul of fidelity, decorum. The Shaper would tip his whitened head, blind eyes staring at the floor whenever the lady spoke, and from time to time, when he sang of heroes, of ship-backs broken, there was no mistaking that he sang the song for her. Nothing came of it. She would leave the hall on her husband's arm: the Shaper would bow politely as she passed.

She hears them coming. I duck back into the gloom to watch and wait. The messenger the Shaper's attendant has sent goes up to the door and has hardly knocked once when the door opens inward and the lady appears, staring through him. "He's dead," says the messenger. The lady nods. When the messenger is gone, the lady comes out onto the steps and stands with her arms locked, expressionless. She looks up the hill toward the meadhall.

"So all of us must sooner or later pass," I am tempted to whisper. "Alas! Woe!" I resist.

Only the wind is alive, pressing her robe to her fat, loose hips and bosom. The woman is as still as the dead man in his bed. I am tempted to snatch her. How her squeals would dance on the icicle-walls of the night! But I back away. I look in on the Shaper one more time. The old women are arranging him, putting gold coins on his eyelids to preserve him from seeing where he goes. At last, unsatisfied as ever, I slink back home.

In my cave the tedium is worse, of course. My mother no longer shows any sign of sanity, hurrying back and forth, wall to wall, sometimes on two legs, sometimes on four, dark forehead furrowed like a new-plowed field, her eyes glittering and crazy as a captured eagle's. Each time I come in she gets between me and the door, as if to lock me up with her forever. I endure it, for the time. When I sleep, she presses close to me, half buries me under her thistly fur and fat. "Dool-dool," she moans. She drools and weeps. "Warovvish," she whimpers, and tears at herself. Hanks of fur come away in her claws. I see gray hide. I study her, cool and objective in my corner, and because now the Shaper is dead, strange thoughts come over me. I think of the pastness of the past: how the moment I am alive in, prisoned in, moves like a slowly tumbling form through darkness, the underground river. Not only ancient history—the mythical age of the brothers' feud—but my own history one second ago, has vanished utterly, dropped out of existence. King Scyld's great deeds do not exist "back there" in Time. "Back there in Time" is an allusion of language. They do not exist at all. My wickedness five years ago, or six, or twelve, has no existence except as now, mumbling, mumbling, sacrificing the slain world to the omnipotence of words, I strain my memory to regain it. I snatch by my wits a time when I was very small and my mama held me softly in her arms. Ah, ah, how I loved you, Mama—dead these many years! I snatch a time when I crouched outside the meadhall hearing the first strange hymns of the Shaper. Beauty! Holiness! How my heart rocked! He is dead. I should have captured him, teased him, tormented him, made a fool of him. I should have cracked his skull midsong and sent his blood spraying out wet through the meadhall like a shocking change of key. One evil deed missed is a loss for all eternity.

I decide, naturally, to attend his funeral. She tries to prevent me. I lift her by the armpits as though she were a child and, gently, I set her aside. Her face trembles, torn, I think, between terror and self-pity. It crosses my mind that she knows something, but she doesn't, I know. The future is as dark, as unreal, as the past. Coolly, objectively, I watch the trembling; it's as if all the muscles are locked to the charge of an eel. Then I push her away. The face shatters, she whoops. I run to the pool and dive, and even now I can hear her. I will forget, tomorrow, so her pain is a matter of indifference.

And so to the funeral.

The Shaper's assistant, cradling the old man's polished harp, sings of Hoc and Hildeburh and Hnaef and Hengest, how Finn's thanes fought with his wife's dear kinsmen and killed King Hnaef, and a terrible thing ensued. When Finn had few men and his enemies had no king, they made a truce, and the terms were these: that Finn would be lord of the lordless Danes, because a king without men is a worthless thing, and thanes without a lord are exiles. Both sides made vows, swore the duty of peace, and so winter came, in its time, to the country of the Jutes.

The people listen silent and solemn to the old Shaper's song on the young man's lips, and the pyre where the old man lies stands waiting for fire. The dead arms are crossed, the features are stiff and blue, as if frozen. Ice glints on the sides of the pyre. The world is white.

> *Young Hengest still*
> *through slaughter-dark winter stayed with Finn,*
> *heart sorrowing. He thought of home,*
> *though he could not drive on the dark sea*
> *his ring-prowed ship; for the sea-air rolled,*
> *dusky with wind, and the waves were locked*
> *in ice. Then another season came,*
> *another year, as the years do yet,*
> *bright shining weather awaiting its time.*
> *The winter was gone, earth's breast was fair,*
> *and the exiled Hengest was eager to go,*
> *unwilling guest from the dwelling.—Yet as*
> *ice-chains locked the land, so Hengest's heart*
> *was locked: revenge called harder to him than home.*
> *He cried in his mind for quarrel, and quarrel came.*
> *Then Finn lay down in blood, bold king*
> *with all his company, and the queen was taken;*
> *and, loaded with rings King Finn could not refuse,*
> *the Danes sailed home. Men's double vows*
> *soon wash away. Spring rain drips down through rafters.*

So he sings, looking down, recalling and repeating the words, hands light on the harp. The king listens, dry-eyed, his mind far, far away. Prince Hrothulf stands with the children of Hrothgar and Wealtheow, his features revealing no more secrets than does snow. Men light the pyre. Unferth stares at the flames with eyes like stones. I too watch the fire, as well as I can. Colorless it seems. A more intense place in the brightness of snow and ice. It flames high at once, as if hungry for the coarse, lean meat. The priests walk slowly around the pyre, saying antique prayers, and the crowd, all in black, ignoring the black priests, keens. I watch the burning head burst, bare of visions, dark blood dripping from the corner of the mouth and ear.

End of an epoch, I could tell the king.

We're on our own again. Abandoned.

I awaken with a start and imagine I hear the goat still picking at the cliffwall, climbing to the mere. Something groans, far out at sea.

My mother makes sounds. I strain my wits toward them, clench my mind. *Beware the fish.*

I get up and walk, filled with restless expectation, though I know there is nothing to expect.

I am not the only monster on these moors.
I met an old woman as wild as the wind
Striding in white out of midnight's den.
Her cloak was in rags, and her flesh it was lean,
And her eyes, her murdered eyes . . .

Scent of the dragon.

I should sleep, drop war till spring as I normally do.

When I sleep I wake up in terror, with hands on my throat.

A stupid business.

Nihil ex nihilo, I always say.

11

I am mad with joy.—At least I think it's joy. Strangers
have come, and it's a whole new game. I kiss the ice on
the frozen creeks, I press my ear to it, honoring the water
that rattles below, for by water they came: the icebergs
parted as if gently pushed back by enormous hands, and
the ship sailed through, sea-eager, foamy-necked, white
sails riding the swan-road, flying like a bird! O happy
Grendel! Fifteen glorious heroes, proud in their battle
dress, fat as cows!

I could feel them coming as I lay in the dark of my
cave. I stirred, baffled by the strange sensation, squinting
into dark corners to learn the cause. It drew me as the

mind of the dragon did once. *It's coming!* I said. More clearly than ever I heard the muffled footsteps on the dome of the world, and even when I realized that the footsteps were nothing but the sound of my own heart, I knew more surely than before that something was coming. I got up, moved past stone icicles to the pool and the sunken door. My mother made no move to prevent me. At the pool, firesnakes shot away from me in all directions, bristling, hissing, mysteriously wrought up. They had sensed it too. That beat—steady, inhumanly steady; inexorable. And so, an hour before dawn, I crouched in shadows at the rocky sea-wall, foot of the giants' work. Low tide. Lead-gray water sucked quietly, stubborn and deliberate, at icy gray boulders. Gray wind teased leafless trees. There was no sound but the ice-cold surge, the cry of a gannet, invisible in grayness above me. A whale passed, long dark shadow two miles out. The sky grew light at my back. Then I saw the sail.

I was not the only one who saw them coming. A lone Danish coastguard stood bundled in furs, his horse beside him, and he shaded his eyes against the glint of the icebergs beyond the sail and watched the strangers come swiftly in toward land. The wooden keel struck sand and cut a gouge toward the boulders on the shore—a forty-foot cut, half the length of the ship—and then, quick as wolves—but mechanical, terrible—the strangers leaped down, and with stiff, ice-crusted ropes as gray as the sea, the sky, the stones, they moored their craft. Their chain-mail rattled as they worked—never speaking, walking dead men—lashing the helm-bar, lowering the sail, unloading ashspear shafts and battle-axes. The coastguard mounted, snatched up his spear, and rode loudly down to meet them. His horse's hooves shot sparks. I laughed. If they were here for war, the coastguard was a goner.

"What are ye, bearers of armor, dressed in mail-coats, that have thus come riding your tall ship over the sea-road, winter-cold ocean, here to Daneland?" Thus spake the coastguard. Wind took his words and sent them tumbling.

I bent double, soundlessly laughing till I thought I'd split. They were like trees, these strangers. Their leader was big as a mountain, moving with his forest toward the guard. Nevertheless, the Dane shook his spear the way at-tackers do when they're telling a man what they're going to do with his testicles. "Attaboy!" I whisper. I shadow box. "If they come at you, bite 'em in the leg!"

He scolded and fumed and demanded their lineage; they listened with folded arms. The wind blew colder. At last the coastguard's voice gave out—he bent over the pommel, coughing into his fist—and the leader answered. His voice, though powerful, was mild. Voice of a dead thing, calm as dry sticks and ice when the wind blows over them. He had a strange face that, little by little, grew unsettling to me: it was a face, or so it seemed for an instant, from a dream I had almost forgotten. The eyes slanted downward, never blinking, unfeeling as a snake's. He had no more beard than a fish. He smiled as he spoke, but it was as if the gentle voice, the childlike yet faintly ironic smile were holding something back, some magician-power that could blast stone cliffs to ashes as lightning blasts trees.

"We're Geats," he said, "the hearth-companions of King Hygilac. You've heard of my father. A famous old man named Ecgtheow." His mind, as he spoke, seemed far away, as if, though polite, he were indifferent to all this —an outsider not only among the Danes but everywhere. He said: "We've come as friends for a visit with your lord King Hrothgar, protector of the people." He tipped his head, pausing. You'd have thought he had centuries. At last with a little shrug, he said, "Be so kind as to give us some advice, old man. We've come on a fairly important errand." The hint of irony in the smile grew darker, and he looked now not at the coastguard but at the coastguard's horse. "A certain thing can't very well be kept hidden, I think. You'll know if it's true, as we heard back home, that I don't know what kind of enemy stalks your hall at night—kills men, so they say, and for some reason scorns your warriors. If it's so—" He paused, his eyebrows cocked, and glanced at the coastguard and smiled. "I've come to give Hrothgar advice."

You could see pretty well what advice he'd give. His chest was as wide as an oven. His arms were like beams. "Come ahead," I whispered. "Make your play. Do your worst." But I was less sure of myself than I pretended. Staring at his grotesquely muscled shoulders—stooped, naked despite the cold, sleek as the belly of a shark and as rippled with power as the shoulders of a horse—I found my mind wandering. If I let myself, I could drop into a trance just looking at those shoulders. He was dangerous. And yet I was excited, suddenly alive. He talked on. I found myself not listening, merely looking at his mouth, which moved—or so it seemed to me—independent of the words, as if the body of the stranger were a ruse, a disguise for something infinitely more terrible. Then the coastguard turned his horse and led them up to where the stone-paved road began, gray as the sea, between snow-banks. "I'll have men guard your ship," he said. He pointed out the meadhall, high on its hill above the town. Then he turned back. The sea-pale eyes of the stranger were focused on nothing. He and his company went on, their weapons clinking, chain-mail jangling, solemn and ominous as drums. They moved like one creature, huge strange machine. Sunlight gleamed on their helmets and cheekguards and flashed off their spearpoints, blinding.

I did not follow. I stayed in the ruin, prowling where long-dead giants prowled, my heart aching to know what the strangers were doing now, up at the meadhall. But it was daylight; I'd be a fool to go up and see.

I couldn't tell, back in my cave, whether I was afraid of them or not. My head ached from staying too long in the sunlight, and my hands had no grip. It was as if they were asleep. I was unnaturally conscious, for some reason, of the sounds in the cave: the roar of the underground river hundreds of feet below our rooms, reaming out walls, driving deeper and deeper; the centuries-old drip-drip of seepage building stalagmites, an inch in a hundred years; the spatter of the spring three rooms away —the room of the pictures half buried in stone—where the spring breaks through the roof. Half awake, half asleep, I felt as if I were myself the cave, my thoughts coursing downward through my own strange hollows . . . or some impulse older and darker than thought, as old as the mindless mechanics of a bear, the twilight meditations of a wolf, a tree . . .

Who knows what all this means? Neither awake nor asleep, my chest filled with an excitement like joy, I tried to think whether or not I was afraid of the strangers, and the thought made no sense. It was unreal—insubstantial as spiderweb-strands blowing lightly across a window that looks out on trees. I have sometimes watched men do mysterious things. A man with a wife and seven children, a carpenter with a fair reputation as wise, not maddened by passions, not given to foolishness—regular of habit, dignified in bearing, a dedicated craftsman (no edge unbeveled, no ragged peg, no gouge or split)—once crept from his house at the edge of the town while his family slept, and fled down snowy paths through woods to the house of a hunter away in search of game. The hunter's wife admitted him, and he slept with her until the second rooster crowed; then he fled back home. Who knows why? Tedium is the worst pain. The mind lays out the world in blocks, and the hushed blood waits for revenge. All order, I've come to understand, is theoretical, unreal— a harmless, sensible, smiling mask men slide between the two great, dark realities, the self and the world—two snake-pits. The watchful mind lies, cunning and swift, about the dark blood's lust, lies and lies and lies until, weary of talk, the watchman sleeps. Then sudden and swift the enemy strikes from nowhere, the cavernous heart. Violence is truth, as the crazy old peasant told Hrothulf. But the old fool only half grasped what he said. He had never conversed with a dragon. And the stranger?

Afraid or not, I would go to the meadhall, I knew. I toyed, of course, with the ridiculous theory that I'd stay where I was safe, like a sensible beast. "Am I not free?— as free as a bird?" I whispered, leering, maniacal. I have seen—I embody—the vision of the dragon: absolute, final waste. I saw long ago the whole universe as not-my-mother, and I glimpsed my place in it, a hole. *Yet I exist,* I knew. *Then I alone exist,* I said. *It's me or it.* What glee, that glorious recognition! (The cave my cave is a jealous cave.) For even my mama loves me not for myself, my holy specialness (he he ho ha), but for my son-ness, my possessedness, my displacement of air as visible proof of her power. I have set her aside—gently, picking her up by the armpits as I would a child—and so have proved that she has no power but the little I give her by momentary whim. So I might set aside Hrothgar's whole kingdom and all his thanes if I did not, for sweet desire's sake, set limits to desire. If I murdered the last of the Scyldings, what would I live for? I'd have to move.

So now, for once unsure of victory, I might set limits to desire: go to sleep, put off further raids till the Geats go home. For the world is divided, experience teaches, into two parts: things to be murdered, and things that would hinder the murder of things: and the Geats might reasonably be defined either way. So I whispered, wading through drifts waist-high, inexorably on my way to Hrothgar's meadhall. Darkness lay over the world like a coffin lid. I hurried. It would be a shame to miss the boasting. I came to the hall, bent down at my chink, peered in. The wind was shrill, full of patterns.

It was a scene to warm the cockles of your heart. The Danes were not pleased, to say the least, that the Geats had come to save them. Honor is very big with them; they'd rather be eaten alive than be bailed out by strangers. The priests weren't happy either. They'd been saying for years that the ghostly Destroyer would take care of things in time. Now here were these foreigner upstarts unmasking religion! My old friend Ork sat shaking his head in dismay, saying nothing, brooding, no doubt, on the dark metaphysical implications. Things fade; alternatives exclude. Whichever of us might exclude the other, when the time came for me and the stranger to meet, the eyes of the people would be drawn to the instance, they would fail to rise to the holy idea of process. Theology does not thrive in the world of action and reaction, change: it grows on calm, like the scum on a stagnant pool. And it flourishes, it prospers, on decline. Only in a world where everything is patently being lost can a priest stir men's hearts as a poet would by maintaining that nothing is in vain. For old times' sake, for the old priest's honor, I would have to kill the stranger. And for the honor of Hrothgar's thanes.

The Danes sat sulking, watching the strangers eat, wishing some one of them would give them an excuse to use their daggers. I covered my mouth to keep from cackling. The king presided, solemn and irritable. He knew that his thanes couldn't handle me alone, and he was too old and tired to be much impressed—however useful it might be to his kingdom—by their fathead ideas of honor. *Get through the meal, that's the thing,* he was thinking. *Keep them from wasting their much touted skills on one another.* The queen wasn't present. Situation much too touchy.

Then up spoke Unferth, Ecglaf's son, top man in Hrothgar's hall. He had a nose like a black, deformed potato, eyes like a couple of fangs. He leaned forward over the table and pointed the dagger he'd been eating with. "Say, friend," he said to the beardless leader of the Geats, "are you the same man that went swimming that time with young Breca—risked your lives in the middle of the winter for nothing—for a crazy meadboast?"

The stranger stopped eating, smiled.

"We heard about that," Unferth said. "Nobody could stop you—kings, priests, councilors—nobody. Splash! *Uh, uh, uh!*" Unferth made swimming motions, eyes rolled up, mouth gasping. The thanes around him laughed. "The sea boiled with waves, fierce winter swells. Seven nights you swam, so people say." He made his face credulous, and the Danes laughed again. "And at last Breca beat you, much stronger than you were. He proved his boast against you—for what it may be worth." The Danish thanes laughed. Even Hrothgar smiled. Unferth grew serious, and now only the stranger went on smiling, he alone and the huge Geats next to him, patient as timberwolves. Unferth pointed with his dagger, giving friendly advice. "I predict it will go even worse for you tonight. You may have had successes—I haven't heard. But wait up for Grendel for one night's space and all your glorious successes will be done with."

The Danes applauded. The stranger smiled on, his downward-slanting eyes like empty pits. I could see his mind working, stone-cold, grinding like a millwheel. When the hall was still, he spoke, soft-voiced, his weird gaze focused nowhere. "Ah, friend Unferth, drunk with mead you've said a good deal about Breca. The truth is, nevertheless, that I beat him. I'm stronger in the ocean than any other man alive. Like foolish boys we agreed on the match and boasted, yes . . . we were both very young . . . swore we'd risk our lives in the sea, and did so. We took swords with us, swimming one-handed, to fight off whales."

Unferth laughed, and the others followed, as was right. It was preposterous.

The stranger said, "Breca couldn't swim away from me, for all his strength—a man with arms like yours, friend Unferth—and as for myself, I chose not to swim away from him. Thus we swam for five nights, and then a storm came up, icy wind from the north, black sky, raging waves, and we were separated. The turmoil stirred up the sea-monsters. One of them attacked me, dragged me down to the bottom where the weight of the sea would have crushed any other man. But it was granted to me that I might kill him with my sword, which same I did. Then others attacked. They pressed me hard. I killed them, nine old water nickers, robbed them of the feast they expected at the bottom of the sea. In the morning, sword-ripped, they lay belly-up near shore. They'd trouble no more passing sailors after that. Light came from the east and, behold, I saw headlands, and I swam to them. Fate often enough will spare a man if his courage holds."

Now the Danes weren't laughing. The stranger said it all so calmly, so softly, that it was impossible to laugh. He believed every word he said. I understood at last the look in his eyes. He was insane.

Even so, I wasn't prepared for what came next. Nobody was. Solemn, humorless despite the slightly ironic smile, he suddenly cut deep—yet with the same mildness, the same almost inhuman indifference except for the pale flash of fire in his eyes. "Neither Breca nor you ever fought such battles," he said. "I don't boast much of that. Nevertheless, I don't recall hearing any glorious deeds of yours, except that you murdered your brothers. You'll prowl the stalagmites of hell for that, friend Unferth—clever though you are."

The hall was numb. The stranger was no player of games.

And yet he was shrewd, you had to grant. Whether or not they believed his wild tale of superhuman strength, no thane in the hall would attack him again and risk the slash of that mild, coolly murderous tongue.

Old King Hrothgar, for one, was pleased. The madman's single-mindedness would be useful in a monster fight. He spoke: "Where's the queen? We're all friends in this hall! Let her come to us and pass the bowl!"

She must have been listening behind her door. She came out, radiant, and crossed swiftly to the great golden bowl on the table by the hearth. As if she'd brought light and warmth with her, men began talking, joking, laughing, both Danes and Geats together. When she'd served all the Danes and the lesser Geats, she stood, red hair flowing, her neck and arms adorned in gold, by the leader of the strangers. "I thank God," she said, "that my wish has been granted, that at last I have found a man whose courage I can trust."

The stranger smiled, glanced at Unferth. Hrothgar's top man had recovered a little, though his neck was still dark red.

"We'll see," the stranger said.

And again I found something peculiar happening to my mind. His mouth did not seem to move with his words, and the harder I stared at his gleaming shoulders, the more uncertain I was of their shape. The room was full of a heavy, unpleasant scent I couldn't place. I labor to remember something: twisted roots, an abyss . . . I lose it. The queer little spasm of terror passes. Except for his curious beard-lessness, there is nothing frightening about the stranger. I've broken the backs of bulls no weaker than he is.

Hrothgar made speeches, his hand on the queen's. Un-ferth sat perfectly still, no longer blushing. He was strug-gling to make himself hope for the stranger's success, no doubt. *Heroism is more than noble language, dignity. Inner heroism, that's the trick! Glorious carbuncle of the soul! Except in the life of the hero the whole world's meaningless.* He took a deep breath. He would try to be a better person, yes. He forced a smile, but it twisted, out of his control. Tears! He got up suddenly and, without a word, walked out.

Hrothgar told the hall that the stranger was like a son to him. The queen's smile was distant, and the nephew, Hrothulf, picked at the table with a dirty fingernail. "You already have more sons than you need," the queen laughed lightly. Hrothgar laughed too, though he didn't seem to get it. He was tipsy. The stranger went on sitting with the same unlighted smile. The old king chatted of his plans for Freawaru, how he would marry her off to his enemy, the king of the Heathobards. The stranger smiled on, but closed his eyes. He knew a doomed house when he saw it, I had a feeling; but for one reason or another he kept his peace. I grew more and more afraid of him and at the same time—who can explain it?—more and more eager for the hour of our meeting.

The queen rose, at last, and retired. The fire in the hearth had now died down. The priests filed out to the god-ring to do their devotions. Nobody followed. I could hear them in the distance: "O ghostly Destroyer . . ." The cold ring of gods stared inward with large, dead eyes.

It is the business of rams to be rams and of goats to be goats, the business of shapers to sing and of kings to rule. The stranger waits on, as patient as a grave-mound. I too wait, whispering, whispering, mad like him. Time grows, obeying its mechanics, like all of us. So the young Shaper observes, singing to the few who remain, fingertips troubling a dead man's harp.

> *Frost shall freeze, and fire melt wood;*
> *the earth shall give fruit, and ice shall bridge*
> *dark water, make roofs, mysteriously lock*
> *earth's flourishings; but the fetters of frost*
> *shall also fall, fair weather return,*
> *and the reaching sun restore the restless sea. . . .*

We wait.

The king retires, and his people leave.

The Geats build up the fire, prepare to sleep.

And now, silence.

Darkness.

It is time.

12

I touch the door with my fingertips and it bursts, for all its fire-forged bands—it jumps away like a terrified deer—and I plunge into the silent, hearth-lit hall with a laugh that I wouldn't much care to wake up to myself. I trample the planks that a moment before protected the hall like a hand raised in horror to a terrified mouth (sheer poetry, ah!) and the broken hinges rattle like swords down the timbered walls. The Geats are stones, and whether it's because they're numb with terror or stiff from too much mead, I cannot tell. I am swollen with excitement, bloodlust and joy and a strange fear that mingle in my chest like the twisting rage of a bone-fire. I step onto the brightly shining floor and angrily advance on them. They're all asleep, the whole company! I can hardly believe my luck, and my wild heart laughs, but I let out no sound. Swiftly, softly, I will move from bed to bed and destroy them all, swallow every last man. I am blazing, half-crazy with joy. For pure, mad prank, I snatch a cloth from the nearest table and tie it around my neck to make a napkin. I delay no longer. I seize up a sleeping man, tear at him hungrily, bite through his bone-locks and suck hot, slippery blood. He goes down in huge morsels, head, chest, hips, legs, even the hands and feet. My face and arms are wet, matted. The napkin is sopping. The dark floor steams. I move on at once and I reach for another one (whispering, whispering, chewing the universe down to words), and I seize a wrist. A shock goes through me. Mistake!

It's a trick! His eyes are open, were open all the time, cold-bloodedly watching to see how I work. The eyes nail me now as his hand nails down my arm. I jump back without thinking (whispering wildly: *jump back without thinking*). Now he's out of his bed, his hand still closed like a dragon's jaws on mine. Nowhere on middle-earth, I realize, have I encountered a grip like his. My whole arm's on fire, incredible, searing pain— it's as if his crushing fingers are charged like fangs with poison. I scream, facing him, grotesquely shaking hands

—dear long-lost brother, kinsman-thane—and the timbered hall screams back at me. I feel the bones go, ground from their sockets, and I scream again. I am suddenly awake. The long pale dream, my history, falls away. The meadhall is alive, great cavernous belly, gold-adorned, bloodstained, howling back at me, lit by the flickering fire in the stranger's eyes. He has wings. Is it possible? And yet it's true: out of his shoulders come terrible fiery wings. I jerk my head, trying to drive out illusion. The world is what it is and always was. That's our hope, our chance. Yet even in times of catastrophe we people it with tricks. Grendel, Grendel, hold fast to what is true!

Suddenly, darkness. My sanity has won. He's only a man; I can escape him. I plan. I feel the plan moving inside me like thaw-time waters rising between cliffs. When I'm ready, I give a ferocious kick—but something's wrong: I am spinning—*Wa!*—falling through bottomless space—*Wa!*—snatching at the huge twisted roots of an oak . . . a blinding flash of fire . . . no, darkness. I concentrate. I have fallen! Slipped on blood. He viciously twists my arm behind my back. By accident, it comes to me, I have given him a greater advantage. I could laugh. *Woe, woe!*

And now something worse. He's whispering—spilling words like showers of sleet, his mouth three inches from my ear. I will not listen. I continue whispering. As long as I whisper myself I need not hear. His syllables lick at me, chilly fire. His syllables lick at me, chilly fire. His syllables lick at me, chilly fire. His syllables lick . . .

A meaningless swirl in the stream of time, a temporary gathering of bits, a few random specks, a cloud . . . Complexities: green dust, purple dust, gold. Additional refinements: sensitive dust, copulating dust . . .

The world is my bone-cave, I shall not want . . . (He laughs as he whispers. I roll my eyes back. Flames slip out at the corners of his mouth.) *As you see it it is, while the seeing lasts, dark nightmare-history, time-as-coffin; but where the water was rigid there will be fish, and men will survive on their flesh till spring. It's coming, my brother. Believe it or not. Though you murder the world, turn plains to stone, transmogrify life into I and it, strong searching roots will crack your cave and rain will cleanse it: The world will burn green, sperm build again. My promise. Time is the mind, the hand that makes (fingers on harpstrings, hero-swords, the acts, the eyes of queens). By that I kill you.*

I do not listen. I am sick at heart. I have been betrayed before by talk like that. "Mama!" I bawl. Shapes vague as lurking seaweed surround us. My vision clears. The stranger's companions encircle us, useless swords. I could laugh if it weren't for the pain that makes me howl. And yet I address him, whispering, whimpering, whining.

"If you win, it's by mindless chance. Make no mistake. First you tricked me, and then I slipped. Accident."

He answers with a twist that hurls me forward screaming. The thanes make way. I fall against a table and smash it, and wall timbers crack. And still he whispers.

Grendel, Grendel! You make the world by whispers, second by second. Are you blind to that? Whether you make it a grave or a garden of roses is not the point. Feel the wall: is it not hard? He smashes me against it, breaks open my forehead. *Hard, yes! Observe the hardness, write it down in careful runes. Now sing of walls! Sing!*

I howl.

Sing!

"I'm singing!"

Sing words! Sing raving hymns!

"You're crazy. Ow!"

Sing!

"I sing of walls," I howl. "Hooray for the hardness of walls!"

Terrible, he whispers. *Terrible.* He laughs and lets out fire.

"You're crazy," I say. "If you think I created that wall that cracked my head, you're a fucking lunatic."

Sing walls, he hisses.

I have no choice.

"The wall will fall to the wind as the windy hill
will fall, and all things thought in former times:
Nothing made remains, nor man remembers.
And these towns shall be called the shining towns!"

Better, he whispers. *That's better.* He laughs again, and
the nasty laugh admits I'm slyer than he guessed.

He's crazy. I understand him all right, make no mistake.
Understand his lunatic theory of matter and mind, the
chilly intellect, the hot imagination, blocks and builder,
reality as stress. Nevertheless, it was by accident that he
got my arm behind me. He penetrated no mysteries. He
was lucky. If I'd known he was awake, if I'd known there
was blood on the floor when I gave him that kick . . .

The room goes suddenly white, as if struck by lightning.
I stare down, amazed. He has torn off my arm at the
shoulder! Blood pours down where the limb was. I cry,
I bawl like a baby. He stretches his blinding white wings
and breathes out fire. I run for the door and through it.
I move like wind. I stumble and fall, get up again. I'll die!
I howl. The night is aflame with winged men. *No, no!*
Think! I come suddenly awake once more from the night-
mare. Darkness. I really will die! Every rock, every tree,
every crystal of snow cries out cold-blooded objectness.
Cold, sharp outlines, everything around me: distinct, de-
tached as dead men. I understand. "Mama!" I bellow.

"Mama, Mama! I'm dying!" But her love is history. His whispering follows me into the woods, though I've outrun him. "It was an accident," I bellow back. I will cling to what is true. "Blind, mindless, mechanical. Mere logic of chance." I am weak from loss of blood. No one follows me now. I stumble again and with my one weak arm I cling to the huge twisted roots of an oak. I look down past stars to a terrifying darkness. I seem to recognize the place, but it's impossible. "Accident," I whisper. I will fall. I seem to desire the fall, and though I fight it with all my will I know in advance that I can't win. Standing baffled, quaking with fear, three feet from the edge of a nightmare cliff, I find myself, incredibly, moving toward it. I look down, down, into bottomless blackness, feeling the dark power moving in me like an ocean current, some monster inside me, deep sea wonder, dread night monarch astir in his cave, moving me slowly to my voluntary tumble into death.

Again sight clears. I am slick with blood. I discover I no longer feel pain. Animals gather around me, enemies of old, to watch me die. I give them what I hope will appear a sheepish smile. My heart booms terror. Will the last of my life slide out if I let out breath? They watch with mindless, indifferent eyes, as calm and midnight black as the chasm below me.

Is it joy I feel?

They watch on, evil, incredibly stupid, enjoying my destruction.

"Poor Grendel's had an accident," I whisper. "*So may you all.*"

ABOUT THE AUTHOR

John Gardner received wide acclaim for his novels, his collections of short stories and his critical works. He was born in Batavia, New York, in 1933 and taught English, Anglo-Saxon and creative writing at Oberlin, Chico State College, San Francisco State, Southern Illinois, Bennington, and SUNY-Binghamton. His books include *The Art of Fiction, The Art of Living, Grendel, Jason and Medeia, The Life and Times of Chaucer, Mickelsson's Ghosts, Nickel Mountain, October Light, The Resurrection, The Sunlight Dialogues, Stillness and Shadows,* and various books for children. He died in a motorcycle accident in 1982.

WILLIAM SOMERSET MAUGHAM was born in 1874 and lived in Paris until he was ten years old. He was educated at The King's School, Canterbury, and at Heidelberg University. He later walked the wards of St. Thomas's Hospital with a view to practicing medicine, but when he had qualified, the success of his first novel, *Liza of Lambeth* (1897), won him over to letters. Some of his hospital experience is reflected in the story, as well as in his later masterpiece *Of Human Bondage* (1915). With *The Moon and Sixpence* (1919) and *Cakes and Ale* (1930), his reputation as a novelist was further enhanced.

A celebrity by the age of thirty-three when he became one of most successful playwrights on the London stage, Maugham's Edwardian comedy *Lady Frederick,* his first hit (1907), was followed by a string of successes just before and then after the First World War. At one point Maugham had four plays running at the same time in London's West End. His theater career ended with *Sheppey* (1933).

His fame as a short-story writer began in 1921 with *The Trembling of a Leaf,* subtitled *Little Stories of the South Sea Islands,* which contained "Rain." After initial magazine publication of each story he wrote, there were ten more collections. Somerset Maugham's general nonfiction books also reflect his love of travel; they include *On a Chinese Screen* (1922) and *Don Fernando* (1935), essays, criticism, and the self-revealing *The Summing Up* (1938) and *A Writer's Notebook* (1949).

He traveled widely in the Far East and throughout Europe. His permanent home since before the Second World War was on the French Riviera, which he vacated temporarily in 1940. He became Companion of Honor in 1954 and he died in 1965.

ROBERT CALDER is Professor of English at the University of Saskatchewan. He is the author of *W. Somerset Maugham and the Quest for Freedom* and *Willie: The Life of W. Somerset Maugham,* which won the 1989 Governor General's Literary Award for Non-Fiction. Most recently he has written *Beware the British Serpent: The Role of Writers in British Propaganda in the United States, 1939–1945* and *A Richer Dust: Family, Memory and the Second World War.*

W. SOMERSET MAUGHAM

The Moon and Sixpence

Introduction and Notes by
ROBERT CALDER

PENGUIN BOOKS

PENGUIN BOOKS

Published by the Penguin Group

Penguin Group (USA) Inc., 375 Hudson Street, New York, New York 10014, U.S.A.
Penguin Group (Canada), 90 Eglinton Avenue East, Suite 700, Toronto, Ontario,
Canada M4P 2Y3 (a division of Pearson Penguin Canada Inc.)
Penguin Books Ltd, 80 Strand, London WC2R 0RL, England
Penguin Ireland, 25 St Stephen's Green, Dublin 2, Ireland
(a division of Penguin Books Ltd)
Penguin Group (Australia), 250 Camberwell Road, Camberwell, Victoria 3124,
Australia (a division of Pearson Australia Group Pty Ltd)
Penguin Books India Pvt Ltd, 11 Community Centre, Panchsheel Park,
New Delhi – 110 017, India
Penguin Group (NZ), 67 Apollo Drive, Rosedale, North Shore 0745,
Auckland, New Zealand (a division of Pearson New Zealand Ltd)
Penguin Books (South Africa) (Pty) Ltd, 24 Sturdee Avenue, Rosebank,
Johannesburg 2196, South Africa

Penguin Books Ltd, Registered Offices: 80 Strand, London WC2R 0RL, England

First published in Great Britain by William Heinemann Ltd 1919
First published in the United States of America by George H. Doran Company 1919
Published in Penguin Books (U.S.A.) 1977
This edition with an introduction and notes by Robert Calder published in Penguin Books (U.S.A.) 2005

10

Introduction and notes copyright © Robert Calder, 2005
All rights reserved

LIBRARY OF CONGRESS CATALOGING IN PUBLICATION DATA
Maugham, W. Somerset (William Somerset), 1874–1965.
The Moon and Sixpence / W. Somerset Maugham ; introduction and notes by Robert Calder.
p.   cm.—(Penguin classics)
Includes bibliographical references.
ISBN 978-0-14-303934-1
1. Painters—Fiction.   2. England—Fiction.   3. Tahiti—Fiction.   I. Calder, Robert, 1941–   II. Title.
III. Series.
PR6025.A86M6 2005
823'.912—dc22   2005051352

Printed in the United States of America
Set in Adobe Sabon

Contents

Introduction

Book reviewers, once they have taken their fees to the bank, occasionally imagine that their commentaries actually serve to inform and instruct the authors whose work they dissect. More often than not this is a mere fancy, but on at least one occasion Somerset Maugham, who always claimed to be indifferent to the critics, gained from a reviewer's suggestion. When *Of Human Bondage,* which was to become his most widely read book, appeared in 1915, an anonymous review in the *Times Literary Supplement* observed of the novel's protagonist, Philip Carey, that "like so many young men he was so busy yearning for the moon that he never saw the sixpence at his feet." On completing his next novel four years later, Maugham adopted the metaphor for its title: *The Moon and Sixpence* (called first and more awkwardly "Sixpence and the Moon" in his contract with William Heinemann).

Though this connection may seem to be merely a footnote in literary history, there are significant reasons to consider these two novels together. Even as he was writing *Of Human Bondage,* Maugham was looking ahead to his next novel, whose plot is briefly outlined in Philip's conversations with fellow art students in bohemian Paris. There he learns from his friend Clutton that "in Brittany he had come across a painter whom nobody else had heard of, a queer fellow who had been a stockbroker and taken up painting at middle age, and he was greatly impressed by his work. He was turning his back on impressionism and working out for himself painfully an individual way not only of painting but of seeing." Some

time later, Clutton tells Philip that this odd painter is leaving
for Tahiti:

> "He was broke to the world. He was a *brasseur d'affaires,* a
> stockbroker I suppose you call it in English; and he had a wife
> and family, and he was earning a large income. He chucked it all
> to become a painter. He just went off and settled down in Brit-
> tany and began to paint. He hadn't got any money and did the
> next best thing to starving."
>
> "And what about his wife and family?" asked Philip.
>
> "Oh, he dropped them. He left them to starve on their own ac-
> count. . . . He's behaved like a perfect cad to his wife and chil-
> dren, he's always behaving like a perfect cad; the way he treats
> the people who've helped him—and sometimes he's been saved
> from starvation merely by the kindness of friends—is simply
> beastly. He just happens to be a great artist."

Clutton's account is, of course, a bare bones sketch of the life
and career of the French painter Paul Gauguin which Maugham
had heard in Paris in 1905, when he lived in Montparnasse for a
year among a group of artists and writers which he described at
length in *Of Human Bondage.* Clutton is modeled on the sharp-
tongued and iconoclastic Irish painter Roderick O'Conor, a dis-
ciple of Gauguin from the time he had met him in Brittany and
both an exponent of his aesthetic theories and an apologist for
his antisocial attitude. Maugham, "already greatly interested in
that mysterious, talented man, would have liked to learn from
O'Conor what he could tell me about him; but unfortunately he
took an immediate dislike to me." Thus denied the detail that
O'Conor might have provided about Gauguin, Maugham, as he
confessed years later, was forced to fall back on "using the novelist's privilege" and devising "a number of incidents to illus-
trate the character I had created on the suggestions afforded me
by the scanty facts I knew about the French artist."
What Maugham did manage to glean from O'Conor were
largely the myths which had then grown around Gauguin—his
instantaneous conversion to art, his abandonment of family, his
ruthlessness, his idyllic life in Tahiti, and his death from leprosy

(a fallacy which *The Moon and Sixpence* helped perpetuate). We now know that the reality was considerably different. Gauguin had painted industriously in his spare time for ten years before losing his job as a stockbroker, while Maugham's protagonist, Charles Strickland, develops his interest in art very suddenly. Gauguin was concerned about his wife and children, and he hoped to achieve things for them through his art, even planning that they would eventually join him in Tahiti; Strickland, however, feels nothing for his family. Gauguin continually analyzed and discussed his painting, while Strickland is almost inarticulate and indifferent to artistic theory. Gauguin died of complications from syphilis in the Marquesas Islands whereas Strickland is killed by leprosy in Tahiti. With this in mind, it is understandable that the artist's son Pola might write that in *The Moon and Sixpence* his mother "did not find a single trait of Strickland which had anything in common with her husband."

Maugham, however, was not producing a biography; he was writing a novel and his interest lay more in the source of the "mysterious" talent of someone like Gauguin than in the details of his life. And in making an artist the focus of his story—in writing a *kunstlerroman,* or artist-hero novel—in 1919 he was hardly alone. Surveying the fiction of the early decades of the twentieth century, Van Wyck Brooks wrote:

> The artist, one might almost say, is the typical hero in contemporary fiction From *Jean-Christophe* to *Mendel,* from *The Flame of Life* to *The Moon and Sixpence,* and how much further, as one glances over the list of significant novels of the last two decades, one is surprised to find how often the leading character is a painter, a musician or a writer. The artist has always appeared as a character in fiction, but never before, surely, has he so filled the novelist's stage.

Although the occasional creative figure can be found in the earliest novels, it was not until the late nineteenth century that the artist appeared with any frequency, and even then his portrayal was usually sketchy and followed one of several stereotypes: the high-spirited bohemian, the casual dilettante, the

precious aesthete, or the refined intellectual. The common
method of presenting them, complained Katherine de Mattos in
1894, was "to huddle together a few of the 'novelist's proper-
ties,' bind them around with certain tricks of speech and manner, push the scarecrow about a bit, and label it 'painter.' So
long as there are plenty of pipes and pewters, incident and character will matter little." Beneath this veneer, these caricature
artists were most often socially-minded, with relatively conventional moral outlooks, and most of the emphasis was placed on
the events of their lives rather than on the practice of their art.

At the turn of the twentieth century the artist moved out
from the fictional background to become the central focus of a
great many novels, and the *kunstlerroman* became one of the
most widespread genres in English. Among many others, there
were George Gissing's *The Private Papers of Henry Ryecroft*
(1903), Thomas Hardy's *The Well-Beloved* (1903), Jack London's *Martin Eden* (1909), Henry Handel Richardson's *Maurice Guest* (1910), Stephen French Whitman's *Predestined*
(1910), Mary Austin's *A Woman of Genius* (1912), D. H.
Lawrence's *Sons and Lovers* (1913), Frank Norris's *Vandover
and the Brute* (1914), Willa Cather's *The Song of the Lark*
(1915), Theodore Dreiser's *The Genius* (1915), May Sinclair's
Tasker Jevons (1916), James Joyce's *A Portrait of the Artist as a
Young Man* (1916), Gilbert Cannan's *Mendel: A Story of
Youth* (1916), and Wyndham Lewis's *Tarr* (1918).

With this proliferation of the *kunstlerroman* came a significant shift in the portrayal of the artist-hero. In place of
the conventional and relatively harmless bohemianism of the
nineteenth-century fictional artists, those in twentieth-century
fiction rebel in a genuine and often profound manner. They frequently become more isolated than their predecessors, and their
sensitivity, introspection, and artistic drive demands that they
break loose from conventional society. As Gerald Jay Goldberg
observed, the new artist-hero no longer feels "that it is incum-
bent upon him to represent the 'collected ideology' of his community. Didacticism in art is supplanted by self-expression and
the individual sensibility becomes paramount." In many cases,
the artist not only no longer articulates the beliefs of his society;

he sees himself as a gadfly stinging a complacent, myopic public to action—or at least to comprehension.

In part, this growth of the *kunstlerroman* and reconfiguring of the artist-hero was a response to the concerns and anxieties of the modern age. Inspired by the myth of the genius or superman advanced in the writings of Nietzsche, many people looked back with fascination to the generation of antisocial artists that came to prominence at the turn of the century. In Verlaine, Wagner, Van Gogh, Rimbaud, and Gauguin they saw men who had defiantly rejected conventional morality and orthodox social attitudes. This interest in individuality, creativity, and rebellion was a form of romanticism engendered by the widespread disillusionment with the waste and futility of the Great War and by a growing feeling that increased mechanization and industrialism were destroying people's instinctual qualities. "Industrialisation," explained David Paul, "imposes a routine, not based on tradition or any system of beliefs, but simply of the motives of the machine—the saving of time, the noncreative multiplication of production, speed, money. The process of production becomes so sectionalised that all creative sense is lost." The artist, said Van Wyck Brooks, had come to represent someone whose essential humanity had not been ground down by mechanization:

> Thanks to the universal blocking and checking of instinct that modern industrialism implies for the run of men and even women, the type of life that still, at whatever cost, affords scope for the creative impulses is haloed with an immense desirability. In our age in which everything tends toward a regimentation of character, the average man, presented with no ideal but that of success, finds himself almost obliged to yield up one by one the attributes of a generous humanity. No wonder the artist has come to be the lodestone of so many wishes. He alone seems to be able to keep open the human right of way, to test and explore the possibilities of life.

Throughout his career, Maugham always had a shrewd sense of public tastes and opinion, and he must have been aware of the widely held desire of readers to experience, even vicariously, the breaking of bonds of a character like Strickland. As he revealed in *The Summing Up,* the artist was especially attractive because he was one of the very few types of people who can carve his own path in life:

> The artist can within certain limits make whatever he likes of his life. In other callings, in medicine for instance or the law, you are free to choose whether you will adopt them or not, but having chosen, you are free no longer. You are bound by the rules of your profession; a standard of conduct is imposed on you. The pattern is predetermined. It is only the artist, and maybe the criminal, who can make his own.

In *The Moon and Sixpence,* Maugham emphasizes the striking disparity between the constraints of social convention and the autonomy of the artist by framing Strickland's story with a detailed picture of a London life that is both stultifying and petty; and, though it is a particular existence not shared by many of his readers, its tedium, routine, and banality are enough to remind them of the circumscribed nature of their own lives.

Maugham begins to build this picture in the first chapter, where, adopting the technique of Swift in *Gulliver's Travels* and Defoe in *Robinson Crusoe,* he acts as if he were writing not a novel, but a memoir of a real and famous painter. With mock gravity his narrator analyzes the range of solid, pedantic studies of Charles Strickland: the earliest critical article, the subsequent book of "notes," the family apologia, and the inevitable caustic dissection. Each is found to miss the essential genius of the painter. Claiming to have known the great man more intimately than most people, the narrator suggests that he has a special knowledge of a part of Strickland's career that has been obscured in the public accounts. At the end of the novel, when he has told his tale and his readers have seen more deeply into the artist, his journey, and his creativity, he reminds them of where they sit by bringing them back both to the pretensions and superficiality of modern "civilized" London life and to another sanitized examination of Strickland, this in a

book being written by a "distinguished American critic," Mr.
Van Busche Taylor.

The misunderstanding and misrepresenting of a famous artist
after his death by those—widows, family, friends, and critics—
with vested interests in advancing their own versions of the man
is an idea that Maugham developed more fully and skillfully in
Cakes and Ale (1930). The first eight chapters of *The Moon
and Sixpence* provide a taste of the later novel's satiric treatment of the London social and literary scene in its acerbic
picture of literary luncheons, lionizing society hostesses, and
commercially-minded authors. It was a milieu that Maugham
knew well, and his early readers would have recognized a number of celebrated figures among its characters: Richard Twining
and George Road are clearly the Edwardian authors Richard
Whiting and George Street, and Rose Waterford is very likely
based on Maugham's friend Violet Hunt. Mrs. Strickland, moreover, bears a considerable resemblance to the prominent society
hostess of the time Lady (Sibyl) Colefax.

The main focus of the early chapters is, of course, on the
Strickland family from which the painter surprisingly emerges,
and it is meant to epitomize the dull, pretentious, and stifling
life of society at large. Impelled by the aspirations of Mrs.
Strickland, the household seems governed by mediocrity and
oppressive conformity. The dining-room, like five hundred others decorated in the same "good taste of the period," is "chaste,
artistic and dull." The children are "clean, healthy and normal," with a father apparently so dull that his wife is reluctant
to inflict his company on the guests at her many dinner parties,
occasions which, in any case, are attended with indifference
and left with relief. All in all, the Strickland family is a well-
integrated and typical specimen of its class and milieu:

> There was just that shadowiness about them which you find in
> people whose lives are part of the social organism, so that they
> exist in it and by it only. They are like cells in the body, essential,
> but, so long as they remain healthy, engulfed in the momentous
> whole. The Stricklands were an average family in the middle
> class. . . . Nothing could be more ordinary.

When the apparently ordinary Strickland abandons this conventional family, it is shocked and the social set, its boredom relieved by such drama, is delighted. In fleeing from domesticity and the society in which it is embedded, Strickland is typical of twentieth-century artist-heroes. Analyzing the artistry of the figures in *A Portrait of the Artist as a Young Man* and Proust's *À la Recherche du Temps Perdu*, Maurice Beebe has written:

> In both instances . . . the hero attains this state only after he has sloughed off the domestic, social, and religious demands imposed upon him by his environment. Narrative development in the typical artist-novel requires that the hero test and reject the claims of love and life, of God, home and country, until nothing is left but his true self and his consecration as artist. Quest for self is the dominant theme of the artist-novel, and because the self is almost always in conflict with society, a closely related theme is the opposition of art to life. The artist-as-hero is usually therefore the artist-as-exile.

When the narrator is sent to Paris to persuade the absconded Strickland to return to his family, he goes armed with every appeal to the man's social conscience, which he characterizes as "the guardian in the individual of the rules which the community has evolved for its own preservation. . . . It keeps watch over him, vigilant always in the interests of its master to crush any half-formed desire to break away from the herd. It will force him to place the good of society before his own. It is the very strong link that attaches the individual to the whole." To his professed horror, the narrator discovers that Strickland has no qualms about abandoning his wife and children, that he in fact has no social conscience. "Here was a man," he says, "who sincerely did not mind what people thought of him, and so convention had no hold on him; he was like a wrestler whose body is oiled; you could not get a grip on him; it gave him a freedom which was an outrage."

In the Paris section of *The Moon and Sixpence* Maugham shows his artist-hero's complete lack of conscience in Strickland's behavior in different ways with Dirk and Blanche Stroeve.

In one sense Stroeve represents the kind of art Strickland is rejecting: the "Master of the Chocolate Box," Stroeve paints picturesque scenes of colorful peasants, urchins, and brightly petticoated women lounging on church steps or wandering through the Italian countryside. As if Impressionism had never arisen, his paintings are as realistic as photographs and are designed to "bring romance" into the homes of affluent merchants in northern Europe. Stroeve's canvases, though "common and shop-soiled" and old-fashioned, are not outdated because there is always a widespread market for art which is familiar, comfortable, and reassuring. They are the paintings that are decorative, unprovocative, and unchallenging, and their public is one that is complacent, comfortable, and self-satisfied.

Stroeve is a poor, commonplace artist and he cuts an absurd figure—"Nature had made him a buffoon"—but he is a good man. Though treated with contempt by his fellow painters and made the butt of their jokes, he is sympathetic to their difficulties and generous with those in need. Possessing a delicate sensibility for art belied by his own pedestrian work, he is no Salieri consumed by jealousy of an emerging Mozart, and he is generous in his praise of the paintings of others. It is, in fact, Stroeve who first recognizes Strickland's greatness and brings it to the narrator's attention.

As artists and men Stroeve and Strickland could not be more strikingly different; and in bringing them together Maugham confronts his readers with a difficult question: how much amoral behavior should society tolerate from a great artist in order to be enriched by his art? Shaw had dramatized the problem in *The Doctor's Dilemma,* where a physician has the medical resources to save only one dying man—a good but useless colleague or an unscrupulous, immoral but gifted artist. Shaw's audience was forced uncomfortably to weigh the relative value of goodness and art, to choose the man or the art.

With Stroeve and Strickland Maugham presents a similar problem, though the choice here is not so much who should live but which man's way of life the reader finds more acceptable and ultimately more valuable. The situation is, moreover, made more complicated by the interaction of the men. Shaw's

Dr. Blenkinsop, a minor character whose goodness is conveyed by reports and conversations, has few direct dealings with the artist, Louis Dubedat, who is simply a cheap swindler and social misfit. Stroeve, who is in the forefront of the Paris chapters, is shown in various acts of warmth, generosity, and kindness. Strickland is completely amoral and unconcerned as he sponges off Stroeve and destroys his life by exploiting Blanche and driving her to a grotesque suicide.

Strickland's behavior is cruel, remorseless, and indefensible, and few readers' sympathies would not lie with the shattered Stroeve. Moreover, faced themselves with a choice of which man to have as a friend, neighbor, or colleague, few readers would choose Strickland. Maugham, however, provides a good deal of justification for his artist-hero's conduct, and ironically this defence is launched by Stroeve himself. After Blanche's death he returns to their apartment, which Strickland had taken over after being nursed back to health by Blanche, and he discovers a nude portrait that Strickland had painted of her. After an initial, entirely human impulse to slash the picture to ribbons, Stroeve recognizes that it is a great work of art and he stays his hand. Strickland, he tells the narrator,

> had burst the bonds that hitherto had held him. He had found, not himself, as the phrase goes, but a new soul with unsuspected powers. . . . it was not only the painting, though the flesh was painted with a passionate sensuality which had in it something miraculous; it was not only the solidity, so that you felt extraordinarily the weight of the body; there was also a spirituality, troubling and new, which led the imagination along unsuspected ways, and suggested dim empty spaces, lit only by the eternal stars, where the soul, all naked, adventured fearful to the discovery of new mysteries.

Blanche had been the raw material for a transcendent work of art, and her suffering and her husband's torture become the background to Strickland's emergence as a great artist. When the narrator confronts him with his callousness in sacrificing the pair to his own creative urge, the painter replies: "Do you really care a twopenny damn if Blanche Stroeve is alive or dead?" The narrator, reflecting on the point, is forced to admit what Philip Carey comes to believe in *Of Human Bondage*: that the individual human life is meaningless:

> The cruellest thing of all was that in fact it made no great difference. The world went on, and no one was a penny the worse for all that wretchedness. I had an idea that Dirk, a man of greater emotional reactions than depth of feeling, would soon forget; and Blanche's life, begun with who know what bright hopes and what dreams, might just as well have never been lived. It all seemed useless and inane.

The implication of this is that, though the lives of the Stroeves have been futile in themselves, the great art that has come out of their suffering has meaning and worth. While Dirk and Blanche have lived banally and without any lasting impact on the world, Strickland, for all his ruthlessness, has succeeded in producing something which transcends his daily existence. Given the choice between the happiness of a good but commonplace man and woman, and the creation of a masterpiece at their sacrifice, Maugham's narrator seems to prefer the painting.

Blanche Stroeve, however, is important to *The Moon and Sixpence* in another way: as one of three women with whom Strickland is involved in the course of the novel, she is an essential part of Maugham's examination of the relationship between the artistic temperament and love or sex. In Maxwell Anderson's words, "Mrs Strickland and Blanche Stroeve and Ata, the Tahitian girl, make up a trio from which we can derive a whole conception of womanhood." And in the end only one of these forms of womanhood is shown to allow the artist the freedom to express his creative genius.

Amy Strickland is the socially conscious and convention-bound woman who is often harshly treated in Maugham's writings. Like *Cakes and Ale*'s the second Mrs. Driffield (also, interestingly, called "Amy"), "The Fall of Edward Barnard" 's

Isabel Longstaffe, and *The Razor's Edge*'s Isabel Bradley, she represents a threat to the man who seeks to preserve his freedom. Through this kind of woman, a man can be drawn into the mainstream and trapped into a social posture which smothers his individuality—and more importantly for Strickland, his artistic sensibility. It takes a ruthless desertion for Strickland to escape from his life with Amy, and when he absconds to Paris, his family and friends assume without question that he has left with a woman, driven to it by a sexual urge. Mrs. Strickland later finds this a more acceptable explanation for her husband's behavior than the idea that he might have forsaken her for art; however, he is in the grip of a passion which may be sensual but certainly not sexual.

Later in Paris, of course, Strickland becomes sexually attracted to Blanche and, in spite of his hatred of "the instincts that robbed him of his self-possession," he satisfies his sexual instincts in a brief period with her. Her passion, long dormant in her marriage to Stroeve, becomes aroused beyond her control and, being both sensual and emotional, she begins to demand a deeper response from Strickland than mere physicality. Like many of Maugham's female characters, Blanche tries to bind him to her through her sensuality, and, as he later confesses, this is a threat to his independence and his art:

> "When a woman loves you she's not satisfied until she possesses your soul. Because she's weak she has a rage for domination, and nothing less will satisfy her. . . . The soul of man wanders through the uttermost regions of the universe, and she seeks to imprison it in the circle of her account book. . . . I saw Blanche little by little trying all her tricks. With infinite patience she prepared to snare me and bind me. She wanted to bring me down to her level; she cared nothing for me, she only wanted me to be hers. She was willing to do everything in the world for me except the one thing I wanted: to leave me alone."

In his treatment of sex and the artist, Maugham adheres to the common idea in artist novels that a woman can inhibit and destroy the artist. Throughout Strickland's development as a painter, love and sexual passion impose a form of bondage from which, for the sake of his art, he must remain free. There is not enough space or time in his life for both love and art:

> "I don't want love. I haven't time for it. It's weakness. I am a man, and sometimes I want a woman. When I've satisfied my passion I'm ready for other things. I can't overcome my desire, but I hate it; it imprisons my spirit; I look forward to the time when I shall be free from all desires and can give myself without hindrance to my work."

Strickland's responses to Amy and Blanche suggest that a commitment to a loved one and a commitment to art are incompatible and mutually destructive. The creative man, he seems to say, can compartmentalize his life, pursuing artistic expression at one time and sexual satisfaction at another. Women resent this separation, however, and their attempts to invade the man's creative world impede and destroy his art.

Strickland's happiest years, and more importantly his most artistically productive ones, are nonetheless those spent living with a woman, Ata, but she is as different from Amy and Blanche as Tahiti is from Europe. Like Maugham's other attractive female characters—Sally (*Of Human Bondage*), Rosie (*Cakes and Ale*), or Suzanne Rouvier (*The Razor's Edge*)—Ata is warm, generous, and open; and she is both sensual and maternal. Above all, she makes few demands of Strickland, neither Amy's expectation that he should play a public, social role nor Blanche's that he should be passionately in love with her. Life with Ata requires no deep commitment or emotional involvement from him and, when he is asked if he is happy with her, he replies: "She leaves me alone . . . She cooks my food and looks after her babies. She does what I tell her. She gives me what I want from a woman."

What Strickland wants from a woman is anything but a full, intimate, and equitable relationship, and this has disturbed many readers. Its underlying thesis that love and art are essentially irreconcilable and even antagonistic is nonetheless one that can be found in a number of Maugham's works. Only three years after the publication of *The Moon and Sixpence,* for example, he wrote of the ideal relationship between love and art in "Princess September and the Nightingale." In this fairy tale the princess is befriended by a nightingale that comes to sing for her each day. When her jealous sisters suggest that the bird might leave her someday, she is persuaded to put him in a golden cage. Now, however, the nightingale cannot sing; denied the freedom to fly outdoors and gather inspiration from the outside world, his artistic sense is inhibited. When the princess protests that she loves him and will take him out every day, he replies that it is not the same thing, that the rice fields and the lake and the willow trees look quite different when you see them through the bars of a cage. When the nightingale claims that "I cannot sing unless I'm free, and if I cannot sing I die," the princess reluctantly gives him his liberty. The story ends with the nightingale free to come and go, returning to sing for the princess when he is so inclined. With no restraints, his artistic temperament thrives.

Freedom, here seen as essential to creativity, was a fundamental concern of Maugham throughout his ninety-one years. "The main thing I've always asked of life," he said in old age, "is freedom. Outer and inner freedom, both in my way of living and my way of writing." It is also the most recurrent theme in his large and varied body of work. *Of Human Bondage* is his most thorough exploration of what he called "the strange and ruthless forces that are beyond our control": the many constraints—physical, emotional, intellectual, social, and financial—that are part of the human condition. A great many of his other writings—for example, the novels *Liza of Lambeth, Cakes and Ale,* and *The Narrow Corner*; the plays *The Circle* and *The Constant Wife,* and the short stories "The Fall of Edward Barnard," "The Unconquered," and "The Alien Corn"—are, however, concerned with characters who seek to free themselves from a variety of restrictions and controls. Even his last good piece of fiction, *The Razor's Edge,* written in his old age, deals with a young man escaping from the pervasive grip of American materialism and finding spiritual liberation in Indian mysticism.

Strickland resembles the protagonists of these works in his struggle to free himself from the familial, social, physical, sexual,

and moral constraints that stand in the way of his becoming
what he wants to be. His pursuit of freedom, however, is much
more complicated than that of the others in that his escape from
the limitations of family, home, honor, comfort, and love is compelled by the need to free himself from a greater force that controls him at a much more profound level. For reasons that are
never explained, Strickland has become possessed by an aesthetic
sensibility that haunts and obsesses him and that can be liberated
only through the medium of paint. The need to exorcise these
artistic visions comes to overshadow everything else in his life.

Strickland's possession is a variation of what Henry James
called the "sacred fire," the almost holy inspiration by which
the romantics explained the artistic temperament, but with a
slightly more insidious and terrifying quality. This nearly de-
monic force is primitive, awe-inspiring and inescapable. After
Strickland's flight to Paris, but before he has shown his genius
as an artist, he tells the narrator that

> "I've got to paint. I can't help myself. When a man falls into the
> water it doesn't matter how he swims, well or badly; he's got to
> get out or else he'll drown."
>
> I seemed to feel in him some vehement power that was strug-
> gling within him; it gave me the sensation of something very
> strong, overmastering, that held him, as it were, against his will.
> I could not understand. He seemed really to be possessed of a de-
> vil, and I felt that it might suddenly turn and rend him.

When the narrator returns to England, he reports to Amy that
her husband "seems to me to be possessed by some power
which is using him for its own ends, and in whose hold he is as
helpless as a fly in a spider's web."

When Maugham began to write and publish at the turn of the
nineteenth century, he was a realist author in the tradition of
George Moore, George Gissing, and Arnold Bennett, and *Of
Human Bondage,* with its detailed descriptions of environment
and appearance and in its determinism, is a textbook example of
the realistic novel. *The Moon and Sixpence,* however, presents a
highly romantic interpretation of the artistic temperament.

Strickland's creativity is not something which has always been present in him and which has developed over a long period of application and apprenticeship. It is an inexplicable force that overwhelms him, and, because he is by nature inarticulate and uncommunicative, it demands expression through painting. The artist, Maugham is saying, cannot avoid its grip, and he can throw it off—temporarily, because it is bound to return—only by the act of creation. "The artist," he observed in *Don Fernando*, "can no more help creating than water can help running down hill. It is a release from the burden on his soul. It is a spiritual exercise which is ... accompanied by a sense of power that is itself delightful. When production fulfils it he enjoys a heavenly sense of liberation. For one delicious moment he rests in a state of equilibrium."

The artist who is in bondage to an urge to create is a figure who fascinated Maugham. In the Paris art colony scenes of *Of Human Bondage*, Fanny Price is an English woman determined to be a capable painter but she has no talent, and when her money runs out she hangs herself. The Spaniard Miguel Ajuria strives to become a published author but his superficiality dooms him to nothing more than mediocrity. Both failures show Philip Carey the futility and pain of pursuing art when one does not have the ability to convey one's vision on canvas or the page, and he wisely abandons his goal of becoming a painter. In Maugham's short story "The Alien Corn," on the other hand, when the young protagonist George Bland's dreams of being a concert pianist are shattered on being told that he will never be more than a competent amateur, he is unable to accept this failure and kills himself.

Strickland, however, achieves artistic greatness and, in Tahiti where the milieu demands little of him and with a woman who puts no ties on him, he paints his masterpiece. Something of the primal force of this last great work, painted on the walls of Strickland's house, is conveyed to the narrator by the doctor attending the dying artist:

> From floor to ceiling the walls were covered with a strange and elaborate composition. It was indescribably wonderful and mys-

terious. It took his breath away. It filled him with an emotion which he could not understand or analyse. He felt the awe and delight which a man might feel who watched the beginning of the world. It was tremendous, sensual, passionate; and yet there was something horrible there, too, something which made him afraid. It was the work of a man who had delved into the hidden depths of nature and discovered the secrets which were beautiful and fearful too. It was the work of a man who knew things which it is unholy for men to know. There was something primeval there and terrible. It was not human. It brought to his mind vague recollections of black magic. It was beautiful and obscene.

"*Mon Dieu*, this is genius."

There, in a native hut in Tahiti, Strickland has created a work whose power reminds Dr. Coutras of Michelangelo's ceiling in the Sistine Chapel.

In this final, monumental painting, Strickland has found the means to communicate the vision that has been tormenting him and he thus achieves liberation. Maugham wrestles with the nearly impossible task of recreating a painting in words, and his depiction is consistent with the necessarily vague illumination the narrator is given of the artist's obsession: huge, sensual, passionate, horrible, primeval, mystical. It is Strickland's soul in paint, and by its expression the demon has been exorcised. To underline that this masterpiece is a personal act of catharsis, rather than a wish for justification or fame, the narrator adds almost as a postscript that its creator left orders that it be destroyed after his death. This destruction is, in Mildred C. Kuner's words, "a supreme gesture of contempt for the world's opinion. Here is a study of revolt and ultimate freedom rivalling even the Gidean ideal."

To remind us of the inadequacy of the world's opinion of Strickland and his art, Maugham ends *The Moon and Sixpence* with the narrator's return to London and to Amy Strickland's comfortable middle-class home. There he finds several reproductions of her husband's paintings placed on the walls of her drawing-room because, as she says, "they're so essentially decorative." Declaring that "great art is always decorative," the

American art critic Mr. Van Bushe Taylor broaches no awkward or embarrassing issues about Strickland and neither does the narrator, who notices that the figures in one of the paintings are Ata and her first son by the painter. Having told his story because he had a special knowledge of Strickland's life and art, the narrator now suppresses that knowledge from both Amy and from the critic who is writing another bland and superficial book about them. Only the teller of the tale and the readers of Maugham's novel understand Strickland's art at its greatest and how little the public knows of it.

But does Maugham succeed in persuading his readers of the greatness of Strickland's paintings or that they have seen the unique and subtle workings of the artistic temperament? If he fails to convince his readers that Strickland's paintings are monumental works of art, he is not alone among writers. Nineteenth-century fiction focused on the life of its artist characters and rarely examined their work, and twentieth-century authors, even with increased interest in the artistic experience, have produced few credible recreations of a painting or composition or piece of sculpture. For example, Shaw's Louis Dubedat, Theodore Dreiser's Eugene Witla (*The Genius*), and Henry Handel Richardson's Maurice Guest (*Maurice Guest*), notable artist figures of the period, do not in any way have their artistic work explored. D. H. Lawrence's *Sons and Lovers* treats Paul Morel as a sensitive and artistic young man trying to break away from his mining community, but the reader never sees any of his work, and Joyce's *A Portrait of the Artist as a Young Man* illustrates the gestation of an artistic temperament without showing any of the results of the birth of the artist.

It should hardly be surprising that wordsmiths have rarely succeeded in recreating the work of another art form in their writing. When the effect of a great poem can never be fully explained even in prose nor its meaning wholly translated from its particular literary form, how much more difficult it is to render color, shape, movement, and sound in words. In the end the writer most often falls back on metaphor, saying one thing in terms of something else, and this rarely captures the elusive uniqueness of the work described. Thus the impossibility of the music reviewer trying to describe the full effect of hearing a Mozart string quintet superbly played in the concert hall, or the futility of the art critic writing of the showing of a new Jackson Pollock or Kandinsky. Skillful writers can enhance and elevate much of lived experience—Norman Mailer's description of the boxing match between Muhammed Ali and George Foreman in Zaire was, for example, arguably better than the fight itself—but a truly great work of art can never be reproduced in another medium.

Maugham, it seems, never assumed that his descriptions of Strickland's paintings would have a profound, direct impact on his readers, and so he attempts to persuade them of his artist's genius through the testimonies of a number of witnesses. Chief among them, of course, is the narrator, who, acting as a mediator between the conventional London society and the painter who turns his back on it, records the recollections of a wide variety of observers: Rose Waterford, Dirk Stroeve, Captain Nichols, Captain Brunot, Tiaré Johnson, and Dr. Coutras. Though the narrator attempts to put their observations of Strickland into evocative word pictures, readers ultimately have to accept on trust that their awe of the man's art is well founded.

Readers have generally appreciated that Maugham cannot be expected to reproduce the power of Strickland's paintings in words, but for many critics the great failing of *The Moon and Sixpence* is the lack of real insight into the artistic temperament and the creative process. An early reviewer, Robert M. Lovett, for example, argued that the painter's conversion to art is too sudden and ungrounded and that this leaves his character too vague: "The one thing interesting above all, we are not allowed to see: through what fiery inner struggle did Strickland break loose to follow his ambition, and what innate chemistry of soul caused his sudden lapse into the freakish behavior that alone characterises his genius?" Katherine Mansfield went beyond Lovett and criticized the absence of any deep probing of the painter's mind throughout the novel. Maugham failed, she said, to reveal enough of what makes the artistic temperament, that extraordinary kind of sensitivity or perception that makes the artist a unique man or woman. "We must be shown," she said, "something of the workings of his mind; we must have some comment of his upon what he feels, fuller and more exhaustive than his perpetual 'Go to hell.' If to be a great artist were to push over everything that comes in one's way, topple over the table, lunge out right and left like a drunken man in a café and send the pots flying, then Strickland was a great artist. But great artists are not drunken men; they are men who are divinely sober."

If the workings of Strickland's mind remain opaque, much of the blame must lie with Maugham's use of a narrator, a device which always distances readers from the characters and experiences being described. The first-person voice was a narrative strategy that Maugham employed frequently over his long career and which he honed to a fine edge. Half of his prodigious output of short stories are told in this way, and in *Cakes and Ale* the various characters, settings, and chronological leaps are seamlessly woven together in the memory of a narrator called "Willie Ashenden." Similarly, Larry Darrell's search for spiritual truth in *The Razor's Edge,* a wandering tale that takes a number of characters from America to Europe and India over many years, is told by a first-person narrator, an urbane and observant novelist.

Anthony Burgess considered the Maugham persona, whether it is Ashenden, the unnamed narrator of the short stories, or the "gentleman in the parlor" of the travel books, to be the author's finest creation. V. S. Pritchett called him "the Great Dry Martini in person," and in the later works Maugham's narrator is a cosmopolitan, worldly-wise raconteur equally at home in London's Mayfair society, the Riviera, the South Pacific, or the Far East. He can tell of sailing to India by P & O liner or of traveling across Burma by ox-cart, and he can recall tiffin at the Raffles Hotel in Singapore or cocktails with beachcombers in Papeete. He is the congenial gentleman recounting a tale—with all its digressions, interjections, and hypotheses about human nature—in front of the fireplace over cigars and port.

Maugham had rarely used the first-person voice before writing *The Moon and Sixpence,* however, and his narrator here is not the shrewd and experienced observer of life of his later works, but a naive, somewhat priggish and pretentious young man. His experience of the world is limited and his outlook narrow. This makes him, in part, a foil for the impulsive, passionate and amoral Strickland, much as the English narrator of Nikos Kazantzakis's *Zorba the Greek* is the antithesis of the fiery, Mediterranean Zorba. Indeed, the teller of the tale in *The Moon and Sixpence* confesses to enjoying someone who can give him "a Roland for my Oliver."

Seeing himself as "Oliver" to Strickland's "Roland," legendary figures from the twelfth-century epic poem *Chanson de Roland*, suggests that the narrator is playing a more prominent and intrusive role in *The Moon and Sixpence* than is usual for the teller of a tale. In recent years, when much of literary criticism has focused on metafiction, voice, and self-referential narrative, this prominence has led scholars to suggest that Maugham's novel is as much about the narrator as about the artist. Sheldon W. Liebman, for example, argues that the narrator does not confine himself to the customary activities of observation, analysis, and discovery, but goes far beyond this descriptive role into speculation, interpretation, and judgment. Because he has only a limited direct experience of Strickland—"I am exasperated by the fragmentariness of the facts at my disposal"—he is reduced to conjecturing, signaled by his frequent use of "may be," "I wonder," "I suppose," "it appears," "it seemed to me," "might have been," and other speculative phrases. Seeing the man's paintings for the first time, he reports that "I *fancy* that Strickland saw vaguely some spiritual meaning in material things," that his interpretation is perhaps "fanciful," and that he "fancied" that the art was the result of a great effort to express its creator's soul. Hearing of Strickland's Tahitian paintings from Dr. Coutras, the narrator tells us that "working silently, knowing that it was his last chance, I *fancied* that here he must have said all that he knew of life and all that he divined. And I *fancied* that perhaps here he had at last found peace" (emphasis added).

The narrator's portrait of Strickland and his art, concludes Liebman, is thus highly unreliable, and he goes further to maintain that it is very largely a projection of the storyteller's own needs, values, and expectations. Strickland is "a cipher onto which anyone may project his own fancies" and the novel is really an exploration of "the process of projection, the biases from which it derives, the moral shallowness that it reflects, and the consequences that it engenders." The subtlety of this examination, says Liebman, is worthy of Henry James, and makes *The Moon and Sixpence* one of the best works of fiction of the twentieth century.

Though Liebman's thoughtful dissection of the novel's unreliable narrative, revealing as it does the complexity of Maugham's writing, is convincing, his claim that Strickland is merely a cipher is unlikely to persuade many readers. In a carefully reasoned response to Liebman, J. David Macey argues that the narrator's inability to penetrate deeply into the painter's psyche—and the resulting shift of his proposed biography into autobiography and myth-making—is inevitable because true artistic genius is beyond his comprehension or that of any conventional person. Thus when Maugham places his narrator back in Amy Strickland's drawing room, that is, back in the civilized London society from which he started, he is reminding his readers that Strickland had to leave civilization in order to create his great painting. Why, then, should we be surprised if civilization cannot understand his work? "Strickland's paintings," says Macey, "possess the virtue of originality, but originality has no place in civilized society, which depends for stability on the reproduction of the familiar patterns embodied by myth and narrative fiction. . . . Strickland's greatness consists in having created works that *cannot* be described in the 'civilized' vocabulary of the drawing room because civilization has no language adequate to the genuine and terrifying originality of true artistic genius."

Behind the enigma of Strickland and the narrator who attempts to understand his art is, of course, the important question of where Maugham himself stands on these matters. According to Macey, if biography, which *The Moon and Sixpence* purports to be, "is an indirect form of self-expression, then the novel points not outward, to the receding figure of Charles Strickland, but inward, to the fictional narrator and, beyond, to the novelist whom the narrator both does and does not represent." Determining the degree to which the narrator does in fact speak for the author, and why Maugham would choose to write a novel from behind a narrative mask for the first time since 1898, is essential in two ways: it helps to explain where Maugham himself stands in regard to Strickland's behavior and art, and it accounts for the apparently conflicting themes of *The Moon and Sixpence* and *Of Human Bondage*, published only four years apart.

One must always exercise great caution in associating a fictional narrator with his or her author, but we know that Maugham's storytellers were often autobiographical and grew increasingly to resemble him as he aged. Eleven years after writing *The Moon and Sixpence*, he gave the narrator of *Cakes and Ale* the name "Willie Ashenden," "Willie" being the name by which Maugham was known to his friends and "Ashenden" the surname of a family he knew as a boy in Kent. It was the name he had used in 1928 as the title of his collection of short stories based on his espionage experiences in the Great War, and when he introduced the film *Trio* in 1950, he told his audience: "if you like to take the character of Ashenden as a flattering portrait of the old party who stands before you, you are perfectly at liberty to do so." By the time he came to write *The Razor's Edge,* in 1944, he threw off the mask and called his narrator, a cosmopolitan novelist, simply "Mr. Maugham."

The narrator of *The Moon and Sixpence* is unnamed but readers can be forgiven for seeing him as a young version of the author. Like Maugham, he has been a medical student at St. Thomas's Hospital and lived in flat near Victoria Station. He too has enjoyed acclaim for his first novel and, now a professional author, he also has been drawn into the London literary/social world. Just as Maugham was pursued by the lion-hunting hostesses of his youth—notably Sibyl Colefax and Emerald Cunard—the young writer in *The Moon and Sixpence* is taken up by the socially ambitious Amy Strickland.

On closer examination, it is clear that Maugham is standing somewhat back of the narrator, with as much of himself in Strickland as in his storyteller. At one point, for example, the narrator says to the artist: "You evidently don't believe in the maxim: Act so that every one of your actions is capable of being made into a universal rule." Strickland replies that it is "rotten nonsense," voicing Maugham's own opinion, as recorded in his *A Writer's Notebook*: "One of the commonest errors of the human intelligence is to insist that a rule should be universally applicable." The relationship between Maugham and his amoral artist-hero is further underlined when the narrator explains that "in his rogues the writer gratifies instincts deep-rooted in him, which the manners and customs of a civilized world have forced back into the recesses of the subconscious." The expression of these instincts in his fiction, he says, gives the author "a sense of liberation."

Maugham's portrayal of aspects of himself in both the intense, antisocial Strickland and the restrained, conventional narrator is a reflection of his ambivalence about his own life and work at that time. He had ended *Of Human Bondage,* written as a form of catharsis, with the autobiographical Philip abandoning his dreams of art and world travel in order to settle down to an ordinary career as a country doctor married to the maternal Sally Athelny. At the end of a long search for meaning in his life, he has recognized that "the simplest pattern, that in which a man was born, worked, married, had children, and died, was likewise the most perfect." The marriage was, Maugham later wrote, a picture of the kind of union that in 1913 he thought he would like to make, and he came to realize that most readers found it the most unconvincing part of the novel.

Neither is the future mapped out for Philip at the end of the novel an accurate description of Maugham's own life. Even before the publication of *Of Human Bondage* in 1915, he had begun an affair with Syrie Barnardo Wellcome, an ambitious and gregarious society beauty who was a far cry from the simple and generous Sally, and they were married in 1917. By then, however, he had met and fallen in love with Gerald Haxton, and together the men began to travel the world, first to Tahiti in 1916, where he gathered material for *The Moon and Sixpence,* and then to China in the winter of 1919–20. This extensive travel was impelled in part by Maugham's desire to leave what he had quickly come to realize was an ill-advised marriage and in part by his growing dissatisfaction with London's cultural and social life. "On the surface," he later wrote, "my life was varied and exciting; but beneath it was narrow."

The thematic shift from *Of Human Bondage* to *The Moon and Sixpence* is clearly revealed in an explanatory comment Maugham had intended would precede the text of the latter novel but which was never published: "in his childhood [the author] was urged to make merry over the man who, looking for the moon, missed the sixpence at his feet, but having reached years of maturity, he is not so sure that this was so great an absurdity as he was bidden to believe. Let him who will pick up the sixpence, to pursue the moon seems the most amusing diversion." Philip Carey had abandoned his search for the moon to pick up the sixpence, but Maugham was no longer prepared to do so. For the rest of his life he traveled extensively, seeking out the exotic, the romantic, and the unconventional.

Maugham, however, could never entirely free himself from the London literary/social circles in which he had moved for twenty years. Part of him enjoyed being lionized, and for the remainder of his life no one savored the latest gossip, news of sexual misadventures, infidelities, misadventures, and reputations made and lost, than him. He delighted in an evening at his club, a dinner at the Café Royale, and his suite at the Dorchester Hotel. Even when he began living at Cap Ferrat, he brought the literary/social world to him by inviting authors, artists, university dons, politicians, and socialites to his luxurious villa. An inveterate snob, he could boast of offering his table to the many titled aristocrats and minor royal figures who, dispossessed and down of their luck had sought refuge along the Riviera.

Maugham was a man of many contradictions and internal conflicts, not the least of which was that between his attraction to, and acceptance by, the social world and his desire for adventure, unorthodoxy, and a simple life. By 1918, when he began writing *The Moon and Sixpence,* he was forty-four, and, though he could admire and envy the boldness and individuality of a Strickland, he could no longer emulate it. The artist's rebellion and rejection of civilization is therefore filtered through the eyes of a narrator, and the author and reader thus stand apart from Strickland's quest, awestruck and mystified, perhaps, but not fully engaged in it.

In the end, perhaps Maugham's portrait of artistic genius through the eyes of a narrator who can observe but not participate is what has given *The Moon and Sixpence* its lasting appeal. Constrained by the demands of family, community, profession, trapped by the particular conditions of their time and place, and subject to the larger forces of history itself, few readers can ever contemplate following Charles Strickland's path. They can nonetheless be fascinated by his defiance of such restraints and by his artistic achievement, and through him they can perhaps satisfy, even vicariously, some of their desires to break free from the narrowness of their own lives.

Suggestions for Further Reading

Burt, Forrest D. *W. Somerset Maugham*. Boston: Twayne, 1985.

Calder, Robert. *Willie: The Life of W. Somerset Maugham*. London: Heinemann, 1989.

Curtis, Anthony. *The Pattern of Maugham*. London: Hamish Hamilton, 1974.

Holden, Philip. *Orienting Masculinity, Orienting Nation: W. Somerset Maugham's Exotic Fiction*. London: Greenwood Press, 1996.

Liebman, Sheldon W. "Fiction as Fantasy: The Unreliable Narrator in *The Moon and Sixpence*." *English Literature in Transition 1880–1920* 38 (1995): 329–43.

Macey, David J. "Fantasy as Necessity: The Role of the Biographer in *The Moon and Sixpence*." *Studies in the Novel* 30 (1997): 61–73.

Meyers, Jeffrey. *Somerset Maugham: A Life*. New York: Knopf, 2004.

Whitehead, John. *Maugham: A Reappraisal*. Towota, N.J.: Barnes and Noble, 1978.

The Moon and
Sixpence

I

I confess that when first I made acquaintance with Charles Strickland I never for a moment discerned that there was in him anything out of the ordinary. Yet now few will be found to deny his greatness. I do not speak of that greatness which is achieved by the fortunate politician or the successful soldier; that is a quality which belongs to the place he occupies rather than to the man; and a change of circumstance reduces it to very discreet proportions. The Prime Minister out of office is seen, too often, to have been but a pompous rhetorician, and the General without an army is but the tame hero of a market town. The greatness of Charles Strickland was authentic. It may be that you do not like his art, but at all events you can hardly refuse it the tribute of your interest. He disturbs and arrests. The time has passed when he was an object of ridicule, and it is no longer a mark of eccentricity to defend or of perversity to extol him. His faults are accepted as the necessary complement to his merits. It is still possible to discuss his place in art, and the adulation of his admirers is perhaps no less capricious than the disparagement of his detractors; but one thing can never be doubtful, and that is that he had genius. To my mind the most interesting thing in art is the personality of the artist; and if that is singular, I am willing to excuse a thousand faults. I suppose Velasquez was a better painter than El Greco, but custom stales one's admiration for him: the Cretan, sensual and tragic, proffers the mystery of his soul like a standing sacrifice. The artist, painter, poet, or musician, by his decoration, sublime or beautiful,

satisfies the aesthetic sense; but that is akin to the sexual instinct, and shares its barbarity: he lays before you also the
greater gift of himself. To pursue his secret has something of
the fascination of a detective story. It is a riddle which shares
with the universe the merit of having no answer. The most insignificant of Strickland's works suggests a personality which is
strange, tormented, and complex; and it is this surely which
prevents even those who do not like his pictures from being indifferent to them; it is this which has excited so curious an interest in his life and character.

It was not till four years after Strickland's death that Maurice
Huret wrote that article in the *Mercure de France* which rescued
the unknown painter from oblivion and blazed the trail which
succeeding writers, with more or less docility, have followed.
For a long time no critic has enjoyed in France a more incon-
testable authority, and it was impossible not to be impressed by
the claims he made; they seemed extravagant; but later judge-
ments have confirmed his estimate, and the reputation of Charles
Strickland is now firmly established on the lines which he laid
down. The rise of this reputation is one of the most romantic incidents in the history of art. But I do not propose to deal with
Charles Strickland's work except in so far as it touches upon his
character. I cannot agree with the painters who claim supercil-
iously that the layman can understand nothing of painting, and
that he can best show his appreciation of their works by silence
and a cheque-book. It is a grotesque misapprehension which
sees in art no more than a craft comprehensible perfectly only to
the craftsman: art is a manifestation of emotion, and emotion
speaks a language that all may understand. But I will allow that
the critic who has not a practical knowledge of technique is seldom able to say anything on the subject of real value, and my ignorance of painting is extreme. Fortunately, there is no need for
me to risk the adventure, since my friend, Mr Edward Leggatt,
an able writer as well as an admirable painter, has exhaustively
discussed Charles Strickland's work in a little book* which is a

---

A Modern Artist: Notes on the work of Charles Strickland, by Edward Leggatt, A.R.H.A. Martin Secker, 1917.

charming example of a style, for the most part, less happily cultivated in England than in France.

Maurice Huret in his famous article gave an outline of Charles Strickland's life which was well calculated to whet the appetites of the inquiring. With his disinterested passion for art, he had a real desire to call the attention of the wise to a talent which was in the highest degree original; but he was too good a journalist to be unaware that the 'human interest' would enable him more easily to effect his purpose. And when such as had come in contact with Strickland in the past, writers who had known him in London, painters who had met him in the cafés of Montmartre, discovered to their amazement that where they had seen but an unsuccessful artist, like another, authentic genius had rubbed shoulders with them, there began to appear in the magazines of France and America a succession of articles, the reminiscences of one, the appreciation of another, which added to Strickland's notoriety, and fed without satisfying the curiosity of the public. The subject was grateful, and the industrious Weitbrecht-Rotholz in his imposing monograph* has been able to give a remarkable list of authorities.

The faculty for myth is innate in the human race. It seizes with avidity upon any incidents, surprising or mysterious, in the career of those who have at all distinguished themselves from their fellows, and invents a legend to which it then attaches a fanatical belief. It is the protest of romance against the commonplace of life. The incidents of the legend become the hero's surest passport to immortality. The ironic philosopher reflects with a smile that Sir Walter Raleigh is more safely enshrined in the memory of mankind because he set his cloak for the Virgin Queen to walk on than because he carried the English name to undiscovered countries. Charles Strickland lived obscurely. He made enemies rather than friends. It is not strange, then, that those who wrote of him should have eked out their scanty recollections with a lively fancy, and it is evident that there was enough in the little that was known of him to give opportunity

*Karl Strickland: sein Leben und seine Kunst, by Hugo Weitbrecht-Rotholz, Ph.D. Schwingel und Hanisch. Leipzig, 1914.

to the romantic scribe; there was much in his life which was strange and terrible, in his character something outrageous, and in his fate not a little that was pathetic. In due course a legend arose of such circumstantiality that the wise historian would hesitate to attack it.

But a wise historian is precisely what the Rev. Robert Strickland is not. He wrote his biography* avowedly to 'remove certain misconceptions which had gained currency' in regard to the later part of his father's life, and which had 'caused considerable pain to persons still living'. It is obvious that there was much in the commonly received account of Strickland's life to embarrass a respectable family. I have read this work with a good deal of amusement, and upon this I congratulate myself, since it is colourless and dull. Mr Strickland has drawn the portrait of an excellent husband and father, a man of kindly temper, industrious habits, and moral disposition. The modern clergyman has acquired in his study of the science which I believe is called exegesis an astonishing facility for explaining things away, but the subtlety with which the Rev. Robert Strickland has 'interpreted' all the facts in his father's life which a dutiful son might find it convenient to remember must surely lead him in the fullness of time to the highest dignities of the Church. I see already his muscular calves encased in the gaiters episcopal. It was a hazardous, though maybe a gallant thing to do, since it is probable that the legend commonly received has had no small share in the growth of Strickland's reputation; for there are many who have been attracted to his art by the detestation in which they held his character or the compassion with which they regarded his death; and the son's well-meaning efforts threw a singular chill upon the father's admirers. It is due to no accident that when one of his most important works, *The Woman of Samaria*,† was sold to Christie's shortly after the

---

Strickland: The Man and His Work, by his son, Robert Strickland. Wm Heinemann, 1913.

†This was described in Christie's catalogue as follows: A nude woman, a native of the Society Islands, is lying on the ground beside a brook. Behind is a tropical landscape with palm-trees, bananas, etc., 60 in. by 48 in.

discussion which followed the publication of Mr Strickland's biography, it fetched £235 less than it had done nine months before, when it was bought by the distinguished collector whose sudden death had brought it once more under the hammer. Perhaps Charles Strickland's power and originality would scarcely have sufficed to turn the scale if the remarkable mythopoeic faculty of mankind had not brushed aside with impatience a story which disappointed all its craving for the extraordinary. And presently Dr Weitbrecht-Rotholz produced the work which finally set at rest the misgivings of all lovers of art.

Dr Weitbrecht-Rotholz belongs to that school of historians which believes that human nature is not only about as bad as it can be, but a great deal worse; and certainly the reader is safer of entertainment in their hands than in those of the writers who take a malicious pleasure in representing the great figures of romance as patterns of the domestic virtues. For my part, I should be sorry to think that there was nothing between Antony and Cleopatra but an economic situation; and it will require a great deal more evidence than is ever likely to be available, thank God, to persuade me that Tiberius was as blameless a monarch as King George V. Dr Weitbrecht-Rotholz has dealt in such terms with the Rev. Robert Strickland's innocent biography that it is difficult to avoid feeling a certain sympathy for the unlucky parson. His decent reticence is branded as hypocrisy, his circumlocutions are roundly called lies, and his silence is vilified as treachery. And on the strength of peccadilloes, reprehensible in an author, but excusable in a son, the Anglo-Saxon race is accused of prudishness, humbug, pretentiousness, deceit, cunning, and bad cooking. Personally I think it was rash of Mr Strickland, in refuting the account which had gained belief of a certain 'unpleasantness' between his father and mother, to state that Charles Strickland in a letter written from Paris had described her as 'an excellent woman', since Dr Weitbrecht-Rotholz was able to print the letter in facsimile, and it appears that the passage referred to ran in fact as follows: *God damn my wife. She is an excellent woman. I wish she was in hell.* It is not thus that the Church in its great days dealt with evidence that was unwelcome.

Dr Weitbrecht-Rotholz was an enthusiastic admirer of Charles Strickland, and there was no danger that he would whitewash him. He had an unerring eye for the despicable motive in actions that had all the appearance of innocence. He was a psycho-pathologist as well as a student of art, and the subconscious had few secrets from him. No mystic ever saw deeper meaning in common things. The mystic sees the ineffable and the psycho-pathologist the unspeakable. There is a singular fascination in watching the eagerness with which the learned author ferrets out every circumstance which may throw discredit on his hero. His heart warms to him when he can bring forward some example of cruelty or meanness, and he exults like an inquisitor at the *auto da fé* of an heretic when with some forgotten story he can confound the filial piety of the Rev. Robert Strickland. His industry has been amazing. Nothing has been too small to escape him, and you may be sure that if Charles Strickland left a laundry bill unpaid it will be given you *in extenso,* and if he forbore to return a borrowed half-crown no detail of the transaction will be omitted.

II

When so much has been written about Charles Strickland, it may seem unnecessary that I should write more. A painter's monument is his work. It is true I knew him more intimately than most: I met him first before ever he became a painter, and I saw him not infrequently during the difficult years he spent in Paris; but I do not suppose I should ever have set down my recollections if the hazards of the war had not taken me to Tahiti. There, as is notorious, he spent the last years of his life; and there I came across persons who were familiar with him. I find myself in a position to throw light on just that part of his tragic career which has remained most obscure. If they who believe in Strickland's greatness are right, the personal narratives of such as knew him in the flesh can hardly be superfluous. What would we not give for the reminiscences of someone who had been as intimately acquainted with El Greco as I was with Strickland?

But I seek refuge in no such excuses. I forget who it was that recommended men for their soul's good to do each day two things they disliked: it was a wise man, and it is a precept that I have followed scrupulously; for every day I have got up and I have gone to bed. But there is in my nature a strain of asceticism, and I have subjected my flesh each week to a more severe mortification. I have never failed to read the Literary Supplement of *The Times*. It is a salutary discipline to consider the vast number of books that are written, the fair hopes with which their authors see them published, and the fate which awaits them. What chance is there that any book will make its way among that multitude? And the successful books are but the successes of a season. Heaven knows what pains the author has been at, what bitter experiences he has endured and what heartache suffered, to give some chance reader a few hours' relaxation or to while away the tedium of a journey. And if I may judge from the reviews, many of these books are well and carefully written; much thought has gone to their composition; to some even has been given the anxious labour of a lifetime. The moral I draw is that the writer should seek his reward in the pleasure of his work and in release from the burden of his thoughts; and, indifferent to aught else, care nothing for praise or censure, failure or success.

Now the war has come, bringing with it a new attitude. Youth has turned to gods we of an earlier day knew not, and it is possible to see already the direction in which those who come after us will move. The younger generation, conscious of strength and tumultuous, have done with knocking at the door; they have burst in and seated themselves in our seats. The air is noisy with their shouts. Of their elders some, by imitating the antics of youth, strive to persuade themselves that their day is not yet over; they shout with the lustiest, but the war-cry sounds hollow in their mouth; they are like poor wantons attempting with pencil, paint, and powder, with shrill gaiety, to recover the illusion of their spring. The wiser go their way with a decent grace. In their chastened smile is an indulgent mockery. They remember that they too trod down a sated generation, with just such clamour and with just such scorn, and they foresee that these brave torchbearers will presently yield their place also.

There is no last word. The new evangel was old when Nineveh reared her greatness to the sky. These gallant words which seem so novel to those that speak them were said in accents scarcely changed a hundred times before. The pendulum swings backwards and forwards. The circle is ever travelled anew.

Sometimes a man survives a considerable time from an era in which he had his place into one which is strange to him, and then the curious are offered one of the most singular spectacles in the human comedy. Who now, for example, thinks of George Crabbe? He was a famous poet in his day, and the world recognized his genius with a unanimity which the greater complexity of modern life has rendered infrequent. He had learnt his craft at the school of Alexander Pope, and he wrote moral stories in rhymed couplets. Then came the French Revolution and the Napoleonic Wars, and the poets sang new songs. Mr Crabbe continued to write moral stories in rhymed couplets. I think he must have read the verse of these young men who were making so great a stir in the world, and I fancy he found it poor stuff. Of course, much of it was. But the odes of Keats and of Wordsworth, a poem or two by Coleridge, a few more by Shelley, discovered vast realms of the spirit that none had explored before. Mr Crabbe was as dead as mutton, but Mr Crabbe continued to write moral stories in rhymed couplets. I have read desultorily the writings of the younger generation. It may be that among them a more fervid Keats, a more ethereal Shelley, has already published numbers the world will willingly remember. I cannot tell. I admire their polish—their youth is already so accomplished that it seems absurd to speak of promise—I marvel at the felicity of their style; but with all their copiousness (their vocabulary suggests that they fingered Roget's *Thesaurus* in their cradles) they say nothing to me: to my mind they know too much and feel too obviously; I cannot stomach the heartiness with which they slap me on the back or the emotion with which they hurl themselves on my bosom; their passion seems to me a little anaemic and their dreams a trifle dull. I do not like them. I am on the shelf. I will continue to write moral stories in rhymed couplets. But I should be thrice a fool if I did it for aught but my own entertainment.

III

But all this is by the way.

I was very young when I wrote my first book. By a lucky chance it excited attention, and various persons sought my acquaintance.

It is not without melancholy that I wander among my recollections of the world of letters in London when first bashful but eager, I was introduced to it. It is long since I frequented it, and if the novels that describe its present singularities are accurate much in it is now changed. The venue is different. Chelsea and Bloomsbury have taken the place of Hampstead, Notting Hill Gate, and High Street, Kensington. Then it was a distinction to be under forty, but now to be more than twenty-five is absurd. I think in those days we were a little shy of our emotions, and the fear of ridicule tempered the more obvious forms of pretentiousness. I do not believe that there was in that genteel Bohemia an intensive culture of chastity, but I do not remember so crude a promiscuity as seems to be practised in the present day. We did not think it hypocritical to draw over our vagaries the curtain of a decent silence. The spade was not invariably called a bloody shovel. Woman had not yet altogether come into her own.

I lived near Victoria Station, and I recall long excursions by bus to the hospitable houses of the literary. In my timidity I wandered up and down the street while I screwed up my courage to ring the bell; and then, sick with apprehension, was ushered into an airless room full of people. I was introduced to this celebrated person after that one, and the kind words they said about my book made me excessively uncomfortable. I felt they expected me to say clever things, and I never could think of any till after the party was over. I tried to conceal my embarrassment by handing round cups of tea and rather ill-cut bread-and-butter. I wanted no one to take notice of me, so that I could observe these famous creatures at my ease and listen to the clever things they said.

I have a recollection of large, unbending women with great noses and rapacious eyes, who wore their clothes as though they were armour; and of little, mouse-like spinsters, with soft voices and a shrewd glance. I never ceased to be fascinated by their persistence in eating buttered toast with their gloves on, and I observed with admiration the unconcern with which they wiped their fingers on their chair when they thought no one was looking. It must have been bad for the furniture, but I suppose the hostess took her revenge on the furniture of her friends when, in turn, she visited them. Some of them were dressed fashionably, and they said they couldn't for the life of them see why you should be dowdy just because you had written a novel; if you had a neat figure you might as well make the most of it, and a smart shoe on a small foot had never prevented an editor from taking your 'stuff'. But others thought this frivolous, and they wore 'art fabrics' and barbaric jewellery. The men were seldom eccentric in appearance. They tried to look as little like authors as possible. They wished to be taken for men of the world, and could have passed anywhere for the managing clerks of a city firm. They always seemed a little tired. I had never known writers before, and I found them very strange, but I do not think they ever seemed to me quite real.

I remember that I thought their conversation brilliant, and I used to listen with astonishment to the stinging humour with which they would tear a brother-author to pieces the moment that his back was turned. The artist has this advantage over the rest of the world, that his friends offer not only their appearance and their character to his satire, but also their work. I despaired of ever expressing myself with such aptness or with such fluency. In those days conversation was still cultivated as an art; a neat repartee was more highly valued than the crackling of thorns under a pot; and the epigram, not yet a mechanical appliance by which the dull may achieve a semblance of wit, gave sprightliness to the small talk of the urbane. It is sad that I can remember nothing of all this scintillation. But I think the conversation never settled down so comfortably as when it turned to the details of the trade which was the other side of the art we practised. When we had done discussing the merits of the latest book, it was natural to wonder how many copies had been sold, what advance the author had received, and how much he was likely to make out of it. Then we would speak of this publisher and of that, comparing the generosity of one with the meanness of another; we would argue whether it was better to go to one who gave handsome royalties or to another who 'pushed' a book for all it was worth. Some advertised badly and some well. Some were modern and some were old-fashioned. Then we would talk of agents and the offers they had obtained for us; of editors and the sort of contributions they welcomed, how much they paid a thousand, and whether they paid promptly or otherwise. To me it was all very romantic. It gave me an intimate sense of being a member of some mystic brotherhood.

IV

No one was kinder to me at that time than Rose Waterford. She combined a masculine intelligence with a feminine perversity, and the novels she wrote were original and disconcerting. It was at her house one day that I met Charles Strickland's wife. Miss Waterford was giving a tea-party, and her small room was more than usually full. Everyone seemed to be talking, and I, sitting in silence, felt awkward; but I was too shy to break into any of the groups that seemed absorbed in their own affairs. Miss Waterford was a good hostess, and seeing my embarrassment came up to me.

'I want you to talk to Mrs Strickland,' she said. 'She's raving about your book.'

'What does she do?' I asked.

I was conscious of my ignorance, and if Mrs Strickland was a well-known writer I thought it as well to ascertain the fact before I spoke to her.

Rose Waterford cast down her eyes demurely to give greater effect to her reply.

'She gives luncheon-parties. You've only got to roar a little, and she'll ask you.'

Rose Waterford was a cynic. She looked upon life as an opportunity for writing novels and the public as her raw material. Now and then she invited members of it to her house if they showed an appreciation of her talent and entertained with proper lavishness.

She held their weakness for lions in good-humoured contempt, but played to them her part of the distinguished woman of letters with decorum.

I was led up to Mrs Strickland, and for ten minutes we talked together. I noticed nothing about her except that she had a pleasant voice. She had a flat in Westminster, overlooking the unfinished cathedral, and because we lived in the same neighbourhood we felt friendly disposed to one another. The Army and Navy Stores are a bond of union between all who dwell between the river and St James's Park. Mrs Strickland asked me for my address, and a few days later I received an invitation to luncheon.

My engagements were few, and I was glad to accept. When I arrived, a little late, because in my fear of being too early I had walked three times round the cathedral, I found the party already complete. Miss Waterford was there and Mrs Jay, Richard Twining, and George Road. We were all writers. It was a fine day, early in spring, and we were in a good humour. We talked about a hundred things. Miss Waterford, torn between the aestheticism of her early youth, when she used to go to parties in sage green, holding a daffodil, and the flippancy of her maturer years, which tended to high heels and Paris frocks, wore a new hat. It put her in high spirits. I had never heard her more malicious about our common friends. Mrs Jay, aware that impropriety is the soul of wit, made observations in tones hardly above a whisper that might well have tinged the snowy table-cloth with a rosy hue. Richard Twining bubbled over with quaint absurdities, and George Road, conscious that he need not exhibit a brilliancy which was almost a byword, opened his mouth only to put food into it. Mrs Strickland did not talk much, but she had a pleasant gift for keeping the conversation general; and when there was a pause she threw in just the right remark to set it going once more. She was a woman of thirty-seven, rather tall, and plump, without being fat; she was not pretty, but her face was pleasing, chiefly, perhaps, on account of her kind brown eyes. Her skin was rather sallow. Her dark hair was elaborately dressed. She was the only woman of the three whose face was free of make-up, and by contrast with the others she seemed simple and unaffected.

The dining-room was in the good taste of the period. It was very severe. There was a high dado of white wood and a green paper on which were etchings by Whistler in neat black frames. The green curtains with their peacock design, hung in straight lines, and the green carpet, in the pattern of which pale rabbits frolicked among leafy trees, suggested the influence of William Morris. There was blue delft on the chimneypiece. At that time there must have been five hundred dining-rooms in London decorated in exactly the same manner. It was chaste, artistic, and dull.

When we left I walked away with Miss Waterford, and the fine day and her new hat persuaded us to saunter through the Park.

'That was a very nice party', I said.

'Did you think the food was good? I told her that if she wanted writers she must feed them well.'

'Admirable advice', I answered. 'But why does she want them?'

Miss Waterford shrugged her shoulders.

'She finds them amusing. She wants to be in the movement. I fancy she's rather simple, poor dear, and she thinks we're all wonderful. After all, it pleases her to ask us to luncheon, and it doesn't hurt us. I like her for it.'

Looking back, I think that Mrs Strickland was the most harmless of all the lion-hunters that pursue their quarry from the rarified heights of Hampstead to the nethermost studios of Cheyne Walk. She had led a very quiet youth in the country, and the books that came down from Mudie's Library brought with them not only their own romance, but the romance of London. She had a real passion for reading (rare in her kind, who for the most part are more interested in the author than in his book, in the painter than in his pictures), and she invented a world of the imagination in which she lived with a freedom she never acquired in the world of every day. When she came to know writers it was like adventuring upon a stage which till then she had known only from the other side of the footlights. She saw them dramatically, and really seemed herself to live a larger life because she entertained them and visited them in their fastnesses. She accepted the rules with which they played the game of life as valid for them, but never for a moment thought of regulating her own conduct in accordance with them. Their moral eccentricities, like their oddities of dress, their wild theories and paradoxes, were an entertainment which amused her, but had not the slightest influence on her convictions.

'Is there a Mr Strickland?' I asked.

'Oh yes; he's something in the city. I believe he's a stockbroker. He's very dull.'

'Are they good friends?'

'They adore one another. You'll meet him if you dine there. But she doesn't often have people to dinner. He's very quiet. He's not in the least interested in literature or the arts.'

'Why do nice women marry dull men?'

'Because intelligent men won't marry nice women.'

I could not think of any retort to this, so I asked if Mrs Strickland had children.

'Yes; she has a boy and a girl. They're both at school.'

The subject was exhausted, and we began to talk of other things.

V

During the summer I met Mrs Strickland not infrequently. I went now and then to pleasant little luncheons at her flat, and to rather more formidable tea-parties. We took a fancy to one another. I was very young, and perhaps she liked the idea of guiding my virgin steps on the hard road of letters; while for me it was pleasant to have someone I could go to with my small troubles, certain of an attentive ear and reasonable counsel. Mrs Strickland had the gift of sympathy. It is a charming faculty, but one often abused by those who are conscious of its possession: for there is something ghoulish in the avidity with which they will pounce upon the misfortune of their friends so that they may exercise their dexterity. It gushes forth like an oil-well, and the sympathetic pour out their sympathy with an abandon that is sometimes embarrassing to their victims. There are bosoms on which so many tears have been shed that I cannot bedew them with mine. Mrs Strickland used her advantage with tact. You felt that you obliged her by accepting her sympathy. When, in the enthusiasm of my youth, I remarked on this to Rose Waterford, she said:

'Milk is very nice, especially with a drop of brandy in it, but the domestic cow is only too glad to be rid of it. A swollen udder is very uncomfortable.'

Rose Waterford had a blistering tongue. No one could say such bitter things; on the other hand, no one could do more charming ones.

There was another thing I liked in Mrs Strickland. She managed her surroundings with elegance. Her flat was always neat and cheerful, gay with flowers, and the chintzes in the drawing-room, notwithstanding their severe design, were bright and pretty. The meals in the artistic little dining-room were pleasant; the table looked nice, the two maids were trim and comely, the food was well cooked. It was impossible not to see that Mrs Strickland was an excellent housekeeper. And you felt sure that she was an admirable mother. There were photographs in the drawing-room of her son and daughter. The son—his name was Robert—was a boy of sixteen at Rugby; and you saw him in flannels and a cricket cap, and again in a tail-coat and a stand-up collar. He had his mother's candid brow and fine, reflective eyes. He looked clean, healthy, and normal.

'I don't know that he's very clever', she said one day, when I was looking at the photograph, 'but I know he's good. He has a charming character.'

The daughter was fourteen. Her hair, thick and dark like her mother's, fell over her shoulders in fine profusion, and she had the same kindly expression and sedate, untroubled eyes.

'They're both of them the image of you', I said.

'Yes; I think they are more like me than their father.'

'Why have you never let me meet him?' I asked.

'Would you like to?'

She smiled, her smile was really very sweet, and she blushed a little; it was singular that a woman of that age should flush so readily. Perhaps her naïveté was her greatest charm.

'You know, he's not at all literary', she said. 'He's a perfect philistine.'

She said this not disparagingly, but affectionately rather, as though, by acknowledging the worst about him, she wished to protect him from the aspersions of her friends.

'He's on the Stock Exchange, and he's a typical broker. I think he'd bore you to death.'

'Does he bore you?' I asked.

'You see, I happen to be his wife. I'm very fond of him.'

She smiled to cover her shyness, and I fancied she had a fear that I would make the sort of gibe that such a confession could hardly have failed to elicit from Rose Waterford. She hesitated a little. Her eyes grew tender.

'He doesn't pretend to be a genius. He doesn't even make much money on the Stock Exchange. But he's awfully good and kind.'

'I think I should like him very much.'

'I'll ask you to dine with us quietly some time, but mind, you come at your own risk; don't blame me if you have a very dull evening.'

VI

But when at last I met Charles Strickland, it was under circumstances which allowed me to do no more than just make his acquaintance. One morning Mrs Strickland sent me round a note to say that she was giving a dinner-party that evening, and one of her guests had failed her. She asked me to stop the gap. She wrote:

It's only decent to warn you that you will be bored to extinction. It was a thoroughly dull party from the beginning, but if you will come I shall be uncommonly grateful. And you and I can have a little chat by ourselves.

It was only neighbourly to accept.

When Mrs Strickland introduced me to her husband, he gave me a rather indifferent hand to shake. Turning to him gaily, she attempted a small jest.

'I asked him to show him that I really had a husband. I think he was beginning to doubt it.'

Strickland gave the polite little laugh with which people acknowledge a facetiousness in which they see nothing funny, but did not speak. New arrivals claimed my host's attention, and I was left to myself. When at last we were all assembled, waiting for dinner to be announced, I reflected, while I chatted with the woman I had been asked to 'take in', that civilized man practises a strange ingenuity in wasting on tedious exercises the brief span of his life. It was the kind of party which makes you wonder why the hostess has troubled to bid her guests, and why the guests have troubled to come. There were ten people. They met with indifference, and would part with relief. It was, of course, a purely social function. The Stricklands 'owed' dinners to a number of persons, whom they took no interest in, and so had asked them; these persons had accepted. Why? To avoid the tedium of dining *tête-à-tête*, to give their servants a rest, because there was no reason to refuse, because they were 'owed' a dinner.

The dining-room was inconveniently crowded. There was a K.C. and his wife, a Government official and his wife, Mrs Strickland's sister and her husband, Colonel MacAndrew, and the wife of a Member of Parliament. It was because the Member of Parliament found that he could not leave the House that I had been invited. The respectability of the party was portentous. The women were too nice to be well dressed, and too sure of their position to be amusing. The men were solid. There was about all of them an air of well-satisfied prosperity.

Everyone talked a little louder than natural in an instinctive desire to make the party go, and there was a great deal of noise in the room. But there was no general conversation. Each one talked to his neighbour; to his neighbour on the right during the soup, fish, and entrée; to his neighbour on the left during the roast, sweet, and savoury. They talked of the political situation, and of golf, of their children and the latest play, of the pictures at the Royal Academy, of the weather, and their plans for the holidays. There was never a pause, and the noise grew louder. Mrs Strickland might congratulate herself that her party was a success. Her husband played his part with decorum. Perhaps he did not talk very much, and I fancied there was towards the end a look of fatigue in the faces of the women on either side of him. They were finding him heavy. Once or twice Mrs Strickland's eyes rested on him somewhat anxiously.

At last she rose and shepherded the ladies out of the room. Strickland shut the door behind her, and, moving to the other end of the table, took his place between the K.C. and the Government official. He passed round the port again and handed us cigars. The K.C. remarked on the excellence of the wine, and Strickland told us where he got it. We began to chat about vintages and tobacco. The K.C. told us of a case he was engaged in, and the Colonel talked about polo. I had nothing to say and so sat silent, trying politely to show interest in the conversation; and because I thought no one was in the least concerned with me, examined Strickland at my ease. He was bigger than I expected: I do not know why I had imagined him slender and of insignificant appearance; in point of fact he was broad and heavy, with large hands and feet, and he wore his evening clothes clumsily. He gave you somewhat the idea of a coachman dressed up for the occasion. He was a man of forty, not good-looking, and yet not ugly, for his features were rather good; but they were all a little larger than life-size, and the effect was ungainly. He was clean shaven, and his large face looked uncomfortably naked. His hair was reddish, cut very short, and his eyes were small, blue or grey. He looked commonplace. I no longer wondered that Mrs Strickland felt a certain embarrassment about him; he was scarcely a credit to a woman who wanted to make herself a position in the world of art and letters. It was obvious that he had no social gifts, but these a man can do without; he had no eccentricity even, to take him out of the common run; he was just a good, dull, honest, plain man. One would admire his excellent qualities, but avoid his company. He was null. He was probably a worthy member of society, a good husband and father, an honest broker; but there was no reason to waste one's time over him.

VII

The season was drawing to its dusty end, and everyone I knew was arranging to go away. Mrs Strickland was taking her family to the coast of Norfolk, so that the children might have the sea and her husband golf. We said good-bye to one another, and arranged to meet in the autumn. But on my last day in town, coming out of the Stores, I met her with her son and daughter; like myself, she had been making her final purchases before leaving London, and we were both hot and tired. I proposed that we should all go and eat ices in the park.

I think Mrs Strickland was glad to show me her children, and she accepted my invitation with alacrity. They were even more attractive than their photographs had suggested, and she was right to be proud of them. I was young enough for them not to feel shy, and they chattered merrily about one thing and another. They were extraordinarily nice, healthy young children. It was very agreeable under the trees.

When in an hour they crowded into a cab to go home, I strolled idly to my club. I was perhaps a little lonely, and it was with a touch of envy that I thought of the pleasant family life of which I had had a glimpse. They seemed devoted to one another. They had little private jokes of their own which, unintelligible to the outsider, amused them enormously. Perhaps Charles Strickland was dull judged by a standard that demanded above all things verbal scintillation; but his intelligence was adequate to his surroundings, and that is a passport, not only to reasonable success, but still more to happiness. Mrs Strickland was a charming woman, and she loved him. I pictured their lives, troubled by no untoward adventure, honest, decent, and, by reason of those two upstanding, pleasant children, so obviously destined to carry on the normal traditions of their race and station, not without significance. They would grow old insensibly; they would see their son and daughter come to years of reason, marry in due course—the one a pretty girl, future mother of healthy children; the other a handsome, manly fellow, obviously a soldier; and at last, prosperous in their dignified retirement, beloved by their descendants, after a happy, not unuseful life, in the fullness of their age they would sink into the grave.

That must be the story of innumerable couples, and the pattern of life it offers has a homely grace. It reminds you of a placid rivulet, meandering smoothly through green pastures and shaded by pleasant trees, till at last it falls into the vasty sea; but the sea is so calm, so silent, so indifferent, that you are troubled suddenly by a vague uneasiness. Perhaps it is only by a kink in my nature, strong in me even in those days, that I felt in such an existence, the share of the great majority, something amiss. I recognized its social value. I saw its ordered happiness, but a fever in my blood asked for a wilder course. There seemed to me something alarming in such easy delights. In my heart was a desire to live more dangerously. I was not unprepared for jagged rocks and treacherous shoals if I could only have change—change and the excitement of the unforeseen.

VIII

On reading over what I have written of the Stricklands, I am conscious that they must seem shadowy. I have been able to invest them with none of those characteristics which make the persons of a book exist with a real life of their own; and, wondering if the fault is mine, I rack my brains to remember idiosyncrasies which might lend them vividness. I feel that by dwelling on some trick of speech or some queer habit I should be able to give them a significance peculiar to themselves. As they stand they are like the figures in an old tapestry; they do not separate themselves from the background, and at a distance seem to lose their pattern, so that you have little but a pleasing piece of colour. My only excuse is that the impression they made on me was no other. There was just that shadowiness about them which you find in people whose lives are part of the social organism, so that they exist in it and by it only. They are like cells in the body, essential, but, so long as they remain healthy, engulfed in the momentous whole. The Stricklands were an average family in the middle class. A pleasant, hospitable

woman, with a harmless craze for the small lions of literary society; a rather dull man, doing his duty in that state of life in
which a merciful Providence had placed him; two nice-looking,
healthy children. Nothing could be more ordinary. I do not know
that there was anything about them to excite the attention of
the curious.

When I reflect on all that happened later, I ask myself if I was
thick-witted not to see that there was in Charles Strickland at
least something out of the common. Perhaps. I think that I have
gathered in the years that intervene between then and now a fair
knowledge of mankind, but even if when I first met the Stricklands I had the experience which I have now, I do not believe
that I should have judged them differently. But because I have
learnt that man is incalculable, I should not at this time of day
be so surprised by the news that reached me when in the early
autumn I returned to London.

I had not been back twenty-four hours before I ran across
Rose Waterford in Jermyn Street.

'You look very gay and sprightly', I said. 'What's the matter
with you?'

She smiled, and her eyes shone with a malice I knew already.
It meant that she had heard some scandal about one of her
friends, and the instinct of the literary woman was all alert.

'You did meet Charles Strickland, didn't you?'

Not only her face, but her whole body, gave a sense of alacrity.
I nodded. I wondered if the poor devil had been hammered on
the Stock Exchange or run over by an omnibus.

'Isn't it dreadful? He's run away from his wife.'

Miss Waterford certainly felt that she could not do her subject justice on the kerb of Jermyn Street, and so, like an artist,
flung the bare fact at me and declared that she knew no details.
I could not do her the injustice of supposing that so trifling a
circumstance would have prevented her from giving them, but
she was obstinate.

'I tell you I know nothing', she said, in reply to my agitated
questions, and then, with an airy shrug of the shoulders: 'I believe that a young person in a city tea-shop has left her situation.'

She flashed a smile at me, and, protesting an engagement

with her dentist, jauntily walked on. I was more interested than distressed. In those days my experience of life at first hand was small, and it excited me to come upon an incident among people I knew of the same sort as I had read in books. I confess that time has now accustomed me to incidents of this character among my acquaintance. But I was also a little shocked. Strickland was certainly forty, and I thought it disgusting that a man of his age should concern himself with affairs of the heart. With the superciliousness of extreme youth, I put thirty-five as the utmost limit at which a man might fall in love without making a fool of himself. And this news was slightly disconcerting to me personally, because I had written from the country to Mrs Strickland, announcing my return, and had added that unless I heard from her to the contrary, I would come on a certain day to drink a dish of tea with her. This was the very day, and I had received no word from Mrs Strickland. Did she want to see me or did she not? It was likely enough that in the agitation of the moment my note had escaped her memory. Perhaps I should be wiser not to go. On the other hand, she might wish to keep the affair quiet, and it might be highly indiscreet on my part to give any sign that this strange news had reached me. I was torn between the fear of hurting a nice woman's feelings and the fear of being in the way. I felt she must be suffering, and I did not want to see a pain which I could not help; but in my heart was a desire, that I felt a little ashamed of, to see how she was taking it. I did not know what to do.

Finally it occurred to me that I would call as though nothing had happened, and send a message in by the maid asking Mrs Strickland if it was convenient for her to see me. This would give her the opportunity to send me away. But I was overwhelmed with embarrassment when I said to the maid the phrase I had prepared, and while I waited for the answer in a dark passage I had to call up all my strength of mind not to bolt. The maid came back. Her manner suggested to my excited fancy a complete knowledge of the domestic calamity.

'Will you come this way, sir?' she asked.

I followed her into the drawing-room. The blinds were partly drawn to darken the room, and Mrs Strickland was sitting with her back to the light. Her brother-in-law, Colonel MacAndrew, stood in front of the fireplace, warming his back at an unlit fire. To myself my entrance seemed excessively awkward. I imagined that my arrival had taken them by surprise, and Mrs Strickland had let me come in only because she had forgotten to put me off. I fancied that the Colonel resented the interruption.

'I wasn't quite sure if you expected me', I said, trying to seem unconcerned.

'Of course I did. Anne will bring the tea in a minute.'

Even in the darkened room, I could not help seeing that Mrs Strickland's face was all swollen with tears. Her skin, never very good, was earthy.

'You remember my brother-in-law, don't you? You met at dinner here, just before the holidays.'

We shook hands. I felt so shy that I could think of nothing to say, but Mrs Strickland came to my rescue. She asked me what I had been doing with myself during the summer, and with this help I managed to make some conversation till tea was brought in. The Colonel asked for a whisky-and-soda.

'You'd better have one too, Amy,' he said.

'No; I prefer tea.'

This was the first suggestion that anything untoward had happened. I took no notice, and did my best to engage Mrs Strickland in talk. The Colonel, still standing in front of the fireplace, uttered no word. I wondered how soon I could decently take my leave, and I asked myself why on earth Mrs Strickland had allowed me to come. There were no flowers, and various knick-knacks, put away during the summer, had not been replaced; there was something cheerless and stiff about the room which had always seemed so friendly; it gave you an odd feeling, as though someone were lying dead on the other side of the wall. I finished tea.

'Will you have a cigarette?' asked Mrs Strickland.

She looked about for the box, but it was not to be seen.

'I'm afraid there are none.'

Suddenly she burst into tears, and hurried from the room.

I was startled. I suppose now that the lack of cigarettes, bought as a rule by her husband, forced him back upon her recollection, and the new feeling that the small comforts she was used to were missing gave her a sudden pang. She realized that the old life was gone and done with. It was impossible to keep up our social pretences any longer.

'I dare say you'd like me to go', I said to the Colonel, getting up.

'I suppose you've heard that blackguard has deserted her', he cried explosively.

I hesitated.

'You know how people gossip', I answered. 'I was vaguely told that something was wrong.'

'He's bolted. He's gone off to Paris with a woman. He's left Amy without a penny.'

'I'm awfully sorry', I said, not knowing what else to say.

The Colonel gulped down his whisky. He was a tall, lean man of fifty, with a drooping moustache and grey hair. He had pale blue eyes and a weak mouth. I remembered from my previous meeting with him that he had a foolish face, and was proud of the fact that for the ten years before he left the army he had played polo three days a week.

'I don't suppose Mrs Strickland wants to be bothered with me just now', I said. 'Will you tell her how sorry I am? If there's anything I can do, I shall be delighted to do it.'

He took no notice of me.

'I don't know what's to become of her. And then there are the children. Are they going to live on air? Seventeen years.'

'What about seventeen years?'

'They've been married', he snapped. 'I never liked him. Of course he was my brother-in-law, and I made the best of it. Did you think him a gentleman? She ought never to have married him.'

'Is it absolutely final?'

'There's only one thing for her to do, and that's to divorce him. That's what I was telling her when you came in. "Fire in with your petition, my dear Amy," I said. "You owe it to yourself and you owe it to the children." He'd better not let me catch sight of him. I'd thrash him within an inch of his life.'

I could not help thinking that Colonel MacAndrew might have some difficulty in doing this, since Strickland had struck me as a hefty fellow, but I did not say anything. It is always distressing when outraged morality does not possess the strength of arm to administer direct chastisement on the sinner. I was making up my mind to another attempt at going when Mrs Strickland came back. She had dried her eyes and powdered her nose.

'I'm sorry I broke down', she said. 'I'm glad you didn't go away.'

She sat down. I did not at all know what to say. I felt a certain shyness at referring to matters which were no concern of mine. I did not then know the besetting sin of woman, the passion to discuss her private affairs with anyone who is willing to listen. Mrs Strickland seemed to make an effort over herself.

'Are people talking about it?' she asked.

I was taken aback by her assumption that I knew all about her domestic misfortune.

'I've only just come back. The only person I've seen is Rose Waterford.'

Mrs Strickland clasped her hands.

'Tell me exactly what she said.' And when I hesitated, she insisted. 'I particularly want to know.'

'You know the way people talk. She's not very reliable, is she? She said your husband had left you.'

'Is that all?'

I did not choose to repeat Rose Waterford's parting reference to a girl from a tea-shop. I lied.

'She didn't say anything about his going with anyone?'

'No.'

'That's all I wanted to know.'

I was a little puzzled, but at all events I understood that I might now take my leave. When I shook hands with Mrs Strickland I told her that if I could be of any use to her I should be very glad. She smiled wanly.

'Thank you so much. I don't know that anybody can do anything for me.'

Too shy to express my sympathy, I turned to say good-bye to the Colonel. He did not take my hand.

'I'm just coming. If you're walking up Victoria Street, I'll come along with you.'

'All right', I said. 'Come on.'

IX

'This is a terrible thing', he said, the moment we got out into the street.

I realized that he had come away with me in order to discuss once more what he had been already discussing for hours with his sister-in-law.

'We don't know who the woman is, you know', he said. 'All we know is that the blackguard's gone to Paris.'

'I thought they got on so well.'

'So they did. Why, just before you came in Amy said they'd never had a quarrel in the whole of their married life. You know Amy. There never was a better woman in the world.'

Since these confidences were thrust on me, I saw no harm in asking a few questions.

'But do you mean to say she suspected nothing?'

'Nothing. He spent August with her and the children in Norfolk. He was just the same as he'd always been. We went down for two or three days, my wife and I, and I played golf with him. He came back to town in September to let his partner go away, and Amy stayed on in the country. They'd taken a house for six weeks, and at the end of her tenancy she wrote to tell him on which day she was arriving in London. He answered from Paris. He said he'd made up his mind not to live with her any more.'

'What explanation did he give?'

'My dear fellow, he gave no explanation. I've seen the letter. It wasn't more than ten lines.'

'But that's extraordinary.'

We happened then to cross the street, and the traffic prevented us from speaking. What Colonel MacAndrew had told me seemed very improbable, and I suspected that Mrs Strickland, for reasons of her own, had concealed from him some part of the facts. It was clear that a man after seventeen years of wedlock did not leave his wife without certain occurrences which must have led her to suspect that all was not well with their married life. The Colonel caught me up.

'Of course, there was no explanation he could give except that he'd gone off with a woman. I suppose he thought she could find that out for herself. That's the sort of chap he was.'

'What is Mrs Strickland going to do?'

'Well, the first thing is to get our proofs. I'm going over to Paris myself.'

'And what about his business?'

'That's where he's been so artful. He's been drawing in his horns for the last year.'

'Did he tell his partner he was leaving?'

'Not a word.'

Colonel MacAndrew had a very sketchy knowledge of business matters, and I had none at all, so I did not quite understand under what conditions Strickland had left his affairs. I gathered that the deserted partner was very angry and threatened proceedings. It appeared that when everything was settled he would be four or five hundred pounds out of pocket.

'It's lucky the furniture in the flat is in Amy's name. She'll have that at all events.'

'Did you mean it when you said she wouldn't have a bob?'

'Of course I did. She's got two or three hundred pounds and the furniture.'

'But how is she going to live?'

'God knows.'

The affair seemed to grow more complicated, and the Colonel, with his expletives and his indignation, confused rather than informed me. I was glad that, catching sight of the clock at the Army and Navy Stores, he remembered an engagement to play cards at his club, and so left me to cut across St James's Park.

X

A day or two later Mrs Strickland sent me round a note asking if I could go and see her that evening after dinner. I found her alone. Her black dress, simple to austerity, suggested her bereaved condition, and I was innocently astonished that notwithstanding a real emotion she was able to dress the part she had to play according to her notions of seemliness.

'You said that if I wanted you to do anything you wouldn't mind doing it', she remarked.

'It was quite true.'

'Will you go over to Paris and see Charlie?'

'I?'

I was taken aback. I reflected that I had only seen him once. I did not know what she wanted me to do.

'Fred is set on going.' Fred was Colonel MacAndrew. 'But I'm sure he's not the man to go. He'll only make things worse. I don't know who else to ask.'

Her voice trembled a little, and I felt a brute even to hesitate.

'But I've not spoken ten words to your husband. He doesn't know me. He'll probably just tell me to go to the devil.'

'That wouldn't hurt you', said Mrs Strickland, smiling.

'What is it exactly you want me to do?'

She did not answer directly.

'I think it's rather an advantage that he doesn't know you. You see, he never really liked Fred; he thought him a fool; he didn't understand soldiers. Fred would fly into a passion, and there'd be a quarrel, and things would be worse instead of better. If you said you came on my behalf, he couldn't refuse to listen to you.'

'I haven't known you very long', I answered. 'I don't see how anyone can be expected to tackle a case like this unless he knows all the details. I don't want to pry into what doesn't concern me. Why don't you go and see him yourself?'

'You forget he isn't alone.'

I held my tongue. I saw myself calling on Charles Strickland and sending in my card; I saw him come into the room, holding it between finger and thumb:

'To what do I owe this honour?'

'I've come to see you about your wife.'

'Really. When you are a little older you will doubtless learn the advantage of minding your own business. If you will be so good as to turn your head slightly to the left, you will see the door. I wish you good afternoon.'

I foresaw that it would be difficult to make my exit with dignity, and I wished to goodness that I had not returned to London till Mrs Strickland had composed her difficulties. I stole a glance at her. She was immersed in thought. Presently she looked up at me, sighed deeply, and smiled.

'It was all so unexpected', she said. 'We'd been married seventeen years. I never dreamed that Charlie was the sort of man to get infatuated with anyone. We always got on very well together. Of course, I had a great many interests that he didn't share.'

'Have you found out who'—I did not quite know how to express myself—'who the person, who it is he's gone away with?'

'No. No one seems to have an idea. It's so strange. Generally when a man falls in love with someone people see them about together, lunching or something, and her friends always come and tell the wife. I had no warning—nothing. His letter came like a thunderbolt. I thought he was perfectly happy.'

She began to cry, poor thing, and I felt very sorry for her. But in a little while she grew calmer.

'It's no good making a fool of myself', she said, drying her eyes. 'The only thing is to decide what is the best thing to do.'

She went on, talking somewhat at random, now of the recent past, then of their first meeting and their marriage; but presently I began to form a fairly coherent picture of their lives; and it seemed to me that my surmises had not been incorrect. Mrs Strickland was the daughter of an Indian civilian, who on his retirement had settled in the depths of the country, but it was his habit every August to take his family to Eastbourne for change of air; and it was here, when she was twenty, that she met Charles Strickland. He was twenty-three. They played tennis together, walked on the front together, listened together to the nigger minstrels; and she made up her mind to accept him a week before he proposed to her. They lived in London, first in

Hampstead, and then, as he grew more prosperous, in town. Two children were born to them.

'He always seemed very fond of them. Even if he was tired of me, I wonder that he had the heart to leave them. It's all so incredible. Even now I can hardly believe it's true.'

At last she showed me the letter he had written. I was curious to see it, but had not ventured to ask for it.

MY DEAR AMY,

I think you will find everything all right in the flat. I have given Anne your instructions, and dinner will be ready for you and the children when you come. I shall not be there to meet you. I have made up my mind to live apart from you, and I am going to Paris in the morning. I shall post this letter on my arrival. I shall not come back. My decision is irrevocable.

Yours always,
CHARLES STRICKLAND.

'Not a word of explanation or regret. Don't you think it's inhuman?'

'It's a very strange letter under the circumstances', I replied.

'There's only one explanation, and that is that he's not himself. I don't know who this woman is who's got hold of him, but she's made him into another man. It's evidently been going on a long time.'

'What makes you think that?'

'Fred found that out. My husband said he went to the club three or four nights a week to play bridge. Fred knows one of the members, and said something about Charles being a great bridge-player. The man was surprised. He said he'd never even seen Charles in the card-room. It's quite clear now that when I thought Charles was at his club he was with her.'

I was silent for a moment. Then I thought of the children.

'It must have been very difficult to explain to Robert', I said.

'Oh, I never said a word to either of them. You see, we only came up to town the day before they had to go back to school. I had the presence of mind to say that their father had been called away on business.'

It could not have been very easy to be right and careless with that sudden secret in her heart, nor to give her attention to all the things that needed doing to get her children comfortably packed off. Mrs Strickland's voice broke again.

'And what is to happen to them, poor darlings? How are we going to live?'

She struggled for self-control, and I saw her hands clench and unclench spasmodically. It was dreadfully painful.

'Of course I'll go over to Paris if you think I can do any good, but you must tell me exactly what you want me to do.'

'I want him to come back.'

'I understand from Colonel MacAndrew that you'd made up your mind to divorce him.'

'I'll never divorce him', she answered with a sudden violence. 'Tell him that from me. He'll never be able to marry that woman. I'm as obstinate as he is, and I'll never divorce him. I have to think of my children.'

I think she added this to explain her attitude to me, but I thought it was due to a very natural jealousy rather than to maternal solicitude.

'Are you in love with him still?'

'I don't know. I want him to come back. If he'll do that we'll let bygones be bygones. After all, we've been married for seventeen years. I'm a broad-minded woman. I wouldn't have minded what he did as long as I knew nothing about it. He must know that his infatuation won't last. If he'll come back now everything can be smoothed over, and no one will know anything about it.'

It chilled me a little that Mrs Strickland should be concerned with gossip, for I did not know then how great a part is played in women's life by the opinion of others. It throws a shadow of insincerity over their most deeply felt emotions.

It was known where Strickland was staying. His partner, in a violent letter, sent to his bank, had taunted him with hiding his whereabouts; and Strickland, in a cynical and humorous reply, had told his partner exactly where to find him. He was apparently living in an hotel.

'I've never heard of it', said Mrs Strickland. 'But Fred knows it well. He says it's very expensive.'

She flushed darkly. I imagine that she saw her husband in-
stalled in a luxurious suite of rooms, dining at one smart
restaurant after another, and she pictured his days spent at
race-meetings and his evenings at the play.

'It can't go on at his age', she said. 'After all, he's forty. I could
understand it in a young man, but I think it's horrible in a man
of his years, with children who are nearly grown up. His health
will never stand it.'

Anger struggled in her breast with misery.

'Tell him that our home cries out for him. Everything is just
the same, and yet everything is different. I can't live without
him. I'd sooner kill myself. Talk to him about the past, and all
we've gone through together. What am I to say to the children
when they ask for him? His room is exactly as it was when he
left it. It's waiting for him. We're all waiting for him.'

Now she told me exactly what I should say. She gave me elaborate answers to every possible observation of his.

'You will do everything you can for me?' she said pitifully.
'Tell him what a state I'm in.'

I saw that she wished me to appeal to his sympathies by every
means in my power. She was weeping freely. I was extraordinarily touched. I felt indignant at Strickland's cold cruelty, and I
promised to do all I could to bring him back. I agreed to go over
on the next day but one, and to stay in Paris till I had achieved
something. Then, as it was growing late and we were both exhausted by so much emotion, I left her.

XI

During the journey I thought over my errand with misgiving.
Now that I was free from the spectacle of Mrs Strickland's distress I could consider the matter more calmly. I was puzzled by
the contradictions that I saw in her behaviour. She was very unhappy, but to excite my sympathy she was able to make a show
of her unhappiness. It was evident that she had been prepared
to weep, for she had provided herself with a sufficiency of

handkerchiefs; I admired her forethought, but in retrospect it made her tears perhaps less moving. I could not decide whether she desired the return of her husband because she loved him, or because she dreaded the tongue of scandal; and I was perturbed by the suspicion that the anguish of love contemned was alloyed in her broken heart with the pangs, sordid to my young mind, of wounded vanity. I had not yet learnt how contradictory is human nature; I did not know how much pose there is in the sincere, how much baseness in the noble, or how much goodness in the reprobate.

But there was something of an adventure in my trip, and my spirits rose as I approached Paris. I saw myself, too, from the dramatic standpoint, and I was pleased with my role of the trusted friend bringing back the errant husband to his forgiving wife. I made up my mind to see Strickland the following evening, for I felt instinctively that the hour must be chosen with delicacy. An appeal to the emotions is little likely to be effectual before luncheon. My own thoughts were then constantly occupied with love, but I never could imagine connubial bliss till after tea.

I inquired at my hotel for that in which Charles Strickland was living. It was called the Hôtel des Belges. But the concierge, somewhat to my surprise, had never heard of it. I had understood from Mrs Strickland that it was a large and sumptuous place at the back of the Rue de Rivoli. We looked it out in the directory. The only hotel of that name was in the Rue des Moines. The quarter was not fashionable; it was not even respectable. I shook my head.

'I'm sure that's not it', I said.

The concierge shrugged his shoulders. There was no other hotel of that name in Paris. It occurred to me that Strickland had concealed his address, after all. In giving his partner the one I knew he was perhaps playing a trick on him. I do not know why I had an inkling that it would appeal to Strickland's sense of humour to bring a furious stockbroker over to Paris on a fool's errand to an ill-famed house in a mean street. Still, I thought I had better go and see. Next day about six o'clock I took a cab to the Rue des Moines, but dismissed it at the corner, since I preferred to walk to the hotel and look at it before I went in. It was a street of small shops subservient to the needs of poor people, and about the middle of it, on the left as I walked down, was the Hôtel des Belges. My own hotel was modest enough, but it was magnificent in comparison with this. It was a tall, shabby building, that cannot have been painted for years, and it had so bedraggled an air that the houses on each side of it looked neat and clean. The dirty windows were all shut. It was not here that Charles Strickland lived in guilty splendour with the unknown charmer for whose sake he had abandoned honour and duty. I was vexed, for I felt that I had been made a fool of, and I nearly turned away without making an inquiry. I went in only to be able to tell Mrs Strickland that I had done my best.

The door was at the side of a shop. It stood open, and just within was a sign: *Bureau au premier.* I walked up the narrow stairs, and on the landing found a sort of box, glassed in, within which were a desk and a couple of chairs. There was a bench outside, on which it might be presumed the night porter passed uneasy nights. There was no one about, but under an electric bell was written *Garçon.* I rang, and presently a waiter appeared. He was a young man with furtive eyes and a sullen look. He was in shirt sleeves and carpet slippers.

I do not know why I made my inquiry as casual as possible.

'Does Mr Strickland live here by any chance?' I asked.

'Number thirty-two. On the sixth floor.'

I was so surprised that for a moment I did not answer.

'Is he in?'

The waiter looked at a board in the *bureau.*

'He hasn't left his key. Go up and you'll see.'

I thought it as well to put one more question.

'*Madame est là?*'

'*Monsieur est seul.*'

The waiter looked at me suspiciously as I made my way upstairs. They were dark and airless. There was a foul and musty smell. Three flights up a woman in a dressing-gown, with touzled hair, opened a door and looked at me silently as I passed.

At length I reached the sixth floor, and knocked at the door numbered thirty-two. There was a sound within, and the door was partly opened. Charles Strickland stood before me. He uttered not a word. He evidently did not know me.

I told him my name. I tried my best to assume an airy manner.

'You don't remember me. I had the pleasure of dining with you last July.'

'Come in', he said cheerily. 'I'm delighted to see you. Take a pew.'

I entered. It was a very small room, overcrowded with furniture of the style which the French know as Louis Philippe. There was a large wooden bedstead on which was a billowing red eiderdown, and there was a large wardrobe, a round table, a very small washstand, and two stuffed chairs covered with red rep. Everything was dirty and shabby. There was no sign of the abandoned luxury that Colonel MacAndrew had so confidently described. Strickland threw on the floor the clothes that burdened one of the chairs, and I sat down on it.

'What can I do for you?' he asked.

In that small room he seemed even bigger than I remembered him. He wore an old Norfolk jacket, and he had not shaved for several days. When last I saw him he was spruce enough, but he looked ill at ease: now, untidy and ill-kempt, he looked perfectly at home. I did not know how he would take the remark I had prepared.

'I've come to see you on behalf of your wife.'

'I was just going out to have a drink before dinner. You'd better come too. Do you like absinthe?'

'I can drink it.'

'Come on, then.'

He put on a bowler hat much in need of brushing.

'We might dine together. You owe me a dinner, you know.'

'Certainly. Are you alone?'

I flattered myself that I had got in that important question very naturally.

'Oh yes. In point of fact I've not spoken to a soul for three days. My French isn't exactly brilliant.'

I wondered as I preceded him downstairs what had happened

to the little lady in the tea-shop. Had they quarrelled already, or was his infatuation passed? It seemed hardly likely if, as appeared, he had been taking steps for a year to make his desperate plunge. We walked to the Avenue de Clichy, and sat down at one of the tables on the pavement of a large café.

XII

The Avenue de Clichy was crowded at that hour, and a lively fancy might see in the passers-by the personages of many a sordid romance. There were clerks and shopgirls; old fellows who might have stepped out of the pages of Honoré de Balzac; members, male and female, of the professions which make their profit of the frailties of mankind. There is in the streets of the poorer quarters of Paris a thronging vitality which excites the blood and prepares the soul for the unexpected.

'Do you know Paris well?' I asked.

'No. We came on our honeymoon. I haven't been since.'

'How on earth did you find out your hotel?'

'It was recommended to me. I wanted something cheap.'

The absinthe came, and with due solemnity we dropped water over the melting sugar.

'I thought I'd better tell you at once why I had come to see you', I said, not without embarrassment.

His eyes twinkled.

'I thought somebody would come along sooner or later. I've had a lot of letters from Amy.'

'Then you know pretty well what I've got to say.'

'I've not read them.'

I lit a cigarette to give myself a moment's time. I did not quite know now how to set about my mission. The eloquent phrases I had arranged, pathetic or indignant, seemed out of place on the Avenue de Clichy. Suddenly he gave a chuckle.

'Beastly job for you this, isn't it?'

'Oh, I don't know', I answered.

'Well, look here, you get it over, and then we'll have a jolly evening.'

I hesitated.

'Has it occurred to you that your wife is frightfully unhappy?'

'She'll get over it.'

I cannot describe the extraordinary callousness with which he made this reply. It disconcerted me, but I did my best not to show it. I adopted the tone used by my Uncle Henry, a clergyman, when he was asking one of his relatives for a subscription to the Additional Curates Society.

'You don't mind my talking to you frankly?'

He shook his head, smiling.

'Has she deserved that you should treat her like this?'

'No.'

'Have you any complaint to make against her?'

'None.'

'Then, isn't it monstrous to leave her in this fashion, after seventeen years of married life, without a fault to find with her?'

'Monstrous.'

I glanced at him with surprise. His cordial agreement with all I said cut the ground from under my feet. It made my position complicated, not to say ludicrous. I was prepared to be persuasive, touching, and hortatory, admonitory and expostulating, if need be vituperative even, indignant and sarcastic; but what the devil does a mentor do when the sinner makes no bones about confessing his sin? I had no experience, since my own practice has always been to deny everything.

'What, then?' asked Strickland.

I tried to curl my lip.

'Well, if you acknowledge that, there doesn't seem much more to be said.'

'I don't think there is.'

I felt that I was not carrying out my embassy with any great skill. I was distinctly nettled.

'Hang it all, one can't leave a woman without a bob.'

'Why not?'

'How is she going to live?'

'I've supported her for seventeen years. Why shouldn't she support herself for a change?'

'She can't.'

'Let her try.'

Of course there were many things I might have answered to this. I might have spoken of the economic position of woman, of the contract, tacit and overt, which a man accepts by his marriage, and of much else; but I felt that there was only one point which really signified.

'Don't you care for her any more?'

'Not a bit', he replied.

The matter was immensely serious for all the parties concerned, but there was in the manner of his answers such a cheerful effrontery that I had to bite my lips in order not to laugh. I reminded myself that his behaviour was abominable. I worked myself up into a state of moral indignation.

'Damn it all, there are your children to think of. They've never done you any harm. They didn't ask to be brought into the world. If you chuck everything like this, they'll be thrown on the streets.'

'They've had a good many years of comfort. It's much more than the majority of children have. Besides, somebody will look after them. When it comes to the point, the MacAndrews will pay for their schooling.'

'But aren't you fond of them? They're such awfully nice kids. Do you mean to say you don't want to have anything more to do with them?'

'I liked them all right when they were kids, but now they're growing up I haven't got any particular feeling for them.'

'It's just inhuman.'

'I dare say.'

'You don't seem in the least ashamed.'

'I'm not.'

I tried another tack.

'Everyone will think you a perfect swine.'

'Let them.'

'Won't it mean anything to you to know that people loathe and despise you?'

'No.'

His brief answer was so scornful that it made my question, natural though it was, seem absurd. I reflected for a minute or two.

'I wonder if one can live quite comfortably when one's

conscious of the disapproval of one's fellows? Are you sure it won't begin to worry you? Everyone has some sort of a conscience, and sooner or later it will find you out. Supposing your wife died, wouldn't you be tortured by remorse?'

He did not answer, and I waited for some time for him to speak. At last I had to break the silence myself.

'What have you to say to that?'

'Only that you're a damned fool.'

'At all events, you can be forced to support your wife and children', I retorted, somewhat piqued. 'I suppose the law has some protection to offer them.'

'Can the law get blood out of a stone? I haven't any money. I've got about a hundred pounds.'

I began to be more puzzled than before. It was true that his hotel pointed to the most straitened circumstances.

'What are you going to do when you've spent that?'

'Earn some.'

He was perfectly cool, and his eyes kept that mocking smile which made all I said seem rather foolish. I paused for a little while to consider what I had better say next. But it was he who spoke first.

'Why doesn't Amy marry again? She's comparatively young, and she's not unattractive. I can recommend her as an excellent wife. If she wants to divorce me I don't mind giving her the necessary grounds.'

Now it was my turn to smile. He was very cunning, but it was evidently this that he was aiming at. He had some reason to conceal the fact that he had run away with a woman, and he was using every precaution to hide her whereabouts. I answered with decision.

'Your wife says that nothing you can do will ever induce her to divorce you. She's quite made up her mind. You can put any possibility of that definitely out of your head.'

He looked at me with astonishment that was certainly not feigned. The smile abandoned his lips, and he spoke quite seriously.

'But, my dear fellow, I don't care. It doesn't matter a twopenny damn to me one way or the other.'

I laughed.

'Oh, come now; you mustn't think us such fools as all that. We happen to know that you came away with a woman.'

He gave a little start, and then suddenly burst into a shout of laughter. He laughed so uproariously that the people sitting near us looked round, and some of them began to laugh too.

'I don't see anything very amusing in that.'

'Poor Amy', he grinned.

Then his face grew bitterly scornful.

'What poor minds women have got! Love. It's always love. They think a man leaves them only because he wants others. Do you think I should be such a fool as to do what I've done for a woman?'

'Do you mean to say you didn't leave your wife for another woman?'

'Of course not.'

'On your word of honour?'

I don't know why I asked for that. It was very ingenuous of me.

'On my word of honour.'

'Then, what in God's name have you left her for?'

'I want to paint.'

I looked at him for quite a long time. I did not understand. I thought he was mad. It must be remembered that I was very young, and I looked upon him as a middle-aged man. I forgot everything but my own amazement.

'But you're forty.'

'That's what made me think it was high time to begin.'

'Have you ever painted?'

'I rather wanted to be a painter when I was a boy, but my father made me go into business because he said there was no money in art. I began to paint a bit a year ago. For the last year I've been going to some classes at night.'

'Was that where you went when Mrs Strickland thought you were playing bridge at your club?'

'That's it.'

'Why didn't you tell her?'

'I preferred to keep it to myself.'

'Can you paint?'

'Not yet. But I shall. That's why I've come over here. I couldn't get what I wanted in London. Perhaps I can here.'

'Do you think it's likely that a man will do any good when he starts at your age? Most men begin painting at eighteen.'

'I can learn quicker than I could when I was eighteen.'

'What makes you think you have any talent?'

He did not answer for a minute. His gaze rested on the passing throng, but I do not think he saw it. His answer was no answer.

'I've got to paint.'

'Aren't you taking an awful chance?'

He looked at me then. His eyes had something strange in them, so that I felt rather uncomfortable.

'How old are you? Twenty-three?'

It seemed to me that the question was beside the point. It was natural that I should take chances; but he was a man whose youth was past, a stockbroker with a position of respectability, a wife and two children. A course that would have been natural for me was absurd for him. I wished to be quite fair.

'Of course a miracle may happen, and you may be a great painter, but you must confess the chances are a million to one against it. It'll be an awful sell if at the end you have to acknowledge you've made a hash of it.'

'I've got to paint', he repeated.

'Supposing you're never anything more than third-rate, do you think it will have been worth while to give up everything? After all, in any other walk in life it doesn't matter if you're not very good; you can get along quite comfortably if you're just adequate; but it's different with an artist.'

'You blasted fool', he said.

'I don't see why, unless it's folly to say the obvious.'

'I tell you I've got to paint. I can't help myself. When a man falls into the water it doesn't matter how he swims, well or badly: he's got to get out or else he'll drown.'

There was real passion in his voice, and in spite of myself I was impressed. I seemed to feel in him some vehement power that was struggling within him; it gave me the sensation of something very strong, overmastering, that held him, as it were, against his will. I could not understand. He seemed really to be possessed of a devil, and I felt that it might suddenly turn and rend him. Yet he looked ordinary enough. My eyes, resting on him curiously, caused him no embarrassment. I wondered what a stranger would have taken him to be, sitting there in his old Norfolk jacket and his unbrushed bowler; his trousers were baggy, his hands were not clean; and his face, with the red stubble of the unshaved chin, the little eyes, and the large, aggressive nose, was uncouth and coarse. His mouth was large, his lips were heavy and sensual. No; I could not have placed him.

'You won't go back to your wife?' I said at last.

'Never.'

'She's willing to forget everything that's happened and start afresh. She'll never make you a single reproach.'

'She can go to hell.'

'You don't care if people think you an utter blackguard? You don't care if she and your children have to beg their bread?'

'Not a damn.'

I was silent for a moment in order to give greater force to my next remark. I spoke as deliberately as I could.

'You are a most unmitigated cad.'

'Now that you've got that off your chest, let's go and have dinner.'

XIII

I dare say it would have been more seemly to decline this proposal. I think perhaps I should have made a show of the indignation I really felt, and I am sure that Colonel MacAndrew at least would have thought well of me if I had been able to report my stout refusal to sit at the same table with a man of such character. But the fear of not being able to carry it through effectively has always made me shy of assuming the moral attitude; and in this case the certainty that my sentiments would be lost on Strickland made it peculiarly embarrassing to utter them. Only the poet or the saint can water an asphalt pavement in the confident anticipation that lilies will reward his labour.

I paid for what we had drunk, and we made our way to a

cheap restaurant, crowded and gay, where we dined with pleasure. I had the appetite of youth and he of a hardened conscience. Then we went to a tavern to have coffee and liqueurs.

I had said all I had to say on the subject that had brought me
to Paris, and though I felt it in a manner treacherous to Mrs
Strickland not to pursue it, I could not struggle against his indifference. It requires the feminine temperament to repeat the
same thing three times with unabated zest. I solaced myself by
thinking that it would be useful for me to find out what I could
about Strickland's state of mind. It also interested me much
more. But this was not an easy thing to do, for Strickland was
not a fluent talker. He seemed to express himself with difficulty, as though words were not the medium with which his
mind worked; and you had to guess the intentions of his soul by
hackneyed phrases, slang, and vague, unfinished gestures. But
though he said nothing of any consequence, there was something in his personality which prevented him from being dull.
Perhaps it was sincerity. He did not seem to care much about
the Paris he was now seeing for the first time (I did not count
the visit with his wife), and he accepted sights which must have
been strange to him without any sense of astonishment. I have
been to Paris a hundred times, and it never fails to give me a
thrill of excitement; I can never walk its streets without feeling
myself on the verge of adventure. Strickland remained placid.
Looking back, I think now that he was blind to everything but
to some disturbing vision in his soul.

One rather absurd incident took place. There were a number
of harlots in the tavern: some were sitting with men, others by
themselves; and presently I noticed that one of these was looking at us. When she caught Strickland's eye she smiled. I do not
think he saw her. In a little while she went out, but in a minute
returned and, passing our table, very politely asked us to buy
her something to drink. She sat down and I began to chat with
her; but it was plain that her interest was in Strickland. I explained that he knew no more than two words of French. She
tried to talk to him, partly by signs, partly in pidgin French,
which, for some reason, she thought would be more comprehensible to him, and she had half a dozen phrases of English.

She made me translate what she could only express in her own tongue, and eagerly asked for the meaning of his replies. He was quite good-tempered, a little amused, but his indifference was obvious.

'I think you've made a conquest', I laughed.

'I'm not flattered.'

In his place I should have been more embarrassed and less calm. She had laughing eyes and a most charming mouth. She was young. I wondered what she found so attractive in Strickland. She made no secret of her desires, and I was bidden to translate.

'She wants you to go home with her.'

'I'm not taking any', he replied.

I put his answer as pleasantly as I could. It seemed to me a little ungracious to decline an invitation of that sort, and I ascribed his refusal to lack of money.

'But I like him', she said. 'Tell him it's for love.'

When I translated this, Strickland shrugged his shoulders impatiently.

'Tell her to go to hell', he said.

His manner made his answer quite plain, and the girl threw back her head with a sudden gesture. Perhaps she reddened under her paint. She rose to her feet.

'Monsieur n'est pas poli', she said.

She walked out of the inn. I was slightly vexed.

'There wasn't any need to insult her that I can see', I said. 'After all, it was rather a compliment she was paying you.'

'That sort of thing makes me sick', he said roughly.

I looked at him curiously. There was real distaste in his face, and yet it was the face of a coarse and sensual man. I suppose the girl had been attracted by a certain brutality in it.

'I could have got all the women I wanted in London. I didn't come here for that.'

XIV

During the journey back to England I thought much of Strick-land. I tried to set in order what I had to tell his wife. It was un-satisfactory, and I could not imagine that she would be content with me; I was not content with myself. Strickland perplexed me. I could not understand his motives. When I had asked him what first gave him the idea of being a painter, he was unable or unwilling to tell me. I could make nothing of it. I tried to per-suade myself that an obscure feeling of revolt had been gradu-ally coming to a head in his slow mind, but to challenge this was the undoubted fact that he had never shown any impatience with the monotony of his life. If, seized by an intolerable bore-dom, he had determined to be a painter merely to break with irksome ties, it would have been comprehensible, and common-place; but commonplace is precisely what I felt he was not. At last, because I was romantic, I devised an explanation which I acknowledged to be far-fetched, but which was the only one that in any way satisfied me. It was this: I asked myself whether there was not in his soul some deep-rooted instinct of creation, which the circumstances of his life had obscured, but which grew relentlessly, as a cancer may grow in the living tissues, till at last it took possession of his whole being and forced him ir-resistibly to action. The cuckoo lays its eggs in the strange bird's nest, and when the young one is hatched it shoulders its foster-brothers out and breaks at last the nest that has sheltered it.

But how strange it was that the creative instinct should seize upon this dull stockbroker, to his own ruin, perhaps, and to the misfortune of such as were dependent on him; and yet no stranger than the way in which the spirit of God has seized men, powerful and rich, pursuing them with stubborn vigi-lance till at last, conquered, they have abandoned the joy of the world and the love of women for the painful austerities of the cloister. Conversion may come under many shapes, and it may be brought about in many ways. With some men it needs a cataclysm, as a stone may be broken to fragments by the fury of a torrent; but with some it comes gradually, as a stone may be worn away by the ceaseless fall of a drop of water.

Strickland had the directness of the fanatic and the ferocity of the apostle.

But to my practical mind it remained to be seen whether the passion which obsessed him would be justified of its works. When I asked him what his brother-students at the night classes he had attended in London thought of his painting, he answered with a grin:

'They thought it a joke.'

'Have you begun to go to a studio here?'

'Yes. The blighter came round this morning—the master, you know; when he saw my drawing he just raised his eyebrows and walked on.'

Strickland chuckled. He did not seem discouraged. He was independent of the opinion of his fellows.

And it was just that which had most disconcerted me in my dealings with him. When people say they do not care what others think of them, for the most part they deceive themselves. Generally they mean only that they will do as they choose, in the confidence that no one will know their vagaries; and at the utmost only that they are willing to act contrary to the opinion of the majority because they are supported by the approval of their neighbours. It is not difficult to be unconventional in the eyes of the world when your unconventionality is but the convention of your set. It affords you then an inordinate amount of self-esteem. You have the self-satisfaction of courage without the inconvenience of danger. But the desire for approbation is perhaps the most deeply seated instinct of civilized man. No one runs so hurriedly to the cover of respectability as the unconventional woman who has exposed herself to the slings and arrows of outraged propriety. I do not believe the people who tell me they do not care a row of pins for the opinion of their fellows. It is the bravado of ignorance. They mean only that they do not fear reproaches for peccadilloes which they are convinced none will discover.

But here was a man who sincerely did not mind what people thought of him, and so convention had no hold on him; he was like a wrestler whose body is oiled; you could not get a grip on him; it gave him a freedom which was an outrage. I remember saying to him:

'Look here, if everyone acted like you, the world couldn't go on.'

'That's a damned silly thing to say. Everyone doesn't want to act like me. The great majority are perfectly content to do the ordinary thing.'

And once I sought to be satirical.

'You evidently don't believe in the maxim: Act so that every one of your actions is capable of being made into a universal rule.'

'I never heard it before, but it's rotten nonsense.'

'Well, it was Kant who said it.'

'I don't care; it's rotten nonsense.'

Nor with such a man could you expect the appeal to conscience to be effective. You might as well ask for a reflection without a mirror. I take it that conscience is the guardian in the individual of the rules which the community has evolved for its own preservation. It is the policeman in all our hearts, set there to watch that we do not break its laws. It is the spy seated in the central stronghold of the ego. Man's desire for the approval of his fellows is so strong, his dread of their censure so violent, that himself has brought his enemy within his gates; and it keeps watch over him, vigilant always in the interests of its master to crush any half-formed desire to break away from the herd. It will force him to place the good of society before his own. It is the very strong link that attaches the individual to the whole. And man, subservient to interests he has persuaded himself are greater than his own, makes himself a slave to his taskmaster. He sits him in a seat of honour. At last, like a courtier fawning on the royal stick that is laid about his shoulders, he prides himself on the sensitiveness of his conscience. Then he has no words hard enough for the man who does not recognize its sway; for, a member of society now, he realizes accurately enough that against him he is powerless. When I saw that Strickland was really indifferent to the blame his conduct must excite, I could only draw back in horror as from a monster of hardly human shape.

The last words he said to me when I bade him good night were:

'Tell Amy it's no good coming after me. Anyhow I shall change my hotel, so she wouldn't be able to find me.'

'My own impression is that she's well rid of you', I said.

'My dear fellow, I only hope you'll be able to make her see it. But women are very unintelligent.'

XV

When I reached London I found waiting for me an urgent request that I should go to Mrs Strickland's as soon after dinner as I could. I found her with Colonel MacAndrew and his wife. Mrs Strickland's sister was older than she, not unlike her, but more faded; and she had the efficient air, as though she carried the British Empire in her pocket, which the wives of senior officers acquire from the consciousness of belonging to a superior caste. Her manner was brisk, and her good-breeding scarcely concealed her conviction that if you were not a soldier you might as well be a counter-jumper. She hated the Guards, whom she thought conceited, and she could not trust herself to speak of their ladies, who were so remiss in calling. Her gown was dowdy and expensive.

Mrs Strickland was plainly nervous.

'Well, tell us your news', she said.

'I saw your husband. I'm afraid he's quite made up his mind not to return.' I paused a little. 'He wants to paint.'

'What do you mean?' cried Mrs Strickland, with the utmost astonishment.

'Did you never know that he was keen on that sort of thing?'

'He must be as mad as a hatter', exclaimed the Colonel.

Mrs Strickland frowned a little. She was searching among her recollections.

'I remember before we were married he used to potter about with a paint-box. But you never saw such daubs. We used to chaff him. He had absolutely no gift for anything like that.'

'Of course, it's only an excuse', said Mrs MacAndrew.

Mrs Strickland pondered deeply for some time. It was quite

clear that she could not make head or tail of my announcement. She had put some order into the drawing-room by now, her housewifely instincts having got the better of her dismay; and it no longer bore that deserted look, like a furnished house long to let, which I had noticed on my first visit after the catastrophe. But now that I had seen Strickland in Paris it was difficult to imagine him in those surroundings. I thought it could hardly have failed to strike them that there was something incongruous in him.

'But if he wanted to be an artist, why didn't he say so?' asked Mrs Strickland at last. 'I should have thought I was the last person to be unsympathetic to—to aspiration of that kind.'

Mrs MacAndrew tightened her lips. I imagine that she had never looked with approval on her sister's leaning towards persons who cultivated the arts. She spoke of 'culchaw' derisively.

Mrs Strickland continued:

'After all, if he had any talent I should be the first to encourage it. I wouldn't have minded sacrifices. I'd much rather be married to a painter than to a stockbroker. If it weren't for the children, I wouldn't mind anything. I could be just as happy in a shabby studio in Chelsea as in this flat.'

'My dear, I have no patience with you', cried Mrs MacAndrew. 'You don't mean to say you believe a word of this nonsense?'

'But I think it's true', I put in mildly.

She looked at me with good-humoured contempt.

'A man doesn't throw up his business and leave his wife and children at the age of forty to become a painter unless there's a woman in it. I suppose he met one of your—artistic friends, and she's turned his head.'

A spot of colour rose suddenly to Mrs Strickland's pale cheeks.

'What is she like?'

I hesitated a little. I knew that I had a bombshell.

'There isn't a woman.'

Colonel MacAndrew and his wife uttered expressions of incredulity, and Mrs Strickland sprang to her feet.

'Do you mean to say you never saw her?'

'There's no one to see. He's quite alone.'

'That's preposterous', cried Mrs MacAndrew.

'I knew I ought to have gone over myself', said the Colonel. 'You can bet your boots I'd have routed her out fast enough.'

'I wish you had gone over', I replied, somewhat tartly. 'You'd have seen that every one of your suppositions was wrong. He's not at a smart hotel. He's living in one tiny room in the most squalid way. If he's left his home, it's not to live a gay life. He's got hardly any money.'

'Do you think he's done something that we don't know about, and is lying doggo on account of the police?'

The suggestion sent a ray of hope in all their breasts, but I would have nothing to do with it.

'If that were so, he would hardly have been such a fool as to give his partner his address', I retorted acidly. 'Anyhow, there's one thing I'm positive of, he didn't go away with anyone. He's not in love. Nothing is farther from his thoughts.'

There was a pause while they reflected over my words.

'Well, if what you say is true', said Mrs MacAndrew at last, 'things aren't so bad as I thought.'

Mrs Strickland glanced at her, but said nothing. She was very pale now, and her fine brow was dark and lowering. I could not understand the expression of her face. Mrs MacAndrew continued:

'If it's just a whim, he'll get over it.'

'Why don't you go over to him, Amy?' hazarded the Colonel. 'There's no reason why you shouldn't live with him in Paris for a year. We'll look after the children. I dare say he'd got stale. Sooner or later he'll be quite ready to come back to London, and no great harm will have been done.'

'I wouldn't do that', said Mrs MacAndrew. 'I'd give him all the rope he wants. He'll come back with his tail between his legs and settle down again quite comfortably.' Mrs MacAndrew looked at her sister coolly. 'Perhaps you weren't very wise with him sometimes. Men are queer creatures, and one has to know how to manage them.'

Mrs MacAndrew shared the common opinion of her sex that a man is always a brute to leave a woman who is attached to him, but that a woman is much to blame if he does. *Le cœur a ses raisons que la raison ne connait point.*

Mrs Strickland looked slowly from one to another of us.

'He'll never come back', she said.

'Oh, my dear, remember what we've just heard. He's been used to comfort and to having someone to look after him. How long do you think it'll be before he gets tired of a scrubby room in a scrubby hotel? Besides, he hasn't any money. He must come back.'

'As long as I thought he'd run away with some woman I thought there was a chance. I don't believe that sort of thing ever answers. He'd have got sick to death of her in three months. But if he hasn't gone because he's in love, then it's finished.'

'Oh, I think that's awfully subtle', said the Colonel, putting into the word all the contempt he felt for a quality so alien to the traditions of his calling. 'Don't you believe it. He'll come back, and, as Dorothy says, I dare say he'll be none the worse for having had a bit of a fling.'

'But I don't want him back', she said.

'Amy!'

It was anger that had seized Mrs Strickland, and her pallor was the pallor of a cold and sudden rage. She spoke quickly now, with little gasps.

'I could have forgiven it if he'd fallen desperately in love with someone and gone off with her. I should have thought that natural. I shouldn't really have blamed him. I should have thought he was led away. Men are so weak, and women are so unscrupulous. But this is different. I hate him. I'll never forgive him now.'

Colonel MacAndrew and his wife began to talk to her together. They were astonished. They told her she was mad. They could not understand. Mrs Strickland turned desperately to me.

'Don't *you* see?' she cried.

'I'm not sure. Do you mean that you could have forgiven him if he'd left you for a woman, but not if he's left you for an idea? You think you're a match for the one, but against the other you're helpless?'

Mrs Strickland gave me a look in which I read no great friendliness, but did not answer. Perhaps I had struck home. She went on in a low and trembling voice:

'I never knew it was possible to hate anyone as much as I hate him. Do you know, I've been comforting myself by thinking that however long it lasted he'd want me at the end. I knew when he was dying he'd send for me, and I was ready to go; I'd have nursed him like a mother, and at the last I'd have told him that it didn't matter, I'd loved him always, and I forgave him everything.'

I have always been a little disconcerted by the passion women have for behaving beautifully at the death-bed of those they love. Sometimes it seems as if they grudge the longevity which postpones their chance of an effective scene.

'But now—now it's finished. I'm as indifferent to him as if he were a stranger. I should like him to die miserable, poor, and starving, without a friend. I hope he'll rot with some loathsome disease. I've done with him.'

I thought it as well then to say what Strickland had suggested.

'If you want to divorce him, he's quite willing to do whatever is necessary to make it possible.'

'Why should I give him his freedom?'

'I don't think he wants it. He merely thought it might be more convenient to you.'

Mrs Strickland shrugged her shoulders impatiently. I think I was a little disappointed in her. I expected then people to be more of a piece than I do now, and I was distressed to find so much vindictiveness in so charming a creature. I did not realize how motley are the qualities that go to make up a human being. Now I am well aware that pettiness and grandeur, malice and charity, hatred and love, can find place side by side in the same human heart.

I wondered if there was anything I could say that would ease the sense of bitter humiliation which at present tormented Mrs Strickland. I thought I would try.

'You know, I'm not sure that your husband is quite responsible for his actions. I do not think he is himself. He seems to me to be possessed by some power which is using him for its own ends, and in whose hold he is as helpless as a fly in a spider's web. It's as though someone had cast a spell over him. I'm reminded of those strange stories one sometimes hears of another personality entering into a man and driving out the old one.

The soul lives unstably in the body, and is capable of mysterious transformations. In the old days they would say Charles Strickland had a devil.'

Mrs MacAndrew smoothed down the lap of her gown, and gold bangles fell over her wrists.

'All that seems to me very far-fetched', she said acidly. 'I don't deny that perhaps Amy took her husband a little too much for granted. If she hadn't been so busy with her own affairs, I can't believe that she wouldn't have suspected something was the matter. I don't think that Alec could have something on his mind for a year or more without my having a pretty shrewd idea of it.'

The Colonel stared into vacancy, and I wondered whether anyone could be quite so innocent of guile as he looked.

'But that doesn't prevent the fact that Charles Strickland is a heartless beast.' She looked at me severely. 'I can tell you why he left his wife—from pure selfishness and nothing else whatever.'

'That is certainly the simplest explanation', I said. But I thought it explained nothing. When, saying I was tired, I rose to go, Mrs Strickland made no attempt to detain me.

XVI

What followed showed that Mrs Strickland was a woman of character. Whatever anguish she suffered she concealed. She saw shrewdly that the world is quickly bored by the recital of misfortune, and willingly avoids the sight of distress. Whenever she went out—and compassion for her misadventure made her friends eager to entertain her—she bore a demeanour that was perfect. She was brave, but not too obviously; cheerful, but not brazenly; and she seemed more anxious to listen to the troubles of others than to discuss her own. Whenever she spoke of her husband it was with pity. Her attitude towards him at first perplexed me. One day she said to me:

'You know, I'm convinced you were mistaken about Charles being alone. From what I've been able to gather from certain sources that I can't tell you, I know that he didn't leave England by himself.'

'In that case he has a positive genius for covering up his tracks.'

She looked away and slightly coloured.

'What I mean is, if anyone talks to you about it, please don't contradict it if they say he eloped with somebody.'

'Of course not.'

She changed the conversation as though it were a matter to which she attached no importance. I discovered presently that a peculiar story was circulating among her friends. They said that Charles Strickland had become infatuated with a French dancer, whom he had first seen in the ballet at the Empire, and had accompanied her to Paris. I could not find out how this had arisen, but, singularly enough, it created much sympathy for Mrs Strickland, and at the same time gave her not a little prestige. This was not without its use in the calling which she had decided to follow. Colonel MacAndrew had not exaggerated when he said she would be penniless, and it was necessary for her to earn her living as quickly as she could. She made up her mind to profit by her acquaintance with so many writers, and without loss of time began to learn shorthand and typewriting. Her education made it likely that she would be a typist more efficient than the average, and her story made her claims appealing. Her friends promised to send her work, and took care to recommend her to all theirs.

The MacAndrews, who were childless and in easy circumstances, arranged to undertake the care of the children, and Mrs Strickland had only herself to provide for. She let her flat and sold her furniture. She settled in two tiny rooms in Westminster, and faced the world anew. She was so efficient that it was certain she would make a success of the adventure.

XVII

It was about five years after this that I decided to live in Paris for a while. I was growing stale in London. I was tired of doing much the same thing every day. My friends pursued their course with uneventfulness; they had no longer any surprises for me, and when I met them I knew pretty well what they would say; even their love-affairs had a tedious banality. We were like tram-cars running on their lines from terminus to terminus, and it was possible to calculate within small limits the number of passengers they would carry. Life was ordered too pleasantly. I was seized with panic. I gave up my small apartment, sold my few belongings, and resolved to start afresh.

I called on Mrs Strickland before I left. I had not seen her for some time, and I noticed changes in her; it was not only that she was older, thinner, and more lined; I think her character had altered. She had made a success of her business, and now had an office in Chancery Lane; she did little typing herself, but spent her time correcting the work of the four girls she employed. She had had the idea of giving it a certain daintiness, and she made much use of blue and red inks; she bound the copy in coarse paper, that looked vaguely like watered silk, in various pale colours; and she had acquired a reputation for neatness and accuracy. She was making money. But she could not get over the idea that to earn her living was somewhat undignified, and she was inclined to remind you that she was a lady by birth. She could not help bringing into her conversation the names of people she knew which would satisfy you that she had not sunk in the social scale. She was a little ashamed of her courage and business capacity, but delighted that she was going to dine the next night with a K.C. who lived in South Kensington. She was pleased to be able to tell you that her son was at Cambridge, and it was with a little laugh that she spoke of the rush of dances to which her daughter, just out, was invited. I suppose I said a very stupid thing.

'Is she going into your business?' I asked.

'Oh no; I wouldn't let her do that', Mrs Strickland answered. 'She's so pretty. I'm sure she'll marry well.'

'I should have thought it would be a help to you.'

'Several people have suggested that she should go on the stage, but of course I couldn't consent to that. I know all the chief dramatists, and I could get her a part tomorrow, but I shouldn't like her to mix with all sorts of people.'

I was a little chilled by Mrs Strickland's exclusiveness.

'Do you ever hear of your husband?'

'No; I haven't heard a word. He may be dead for all I know.'

'I may run across him in Paris. Would you like me to let you know about him?'

She hesitated a minute.

'If he's in any real want I'm prepared to help him a little. I'd send you a certain sum of money, and you could give it him gradually, as he needed it.'

'That's very good of you', I said.

But I knew it was not kindness that prompted the offer. It is not true that suffering ennobles the character; happiness does that sometimes, but suffering, for the most part, makes men petty and vindictive.

XVIII

In point of fact, I met Strickland before I had been a fortnight in Paris.

I quickly found myself a tiny apartment on the fifth floor of a house in the Rue des Dames, and for a couple of hundred francs bought at a second-hand dealer's enough furniture to make it habitable. I arranged with the concierge to make my coffee in the morning and to keep the place clean. Then I went to see my friend Dirk Stroeve.

Dirk Stroeve was one of those persons whom, according to your character, you cannot think of without derisive laughter or an embarrassed shrug of the shoulders. Nature had made him a buffoon. He was a painter, but a very bad one, whom I had met in Rome, and I still remembered his pictures. He had a genuine enthusiasm for the commonplace. His soul palpitating with love of art, he painted the models who hung about the stairway of Bernini in the Piazza di Spagna, undaunted by their obvious picturesqueness; and his studio was full of canvases on which were portrayed moustachioed, large-eyed peasants in peaked hats, urchins in becoming rags, and women in bright petticoats. Sometimes they lounged at the steps of a church, and sometimes dallied among cypresses against a cloudless sky; sometimes they made love by a Renaissance well-head, and sometimes they wandered through the Campagna by the side of an ox-wagon. They were carefully drawn and carefully painted. A photograph could not have been more exact. One of the painters at the Villa Medici had called him *Le Maître de la Boîte à Chocolats*. To look at his pictures you would have thought that Monet, Manet, and the rest of the Impressionists had never been.

'I don't pretend to be a great painter', he said. 'I'm not a Michael Angelo, no, but I have something. I sell. I bring romance into the homes of all sorts of people. Do you know, they buy my pictures not only in Holland, but in Norway and Sweden and Denmark? It's mostly merchants who buy them, and rich tradesmen. You can't imagine what the winters are like in those countries, so long and dark and cold. They like to think that Italy is like my pictures. That's what they expect. That's what I expected Italy to be before I came here.'

And I think that was the vision that had remained with him always, dazzling his eyes so that he could not see the truth; and notwithstanding the brutality of fact, he continued to see with the eyes of the spirit an Italy of romantic brigands and picturesque ruins. It was an ideal that he painted—a poor one, common, and shop-soiled, but still it was an ideal; and it gave his character a definite charm.

It was because I felt this that Dirk Stroeve was not to me, as to others, merely an object of ridicule. His fellow-painters made no secret of their contempt for his work, but he earned a fair amount of money, and they did not hesitate to make free use of his purse. He was generous, and the needy, laughing at him because he believed so naïvely their stories of distress, borrowed from him with effrontery. He was very emotional, yet his feeling, so easily aroused, had in it something absurd, so that you accepted his kindness, but felt no gratitude. To take money from him was like robbing a child, and you despised him because he was so foolish. I imagine that a pickpocket, proud of his light fingers, must feel a sort of indignation with the careless woman who leaves in a cab a vanity-bag with all her jewels in it. Nature had made him a butt, but had denied him insensibility. He writhed under the jokes, practical and otherwise, which were perpetually made at his expense, and yet never ceased, it seemed wilfully, to expose himself to them. He was constantly wounded, and yet his good nature was such that he could not bear malice: the viper might sting him, but he never learned by experience, and had no sooner recovered from his pain than he tenderly placed it once more in his bosom. His life was a tragedy written in the terms of knock-about farce. Because I did not laugh at him he was grateful to me, and he used to pour into my sympathetic ear the long list of his troubles. The saddest thing about them was that they were grotesque, and the more pathetic they were, the more you wanted to laugh.

But though so bad a painter, he had a very delicate feeling for art, and to go with him to picture galleries was a rare treat. His enthusiasm was sincere and his criticism acute. He was catholic. He had not only a true appreciation of the old masters, but sympathy with the moderns. He was quick to discover talent, and his praise was generous. I think I have never known a man whose judgement was surer. And he was better educated than most painters. He was not, like most of them, ignorant of kindred arts, and his taste for music and literature gave depth and variety to his comprehension of painting. To a young man like myself his advice and guidance was of incomparable value.

When I left Rome I corresponded with him, and about once in two months received from him long letters in queer English, which brought before me vividly his spluttering, enthusiastic, gesticulating conversation. Some time before I went to Paris he had married an Englishwoman, and was now settled in a studio in Montmartre. I had not seen him for four years, and had never met his wife.

XIX

I had not announced my arrival to Stroeve, and when I rang the bell of his studio, on opening the door himself, for a moment he did not know me. Then he gave a cry of delighted surprise and drew me in. It was charming to be welcomed with so much eagerness. His wife was seated near the stove at her sewing, and she rose as I came in. He introduced me.

'Don't you remember?' he said to her. 'I've talked to you about him often.' And then to me: 'But why didn't you let me know you were coming? How long have you been here? How long are you going to stay? Why didn't you come an hour earlier, and we would have dined together?'

He bombarded me with questions. He sat me down in a chair, patting me as though I were a cushion, pressed cigars upon me, cakes, wine. He could not leave me alone. He was heart-broken because he had no whisky, wanted to make coffee for me, racked his brain for something he could possibly do for me, and beamed and laughed, and in the exuberance of his delight sweated at every pore.

'You haven't changed', I said, smiling, as I looked at him.

He had the same absurd appearance that I remembered. He was a fat little man, with short legs, young still—he could not have been more than thirty—but prematurely bald. His face was perfectly round, and he had a very high colour, a white skin, red cheeks, and red lips. His eyes were blue and round too, he wore large gold-rimmed spectacles, and his eyebrows were so fair that you could not see them. He reminded you of those jolly, fat merchants that Rubens painted.

When I told him that I meant to live in Paris for a while, and had taken an apartment, he reproached me bitterly for not having let him know. He would have found me an apartment himself, and lent me furniture—did I really mean that I had gone to the expense of buying it?—and he would have helped me to move in. He really looked upon it as unfriendly that I had not given him the opportunity of making himself useful to me. Meanwhile, Mrs Stroeve sat quietly mending her stockings, without talking, and she listened to all he said with a quiet smile on her lips.

'So, you see, I'm married', he said suddenly; 'what do you think of my wife?'

He beamed at her, and settled his spectacles on the bridge of his nose. The sweat made them constantly slip down.

'What on earth do you expect me to say to that?' I laughed.

'Really, Dirk', put in Mrs Stroeve, smiling.

'But isn't she wonderful? I tell you, my boy, lose no time; get married as soon as ever you can. I'm the happiest man alive. Look at her sitting there. Doesn't she make a picture? Chardin, eh? I've seen all the most beautiful women in the world; I've never seen anyone more beautiful than Madame Dirk Stroeve.'

'If you don't be quiet, Dirk, I shall go away.'

'Mon petit chou', he said.

She flushed a little, embarrassed by the passion in his tone. His letters had told me that he was very much in love with his wife, and I saw that he could hardly take his eyes off her. I could not tell if she loved him. Poor pantaloon, he was not an object to excite love, but the smile in her eyes was affectionate, and it was possible that her reserve concealed a very deep feeling. She was not the ravishing creature that his love-sick fancy saw, but she had a grave comeliness. She was rather tall, and her grey dress, simple and quite well-cut, did not hide the fact that her figure was beautiful. It was a figure that might have appealed more to the sculptor than to the costumier. Her hair, brown and abundant, was plainly done, her face was very pale, and her features were good without being distinguished. She had quiet grey eyes. She just missed being beautiful, and in missing it was not even pretty. But when Stroeve spoke of Chardin it was not without reason, and she reminded me curiously of that pleasant housewife in her mob-cap and apron whom the great painter has immortalized. I could imagine her sedately busy among her pots and pans, making a ritual of her household duties, so that they acquired a moral significance; I did not suppose that she was clever or could ever be amusing, but there was something in her grave intentness which excited my interest. Her reserve was not without mystery. I wondered why she had married Dirk Stroeve. Though she was English, I could not exactly place her, and it was not obvious from what rank in society she sprang, what had been her upbringing, or how she had lived before her marriage. She was very silent, but when she spoke it was with a pleasant voice, and her manners were natural.

I asked Stroeve if he was working.

'Working? I'm painting better than I've ever painted before.'

We sat in the studio, and he waved his hand to an unfinished picture on an easel. I gave a little start. He was painting a group of Italian peasants, in the costume of the Campagna, lounging on the steps of a Roman church.

'Is that what you're doing now?' I asked.

'Yes. I can get my models here just as well as in Rome.'

'Don't you think it's very beautiful?' said Mrs Stroeve.

'This foolish wife of mine thinks I'm a great artist', said he.

His apologetic laugh did not disguise the pleasure that he felt. His eyes lingered on his picture. It was strange that his critical sense, so accurate and unconventional when he dealt with the work of others, should be satisfied in himself with what was hackneyed and vulgar beyond belief.

'Show him some more of your pictures', she said.

'Shall I?'

Though he had suffered so much from the ridicule of his friends, Dirk Stroeve, eager for praise and naïvely self-satisfied, could never resist displaying his work. He brought out a picture of two curly-headed Italian urchins playing marbles.

'Aren't they sweet?' said Mrs Stroeve.

And then he showed me more. I discovered that in Paris he had been painting just the same stale, obviously picturesque things that he had painted for years in Rome. It was all false, insincere, shoddy; and yet no one was more honest, sincere, and frank than Dirk Stroeve. Who could resolve the contradiction?

I do not know what put it into my head to ask:

'I say, have you by any chance run across a painter called Charles Strickland?'

'You don't mean to say you know him?' cried Stroeve.

'Beast', said his wife.

Stroeve laughed.

'*Ma pauvre chérie.*' He went over to her and kissed both her hands. 'She doesn't like him. How strange that you should know Strickland!'

'I don't like bad manners', said Mrs Stroeve.

Dirk, laughing still, turned to me to explain.

'You see, I asked him to come here one day and look at my pictures. Well, he came, and I showed him everything I had.'

Stroeve hesitated a moment with embarrassment. I do not know why he had begun the story against himself; he felt an awkwardness at finishing it. 'He looked at—at my pictures, and he didn't say anything. I thought he was reserving his judgement till the end. And at last I said: "There, that's the lot!" He said: "I came to ask you to lend me twenty francs."'

'And Dirk actually gave it him', said his wife indignantly.

'I was so taken aback. I didn't like to refuse. He put the money in his pocket, just nodded, said "Thanks", and walked out.'

Dirk Stroeve, telling the story, had such a look of blank astonishment on his round, foolish face that it was almost impossible not to laugh.

'I shouldn't have minded if he'd said my pictures were bad, but he said nothing—nothing.'

'And you *will* tell the story, Dirk', said his wife.

It was lamentable that one was more amused by the ridiculous figure cut by the Dutchman than outraged by Strickland's brutal treatment of him.

'I hope I shall never see him again', said Mrs Stroeve.

Stroeve smiled and shrugged his shoulders. He had already recovered his good humour.

'The fact remains that he's a great artist, a very great artist.'

'Strickland?' I exclaimed. 'It can't be the same man.'

'A big fellow with a red beard. Charles Strickland. An Englishman.'

'He had no beard when I knew him, but if he has grown one it might well be red. The man I'm thinking of only began painting five years ago.'

'That's it. He's a great artist.'

'Impossible.'

'Have I ever been mistaken?' Dirk asked me. 'I tell you he has genius. I'm convinced of it. In a hundred years, if you and I are remembered at all, it will be because we knew Charles Strickland.'

I was astonished, and at the same time I was very much excited. I remembered suddenly my last talk with him.

'Where can one see his work?' I asked. 'Is he having any success? Where is he living?'

'No; he has no success. I don't think he's ever sold a picture. When you speak to men about him they only laugh. But I *know* he's a great artist. After all, they laughed at Manet. Corot never sold a picture. I don't know where he lives, but I can take you to see him. He goes to a café in the Avenue de Clichy at seven o'clock every evening. If you like we'll go there tomorrow.'

'I'm not sure if he'll wish to see me. I think I may remind him of a time he prefers to forget. But I'll come all the same. Is there any chance of seeing any of his pictures?'

'Not from him. He won't show you a thing. There's a little dealer I know who has two or three. But you mustn't go without me; you wouldn't understand. I must show them to you myself.'

'Dirk, you make me impatient', said Mrs Stroeve. 'How can you talk like that about his pictures when he treated you as he did?' She turned to me. 'Do you know, when some Dutch people came here to buy Dirk's pictures he tried to persuade them to buy Strickland's. He insisted on bringing them here to show.'

'What did *you* think of them?' I asked her, smiling.

'They were awful.'

'Ah, sweetheart, you don't understand.'

'Well, your Dutch people were furious with you. They thought you were having a joke with them.'

Dirk Stroeve took off his spectacles and wiped them. His flushed face was shining with excitement.

'Why should you think that beauty, which is the most precious thing in the world, lies like a stone on the beach for the careless passer-by to pick up idly? Beauty is something wonderful and strange that the artist fashions out of the chaos of the world in the torment of his soul. And when he has made it, it is not given to all to know it. To recognize it you must repeat the adventure of the artist. It is a melody that he sings to you, and to hear it again in your own heart you want knowledge and sensitiveness and imagination.'

'Why did I always think your pictures beautiful, Dirk? I admired them the very first time I saw them.'

Stroeve's lips trembled a little.

'Go to bed, my precious. I will walk a few steps with our friend, and then I will come back.'

XX

Dirk Stroeve agreed to fetch me on the following evening and take me to the café at which Strickland was most likely to be found. I was interested to learn that it was the same as that at which Strickland and I had drunk absinthe when I had gone over to Paris to see him. The fact that he had never changed suggested a sluggishness of habit which seemed to me characteristic.

'There he is', said Stroeve, as we reached the café.

Though it was October, the evening was warm, and the tables on the pavement were crowded. I ran my eyes over them, but did not see Strickland.

'Look. Over there, in the corner. He's playing chess.'

I noticed a man bending over a chess-board, but could see only a large felt hat and a red beard. We threaded our way among the tables till we came to him.

'Strickland.'

He looked up.

'Hulloa, fatty. What do you want?'

'I've brought an old friend to see you.'

Strickland gave me a glance, and evidently did not recognize me. He resumed his scrutiny of the chess-board.

'Sit down, and don't make a noise', he said.

He moved a piece and straightway became absorbed in the game. Poor Stroeve gave me a troubled look, but I was not disconcerted by so little. I ordered something to drink, and waited quietly till Strickland had finished. I welcomed the opportunity to examine him at my ease. I certainly should never have known him. In the first place his red beard, ragged and untrimmed, hid much of his face, and his hair was long; but the most surprising change in him was his extreme thinness. It made his great nose protrude more arrogantly; it emphasized his cheek-bones; it made his eyes seem larger. There were deep hollows at his temples. His body was cadaverous. He wore the same suit that I had seen him in five years before; it was torn and stained, threadbare, and it hung upon him loosely, as though it had been made for someone else. I noticed his hands, dirty, with long nails; they were merely bone and sinew, large and strong; but I had forgotten that they were so shapely. He gave me an extraordinary impression as he sat there, his attention riveted on his game—an impression of great strength; and I could not understand why it was that his emaciation somehow made it more striking.

Presently, after moving, he leaned back and gazed with a curious abstraction at his antagonist. This was a fat, bearded Frenchman. The Frenchman considered the position, then broke suddenly into jovial expletives, and with an impatient gesture, gathering up the pieces, flung them into their box. He cursed Strickland freely, then, calling for the waiter, paid for the drinks, and left. Stroeve drew his chair closer to the table.

'Now I suppose we can talk', he said.

Strickland's eyes rested on him, and there was in them a malicious expression. I felt sure he was seeking for some gibe, could think of none, and so was forced to silence.

'I've brought an old friend to see you', repeated Stroeve, beaming cheerfully.

Strickland looked at me thoughtfully for nearly a minute. I did not speak.

'I've never seen him in my life', he said.

I do not know why he said this, for I felt certain I had caught a gleam of recognition in his eyes. I was not so easily abashed as I had been some years earlier.

'I saw your wife the other day', I said. 'I felt sure you'd like to have the latest news of her.'

He gave a short laugh. His eyes twinkled.

'We had a jolly evening together', he said. 'How long ago is it?'

'Five years.'

He called for another absinthe. Stroeve, with voluble tongue, explained how he and I had met, and by what an accident we discovered that we both knew Strickland. I do not know if Strickland listened. He glanced at me once or twice reflectively, but for the most part seemed occupied with his own thoughts; and certainly without Stroeve's babble the conversation would have been difficult. In half an hour the Dutchman, looking at his watch, announced that he must go. He asked whether I would come too. I thought, alone, I might get something out of Strickland, and so answered that I would stay.

When the fat man had left I said:

'Dirk Stroeve thinks you're a great artist.'

'What the hell do you suppose I care?'

'Will you let me see your pictures?'

'Why should I?'

'I might feel inclined to buy one.'

'I might not feel inclined to sell one.'

'Are you making a good living?' I asked, smiling.

He chuckled.

'Do I look it?'

'You look half starved.'

'I am half starved.'

'Then come and let's have a bit of dinner.'

'Why do you ask me?'

'Not out of charity', I answered coolly. 'I don't really care a twopenny damn if you starve or not.'

His eyes lit up again.

'Come on, then', he said, getting up. 'I'd like a decent meal.'

XXI

I let him take me to a restaurant of his choice, but on the way I bought a paper. When he had ordered our dinner, I propped it against a bottle of St Galmier and began to read. We ate in silence. I felt him looking at me now and again, but I took no notice. I meant to force him to conversation.

'Is there anything in the paper?' he said, as we approached the end of our silent meal.

I fancied there was in his tone a slight note of exasperation.

'I always like to read the *feuilleton* on the drama,' I said.

I folded the paper and put it down beside me.

'I've enjoyed my dinner', he remarked.

'I think we might have our coffee here, don't you?'

'Yes.'

We lit our cigars. I smoked in silence. I noticed that now and then his eyes rested on me with a faint smile of amusement. I waited patiently.

'What have you been up to since I saw you last?' he asked at length.

I had not very much to say. It was a record of hard work and of little adventure; of experiments in this direction and in that; of the gradual acquisition of the knowledge of books and of men. I took care to ask Strickland nothing about his own doings. I showed not the least interest in him, and at last I was rewarded. He began to talk of himself. But with his poor gift of expression he gave but indications of what he had gone through, and I had to fill up the gaps with my own imagination. It was tantalizing to get no more than hints into a character that interested me so much. It was like making one's way through a mutilated manuscript. I received the impression of a life which was a bitter struggle against every sort of difficulty; but I realized that much which would have seemed horrible to most people did not in the least affect him. Strickland was distinguished from most Englishmen by his perfect indifference to comfort; it did not irk him to live always in one shabby room; he had no need to be surrounded by beautiful things. I do not suppose he had ever noticed how dingy was the paper on the wall of the room in which on my first visit I found him. He did not want arm-chairs to sit in; he really felt more at his ease on a kitchen-chair. He ate with appetite, but was indifferent to what he ate; to him it was only food that he devoured to still the pangs of hunger; and when no food was to be had he seemed capable of doing without. I learned that for six months he had lived on a loaf of bread and a bottle of milk a day. He was a sensual man, and yet was indifferent to sensual things. He looked upon privation as no hardship. There was something impressive in the manner in which he lived a life wholly of the spirit.

When the small sum of money which he brought with him from London came to an end he suffered from no dismay. He sold no pictures; I think he made little attempt to sell any; he set about finding some way to make a bit of money. He told me with grim humour of the time he had spent acting as guide to

Cockneys who wanted to see the night side of life in Paris; it was an occupation that appealed to his sardonic temper; and somehow or other he had acquired a wide acquaintance with the more disreputable quarters of the city. He told me of the long hours he spent walking about the Boulevard de la Madeleine on the look-out for Englishmen, preferably the worse for liquor, who desired to see things which the law forbade. When in luck he was able to make a tidy sum; but the shabbiness of his clothes at last frightened the sightseers, and he could not find people adventurous enough to trust themselves to him. Then he happened on a job to translate the advertisements of patent medicines which were sent broadcast to the medical profession in England. During a strike he had been employed as a house-painter.

Meanwhile he had never ceased to work at his art; but, soon tiring of the studios, entirely by himself. He had never been so poor that he could not buy canvas and paint, and really he needed nothing else. So far as I could make out, he painted with great difficulty, and in his unwillingness to accept help from anyone lost much time in finding out for himself the solution of technical problems which preceding generations had already worked out one by one. He was aiming at something, I knew not what, and perhaps he hardly knew himself; and I got again more strongly the impression of a man possessed. He did not seem quite sane. It seemed to me that he would not show his pictures because he was really not interested in them. He lived in a dream, and the reality meant nothing to him. I had the feeling that he worked on a canvas with all the force of his violent personality, oblivious of everything in his effort to get what he saw with the mind's eye; and then, having finished, not the picture perhaps, for I had an idea that he seldom brought anything to completion, but the passion that fired him, he lost all care for it. He was never satisfied with what he had done: it seemed to him of no consequence compared with the vision that obsessed his mind.

'Why don't you ever send your work to exhibitions?' I asked. 'I should have thought you'd like to know what people thought about it.'

'Would you?'

I cannot describe the unmeasurable contempt he put into the two words.

'Don't you want fame? It's something that most artists haven't been indifferent to.'

'Children. How can you care for the opinion of the crowd, when you don't care twopence for the opinion of the individual?'

'We're not all reasonable beings', I laughed.

'Who makes fame? Critics, writers, stockbrokers, women.'

'Wouldn't it give you a rather pleasant sensation to think of people you didn't know and had never seen receiving emotions, subtle and passionate, from the work of your hands? Everyone likes power. I can't imagine a more wonderful exercise of it than to move the souls of men to pity or terror.'

'Melodrama.'

'Why do you mind if you paint well or badly?'

'I don't. I only want to paint what I see.'

'I wonder if I could write on a desert island, with the certainty that no eyes but mine would ever see what I had written.'

Strickland did not speak for a long time, but his eyes shone strangely, as though he saw something that kindled his soul to ecstasy.

'Sometimes I've thought of an island lost in a boundless sea, where I could live in some hidden valley, among strange trees, in silence. There I think I could find what I want.'

He did not express himself quite like this. He used gestures instead of adjectives, and he halted. I have put into my own words what I think he wanted to say.

'Looking back on the last five years, do you think it was worth it?' I asked.

He looked at me, and I saw that he did not know what I meant. I explained.

'You gave up a comfortable home and a life as happy as the average. You were fairly prosperous. You seem to have had a rotten time in Paris. If you had your time over again would you do what you did?'

'Rather.'

'Do you know that you haven't asked anything about your wife and children? Do you never think of them?'

'No.'

'I wish you weren't so damned monosyllabic. Have you never had a moment's regret for all the unhappiness you caused them?'

His lips broke into a smile, and he shook his head.

'I should have thought sometimes you couldn't help thinking of the past. I don't mean the past of seven or eight years ago, but further back still, when you first met your wife, and loved her, and married her. Don't you remember the joy with which you first took her in your arms?'

'I don't think of the past. The only thing that matters is the everlasting present.'

I thought for a moment over this reply. It was obscure perhaps, but I thought that I saw dimly his meaning.

'Are you happy?' I asked.

'Yes.'

I was silent. I looked at him reflectively. He held my stare, and presently a sardonic twinkle lit up his eyes.

'I'm afraid you disapprove of me?'

'Nonsense', I answered promptly; 'I don't disapprove of the boa-constrictor; on the contrary, I'm interested in his mental processes.'

'It's a purely professional interest you take in me?'

'Purely.'

'It's only right that you shouldn't disapprove of me. You have a despicable character.'

'Perhaps that's why you feel at home with me', I retorted.

He smiled dryly, but said nothing. I wish I knew how to describe his smile. I do not know that it was attractive, but it lit up his face, changing the expression, which was generally sombre, and gave it a look of not ill-natured malice. It was a slow smile, starting and sometimes ending in the eyes; it was very sensual, neither cruel nor kindly, but suggested rather the inhuman glee of the satyr. It was his smile that made me ask him:

'Haven't you been in love since you came to Paris?'

'I haven't got time for that sort of nonsense. Life isn't long enough for love and art.'

'Your appearance doesn't suggest the anchorite.'

'All that business fills me with disgust.'

'Human nature is a nuisance, isn't it?' I said.

'Why are you sniggering at me?'

'Because I don't believe you.'

'Then you're a damned fool.'

I paused, and I looked at him searchingly.

'What's the good of trying to humbug me?' I said.

'I don't know what you mean.'

I smiled.

'Let me tell you. I imagine that for months the matter never comes into your head, and you're able to persuade yourself that you've finished with it for good and all. You rejoice in your freedom, and you feel that at last you can call your soul your own. You seem to walk with your head among the stars. And then, all of a sudden you can't stand it any more, and you notice that all the time your feet have been walking in the mud. And you want to roll yourself in it. And you find some woman, coarse and low and vulgar, some beastly creature in whom all the horror of sex is blatant, and you fall upon her like a wild animal. You drink till you're blind with rage.'

He stared at me without the slightest movement. I held his eyes with mine. I spoke very slowly.

'I'll tell you what must seem strange, that when it's over you feel so extraordinarily pure. You feel like a disembodied spirit, immaterial; and you seem to be able to touch beauty as though it were a palpable thing; and you feel an intimate communion with the breeze, and with the trees breaking into leaf, and with the iridescence of the river. You feel like God. Can you explain that to me?'

He kept his eyes fixed on mine till I had finished, and then he turned away. There was on his face a strange look, and I thought that so might a man look when he had died under the torture. He was silent. I knew that our conversation was ended.

XXII

I settled down in Paris and began to write a play. I led a very
regular life, working in the morning, and in the afternoon
lounging about the gardens of the Luxembourg or sauntering
through the streets. I spent long hours in the Louvre, the most
friendly of all galleries and the most convenient for meditation;
or idled on the quays, fingering second-hand books that I never
meant to buy. I read a page here and there, and made acquaintance with a great many authors whom I was content to know
thus desultorily. In the evenings I went to see my friends. I
looked in often on the Stroeves, and sometimes shared their
modest fare. Dirk Stroeve flattered himself on his skill in cooking Italian dishes, and I confess that his *spaghetti* were very
much better than his pictures. It was a dinner for a king when
he brought in a huge dish of it, succulent with tomatoes, and
we ate it together with the good household bread and a bottle
of red wine. I grew more intimate with Blanche Stroeve, and I
think, because I was English and she knew few English people,
she was glad to see me. She was pleasant and simple, but she remained always rather silent, and, I knew not why, gave me the
impression that she was concealing something. But I thought
that was perhaps no more than a natural reserve accentuated by
the verbose frankness of her husband. Dirk never concealed
anything. He discussed the most intimate matters with a complete lack of self-consciousness. Sometimes he embarrassed
his wife, and the only time I saw her put out of countenance was
when he insisted on telling me that he had taken a purge, and
went into somewhat realistic details on the subject. The perfect
seriousness with which he narrated his misfortunes convulsed
me with laughter, and this added to Mrs Stroeve's irritation.

'You seem to like making a fool of yourself', she said.

His round eyes grew rounder still, and his brow puckered in
dismay as he saw that she was angry.

'Sweetheart, have I vexed you? I'll never take another. It was
only because I was bilious. I lead a sedentary life. I don't take
enough exercise. For three days I hadn't . . . '

'For goodness' sake, hold your tongue', she interrupted, tears of annoyance in her eyes.

His face fell, and he pouted his lips like a scolded child. He gave me a look of appeal, so that I might put things right, but unable to control myself, I shook with helpless laughter.

We went one day to the picture-dealer in whose shop Stroeve thought he could show me at least two or three of Strickland's pictures, but when we arrived were told that Strickland himself had taken them away. The dealer did not know why.

'But don't imagine to yourself that I make myself bad blood on that account. I took them to oblige Monsieur Stroeve, and I said I would sell them if I could. But really—' He shrugged his shoulders. 'I'm interested in the young men, but *voyons,* you yourself, Monsieur Stroeve, you don't think there's any talent there.'

'I give you my word of honour, there's no one painting today of whose talent I am more convinced. Take my word for it, you are missing a good affair. Some day those pictures will be worth more than all you have in your shop. Remember Monet, who could not get anyone to buy his pictures for a hundred francs. What are they worth now?'

'True. But there were a hundred as good painters as Monet who couldn't sell their pictures at that time, and their pictures are worth nothing still. How can one tell? Is merit enough to bring success? Don't believe it. *Du reste,* it has still to be proved that this friend of yours has merit. No one claims it for him but Monsieur Stroeve.'

'And how, then, will you recognize merit?' asked Dirk, red in the face with anger.

'There is only one way—by success.'

'Philistine', cried Dirk.

'But think of the great artists of the past—Raphael, Michael Angelo, Ingres, Delacroix—they were all successful.'

'Let us go', said Stroeve to me, 'or I shall kill this man.'

XXIII

I saw Strickland not infrequently, and now and then played chess with him. He was of uncertain temper. Sometimes he would sit silent and abstracted, taking no notice of anyone; and at others, when he was in a good humour, he would talk in his own halting way. He never said a clever thing, but he had a vein of brutal sarcasm which was not ineffective, and he always said exactly what he thought. He was indifferent to the susceptibilities of others, and when he wounded them was amused. He was constantly offending Dirk Stroeve so bitterly that he flung away, vowing he would never speak to him again; but there was a solid force in Strickland that attracted the fat Dutchman against his will, so that he came back, fawning like a clumsy dog, though he knew that his only greeting would be the blow he dreaded.

I do not know why Strickland put up with me. Our relations were peculiar. One day he asked me to lend him fifty francs.

'I wouldn't dream of it', I replied.

'Why not?'

'It wouldn't amuse me.'

'I'm frightfully hard up, you know.'

'I don't care.'

'You don't care if I starve?'

'Why on earth should I?' I asked in my turn.

He looked at me for a minute or two, pulling his untidy beard. I smiled at him.

'What are you amused at?' he said, with a gleam of anger in his eyes.

'You're so simple. You recognize no obligations. No one is under any obligation to you.'

'Wouldn't it make you uncomfortable if I went and hanged myself because I'd been turned out of my room as I couldn't pay the rent?'

'Not a bit.'

He chuckled.

'You're bragging. If I really did you'd be overwhelmed with remorse.'

'Try it, and we'll see', I retorted.

A smile flickered in his eyes, and he stirred his absinthe in silence.

'Would you like to play chess?' I asked.

'I don't mind.'

We set up the pieces, and when the board was ready he considered it with a comfortable eye. There is a sense of satisfaction in looking at your men all ready for the fray.

'Did you really think I'd lend you money?' I asked.

'I didn't see why you shouldn't.'

'You surprise me.'

'Why?'

'It's disappointing to find that at heart you are sentimental. I should have liked you better if you hadn't made that ingenuous appeal to my sympathies.'

'I should have despised you if you'd been moved by it', he answered.

'That's better', I laughed.

We began to play. We were both absorbed in the game. When it was finished I said to him:

'Look here, if you're hard up, let me see your pictures. If there's anything I like I'll buy it.'

'Go to hell', he answered.

He got up and was about to go away. I stopped him.

'You haven't paid for your absinthe', I said, smiling.

He cursed me, flung down the money, and left.

I did not see him for several days after that, but one evening, when I was sitting in the café, reading a paper, he came up and sat beside me.

'You haven't hanged yourself after all', I remarked.

'No. I've got a commission. I'm painting the portrait of a retired plumber for two hundred francs.'*

'How did you manage that?'

---

*This picture, formerly in the possession of a wealthy manufacturer at Lille, who fled from that city on the approach of the Germans, is now in the National Gallery at Stockholm. The Swede is adept at the gentle pastime of fishing in troubled waters.

'The woman where I get my bread recommended me. He'd told her he was looking out for someone to paint him. I've got to give her twenty francs.'

'What's he like?'

'Splendid. He's got a great red face like a leg of mutton, and on his right cheek there's an enormous mole with long hairs growing out of it.'

Strickland was in a good humour, and when Dirk Stroeve came up and sat down with us he attacked him with ferocious banter. He showed a skill I should never have credited him with in finding the places where the unhappy Dutchman was most sensitive. Strickland employed not the rapier of sarcasm but the bludgeon of invective. The attack was so unprovoked that Stroeve, taken unawares, was defenceless. He reminded you of a frightened sheep running aimlessly hither and thither. He was startled and amazed. At last the tears ran from his eyes. And the worst of it was that, though you hated Strickland, and the exhibition was horrible, it was impossible not to laugh. Dirk Stroeve was one of those unlucky persons whose most sincere emotions are ridiculous.

But after all when I look back upon that winter in Paris, my pleasantest recollection is of Dirk Stroeve. There was something very charming in his little household. He and his wife made a picture which the imagination gratefully dwelt upon, and the simplicity of his love for her had a deliberate grace. He remained absurd, but the sincerity of his passion excited one's sympathy. I could understand how his wife must feel for him, and I was glad that her affection was so tender. If she had any sense of humour, it must amuse her that he should place her on a pedestal and worship her with such an honest idolatry, but even while she laughed she must have been pleased and touched. He was the constant lover, and though she grew old, losing her rounded lines and her fair comeliness, to him she would certainly never alter. To him she would always be the loveliest woman in the world. There was a pleasing grace in the orderliness of their lives. They had but the studio, a bedroom, and a tiny kitchen. Mrs Stroeve did all the housework herself; and while Dirk painted bad pictures, she went marketing, cooked the luncheon, sewed, occupied herself like a busy ant all the day; and in the evening sat in the studio, sewing again, while Dirk played music which I am sure was far beyond her comprehension. He played with taste, but with more feeling than was always justified, and into his music poured all his honest, sentimental, exuberant soul.

Their life in its own way was an idyll, and it managed to achieve a singular beauty. The absurdity that clung to everything connected with Dirk Stroeve gave it a curious note, like an unresolved discord, but made it somehow more modern, more human; like a rough joke thrown into a serious scene, it heightened the poignancy which all beauty has.

XXIV

Shortly before Christmas Dirk Stroeve came to ask me to spend the holiday with him. He had a characteristic sentimentality about the day and wanted to pass it among his friends with suitable ceremonies. Neither of us had seen Strickland for two or three weeks—I because I had been busy with friends who were spending a little while in Paris, and Stroeve because, having quarrelled with him more violently than usual, he had made up his mind to have nothing more to do with him. Strickland was impossible, and he swore never to speak to him again. But the season touched him with gentle feeling, and he hated the thought of Strickland spending Christmas Day by himself; he ascribed his own emotions to him, and could not bear that on an occasion given up to good fellowship the lonely painter should be abandoned to his own melancholy. Stroeve had set up a Christmas-tree in his studio, and I suspected that we should both find absurd little presents hanging on its festive branches; but he was shy about seeing Strickland again; it was a little humiliating to forgive so easily insults so outrageous, and he wished me to be present at the reconciliation on which he was determined.

We walked together down the Avenue de Clichy, but Strickland was not in the café. It was too cold to sit outside, and we took our places on leather benches within. It was hot and stuffy, and the air was grey with smoke. Strickland did not come, but presently we saw the French painter who occasionally played chess with him. I had formed a casual acquaintance with him, and he sat down at our table. Stroeve asked him if he had seen Strickland.

'He's ill', he said. 'Didn't you know?'

'Seriously?'

'Very, I understand.'

Stroeve's face grew white.

'Why didn't he write and tell me? How stupid of me to quarrel with him! We must go to him at once. He can have no one to look after him. Where does he live?'

'I have no idea', said the Frenchman.

We discovered that none of us knew how to find him. Stroeve grew more and more distressed.

'He might die, and not a soul would know anything about it. It's dreadful. I can't bear the thought. We must find him at once.'

I tried to make Stroeve understand that it was absurd to hunt vaguely about Paris. We must first think of some plan.

'Yes; but all this time he may be dying, and when we get there it may be too late to do anything.'

'Sit still and let us think', I said impatiently.

The only address I knew was the Hôtel des Belges, but Strickland had long left that, and they would have no recollection of him. With that queer idea of his to keep his whereabouts secret, it was unlikely that, on leaving, he had said where he was going. Besides, it was more than five years ago. I felt pretty sure that he had not moved far. If he continued to frequent the same café as when he had stayed at the hotel, it was probably because it was the most convenient. Suddenly I remembered that he had got his commission to paint a portrait through the baker from whom he bought his bread, and it struck me that there one might find his address. I called for a directory and looked out the bakers. There were five in the immediate neighbourhood, and the only thing was to go to all of them. Stroeve accompanied me unwillingly. His own plan was to run up and down the streets that led out of the Avenue de Clichy and ask at every house if Strickland lived there. My commonplace scheme was, after all, effective, for in the second shop we asked at the woman behind the counter acknowledged that she knew him. She was not certain where he lived, but it was in one of the three houses opposite. Luck favoured us, and in the first we tried the concierge told us that we should find him on the top floor.

'It appears that he's ill', said Stroeve.

'It may be', answered the concierge indifferently. '*En effet,* I have not seen him for several days.'

Stroeve ran up the stairs ahead of me, and when I reached the top floor I found him talking to a workman in his shirtsleeves who had opened a door at which Stroeve had knocked. He pointed to another door. He believed that the person who lived there was a painter. He had not seen him for a week. Stroeve made as though he were about to knock, and then turned to me with a gesture of helplessness. I saw that he was panic-stricken.

'Supposing he's dead?'

'Not he', I said.

I knocked. There was no answer. I tried the handle, and found the door unlocked. I walked in, and Stroeve followed me. The room was in darkness. I could only see that it was an attic, with a sloping roof; and a faint glimmer, no more than a less profound obscurity, came from a skylight.

'Strickland', I called.

There was no answer. It was really rather mysterious, and it seemed to me that Stroeve, standing just behind, was trembling in his shoes. For a moment I hesitated to strike a light. I dimly perceived a bed in the corner, and I wondered whether the light would disclose lying on it a dead body.

'Haven't you got a match, you fool?'

Strickland's voice, coming out of the darkness, harshly, made me start.

Stroeve cried out.

'Oh, my God, I thought you were dead.'

I struck a match, and looked about for a candle. I had a rapid glimpse of a tiny apartment, half room, half studio, in which was nothing but a bed, canvases with their faces to the wall, an easel, a table, and a chair. There was no carpet on the floor. There was no fireplace. On the table, crowded with paints, palette-knives, and litter of all kinds, was the end of a candle. I lit it. Strickland was lying in the bed, uncomfortably because it was too small for him, and he had put all his clothes over him for warmth. It was obvious at a glance that he was in a high fever. Stroeve, his voice cracking with emotion, went up to him.

'Oh, my poor friend, what is the matter with you? I had no idea you were ill. Why didn't you let me know? You must know I'd have done anything in the world for you. Were you thinking of what I said? I didn't mean it. I was wrong. It was stupid of me to take offence.'

'Go to hell', said Strickland.

'Now, be reasonable. Let me make you comfortable. Haven't you anyone to look after you?'

He looked round the squalid attic in dismay. He tried to arrange the bedclothes. Strickland, breathing laboriously, kept an angry silence. He gave me a resentful glance. I stood quite quietly, looking at him.

'If you want to do something for me, you can get me some milk', he said at last. 'I haven't been able to get out for two days.'

There was an empty bottle by the side of the bed, which had contained milk, and in a piece of newspaper a few crumbs.

'What have you been having?' I asked.

'Nothing.'

'For how long?' cried Stroeve. 'Do you mean to say you've had nothing to eat or drink for two days? It's horrible.'

'I've had water.'

His eyes dwelt for a moment on a large can within reach of an outstretched arm.

'I'll go immediately,' said Stroeve. 'Is there anything you fancy?'

I suggested that he should get a thermometer, and a few grapes, and some bread. Stroeve, glad to make himself useful, clattered down the stairs.

'Damned fool', muttered Strickland.

I felt his pulse. It was beating quickly and feebly. I asked him one or two questions, but he would not answer, and when I pressed him he turned his face irritably to the wall. The only thing was to wait in silence. In ten minutes Stroeve, panting, came back. Besides what I had suggested, he brought candles, and meat-juice, and a spirit-lamp. He was a practical little fellow, and without delay set about making bread-and-milk. I took Strickland's temperature. It was a hundred and four. He was obviously very ill.

XXV

Presently we left him. Dirk was going home to dinner, and I proposed to find a doctor and bring him to see Strickland; but when we got down into the street, fresh after the stuffy attic, the Dutchman begged me to go immediately to his studio. He had something in mind which he would not tell me, but he insisted that it was very necessary for me to accompany him. Since I did not think a doctor could at the moment do any more than we had done, I consented. We found Blanche Stroeve laying the table for dinner. Dirk went up to her, and took both her hands.

'Dear one, I want you to do something for me', he said.

She looked at him with the grave cheerfulness which was one of her charms. His red face was shining with sweat, and he had a look of comic agitation, but there was in his round, surprised eyes an eager light.

'Strickland is very ill. He may be dying. He is alone in a filthy attic, and there is not a soul to look after him. I want you to let me bring him here.'

She withdrew her hands quickly—I had never seen her make so rapid a movement—and her cheeks flushed.

'Oh no.'

'Oh, my dear one, don't refuse. I couldn't bear to leave him where he is. I shouldn't sleep a wink for thinking of him.'

'I have no objection to your nursing him.'

Her voice was cold and distant.

'But he'll die.'

'Let him.'

Stroeve gave a little gasp. He wiped his face. He turned to me for support, but I did not know what to say.

'He's a great artist.'

'What do I care? I hate him.'

'Oh, my love, my precious, you don't mean that. I beseech you to let me bring him here. We can make him comfortable. Perhaps we can save him. He shall be no trouble to you. I will do everything. We'll make him up a bed in the studio. We can't let him die like a dog. It would be inhuman.'

'Why can't he go to a hospital?'

'A hospital! He needs the care of loving hands. He must be treated with infinite tact.'

I was surprised to see how moved she was. She went on laying the table, but her hands trembled.

'I have no patience with you. Do you think if you were ill he would stir a finger to help you?'

'But what does that matter? I should have you to nurse me. It wouldn't be necessary. And besides, I'm different; I'm not of any importance.'

'You have no more spirit than a mongrel cur. You lie down on the ground and ask people to trample on you.'

Stroeve gave a little laugh. He thought he understood the reason of his wife's attitude.

'Oh, my poor dear, you're thinking of that day he came here to look at my pictures. What does it matter if he didn't think them any good? It was stupid of me to show them to him. I dare say they're not very good.'

He looked round the studio ruefully. On the easel was a half-finished picture of a smiling Italian peasant, holding a bunch of grapes over the head of a dark-eyed girl.

'Even if he didn't like them he should have been civil. He needn't have insulted you. He showed that he despised you, and you lick his hand. Oh, I hate him.'

'Dear child, he has genius. You don't think I believe that I have it. I wish I had; but I know it when I see it, and I honour it with all my heart. It's the most wonderful thing in the world. It's a great burden to its possessors. We should be very tolerant with them, and very patient.'

I stood apart, somewhat embarrassed by the domestic scene, and wondered why Stroeve had insisted on my coming with him. I saw that his wife was on the verge of tears.

'But it's not only because he's a genius that I ask you to let me bring him here; it's because he's a human being, and he is ill and poor.'

'I will never have him in my house—never.'

Stroeve turned to me.

'Tell her that it's a matter of life and death. It's impossible to leave him in that wretched hole.'

'It's quite obvious that it would be much easier to nurse him here', I said, 'but of course it would be very inconvenient. I have an idea that someone will have to be with him day and night.'

'My love, it's not you who would shirk a little trouble.'

'If he comes here, I shall go', said Mrs Stroeve violently.

'I don't recognize you. You're so good and kind.'

'Oh, for goodness' sake, let me be. You drive me to distraction.'

Then at last the tears came. She sank into a chair, and buried her face in her hands. Her shoulders shook convulsively. In a moment Dirk was on his knees beside her, with his arms round her, kissing her, calling her all sorts of pet names, and the facile tears ran down his own cheeks. Presently she released herself and dried her eyes.

'Leave me alone', she said, not unkindly; and then to me, trying to smile: 'What must you think of me?'

Stroeve, looking at her with perplexity, hesitated. His forehead was all puckered, and his red mouth set in a pout. He reminded me oddly of an agitated guinea-pig.

'Then it's No, darling?' he said at last.

She gave a gesture of lassitude. She was exhausted.

'The studio is yours. Everything belongs to you. If you want to bring him here, how can I prevent you?'

A sudden smile flashed across his round face.

'Then you consent? I knew you would. Oh, my precious.'

Suddenly she pulled herself together. She looked at him with haggard eyes. She clasped her hands over her heart as though its beating were intolerable.

'Oh, Dirk, I've never since we met asked you to do anything for me.'

'You know there's nothing in the world that I wouldn't do for you.'

'I beg you not to let Strickland come here. Anyone else you like. Bring a thief, a drunkard, any outcast off the streets, and I promise you I'll do everything I can for them gladly. But I beseech you not to bring Strickland here.'

'But why?'

'I'm frightened of him. I don't know why, but there's something in him that terrifies me. He'll do us some great harm. I know it. I feel it. If you bring him here it can only end badly.'

'But how unreasonable!'

'No, no. I know I'm right. Something terrible will happen to us.'

'Because we do a good action?'

She was panting now, and in her face was a terror which was inexplicable. I do not know what she thought. I felt that she was possessed by some shapeless dread which robbed her of all self-control. As a rule she was so calm; her agitation now was amazing. Stroeve looked at her for a while with puzzled consternation.

'You are my wife; you are dearer to me than anyone in the world. No one shall come here without your entire consent.'

She closed her eyes for a moment, and I thought she was going to faint. I was a little impatient with her. I had not suspected that she was so neurotic a woman. Then I heard Stroeve's voice again. It seemed to break oddly on the silence.

'Haven't you been in bitter distress once when a helping hand was held out to you? You know how much it means. Wouldn't you like to do someone a good turn when you have the chance?'

The words were ordinary enough, and to my mind there was in them something so hortatory that I almost smiled. I was astonished at the effect they had on Blanche Stroeve. She started a little, and gave her husband a long look. His eyes were fixed on the ground. I did not know why he seemed embarrassed. A faint colour came into her cheeks, and then her face became white—more than white, ghastly; you felt that the blood had shrunk away from the whole surface of her body; and even her hands were pale. A shiver passed through her. The silence of the studio seemed to gather body, so that it became an almost palpable presence. I was bewildered.

'Bring Strickland here, Dirk. I'll do my best for him.'

'My precious', he smiled.

He wanted to take her in his arms, but she avoided him.

'Don't be affectionate before strangers, Dirk', she said. 'It makes me feel such a fool.'

Her manner was quite normal again, and no one could have told that so shortly before she had been shaken by such a great emotion.

XXVI

Next day we moved Strickland. It needed a good deal of firmness and still more patience to induce him to come, but he was really too ill to offer any effective resistance to Stroeve's entreaties and to my determination. We dressed him, while he feebly cursed us, got him downstairs, into a cab, and eventually to Stroeve's studio. He was so exhausted by the time we arrived that he allowed us to put him to bed without a word. He was ill for six weeks. At one time it looked as though he could not live more than a few hours, and I am convinced that it was only through the Dutchman's doggedness that he pulled through. I have never known a more difficult patient. It was not that he was exacting and querulous; on the contrary, he never complained, he asked for nothing, he was perfectly silent; but he seemed to resent the care that was taken of him; he received all inquiries about his feelings or his needs with a jibe, a sneer, or an oath. I found him detestable, and as soon as he was out of danger I had no hesitation in telling him so.

'Go to hell', he answered briefly.

Dirk Stroeve, giving up his work entirely, nursed Strickland with tenderness and sympathy. He was dexterous to make him comfortable, and he exercised a cunning of which I should never have thought him capable to induce him to take the medicines prescribed by the doctor. Nothing was too much trouble for him. Though his means were adequate to the needs of himself and his wife, he certainly had no money to waste; but now he was wantonly extravagant in the purchase of delicacies, out of season and dear, which might tempt Strickland's capricious appetite. I shall never forget the tactful patience with which he persuaded him to take nourishment. He was never put out by Strickland's rudeness; if it was merely sullen, he appeared not to notice it; if it was aggressive, he only chuckled. When Strickland, recovering somewhat, was in a good humour and amused himself by laughing at him, he deliberately did absurd things to excite his ridicule. Then he would give me little happy glances, so that I might notice in how much better form the patient was. Stroeve was sublime.

But it was Blanche who most surprised me. She proved herself not only a capable, but a devoted nurse. There was nothing in her to remind you that she had so vehemently struggled against her husband's wish to bring Strickland to the studio. She insisted on doing her share of the offices needful to the sick. She arranged his bed so that it was possible to change the sheet without disturbing him. She washed him. When I remarked on her competence, she told me with that pleasant little smile of hers that for a while she had worked in a hospital. She gave no sign that she hated Strickland so desperately. She did not speak to him much, but she was quick to forestall his wants. For a fortnight it was necessary that someone should stay with him all night, and she took turns at watching with her husband. I wondered what she thought during the long darkness as she sat by the bedside. Strickland was a weird figure as he lay there, thinner than ever, with his ragged red beard and his eyes staring feverishly into vacancy; his illness seemed to have made them larger, and they had an unnatural brightness.

'Does he ever talk to you in the night?' I asked her once.

'Never.'

'Do you dislike him as much as you did?'

'More, if anything.'

She looked at me with her calm grey eyes. Her expression was so placid, it was hard to believe that she was capable of the violent emotion I had witnessed.

'Has he ever thanked you for what you do for him?'

'No', she smiled.

'He's inhuman.'

'He's abominable.'

Stroeve was, of course, delighted with her. He could not do enough to show his gratitude for the whole-hearted devotion with which she had accepted the burden he laid on her. But he was a little puzzled by the behaviour of Blanche and Strickland towards one another.

'Do you know, I've seen them sit there for hours together without saying a word.'

On one occasion, when Strickland was so much better that in a day or two he was to get up, I sat with them in the studio. Dirk and I were talking. Mrs Stroeve sewed, and I thought I recognized the shirt she was mending as Strickland's. He lay on his back; he did not speak. Once I saw that his eyes were fixed on Blanche Stroeve, and there was in them a curious irony. Feeling their gaze, she raised her own, and for a moment they stared at one another. I could not quite understand her expression. Her eyes had in them a strange perplexity, and perhaps—but why?—alarm. In a moment Strickland looked away and idly surveyed the ceiling, but she continued to stare at him, and now her look was quite inexplicable.

In a few days Strickland began to get up. He was nothing but skin and bone. His clothes hung upon him like rags on a scare-crow. With his untidy beard and long hair, his features, always a little larger than life, now emphasized by illness, he had an extraordinary aspect; but it was so odd that it was not quite ugly. There was something monumental in his ungainliness. I do not know how to express precisely the impression he made upon me. It was not exactly spirituality that was obvious, though the screen of the flesh seemed almost transparent, because there was in his face an outrageous sensuality; but, though it sounds nonsense, it seemed as though his sensuality were curiously spiritual. There was in him something primitive. He seemed to partake of those obscure forces of nature which the Greeks personified in shapes part human and part beast, the satyr and the faun. I thought of Marsyas, whom the god flayed because he had dared to rival him in song. Strickland seemed to bear in his heart strange harmonies and unadventured patterns, and I foresaw for him an end of torture and despair. I had again the feeling that he was possessed of a devil; but you could not say that it was a devil of evil, for it was a primitive force that existed before good and ill.

He was still too weak to paint, and he sat in the studio, silent, occupied with God knows what dreams, or reading. The books he liked were queer; sometimes I would find him poring over the poems of Mallarmé, and he read them as a child reads, forming the words with his lips, and I wondered what strange emotion he got from those subtle cadences and obscure phrases; and again I found him absorbed in the detective novels of Gaboriau. I amused myself by thinking that in his choice of books he showed pleasantly the irreconcilable sides of his fantastic nature. It was singular to notice that even in the weak state of his body he had no thought for its comfort. Stroeve liked his ease, and in his studio were a couple of heavily upholstered arm-chairs and a large divan. Strickland would not go near them, not from any affectation of stoicism, for I found him seated on a three-legged stool when I went into the studio one day and he was alone, but because he did not like them. For choice he sat on a kitchen chair without arms. It often exasperated me to see him. I never knew a man so entirely indifferent to his surroundings.

XXVII

Two or three weeks passed. One morning, having come to a pause in my work, I thought I would give myself a holiday, and I went to the Louvre. I wandered about looking at the pictures I knew so well, and let my fancy play idly with the emotions they suggested. I sauntered into the long gallery, and there suddenly saw Stroeve. I smiled, for his appearance, so rotund and yet so startled, could never fail to excite a smile, and then as I came nearer I noticed that he seemed singularly disconsolate. He looked woebegone and yet ridiculous, like a man who has fallen into the water with all his clothes on, and, being rescued from death, frightened still, feels that he only looks a fool. Turning round, he stared at me, but I perceived that he did not see me. His round blue eyes looked harrassed behind his glasses.

'Stroeve', I said.

He gave a little start, and then smiled, but his smile was rueful.

'Why are you idling in this disgraceful fashion?' I asked gaily.

'It's a long time since I was at the Louvre. I thought I'd come and see if they had anything new.'

'But you told me you had to get a picture finished this week.'

'Strickland's painting in my studio.'

'Well?'

'I suggested it myself. He's not strong enough to go back to his own place yet. I thought we could both paint there. Lots of fellows in the Quarter share a studio. I thought it would be fun. I've always thought it would be jolly to have someone to talk to when one was tired of work.'

He said all this slowly, detaching statement from statement with a little awkward silence, and he kept his kind, foolish eyes fixed on mine. They were full of tears.

'I don't think I understand', I said.

'Strickland can't work with anyone else in the studio.'

'Damn it all, it's your studio. That's his look-out.'

He looked at me pitifully. His lips were trembling.

'What happened?' I asked, rather sharply.

He hesitated and flushed. He glanced unhappily at one of the pictures on the wall.

'He wouldn't let me go on painting. He told me to get out.'

'But why didn't you tell him to go to hell?'

'He turned me out. I couldn't very well struggle with him. He threw my hat after me, and locked the door.'

I was furious with Strickland, and was indignant with myself, because Dirk Stroeve cut such an absurd figure that I felt inclined to laugh.

'But what did your wife say?'

'She'd gone out to do some marketing.'

'Is he going to let her in?'

'I don't know.'

I gazed at Stroeve with perplexity. He stood like a schoolboy with whom a master is finding fault.

'Shall I get rid of Strickland for you?' I asked.

He gave a little start, and his shining face grew very red.

'No. You'd better not do anything.'

He nodded to me and walked away. It was clear that for some reason he did not want to discuss the matter. I did not understand.

XXVIII

The explanation came a week later. It was about ten o'clock at night; I had been dining by myself at a restaurant, and having returned to my small apartment, was sitting in my parlour, reading. I heard the cracked tinkling of the bell, and, going into the corridor, opened the door. Stroeve stood before me.

'Can I come in?' he asked.

In the dimness of the landing I could not see him very well, but there was something in his voice that surprised me. I knew he was of abstemious habit or I should have thought he had been drinking. I led the way into my sitting-room and asked him to sit down.

'Thank God I've found you', he said.

'What's the matter?' I asked in astonishment at his vehemence.

I was able now to see him well. As a rule he was neat in his person, but now his clothes were in disorder. He looked suddenly bedraggled. I was convinced he had been drinking, and I smiled. I was on the point of chaffing him on his state.

'I didn't know where to go', he burst out. 'I came here earlier, but you weren't in.'

'I dined late', I said.

I changed my mind: it was not liquor that had driven him to this obvious desperation. His face, usually so rosy, was now strangely mottled. His hands trembled.

'Has anything happened?' I asked.

'My wife has left me.'

He could hardly get the words out. He gave a little gasp, and the tears began to trickle down his round cheeks. I did not know what to say. My first thought was that she had come to the end of her forbearance with his infatuation for Strickland, and, goaded by the latter's cynical behaviour, had insisted that he should be turned out. I knew her capable of temper, for all the calmness of her manner; and if Stroeve still refused, she might easily have flung out of the studio with vows never to return. But the little man was so distressed that I could not smile.

'My dear fellow, don't be unhappy. She'll come back. You mustn't take very seriously what women say when they're in a passion.'

'You don't understand. She's in love with Strickland.'

'What!' I was startled at this, but the idea had no sooner taken possession of me than I saw it was absurd. 'How can you be so silly? You don't mean to say you're jealous of Strickland?' I almost laughed. 'You know very well that she can't bear the sight of him.'

'You don't understand', he moaned.

'You're an hysterical ass', I said a little impatiently. 'Let me give you a whisky-and-soda, and you'll feel better.'

I supposed that for some reason or other—and Heaven knows what ingenuity men exercise to torment themselves—Dirk had got it into his head that his wife cared for Strickland, and with his genius for blundering he might quite well have offended her so that, to anger him, perhaps, she had taken pains to foster his suspicion.

'Look here', I said, 'let's go back to your studio. If you've made a fool of yourself you must eat humble pie. Your wife doesn't strike me as the sort of woman to bear malice.'

'How can I go back to the studio?' he said wearily, 'They're there. I've left it to them.'

'Then it's not your wife who's left you; it's you who've left your wife.'

'For God's sake don't talk to me like that.'

Still I could not take him seriously. I did not for a moment believe what he had told me. But he was in very real distress.

'Well, you've come here to talk to me about it. You'd better tell me the whole story.'

'This afternoon I couldn't stand it any more. I went to Strickland and told him I thought he was quite well enough to go back to his own place. I wanted the studio myself.'

'No one but Strickland would have needed telling', I said. 'What did he say?'

'He laughed a little; you know how he laughs, not as though he were amused, but as though you were a damned fool, and said he'd go at once. He began to put his things together. You remember I fetched from his room what I thought he needed, and he asked Blanche for a piece of paper and some string to make a parcel.'

Stroeve stopped, gasping, and I thought he was going to faint. This was not at all the story I had expected him to tell me.

'She was very pale, but she brought the paper and the string. He didn't say anything. He made the parcel and he whistled a tune. He took no notice of either of us. His eyes had an ironic smile in them. My heart was like lead. I was afraid something was going to happen, and I wished I hadn't spoken. He looked round for his hat. Then she spoke:

'I'm going with Strickland, Dirk', she said. 'I can't live with you any more.'

'I tried to speak, but the words wouldn't come. Strickland didn't say anything. He went on whistling as though it had nothing to do with him.'

Stroeve stopped again and mopped his face. I kept quite still. I believed him now, and I was astounded. But all the same I could not understand.

Then he told me, in a trembling voice, with the tears pouring down his cheeks, how he had gone up to her, trying to take her in his arms, but she had drawn away and begged him not to touch her. He implored her not to leave him. He told her how passionately he loved her, and reminded her of all the devotion he had lavished upon her. He spoke to her of the happiness of their life. He was not angry with her. He did not reproach her.

'Please let me go quietly, Dirk', she said at last. 'Don't you understand that I love Strickland? Where he goes I shall go.'

'But you must know that he'll never make you happy. For your own sake don't go. You don't know what you've got to look forward to.'

'It's your fault. You insisted on his coming here.'

He turned to Strickland.

'Have mercy on her', he implored him. 'You can't let her do anything so mad.'

'She can do as she chooses', said Strickland. 'She's not forced to come.'

'My choice is made', she said, in a dull voice.

Strickland's injurious calm robbed Stroeve of the rest of his self-control. Blind rage seized him, and without knowing what he was doing he flung himself on Strickland. Strickland was taken by surprise and he staggered, but he was very strong, even after his illness, and in a moment, he did not exactly know how, Stroeve found himself on the floor.

'You funny little man', said Strickland.

Stroeve picked himself up. He noticed that his wife had remained perfectly still, and to be made ridiculous before her increased his humiliation. His spectacles had tumbled off in the struggle, and he could not immediately see them. She picked them up and silently handed them to him. He seemed suddenly to realize his unhappiness, and though he knew he was making himself still more absurd, he began to cry. He hid his face in his hands. The others watched him without a word. They did not move from where they stood.

'Oh, my dear', he groaned at last, 'how can you be so cruel?'

'I can't help myself, Dirk', she answered.

'I've worshipped you as no woman was ever worshipped before. If in anything I did I displeased you, why didn't you tell me, and I'd have changed. I've done everything I could for you.'

She did not answer. Her face was set, and he saw that he was only boring her. She put on a coat and her hat. She moved towards the door, and he saw that in a moment she would be gone. He went up to her quickly and fell on his knees before her, seizing her hands: he abandoned all self-respect.

'Oh, don't go, my darling. I can't live without you; I shall kill myself. If I've done anything to offend you I beg you to forgive me. Give me another chance. I'll try harder still to make you happy.'

'Get up, Dirk. You're making yourself a perfect fool.'

He staggered to his feet, but still he would not let her go.

'Where are you going?' he said hastily. 'You don't know what Strickland's place is like. You can't live there. It would be awful.'

'If I don't care, I don't see why you should.'

'Stay a minute longer. I must speak. After all, you can't grudge me that.'

'What is the good? I've made up my mind. Nothing that you can say will make me alter it.'

He gulped, and put his hand to his heart to ease its painful beating.

'I'm not going to ask you to change your mind, but I want you to listen to me for a minute. It's the last thing I shall ever ask you. Don't refuse me that.'

She paused, looking at him with those reflective eyes of hers, which now were so indifferent to him. She came back into the studio and leaned against the table.

'Well?'

Stroeve made a great effort to collect himself.

'You must be a little reasonable. You can't live on air, you know. Strickland hasn't got a penny.'

'I know.'

'You'll suffer the most awful privations. You know why he took so long to get well. He was half starved.'

'I can earn money for him.'

'How?'

'I don't know. I shall find a way.'

A horrible thought passed through the Dutchman's mind, and he shuddered.

'I think you must be mad. I don't know what has come over you.'

She shrugged her shoulders.

'Now may I go?'

'Wait one second longer.'

He looked round his studio wearily; he had loved it because her presence had made it gay and home-like; he shut his eyes for an instant; then he gave her a long look as though to impress on his mind the picture of her. He got up and took his hat.

'No; I'll go.'

'You?'

She was startled. She did not know what he meant.

'I can't bear to think of you living in that horrible, filthy attic. After all, this is your home just as much as mine. You'll be comfortable here. You'll be spared at least the worst privations.'

He went to the drawer in which he kept his money and took out several bank-notes.

'I would like to give you half what I've got here.'

He put them on the table. Neither Strickland nor his wife spoke.

Then he recollected something else.

'Will you pack up my clothes and leave them with the concierge? I'll come and fetch them tomorrow.' He tried to smile. 'Good-bye, my dear. I'm grateful for all the happiness you gave me in the past.'

He walked out and closed the door behind him. With my mind's eye I saw Strickland throw his hat on a table, and, sitting down, begin to smoke a cigarette.

XXIX

I kept silence for a little while, thinking of what Stroeve had told me. I could not stomach his weakness, and he saw my disapproval.

'You know as well as I do how Strickland lived', he said tremulously. 'I couldn't let her live in those circumstances—I simply couldn't.'

'That's your business', I answered.

'What would *you* have done?' he asked.

'She went with her eyes open. If she had to put up with certain inconveniences it was her own look-out.'

'Yes; but, you see, you don't love her.'

'Do you love her still?'

'Oh, more than ever. Strickland isn't the man to make a

woman happy. It can't last. I want her to know that I shall never fail her.'

'Does that mean that you're prepared to take her back?'

'I shouldn't hesitate. Why, she'll want me more than ever then. When she's alone and humiliated and broken it would be dreadful if she had nowhere to go.'

He seemed to bear no resentment. I suppose it was commonplace in me that I felt slightly outraged at his lack of spirit. Perhaps he guessed what was in my mind, for he said:

'I couldn't expect her to love me as I loved her. I'm a buffoon. I'm not the sort of man that women love. I've always known that. I can't blame her if she's fallen in love with Strickland.'

'You certainly have less vanity than any man I've ever known', I said.

'I love her so much better than myself. It seems to me that when vanity comes into love it can only be because really you love yourself best. After all, it constantly happens that a man when he's married falls in love with somebody else; when he gets over it he returns to his wife, and she takes him back, and everyone thinks it very natural. Why should it be different with women?'

'I dare say that's logical,' I smiled, 'but most men are made differently, and they can't.'

But while I talked to Stroeve I was puzzling over the suddenness of the whole affair. I could not imagine that he had had no warning. I remembered the curious look I had seen in Blanche Stroeve's eyes; perhaps its explanation was that she was growing dimly conscious of a feeling in her heart that surprised and alarmed her.

'Did you have no suspicion before today that there was anything between them?' I asked.

He did not answer for a while. There was a pencil on the table, and unconsciously he drew a head on the blotting-paper.

'Please say so, if you hate my asking you questions', I said.

'It eases me to talk. Oh, if you knew the frightful anguish in my heart.' He threw the pencil down. 'Yes, I've known it for a fortnight. I knew it before she did.'

'Why on earth didn't you send Strickland packing?'

'I couldn't believe it. It seemed so improbable. She couldn't bear the sight of him. It was more than improbable; it was incredible. I thought it was merely jealousy. You see, I've always been jealous, but I trained myself never to show it; I was jealous of every man she knew; I was jealous of you. I knew she didn't love me as I loved her. That was only natural, wasn't it? But she allowed me to love her, and that was enough to make me happy. I forced myself to go out for hours together in order to leave them by themselves; I wanted to punish myself for suspicions which were unworthy of me; and when I came back I found they didn't want me—not Strickland, he didn't care if I was there or not, but Blanche. She shuddered when I went to kiss her. When at last I was certain I didn't know what to do; I knew they'd only laugh at me if I made a scene. I thought if I held my tongue and pretended not to see, everything would come right. I made up my mind to get him away quietly, without quarrelling. Oh, if you only knew what I've suffered!'

Then he told me again of his asking Strickland to go. He chose his moment carefully, and tried to make his request sound casual; but he could not master the trembling of his voice, and he felt himself that into words that he wished to seem jovial and friendly there crept the bitterness of his jealousy. He had not expected Strickland to take him up on the spot and make his preparations to go there and then; above all, he had not expected his wife's decision to go with him. I saw that now he wished with all his heart that he had held his tongue. He preferred the anguish of jealousy to the anguish of separation.

'I wanted to kill him, and I only made a fool of myself.'

He was silent for a long time, and then he said what I knew was in his mind.

'If I'd only waited, perhaps it would have gone all right. I shouldn't have been so impatient. Oh, poor child, what have I driven her to?'

I shrugged my shoulders, but did not speak. I had no sympathy for Blanche Stroeve, but knew that it would only pain poor Dirk if I told him exactly what I thought of her.

He had reached that stage of exhaustion when he could not

stop talking. He went over again every word of the scene. Now something occurred to him that he had not told me before; now he discussed what he ought to have said instead of what he did say; then he lamented his blindness. He regretted that he had done this, and blamed himself that he had omitted the other. It grew later and later, and at last I was as tired as he.

'What are you going to do now?' I said finally.

'What can I do? I shall wait till she sends for me.'

'Why don't you go away for a bit?'

'No, no; I must be at hand when she wants me.'

For the present he seemed quite lost. He had made no plans. When I suggested that he should go to bed he said he could not sleep; he wanted to go out and walk about the streets till day. He was evidently in no state to be left alone. I persuaded him to stay the night with me, and I put him into my own bed. I had a divan in my sitting-room, and could very well sleep on that. He was by now so worn out that he could not resist my firmness. I gave him a sufficient dose of veronal to ensure his unconsciousness for several hours. I thought that was the best service I could render him.

XXX

But the bed I made up for myself was sufficiently uncomfortable to give me a wakeful night, and I thought a good deal of what the unlucky Dutchman had told me. I was not so much puzzled by Blanche Stroeve's action, for I saw in that merely the result of a physical appeal. I do not suppose she had ever really cared for her husband, and what I had taken for love was no more than the feminine response to caresses and comfort which in the minds of most women passes for it. It is a passive feeling capable of being roused for any object, as the vine can grow on any tree; and the wisdom of the world recognizes its strength when it urges a girl to marry the man who wants her with the assurance that love will follow. It is an emotion made up of the satisfaction in security, pride of property, the pleasure of being desired, the gratification of a household, and it is only by an amiable vanity that women ascribe to its spiritual value. It is an emotion which is defenceless against passion. I suspected that Blanche Stroeve's violent dislike of Strickland had in it from the beginning a vague element of sexual attraction. Who am I that I should seek to unravel the mysterious intricacies of sex? Perhaps Stroeve's passion excited without satisfying that part of her nature, and she hated Strickland because she felt in him the power to give her what she needed. I think she was quite sincere when she struggled against her husband's desire to bring him into the studio; I think she was frightened of him, though she knew not why; and I remembered how she had foreseen disaster. I think in some curious way the horror which she felt for him was a transference of the horror which she felt for herself because he so strangely troubled her. His appearance was wild and uncouth; there was aloofness in his eyes and sensuality in his mouth; he was big and strong; he gave the impression of untamed passion; and perhaps she felt in him, too, that sinister element which had made me think of those wild beings of the world's early history when matter, retaining its early connexion with the earth, seemed to possess yet a spirit of its own. If he affected her at all, it was inevitable that she should love or hate him. She hated him.

And then I fancy that the daily intimacy with the sick man moved her strangely. She raised his head to give him food, and it was heavy against her hand; when she fed him she wiped his sensual mouth and his red beard. She washed his limbs; they were covered with thick hair; and when she dried his hands, even in his weakness they were strong and sinewy. His fingers were long; they were the capable, fashioning fingers of the artist; and I know not what troubling thoughts they excited in her. He slept very quietly, without a movement, so that he might have been dead, and he was like some wild creature of the woods, resting after a long chase; and she wondered what fancies passed through his dreams. Did he dream of the nymph flying through the woods of Greece with the satyr in hot pursuit? She fled, swift of foot and desperate, but he gained on her step by step, till she felt his hot breath on her cheek; and still she fled silently, and silently he pursued, and when at last he seized her was it terror that thrilled her heart or was it ecstasy?

Blanche Stroeve was in the cruel grip of appetite. Perhaps she hated Strickland still, but she hungered for him, and everything that had made up her life till then became of no account. She ceased to be a woman, complex, kind, and petulant, considerate and thoughtless; she was a Maenad. She was desire.

But perhaps this is very fanciful; and it may be that she was merely bored with her husband and went to Strickland out of a callous curiosity. She may have had no particular feeling for him, but succumbed to his wish from propinquity or idleness, to find then that she was powerless in a snare of her own contriving. How did I know what were the thoughts and emotions behind that placid brow and those cool grey eyes?

But if one could be certain of nothing in dealing with creatures so incalculable as human beings, there were explanations of Blanche Stroeve's behaviour which were at all events plausible. On the other hand, I did not understand Strickland at all. I racked my brain, but could in no way account for an action so contrary to my conception of him. It was not strange that he should so heartlessly have betrayed his friends' confidence, nor that he hesitated not at all to gratify a whim at the cost of another's misery. That was in his character. He was a man without any conception of gratitude. He had no compassion. The emotions common to most of us simply did not exist in him, and it was as absurd to blame him for not feeling them as for blaming the tiger because he is fierce and cruel. But it was the whim I could not understand.

I could not believe that Strickland had fallen in love with Blanche Stroeve. I did not believe him capable of love. That is an emotion in which tenderness is an essential part, but Strickland had no tenderness either for himself or for others; there is in love a sense of weakness, a desire to protect, and eagerness to do good and to give pleasure—if not unselfishness, at all events a selfishness which marvellously conceals itself; it has in it a certain diffidence. These were not traits which I could imagine in Strickland. Love is absorbing; it takes the lover out of himself; the most clearsighted, though he may know, cannot realize that this love will cease; it gives body to what he knows is illusion, and, knowing it is nothing else, he loves it better than reality. It makes a man a little more than himself, and at the same time a little less. He ceases to be himself. He is no longer an individual, but a thing, an instrument to some purpose foreign to his ego. Love is never quite devoid of sentimentality, and Strickland was the least inclined to that infirmity of any man I have known. I could not believe that he would ever suffer that possession of himself which love is; he could never endure a foreign yoke. I believed him capable of uprooting from his heart, though it might be with agony, so that he was left battered and ensanguined, anything that came between himself and that uncomprehended craving that urged him constantly to he knew not what. If I have succeeded at all in giving the complicated impression that Strickland made on me, it will not seem outrageous to say that I felt he was at once too great and too small for love.

But I suppose that everyone's conception of the passion is formed on his own idiosyncrasies and it is different with every different person. A man like Strickland would love in a manner peculiar to himself. It was vain to seek the analysis of his emotion.

XXXI

Next day, though I pressed him to remain, Stroeve left me. I offered to fetch his things from the studio, but he insisted on going himself; I think he hoped they had not thought of getting them together, so that he would have an opportunity of seeing his wife again and perhaps inducing her to come back to him. But he found his traps waiting for him in the porter's lodge, and the concierge told him that Blanche had gone out. I do not think he resisted the temptation of giving her an account of his troubles. I found that he was telling them to everyone he knew; he expected sympathy, but only excited ridicule.

He bore himself most unbecomingly. Knowing at what time his wife did her shopping, one day, unable any longer to bear not seeing her, he waylaid her in the street. She would not speak to him, but he insisted on speaking to her. He spluttered out words of apology for any wrong he had committed towards her; he told her he loved her devotedly and begged her to return to him. She would not answer; she walked hurriedly, with averted face. I imagined him with his fat little legs trying to keep up with her. Panting a little in his haste, he told her how miserable he was; he besought her to have mercy on him; he promised, if she would forgive him, to do everything she wanted. He offered to take her for a journey. He told her that Strickland would soon tire of her. When he repeated to me the whole sordid little scene I was outraged. He had shown neither sense nor dignity. He had omitted nothing that could make his wife despise him. There is no cruelty greater than a woman's to a man who loves her and whom she does not love; she has no kindness then, no tolerance even, she has only an insane irritation. Blanche Stroeve stopped suddenly, and as hard as she could slapped her husband's face. She took advantage of his confusion to escape, and ran up the stairs to the studio. No word had passed her lips.

When he told me this he put his hand to his cheek as though he still felt the smart of the blow, and in his eyes was a pain that was heartrending and an amazement that was ludicrous. He looked like an overblown schoolboy, and though I felt so sorry for him, I could hardly help laughing.

Then he took to walking along the street which she must pass through to get to the shops, and he would stand at the corner, on the other side, as she went along. He dared not speak to her again, but sought to put into his round eyes the appeal that was in his heart. I suppose he had some idea that the sight of his misery would touch her. She never made the smallest sign that she saw him. She never even changed the hour of her errands or sought an alternative route. I have an idea that there was some cruelty in her indifference. Perhaps she got enjoyment out of the torture she inflicted. I wondered why she hated him so much.

I begged Stroeve to behave more wisely. His want of spirit was exasperating.

'You're doing no good at all by going on like this', I said. 'I think you'd have been wiser if you'd hit her over the head with a stick. She wouldn't have despised you as she does now.'

I suggested that he should go home for a while. He had often spoken to me of the silent town, somewhere up in the north of Holland, where his parents still lived. They were poor people. His father was a carpenter, and they dwelt in a little old red-brick house, neat and clean, by the side of a sluggish canal. The streets were wide and empty; for two hundred years the place had been dying, but the houses had the homely stateliness of their time. Rich merchants, sending their wares to the distant Indies, had lived in them calm and prosperous lives, and in their decent decay they kept still an aroma of their splendid past. You could wander along the canal till you came to broad green fields, with windmills here and there, in which cattle, black and white, grazed lazily. I thought that amongst those surroundings, with their recollections of his boyhood, Dirk Stroeve would forget his unhappiness. But he would not go.

'I must be here when she needs me', he repeated. 'It would be dreadful if something terrible happened and I were not at hand.'

'What do you think is going to happen?' I asked.

'I don't know. But I'm afraid.'

I shrugged my shoulders.

For all his pain, Dirk Stroeve remained a ridiculous object. He might have excited sympathy if he had grown worn and thin. He did nothing of the kind. He remained fat, and his round red cheeks shone like ripe apples. He had great neatness of person, and he continued to wear his spruce black coat and his bowler hat, always a little too small for him, in a dapper, jaunty manner. He was getting something of a paunch, and sorrow had no effect on it. He looked more than ever like a prosperous bagman. It is hard that a man's exterior should tally so little sometimes with his soul. Dirk Stroeve had the passion of Romeo in the body of Sir Toby Belch. He had a sweet and generous nature, and yet was always blundering; a real feeling for what was beautiful and the capacity to create only what was commonplace; a peculiar delicacy of sentiment and gross manners. He could exercise tact when dealing with the affairs of others, but none when dealing with his own. What a cruel practical joke old Nature played when she flung so many contradictory elements together, and left the man face to face with the perplexing callousness of the universe.

XXXII

I did not see Strickland for several weeks. I was disgusted with him, and if I had had an opportunity should have been glad to tell him so, but I saw no object in seeking him out for the purpose. I am a little shy of any assumption of moral indignation. There is always in it an element of self-satisfaction which makes it awkward to anyone who has a sense of humour. It requires a very lively passion to steel me to my own ridicule. There was a sardonic sincerity in Strickland which made me sensitive to anything that might suggest a pose.

But one evening, when I was passing along the Avenue de Clichy in front of the café which Strickland frequented and which I now avoided, I ran straight into him. He was accompanied by Blanche Stroeve, and they were just going to Strickland's favourite corner.

'Where the devil have you been all this time?' said he. 'I thought you must be away.'

His cordiality was proof that he knew I had no wish to speak to him. He was not a man with whom it was worth while wasting politeness.

'No', I said; 'I haven't been away.'

'Why haven't you been here?'

'There are more cafés in Paris than one, at which to trifle away an idle hour.'

Blanche then held out her hand and bade me good evening. I do not know why I had expected her to be somehow changed; she wore the same grey dress that she wore so often, neat and becoming, and her brow was as candid, her eyes as untroubled, as when I had been used to see her occupied with her household duties in the studio.

'Come and have a game of chess', said Strickland.

I do not know why at the moment I could think of no excuse. I followed them rather sulkily to the table at which Strickland always sat, and he called for the board and the chessmen. They both took the situation so much as a matter of course that I felt it absurd to do otherwise. Mrs Stroeve watched the game with inscrutable face. She was silent, but she had always been silent. I looked at her mouth for an expression that could give me a clue to what she felt; I watched her eyes for some tell-tale flash, some hint of dismay or bitterness; I scanned her brow for any passing line that might indicate a settling emotion. Her face was a mask that told nothing. Her hands lay on her lap motionless, one in the other loosely clasped. I knew from what I had heard that she was a woman of violent passions; and that injurious blow that she had given Dirk, the man who had loved her so devotedly, betrayed a sudden temper and a horrid cruelty. She had abandoned the safe shelter of her husband's protection and the comfortable ease of a well-provided establishment for what she could not but see was an extreme hazard. It showed an eagerness for adventure, a readiness for the hand-to-mouth, which the care she took of her home and her love of good housewifery made not a little remarkable. She must be a woman of complicated character, and there was something dramatic in the contrast of that with her demure appearance.

I was excited by the encounter, and my fancy worked busily while I sought to concentrate myself on the game I was playing. I always tried my best to beat Strickland, because he was a player who despised the opponent he vanquished; his exultation in victory made defeat more difficult to bear. On the other hand, if he was beaten he took it with complete good humour. He was a bad winner and a good loser. Those who think that a man betrays his character nowhere more clearly than when he is playing a game might on this draw subtle inferences.

When we had finished I called the waiter to pay for the drinks, and left them. The meeting had been devoid of incident. No word had been said to give me anything to think

about, and any surmises I might make were unwarranted. I
was intrigued. I could not tell how they were getting on. I
would have given much to be a disembodied spirit so that
I could see them in the privacy of the studio and hear what
they talked about. I had not the smallest indication on which
to let my imagination work.

XXXIII

Two or three days later Dirk Stroeve called on me.

'I hear you've seen Blanche', he said.

'How on earth did you find out?'

'I was told by someone who saw you sitting with them. Why
didn't you tell me?'

'I thought it would only pain you.'

'What do I care if it does? You must know that I want to hear
the smallest thing about her.'

I waited for him to ask me questions.

'What does she look like?' he said.

'Absolutely unchanged.'

'Does she seem happy?'

I shrugged my shoulders.

'How can I tell? We were in a café; we were playing chess; I
had no opportunity to speak to her.'

'Oh, but couldn't you tell by her face?'

I shook my head. I could only repeat that by no word, by no
hinted gesture, had she given an indication of her feelings. He
must know better than I how great were her powers of self-
control. He clasped his hands emotionally.

'Oh, I'm so frightened. I know something is going to happen,
something terrible, and I can do nothing to stop it.'

'What sort of thing?' I asked.

'Oh, I don't know,' he moaned, seizing his head with his
hands. 'I foresee some terrible catastrophe.'

Stroeve had always been excitable, but now he was beside
himself; there was no reasoning with him. I thought it probable

enough that Blanche Stroeve would not continue to find life with Strickland tolerable, but one of the falsest of proverbs is that you must lie on the bed that you have made. The experience of life shows that people are constantly doing things which must lead to disaster, and yet by some chance manage to evade the result of their folly. When Blanche quarrelled with Strickland she had only to leave him, and her husband was waiting humbly to forgive and forget. I was not prepared to feel any great sympathy for her.

'You see, you don't love her', said Stroeve.

'After all, there's nothing to prove that she is unhappy. For all we know they may have settled down into a most domestic couple.'

Stroeve gave me a look with his woeful eyes.

'Of course, it doesn't much matter to you, but to me it's so serious, so intensely serious.'

I was sorry if I had seemed impatient or flippant.

'Will you do something for me?' asked Stroeve.

'Willingly.'

'Will you write to Blanche for me?'

'Why can't you write yourself?'

'I've written over and over again. I didn't expect her to answer. I don't think she reads the letters.'

'You make no account of feminine curiosity. Do you think she could resist?'

'She could—mine.'

I looked at him quickly. He lowered his eyes. That answer of his seemed to me strangely humiliating. He was conscious that she regarded him with an indifference so profound that the sight of his handwriting would have not the slightest effect on her.

'Do you really believe that she'll ever come back to you?' I asked.

'I want her to know that if the worst comes to the worst she can count on me. That's what I want you to tell her.'

I took a sheet of paper.

'What is it exactly you wish me to say?'

This is what I wrote:

Dear Mrs Stroeve,

Dirk wishes me to tell you that if at any time you want him he will be grateful for the opportunity of being of service to you. He has no ill-feeling towards you on account of anything that has happened. His love for you is unaltered. You will always find him at the following address.

XXXIV

But though I was no less convinced than Stroeve that the connexion between Strickland and Blanche would end disastrously, I did not expect the issue to take the tragic form it did. The summer came, breathless and sultry, and even at night there was no coolness to rest one's jaded nerves. The sun-baked streets seemed to give back the heat that had beat down on them during the day, and the passers-by dragged their feet along them wearily. I had not seen Strickland for weeks. Occupied with other things, I had ceased to think of him and his affairs. Dirk, with his vain lamentations, had begun to bore me, and I avoided his society. It was a sordid business, and I was not inclined to trouble myself with it further.

One morning I was working. I sat in my pyjamas. My thoughts wandered, and I thought of the sunny beaches of Brittany and the freshness of the sea. By my side was the empty bowl in which the concierge had brought me my *café au lait* and the fragment of *croissant* which I had not had appetite enough to eat. I heard the concierge in the next room emptying my bath. There was a tinkle at my bell, and I left her to open the door. In a moment I heard Stroeve's voice asking if I was in. Without moving, I shouted to him to come. He entered the room quickly, and came up to the table at which I sat.

'She's killed herself', he said hoarsely.

'What do you mean?' I cried, startled.

He made movements with his lips as though he were speaking,

but no sound issued from them. He gibbered like an idiot. My heart thumped against my ribs, and, I do not know why, I flew into a temper.

'For God's sake, collect yourself, man', I said. 'What on earth are you talking about?'

He made despairing gestures with his hands, but still no words came from his mouth. He might have been struck dumb. I do not know what came over me; I took him by the shoulders and shook him. Looking back, I am vexed that I made such a fool of myself. I suppose the last restless nights had shaken my nerves more than I knew.

'Let me sit down', he gasped at length.

I filled a glass with St Galmier, and gave it to him to drink. I held it to his mouth as though he were a child. He gulped down a mouthful, and some of it was spilt on his shirt-front.

'Who's killed herself?'

I do not know why I asked, for I knew whom he meant. He made an effort to collect himself.

'They had a row last night. He went away.'

'Is she dead?'

'No; they've taken her to the hospital.'

'Then what are you talking about?' I cried impatiently. 'Why did you say she'd killed herself?'

'Don't be cross with me. I can't tell you anything if you talk to me like that.'

I clenched my hands, seeking to control my irritation. I attempted to smile.

'I'm sorry. Take your time. Don't hurry, there's a good fellow.'

His round blue eyes behind the spectacles were ghastly with terror. The magnifying glasses he wore distorted them.

'When the concierge went up this morning to take a letter she could get no answer to her ring. She heard someone groaning. The door wasn't locked, and she went in. Blanche was lying on the bed. She'd been frightfully sick. There was a bottle of oxalic acid on the table.'

Stroeve hid his face in his hands and swayed backwards and forwards, groaning.

'Was she conscious?'

'Yes. Oh, if you knew how she's suffering. I can't bear it. I can't bear it.'

His voice rose to a shriek.

'Damn it all, you haven't got to bear it', I cried impatiently. 'She's got to bear it.'

'How can you be so cruel?'

'What have you done?'

'They sent for a doctor and for me, and they told the police. I'd given the concierge twenty francs, and told her to send for me if anything happened.'

He paused a minute, and I saw that what he had to tell me was very hard to say.

'When I went she wouldn't speak to me. She told them to send me away. I swore that I forgave her everything, but she wouldn't listen. She tried to beat her head against the wall. The doctor told me that I mustn't remain with her. She kept on saying, "Send him away!" I went, and waited in the studio. And when the ambulance came and they put her on a stretcher, they made me go in the kitchen so that she shouldn't know I was there.'

While I dressed—for Stroeve wished me to go at once with him to the hospital—he told me that he had arranged for his wife to have a private room, so that she might at least be spared the sordid promiscuity of a ward. On our way he explained to me why he desired my presence; if she still refused to see him, perhaps she would see me. He begged me to repeat to her that he loved her still; he would reproach her for nothing, but desired only to help her; he made no claim on her, and on her recovery would not seek to induce her to return to him; she would be perfectly free.

But when we arrived at the hospital, a gaunt, cheerless building, the mere sight of which was enough to make one's heart sick, and after being directed from this official to that, up endless stairs and through long bare corridors, found the doctor in charge of the case, we were told that the patient was too ill to see anyone that day. The doctor was a little bearded man in white, with an off-hand manner. He evidently looked upon a case as a case, and anxious relatives as a nuisance which must be

treated with firmness. Moreover, to him the affair was commonplace; it was just a hysterical woman who had quarrelled with
her lover and taken poison; it was constantly happening. At first
he thought that Dirk was the cause of the disaster, and he was
needlessly brusque with him. When I explained that he was the
husband, anxious to forgive, the doctor looked at him suddenly,
with curious, searching eyes. I seemed to see in them a hint of
mockery; it was true that Stroeve had the head of the husband
who is deceived. The doctor faintly shrugged his shoulders.

'There is no immediate danger', he said, in answer to our ques-
tioning. 'One doesn't know how much she took. It may be that
she will get off with a fright. Women are constantly trying to
commit suicide for love, but generally they take care not to succeed. It's generally a gesture to arouse pity or terror in their lover.'

There was in his tone a frigid contempt. It was obvious that to
him Blanche Stroeve was only a unit to be added to the statistical
list of attempted suicides in the city of Paris during the current
year. He was busy, and could waste no more time on us. He told
us that if we came at a certain hour next day, should Blanche be
better, it might be possible for her husband to see her.

XXXV

I scarcely know how we got through that day. Stroeve could not
bear to be alone, and I exhausted myself in efforts to distract
him. I took him to the Louvre, and he pretended to look at pictures, but I saw that his thoughts were constantly with his wife.
I forced him to eat, and after luncheon I induced him to lie
down, but he could not sleep. He accepted willingly my invitation to remain for a few days in my apartment. I gave him
books to read, but after a page or two he would put the book
down and stare miserably into space. During the evening we
played innumerable games of piquet, and bravely, not to disap-
point my efforts, he tried to appear interested. Finally I gave
him a draught, and he sank into uneasy slumber.

When we went again to the hospital we saw a nursing sister.
She told us that Blanche seemed a little better, and she went in

to ask if she would see her husband. We heard voices in the room in which she lay, and presently the nurse returned to say that the patient refused to see anyone. We had told her that if she refused to see Dirk the nurse was to ask if she would see me, but this she refused also. Dirk's lips trembled.

'I dare not insist', said the nurse. 'She is too ill. Perhaps in a day or two she may change her mind.'

'Is there anyone else she wants to see?' asked Dirk, in a voice so low it was almost a whisper.

'She says she only wants to be left in peace.'

Dirk's hands moved strangely, as though they had nothing to do with his body, with a movement of their own.

'Will you tell her that if there is anyone else she wishes to see I will bring him? I only want her to be happy.'

The nurse looked at him with her calm, kind eyes, which had seen all the horror and pain of the world, and yet, filled with the vision of a world without sin, remained serene.

'I will tell her when she is a little calmer.'

Dirk, filled with compassion, begged her to take the message at once.

'It may cure her. I beseech you to ask her now.'

With a faint smile of pity, the nurse went back into the room. We heard her low voice, and then, in a voice I did not recognize, the answer:

'No. No. No.'

The nurse came out again and shook her head.

'Was that she who spoke then?' I asked. 'Her voice sounded so strange.'

'It appears that her vocal cords have been burnt by the acid.'

Dirk gave a low cry of distress. I asked him to go on and wait for me at the entrance, for I wanted to say something to the nurse. He did not ask what it was, but went silently. He seemed to have lost all power of will; he was like an obedient child.

'Has she told you why she did it?' I asked.

'No. She won't speak. She lies on her back quite quietly. She doesn't move for hours at a time. But she cries always. Her pillow is all wet. She's too weak to use a handkerchief, and the tears just run down her face.'

It gave me a sudden wrench of the heart-strings. I could have killed Strickland then, and I knew that my voice was trembling when I bade the nurse good-bye.

I found Dirk waiting for me on the steps. He seemed to see nothing, and did not notice that I had joined him till I touched him on the arm. We walked along in silence. I tried to imagine what had happened to drive the poor creature to that dreadful step. I presumed that Strickland knew what had happened, for someone must have been to see him from the police, and he must have made his statement. I did not know where he was. I supposed he had gone back to the shabby attic which served him as a studio. It was curious that she should not wish to see him. Perhaps she refused to have him sent for because she knew he would refuse to come. I wondered what an abyss of cruelty she must have looked into that in horror she refused to live.

XXXVI

The next week was dreadful. Stroeve went twice a day to the hospital to inquire after his wife, who still declined to see him; and came away at first relieved and hopeful because he was told that she seemed to be growing better, and then in despair because, the complication which the doctor had feared having ensued, recovery was impossible. The nurse was pitiful to his distress, but she had little to say that could console him. The poor woman lay quite still, refusing to speak, with her eyes intent, as though she watched for the coming of death. It could now be only the question of a day or two; and when, late one evening, Stroeve came to see me I knew it was to tell me she was dead. He was absolutely exhausted. His volubility had left him at last, and he sank down wearily on my sofa. I felt that no words of condolence availed, and I let him lie there quietly. I feared he would think it heartless if I read, so I sat by my window, smoking a pipe, till he felt inclined to speak.

'You've been very kind to me', he said at last. 'Everyone's been very kind.'

'Nonsense', I said, a little embarrassed.

'At the hospital they told me I might wait. They gave me a chair, and I sat outside the door. When she became unconscious they said I might go in. Her mouth and chin were all burnt by the acid. It was awful to see her lovely skin all wounded. She died very peacefully, so that I didn't know she was dead till the sister told me.'

He was too tired to weep. He lay on his back limply, as though all the strength had gone out of his limbs, and presently I saw that he had fallen asleep. It was the first natural sleep he had had for a week. Nature, sometimes so cruel, is sometimes merciful. I covered him and turned down the light. In the morning when I awoke he was still asleep. He had not moved. His gold-rimmed spectacles were still on his nose.

XXXVII

The circumstances of Blanche Stroeve's death necessitated all manner of dreadful formalities, but at last we were allowed to bury her. Dirk and I alone followed the hearse to the cemetery. We went at a foot-pace, but on the way back we trotted, and there was something to my mind singularly horrible in the way the driver of the hearse whipped up his horses. It seemed to dismiss the dead with a shrug of the shoulders. Now and then I caught sight of the swaying hearse in front of us, and our own driver urged his pair so that we might not remain behind. I felt in myself, too, the desire to get the whole thing out of my mind. I was beginning to be bored with a tragedy that did not really concern me, and pretending to myself that I spoke in order to distract Stroeve, I turned with relief to other subjects.

'Don't you think you'd better go away for a bit?' I said. 'There can be no object in your staying in Paris now.'

He did not answer, but I went on ruthlessly:

'Have you made any plans for the immediate future?'

'No.'

'You must try and gather together the threads again. Why don't you go down to Italy and start working?'

Again he made no reply, but the driver of our carriage came

to my rescue. Slackening his pace for a moment, he leaned over and spoke. I could not hear what he said, so I put my head out of the window; he wanted to know where we wished to be set down. I told him to wait a minute.

'You'd better come and have lunch with me', I said to Dirk. 'I'll tell him to drop us in the Place Pigalle.'

'I'd rather not. I want to go to the studio.'

I hesitated a moment.

'Would you like me to come with you?' I asked then.

'No; I should prefer to be alone.'

'All right.'

I gave the driver the necessary direction, and in renewed silence we drove on. Dirk had not been to the studio since the wretched morning on which they had taken Blanche to the hospital. I was glad he did not want me to accompany him, and when I left him at the door I walked away with relief. I took a new pleasure in the streets of Paris, and I looked with smiling eyes at the people who hurried to and fro. The day was fine and sunny, and I felt in myself a more acute delight in life. I could not help it; I put Stroeve and his sorrows out of my mind. I wanted to enjoy.

XXXVIII

I did not see him again for nearly a week. Then he fetched me soon after seven one evening and took me out to dinner. He was dressed in the deepest mourning, and on his bowler was a broad black band. He had even a black border to his handkerchief. His garb of woe suggested that he had lost in one catastrophe every relation he had in the world, even to cousins by marriage twice removed. His plumpness and his red, fat cheeks made his mourning not a little incongruous. It was cruel that his extreme unhappiness should have in it something of buffoonery.

He told me he had made up his mind to go away, though not to Italy, as I had suggested, but to Holland.

'I'm starting tomorrow. This is perhaps the last time we shall ever meet.'

I made an appropriate rejoinder, and he smiled wanly.

'I haven't been home for five years. I think I'd forgotten it all; I seemed to have come so far away from my father's house that I was shy at the idea of revisiting it; but now I feel it's my only refuge.'

He was sore and bruised, and his thoughts went back to the tenderness of his mother's love. The ridicule he had endured for years seemed now to weigh him down, and the final blow of Blanche's treachery had robbed him of the resiliency which had made him take it so gaily. He could no longer laugh with those who laughed at him. He was an outcast. He told me of his childhood in the tidy brick house, and of his mother's passionate orderliness. Her kitchen was a miracle of clean brightness. Everything was always in its place, and nowhere could you see a speck of dust. Cleanliness, indeed, was a mania with her. I saw a neat little old woman, with cheeks like apples, toiling away from morning to night, through the long years, to keep her house trim and spruce. His father was a spare old man, his hands gnarled after the work of a lifetime, silent and upright; in the evening he read the paper aloud, while his wife and daughter (now married to the captain of a fishing smack), unwilling to lose a moment, bent over their sewing. Nothing ever happened in that little town, left behind by the advance of civilization, and one year followed the next till death came, like a friend, to give rest to those who had laboured so diligently.

'My father wished me to become a carpenter like himself. For five generations we've carried on the same trade, from father to son. Perhaps that is the wisdom of life, to tread in your father's steps, and look neither to the right nor to the left. When I was a little boy I said I would marry the daughter of the harness-maker who lived next door. She was a little girl with blue eyes and a flaxen pigtail. She would have kept my house like a new pin, and I should have had a son to carry on the business after me.'

Stroeve sighed a little and was silent. His thoughts dwelt among pictures of what might have been, and the safety of the life he had refused filled him with longing.

'The world is hard and cruel. We are here none knows why,

and we go none knows whither. We must be very humble. We must see the beauty of quietness. We must go through life so inconspicuously that Fate does not notice us. And let us seek the love of simple, ignorant people. Their ignorance is better than all our knowledge. Let us be silent, content in our little corner, meek and gentle like them. That is the wisdom of life.'

To me it was his broken spirit that expressed itself, and I rebelled against his renunciation. But I kept my own counsel.

'What made you think of being a painter?' I asked.

He shrugged his shoulders.

'It happened that I had a knack for drawing. I got prizes for it at school. My poor mother was very proud of my gift, and she gave me a box of water-colours as a present. She showed my sketches to the pastor and the doctor and the judge. They sent me to Amsterdam to try for a scholarship, and I won it. Poor soul, she was so proud; and though it nearly broke her heart to part from me, she smiled, and would not show me her grief. She was pleased that her son should be an artist. They pinched and saved so that I should have enough to live on, and when my first picture was exhibited they came to Amsterdam to see it, my father and mother and my sister, and my mother cried when she looked at it.' His kind eyes glistened. 'And now on every wall of the old house there is one of my pictures in a beautiful gold frame.'

He glowed with happy pride. I thought of those cold scenes of his, with their picturesque peasants and cypresses and olive-trees. They must look queer in their garish frames on the walls of the peasant house.

'The dear soul thought she was doing a wonderful thing for me when she made me an artist, but perhaps, after all, it would have been better for me if my father's will had prevailed and I were now but an honest carpenter.'

'Now that you know what art can offer, would you change your life? Would you have missed all the delight it has given you?'

'Art is the greatest thing in the world', he answered, after a pause.

He looked at me for a minute reflectively; he seemed to hesitate; then he said:

'Did you know that I had been to see Strickland?'

'You?'

I was astonished. I should have thought he could not bear to set eyes on him. Stroeve smiled faintly.

'You know already that I have no proper pride.'

'What do you mean by that?'

He told me a singular story.

XXXIX

When I left him, after we had buried poor Blanche, Stroeve walked into the house with a heavy heart. Something impelled him to go to the studio, some obscure desire for self-torture, and yet he dreaded the anguish that he foresaw. He dragged himself up the stairs; his feet seemed unwilling to carry him; and outside the door he lingered for a long time, trying to summon up courage to go in. He felt horribly sick. He had an impulse to run down the stairs after me and beg me to go in with him; he had a feeling that there was somebody in the studio. He remembered how often he had waited for a minute or two on the landing to get his breath after the ascent, and how absurdly his impatience to see Blanche had taken it away again. To see her was a delight that never staled, and even though he had not been out an hour he was as excited at the prospect as if they had been parted for a month. Suddenly he could not believe that she was dead. What had happened could only be a dream, a frightful dream; and when he turned the key and opened the door, he would see her bending slightly over the table in the gracious attitude of the woman in Chardin's *Benedicite,* which always seemed to him so exquisite. Hurriedly he took the key out of his pocket, opened, and walked in.

The apartment had no look of desertion. His wife's tidiness was one of the traits which had so much pleased him; his own upbringing had given him a tender sympathy for the delight in orderliness; and when he had seen her instinctive desire to put each thing in its appointed place it had given him a little warm feeling in his heart. The bedroom looked as though she had just left it: the brushes were neatly placed on the toilet-table, one on each side of the comb; someone had smoothed down the bed on which she had spent her last night in the studio, and her night-dress in a little case lay on the pillow. It was impossible to believe that she would never come into that room again.

But he felt thirsty, and went into the kitchen to get himself some water. Here, too, was order. On a rack were the plates that she had used for dinner on the night of her quarrel with Strickland, and they had been carefully washed. The knives and forks were put away in a drawer. Under a cover were the remains of a piece of cheese, and in a tin box was a crust of bread. She had done her marketing from day to day, buying only what was strictly needful, so that nothing was left over from one day to the next. Stroeve knew from the inquiries made by the police that Strickland had walked out of the house immediately after dinner, and the fact that Blanche had washed up the things as usual gave him a little thrill of horror. Her methodicalness made her suicide more deliberate. Her self-possession was frightening. A sudden pang seized him, and his knees felt so weak that he almost fell. He went back into the bedroom and threw himself on the bed. He cried out her name:

'Blanche. Blanche.'

The thought of her suffering was intolerable. He had a sudden vision of her standing in the kitchen—it was hardly larger than a cupboard—washing the plates and glasses, the forks and spoons, giving the knives a rapid polish on the knife-board; then putting everything away, giving the sink a scrub, and hanging the dish-cloth up to dry—it was there still, a grey, torn rag. Then looking round to see that everything was clean and nice. He saw her roll down her sleeves and remove her apron—the apron hung on a peg behind the door—and take the bottle of oxalic acid and go with it into the bedroom.

The agony of it drove him up from the bed and out of the room. He went into the studio. It was dark, for the curtains had been drawn over the great window, and he pulled them quickly back; but a sob broke from him as with a rapid glance he took in the place where he had been so happy. Nothing was changed here, either. Strickland was indifferent to his surroundings, and he had lived in the other's studio without thinking of altering a thing. It was deliberately artistic. It represented Stroeve's idea of the proper environment for an artist. There were bits of old brocade on the walls, and the piano was covered with a piece of silk, beautiful and tarnished; in one corner was a copy of the Venus of Milo, and in another of the Venus of the Medici. Here and there was an Italian cabinet surmounted with Delft, and here and there a bas-relief. In a handsome gold frame was a copy of Velasquez' Innocent X, that Stroeve had made in Rome, and placed so as to make the most of their decorative effect were a number of Stroeve's pictures, all in splendid frames. Stroeve had always been very proud of his taste. He had never lost his appreciation for the romantic atmosphere of a studio, and though now the sight of it was like a stab at his heart, without thinking what he was at, he changed slightly the position of a Louis XV table which was one of his treasures. Suddenly he caught sight of a canvas with its face to the wall. It was a much larger one than he himself was in the habit of using, and he wondered what it did there. He went over to it and leaned it towards him so that he could see the painting. It was a nude. His heart began to beat quickly, for he guessed at once that it was one of Strickland's pictures. He flung it back against the wall angrily—what did he mean by leaving it there?—but his movement caused it to fall, face downward, on the ground. No matter whose the picture, he could not leave it there in the dust, and he raised it; but then curiosity got the better of him. He thought he would like to have a proper look at it, so he brought it along and set it on the easel. Then he stood back in order to see it at his ease.

He gave a gasp. It was the picture of a woman lying on a sofa, with one arm beneath her head and the other along her body; one knee was raised, and the other leg was stretched out. The pose was classic. Stroeve's head swam. It was Blanche. Grief and jealousy and rage seized him, and he cried out hoarsely; he was inarticulate; he clenched his fists and raised them threateningly at an invisible enemy. He screamed at the top of his voice. He was beside himself. He could not bear it. That was too much. He looked round wildly for some instrument; he wanted to hack the picture to pieces; it should not exist another minute. He could see nothing that would serve his purpose; he rummaged about his painting things; somehow he could not find a thing; he was frantic. At last he came upon what he sought, a large scraper, and he pounced on it with a cry of triumph. He seized it as though it were a dagger, and ran to the picture.

As Stroeve told me this he became as excited as when the incident occurred, and he took hold of a dinner-knife on the table between us, and brandished it. He lifted his arm as though to strike, and then, opening his hand, let it fall with a clatter to the ground. He looked at me with a tremulous smile. He did not speak.

'Fire away', I said.

'I don't know what happened to me. I was just going to make a great hole in the picture, I had my arm all ready for the blow, when suddenly I seemed to see it.'

'See what?'

'The picture. It was a work of art. I couldn't touch it. I was afraid.'

Stroeve was silent again, and he stared at me with his mouth open and his round blue eyes starting out of his head.

'It was a great, a wonderful picture. I was seized with awe. I had nearly committed a dreadful crime. I moved a little to see it better, and my foot knocked against the scraper. I shuddered.'

I really felt something of the emotion that had caught him. I was strangely impressed. It was as though I were suddenly transported into a world in which the values were changed. I stood by, at a loss, like a stranger in a land where the reactions of man to familiar things are all different from those he has known. Stroeve tried to talk to me about the picture, but he was incoherent, and I had to guess at what he meant. Strickland had burst the bonds that hitherto had held him. He had found, not himself, as the phrase goes, but a new soul with unsuspected powers. It was not only the bold simplification of the drawing which showed so rich and so singular a personality; it was not only the painting, though the flesh was painted with a passionate sensuality which had in it something miraculous; it was not only the solidity, so that you felt extraordinarily the weight of the body; there was also a spirituality, troubling and new, which led the imagination along unsuspected ways, and suggested dim empty spaces, lit only by the eternal stars, where the soul, all naked, adventured fearful to the discovery of new mysteries.

If I am rhetorical it was because Stroeve was rhetorical. (Do we not know that man in moments of emotion expresses himself naturally in the terms of a novelette?) Stroeve was trying to express a feeling which he had never known before, and he did not know how to put it into common terms. He was like the mystic seeking to describe the ineffable. But one fact was made clear to me: people talk of beauty lightly, and having no feeling for words, they use that one carelessly, so that it loses its force; and the thing it stands for, sharing its name with a hundred trivial objects, is deprived of dignity. They call beautiful a dress, a dog, a sermon; and when they are face to face with Beauty cannot recognize it. The false emphasis with which they try to deck their worthless thoughts blunts their susceptibilities. Like the charlatan who counterfeits a spiritual force he has sometimes felt, they lose the power they have abused. But Stroeve, the unconquerable buffoon, had a love and an understanding of beauty which were as honest and sincere as was his own sincere and honest soul. It meant to him what God means to the believer, and when he saw it he was afraid.

'What did you say to Strickland when you saw him?'

'I asked him to come with me to Holland.'

I was dumbfounded. I could only look at Stroeve in stupid amazement.

'We both loved Blanche. There would have been room for him in my mother's house. I think the company of poor, simple people would have done his soul a great good. I think he might have learnt from them something that would be very useful to him.'

'What did he say?'

'He smiled a little. I suppose he thought me very silly. He said he had other fish to fry.'

I could have wished that Strickland had used some other phrase to indicate his refusal.

'He gave me the picture of Blanche.'

I wondered why Strickland had done that. But I made no re-mark, and for some time we kept silence.

'What have you done with all your things?' I said at last.

'I got a Jew in, and he gave me a round sum for the lot. I'm taking my pictures home with me. Besides them I own nothing in the world now but a box of clothes and a few books.'

'I'm glad you're going home', I said.

I felt that his chance was to put all the past behind him. I hoped that the grief which now seemed intolerable would be softened by the lapse of time, and a merciful forgetfulness would help him to take up once more the burden of life. He was young still, and in a few years he would look back on all his misery with a sadness in which there would be something not unpleasurable. Sooner or later he would marry some honest soul in Holland, and I felt sure he would be happy. I smiled at the thought of the vast number of bad pictures he would paint be-fore he died.

Next day I saw him off for Amsterdam.

XL

For the next month, occupied with my own affairs, I saw no one connected with this lamentable business, and my mind ceased to be occupied with it. But one day, when I was walking along, bent on some errand, I passed Charles Strickland. The sight of him brought back to me all the horror which I was not unwilling to forget, and I felt in me a sudden repulsion for the cause of it. Nodding, for it would have been childish to cut him, I walked on quickly; but in a minute I felt a hand on my shoulder.

'You're in a great hurry', he said cordially.

It was characteristic of him to display geniality with anyone who showed a disinclination to meet him, and the coolness of my greeting can have left him in little doubt of that.

'I am', I answered briefly.

'I'll walk along with you', he said.

'Why?' I asked.

'For the pleasure of your society.'

I did not answer, and he walked by my side silently. We continued thus for perhaps a quarter of a mile. I began to feel a little ridiculous. At last we passed a stationer's, and it occurred to me that I might as well buy some paper. It would be an excuse to be rid of him.

'I'm going in here', I said. 'Good-bye.'

'I'll wait for you.'

I shrugged my shoulders, and went into the shop. I reflected that French paper was bad, and that, foiled of my purpose, I need not burden myself with a purchase I did not need. I asked for something I knew could not be provided, and in a minute came out into the street.

'Did you get what you wanted?' he asked.

'No.'

We walked on in silence, and then came to a place where several streets met. I stopped at the kerb.

'Which way do you go?' I inquired.

'Your way', he smiled.

'I'm going home.'

'I'll come along with you and smoke a pipe.'

'You might wait for an invitation', I retorted frigidly.

'I would if I thought there was any chance of getting one.'

'Do you see that wall in front of you?' I said, pointing.

'Yes.'

'In that case I should have thought you could see also that I don't want your company.'

'I vaguely suspected it, I confess.'

I could not help a chuckle. It is one of the defects of my character that I cannot altogether dislike anyone who makes me laugh. But I pulled myself together.

'I think you're detestable. You're the most loathsome beast that it's ever been my misfortune to meet. Why do you seek the society of someone who hates and despises you?'

'My dear fellow, what the hell do you suppose I care what you think of me?'

'Damn it all,' I said, more violently because I had an inkling my motive was none too creditable, 'I don't want to know you.'

'Are you afraid I shall corrupt you?'

His tone made me feel not a little ridiculous. I knew that he was looking at me sideways, with a sardonic smile.

'I suppose you are hard up', I remarked insolently.

'I should be a damned fool if I thought I had any chance of borrowing money from you.'

'You've come down in the world if you can bring yourself to flatter.'

He grinned.

'You'll never really dislike me so long as I give you the opportunity to get off a good thing now and then.'

I had to bite my lip to prevent myself from laughing. What he said had a hateful truth in it, and another defect of my character is that I enjoy the company of those, however depraved, who can give me a Roland for my Oliver. I began to feel that my abhorrence for Strickland could only be sustained by an effort on my part. I recognized my moral weakness, but saw that my disapprobation had in it already something of a pose; and I knew that if I felt it, his own keen instinct had discovered it too. He was certainly laughing at me up his sleeve. I left him the last word, and sought refuge in a shrug of the shoulders and taciturnity.

XLI

We arrived at the house in which I lived. I would not ask him to come in with me, but walked up the stairs without a word. He followed me, and entered the apartment on my heels. He had not been in it before, but he never gave a glance at the room I had been at pains to make pleasing to the eye. There was a tin of tobacco on the table, and, taking out his pipe, he filled it. He sat down on the only chair that had no arms and tilted himself on the back legs.

'If you're going to make yourself at home, why don't you sit in an arm-chair?' I asked irritably.

'Why are you concerned about my comfort?'

'I'm not,' I retorted, 'but only about my own. It makes me uncomfortable to see someone sit on an uncomfortable chair.'

He chuckled, but did not move. He smoked on in silence, taking no further notice of me, and apparently was absorbed in thought. I wondered why he had come.

Until long habit has blunted the sensibility, there is something disconcerting to the writer in the instinct which causes him to take an interest in the singularities of human nature so absorbing that his moral sense is powerless against it. He recognizes in himself an artistic satisfaction in the contemplation of evil which a little startles him; but sincerity forces him to confess that the disapproval he feels for certain actions is not nearly so strong as his curiosity in their reasons. The character of a scoundrel, logical and complete, has a fascination for his creator which is an outrage to law and order. I expect that Shakespeare devised Iago with a gusto which he never knew when, weaving moonbeams with his fancy, he imagined Desdemona. It may be that in his rogues the writer gratifies instincts deep-rooted in him, which the manners and customs of a civilized world have forced back to the mysterious recesses of the subconscious. In giving to the character of his invention flesh and bones he is giving life to that part of himself which finds no other means of expression. His satisfaction is a sense of liberation.

The writer is more concerned to know than to judge.

There was in my soul a perfectly genuine horror of Strickland, and side by side with it a cold curiosity to discover his motives. I was puzzled by him, and I was eager to see how he regarded the tragedy he had caused in the lives of people who had used him with so much kindness. I applied the scalpel boldly.

'Stroeve told me that picture you painted of his wife was the best thing you've ever done.'

Strickland took his pipe out of his mouth, and a smile lit up his eyes.

'It was great fun to do.'

'Why did you give it him?'

'I'd finished it. It wasn't any good to me.'

'Do you know that Stroeve nearly destroyed it?'

'It wasn't altogether satisfactory.'

He was quiet for a moment or two, then he took his pipe out of his mouth again, and chuckled.

'Do you know that the little man came to see me?'

'Weren't you rather touched by what he had to say?'

'No; I thought it damned silly and sentimental.'

'I suppose it escaped your memory that you'd ruined his life?' I remarked.

He rubbed his bearded chin reflectively.

'He's a very bad painter.'

'But a very good man.'

'And an excellent cook', Strickland added derisively.

His callousness was inhuman, and in my indignation I was not inclined to mince my words.

'As a mere matter of curiosity I wish you'd tell me, have you felt the smallest twinge of remorse for Blanche Stroeve's death?'

I watched his face for some change of expression, but it remained impassive.

'Why should I?' he asked.

'Let me put the facts before you. You were dying, and Dirk Stroeve took you into his own house. He nursed you like a mother. He sacrificed his time and his comfort and his money for you. He snatched you from the jaws of death.'

Strickland shrugged his shoulders.

'The absurd little man enjoys doing things for other people. That's his life.'

'Granting that you owed him no gratitude, were you obliged to go out of your way to take his wife from him? Until you came on the scene they were happy. Why couldn't you leave them alone?'

'What makes you think they were happy?'

'It was evident.'

'You are a discerning fellow. Do you think she could ever have forgiven him for what he did for her?'

'What do you mean by that?'

'Don't you know why he married her?'

I shook my head.

'She was a governess in the family of some Roman prince, and the son of the house seduced her. She thought he was going to marry her. They turned her out into the street neck and crop. She was going to have a baby, and she tried to commit suicide. Stroeve found her and married her.'

'It was just like him. I never knew anyone with so compassionate a heart.'

I had often wondered why that ill-assorted pair had married, but just that explanation had never occurred to me. That was perhaps the cause of the peculiar quality of Dirk's love for his wife. I had noticed in it something more than passion. I remembered also how I had always fancied that her reserve concealed I knew not what; but now I saw in it more than the desire to hide a shameful secret. Her tranquility was like the sullen calm that broods over an island which has been swept by a hurricane. Her cheerfulness was the cheerfulness of despair. Strickland interrupted my reflections with an observation the profound cynicism of which startled me.

'A woman can forgive a man for the harm he does her', he said, 'but she can never forgive him for the sacrifices he makes on her account.'

'It must be reassuring to you to know that you certainly run no risk of incurring the resentment of the women you come in contact with', I retorted.

A slight smile broke on his lips.

'You are always prepared to sacrifice your principles for a repartee', he answered.

'What happened to the child?'

'Oh, it was still-born, three or four months after they were married.'

Then I came to the question which had seemed to me most puzzling.

'Will you tell me why you bothered about Blanche Stroeve at all?'

He did not answer for so long that I nearly repeated it.

'How do I know?' he said at last. 'She couldn't bear the sight of me. It amused me.'

'I see.'

He gave a sudden flash of anger.

'Damn it all, I wanted her.'

But he recovered his temper immediately, and looked at me with a smile.

'At first she was horrified.'

'Did you tell her?'

'There wasn't any need. She knew. I never said a word. She was frightened. At last I took her.'

I do not know what there was in the way he told me this that extraordinarily suggested the violence of his desire. It was disconcerting and rather horrible. His life was strangely divorced from material things, and it was as though his body at times wreaked a fearful revenge on his spirit. The satyr in him suddenly took possession, and he was powerless in the grip of an instinct which had all the strength of the primitive forces of nature. It was an obsession so complete that there was no room in his soul for prudence or gratitude.

'But why did you want to take her away with you?' I asked.

'I didn't', he answered, frowning. 'When she said she was coming I was nearly as surprised as Stroeve. I told her that when I'd had enough of her she'd have to go, and she said she'd risk that.' He paused a little. 'She had a wonderful body, and I wanted to paint a nude. When I'd finished my picture I took no more interest in her.'

'And she loved you with all her heart.'

He sprang to his feet and walked up and down the small room.

'I don't want love. I haven't time for it. It's weakness. I am a man, and sometimes I want a woman. When I've satisfied my passion I'm ready for other things. I can't overcome my desire, but I hate it; it imprisons my spirit; I look forward to the time when I shall be free from all desire and can give myself without hindrance to my work. Because women can do nothing except love, they've given it a ridiculous importance. They want to persuade us that it's the whole of life. It's an insignificant part. I know lust. That's normal and healthy. Love is a disease. Women are the instruments of my pleasure; I have no patience with their claim to be helpmates, partners, companions.'

I had never heard Strickland speak so much at one time. He

132 W. SOMERSET MAUGHAM

spoke with a passion of indignation. But neither here nor else-where do I pretend to give his exact words; his vocabulary was small, and he had no gift for framing sentences, so that one had to piece his meaning together out of interjections, the expression of his face, gestures and hackneyed phrases.

'You should have lived at a time when women were chattels and men the masters of slaves', I said.

'It just happens that I am a completely normal man.'

I could not help laughing at this remark, made in all serious-ness; but he went on, walking up and down the room like a caged beast, intent on expressing what he felt, but found such difficulty in putting coherently.

'When a woman loves you she's not satisfied until she pos-sesses your soul. Because she's weak she has a rage for domina-tion, and nothing less will satisfy her. She has a small mind, and she resents the abstract which she is unable to grasp. She is oc-cupied with material things, and she is jealous of the ideal. The soul of man wanders through the uttermost regions of the uni-verse, and she seeks to imprison it in the circle of her account-book. Do you remember my wife? I saw Blanche little by little trying all her tricks. With infinite patience she prepared to snare me and bind me. She wanted to bring me down to her level; she cared nothing for me, she only wanted me to be hers. She was willing to do everything in the world for me except the one thing I wanted: to leave me alone.'

I was silent for a while.

'What did you expect her to do when you left her?'

'She could have gone back to Stroeve', he said irritably. 'He was ready to take her.'

'You're inhuman', I answered. 'It's as useless to talk to you about these things as to describe colours to a man who was born blind.'

He stopped in front of my chair, and stood looking down at me with an expression in which I read a contemptuous amazement.

'Do you really care a twopenny damn if Blanche Stroeve is alive or dead?'

I thought over his question, for I wanted to answer it truth-fully, at all events to my soul.

'It may be a lack of sympathy in myself if it does not make any great difference to me that she is dead. Life had a great deal to offer her. I think it's terrible that she should have been deprived of it in that cruel way, and I am ashamed because I do not really care.'

'You have not the courage of your convictions. Life has no value. Blanche Stroeve didn't commit suicide because I left her, but because she was a foolish and unbalanced woman. But we've talked about her quite enough; she was an entirely unimportant person. Come, and I'll show you my pictures.'

He spoke as though I were a child that needed to be distracted. I was sore, but not with him so much as with myself. I thought of the happy life that pair had led in the cosy studio in Montmartre, Stroeve and his wife, their simplicity, kindness, and hospitality; it seemed to me cruel that it should have been broken to pieces by a ruthless chance; but the cruellest thing of all was that in fact it made no great difference. The world went on, and no one was a penny the worse for all that wretchedness. I had an idea that Dirk, a man of greater emotional reactions than depth of feeling, would soon forget; and Blanche's life, begun with who knows what bright hopes and what dreams, might just as well have never been lived. It all seemed useless and inane.

Strickland had found his hat, and stood looking at me.

'Are you coming?'

'Why do you seek my acquaintance?' I asked him. 'You know that I hate and despise you.'

He chuckled good-humouredly.

'Your only quarrel with me really is that I don't care a twopenny damn what you think about me.'

I felt my cheeks grow red with sudden anger. It was impossible to make him understand that one might be outraged by his callous selfishness. I longed to pierce his armour of complete indifference. I knew also that in the end there was truth in what he said. Unconsciously, perhaps, we treasure the power we have over people by their regard for our opinion of them, and we hate those upon whom we have no such influence. I suppose it is the bitterest wound to human pride. But I would not let him see that I was put out.

'Is it possible for any man to disregard others entirely?' I said, though more to myself than to him. 'You're dependent on others for everything in existence. It's a preposterous attempt to try to live only for yourself and by yourself. Sooner or later you'll be ill and tired and old, and then you'll crawl back into the herd. Won't you be ashamed when you feel in your heart the desire for comfort and sympathy? You're trying an impossible thing. Sooner or later the human being in you will yearn for the common bonds of humanity.'

'Come and look at my pictures.'

'Have you ever thought of death?'

'Why should I? It doesn't matter.'

I stared at him. He stood before me, motionless, with a mocking smile in his eyes; but for all that, for a moment I had an inkling of a fiery, tortured spirit, aiming at something greater than could be conceived by anything that was bound up with the flesh. I had a fleeting glimpse of a pursuit of the ineffable. I looked at the man before me in his shabby clothes, with his great nose and shining eyes, his red beard and untidy hair; and I had a strange sensation that it was only an envelope, and I was in the presence of a disembodied spirit.

'Let us go and look at your pictures', I said.

XLII

I did not know why Strickland had suddenly offered to show them to me. I welcomed the opportunity. A man's work reveals him. In social intercourse he gives you the surface that he wishes the world to accept, and you can only gain a true knowledge of him by inferences from little actions, of which he is unconscious, and from fleeting expressions, which cross his face unknown to him. Sometimes people carry to such perfection the mask they have assumed that in due course they actually become the person they seem. But in his book or his picture the real man delivers himself defenceless. His pretentiousness will only expose his vacuity. The lath painted to look like iron is seen to be but a lath. No affectation of peculiarity can conceal a commonplace mind. To the acute observer no one can produce the most casual work without disclosing the innermost secrets of his soul.

As I walked up the endless stairs of the house in which Strickland lived, I confess that I was a little excited. It seemed to me that I was on the threshold of a surprising adventure. I looked about the room with curiosity. It was even smaller and more bare than I remembered it. I wondered what those friends of mine would say who demanded vast studios, and vowed they could not work unless all the conditions were to their liking.

'You'd better stand there', he said, pointing to a spot from which, presumably, he fancied I could see to best advantage what he had to show me.

'You don't want me to talk, I suppose', I said.

'No, blast you; I want you to hold your tongue.'

He placed a picture on the easel, and let me look at it for a minute or two; then took it down and put another in its place. I think he showed me about thirty canvases. It was the result of the six years during which he had been painting. He had never sold a picture. The canvases were of different sizes. The smaller were pictures of still-life and the largest were landscapes. There were about half a dozen portraits.

'That is the lot', he said at last.

I wish I could say that I recognized at once their beauty and their great originality. Now that I have seen many of them again and the rest are familiar to me in reproductions, I am astonished that at first sight I was bitterly disappointed. I felt nothing of the peculiar thrill which it is the property of art to give. The impression that Strickland's pictures gave me was disconcerting; and the fact remains, always to reproach me, that I never even thought of buying any. I missed a wonderful chance. Most of them have found their way into museums, and the rest are the treasured possessions of wealthy amateurs. I try to find excuses for myself. I think that my taste is good, but I am conscious that it has no originality. I know very little about painting, and I wander along trails that others have blazed for me. At that time I had the greatest admiration for the Impressionists. I longed to possess a Sisley and a Degas, and I worshipped Manet. His *Olympia* seemed to me the greatest picture of modern times, and *Le Déjeuner sur l'Herbe* moved me profoundly. These works seemed to me the last word in painting.

I will not describe the pictures that Strickland showed me. Descriptions of pictures are always dull, and these, besides, are familiar to all who take an interest in such things. Now that his influence has so enormously affected modern painting, now that others have charted the country which he was among the first to explore, Strickland's pictures, seen for the first time, would find the mind more prepared for them; but it must be remembered that I had never seen anything of the sort. First of all I was taken aback by what seemed to me the clumsiness of his technique. Accustomed to the drawing of the old masters, and convinced that Ingres was the greatest draughtsman of recent times, I thought that Strickland drew very badly. I knew nothing of the simplification at which he aimed. I remembered a still-life of oranges on a plate, and I was bothered because the plate was not round and the oranges were lop-sided. The portraits were a little larger than life-size, and this gave them an ungainly look. To my eyes the faces looked like caricatures. They were painted in a way that was entirely new to me. The landscape puzzled me even more. There were two or three pictures of the forest at Fontainebleau and several of streets in Paris: my first feeling was that they might have been painted by a drunken cab-driver. I was perfectly bewildered. The colour seemed to me extraordinarily crude. It passed through my mind that the whole thing was a stupendous, incomprehensible farce. Now that I look back I am more than ever impressed by Stroeve's acuteness. He saw from the first that here was a revolution in art, and he recognized in its beginnings the genius which now all the world allows.

But if I was puzzled and disconcerted, I was not unimpressed. Even I, in my colossal ignorance, could not but feel that here, trying to express itself, was real power. I was excited and interested. I felt that these pictures had something to say to me that was very important for me to know, but I could not tell what it

was. They seemed to me ugly, but they suggested without disclosing a secret of momentous significance. They were strangely
tantalizing. They gave me an emotion that I could not analyse.
They said something that words were powerless to utter. I
fancy that Strickland saw vaguely some spiritual meaning in
material things that was so strange that he could only suggest it
with halting symbols. It was as though he found in the chaos of
the universe a new pattern, and were attempting clumsily, with
anguish of soul, to set it down. I saw a tormented spirit striving
for the release of expression. I turned to him.

'I wonder if you haven't mistaken your medium', I said.

'What the hell do you mean?'

'I think you're trying to say something; I don't quite know
what it is, but I'm not sure that the best way of saying it is by
means of painting.'

When I imagined that on seeing his pictures I should get a
clue to the understanding of his strange character I was mistaken. They merely increased the astonishment with which he
filled me. I was more at sea than ever. The only thing that
seemed clear to me—and perhaps even this was fanciful—was
that he was passionately striving for liberation from some
power that held him. But what the power was and what line the
liberation would take remained obscure. Each one of us is
alone in the world. He is shut in a tower of brass, and can communicate with his fellows only by signs, and the signs have no
common value, so that their sense is vague and uncertain. We
seek pitifully to convey to others the treasures of our heart, but
they have not the power to accept them, and so we go lonely,
side by side but not together, unable to know our fellows and
unknown by them. We are like people living in a country whose
language they know so little that, with all manner of beautiful
and profound things to say, they are condemned to the banali-
ties of the conversation manual. Their brain is seething with
ideas, and they can only tell you that the umbrella of the gar-
dener's aunt is in the house.

The final impression I received was of a prodigious effort to
express some state of the soul, and in this effect, I fancied, must
be sought the explanation of what so utterly perplexed me. It

was evident that colours and forms had a significance for Strickland that was peculiar to himself. He was under an intolerable necessity to convey something that he felt, and he created them with that intention alone. He did not hesitate to simplify or to distort if he could get nearer to that unknown thing he sought. Facts were nothing to him, for beneath the mass of irrelevant incidents he looked for something significant to himself. It was as though he had become aware of the soul of the universe and were compelled to express it. Though these pictures confused and puzzled me, I could not be unmoved by the emotion that was patent in them; and, I knew not why, I felt in myself a feeling that with regard to Strickland was the last I had ever expected to experience. I felt an overwhelming compassion.

'I think I know now why you surrendered to your feeling for Blanche Stroeve', I said to him.

'Why?'

'I think your courage failed. The weakness of your body communicated itself to your soul. I do not know what infinite yearning possesses you, so that you are driven to a perilous, lonely search for some goal where you expect to find a final release from the spirit that torments you. I see you as the eternal pilgrim to some shrine that perhaps does not exist. I do not know at what inscrutable Nirvana you aim. Do you know yourself? Perhaps it is Truth and Freedom that you seek, and for a moment you thought that you might find release in Love. I think your tired soul sought rest in a woman's arms, and when you found no rest there you hated her. You had no pity for her, because you have no pity for yourself. And you killed her out of fear, because you trembled still at the danger you had barely escaped.'

He smiled dryly and pulled his beard.

'You are a dreadful sentimentalist, my poor friend.'

A week later I heard by chance that Strickland had gone to Marseilles. I never saw him again.

XLIII

Looking back, I realize that what I have written about Charles Strickland must seem very unsatisfactory. I have given incidents that came to my knowledge, but they remain obscure because I do not know the reason that led to them. The strangest, Strickland's determination to become a painter, seems to be arbitrary; and though it must have had causes in the circumstances of his life, I am ignorant of them. From his own conversation I was able to glean nothing. If I were writing a novel, rather than narrating such facts as I know of a curious personality, I should have invented much to account for this change of heart. I think I should have shown a strong vocation in boyhood, crushed by the will of his father or sacrificed to the necessity of earning a living; I should have pictured him impatient of the restraints of life; and in the struggle between his passion for art and the duties of his station I could have aroused sympathy for him. I should so have made him a more imposing figure. Perhaps it would have been possible to see in him a new Prometheus. There was here, maybe, the opportunity for a modern version of the hero who for the good of mankind exposes himself to the agonies of the damned. It is always a moving subject.

On the other hand, I might have found his motives in the influence of the marriage relation. There are a dozen ways in which this might be managed. A latent gift might reveal itself on acquaintance with the painters and writers whose society his wife sought; or domestic incompatibility might turn him upon himself; a love affair might fan into bright flame a fire which I could have shown smouldering dimly in his heart. I think then I should have drawn Mrs Strickland quite differently. I should have abandoned the facts and made her a nagging, tiresome woman, or else a bigoted one with no sympathy for the claims of the spirit. I should have made Strickland's marriage a long torment from which escape was the only possible issue. I think I should have emphasized his patience with the unsuitable mate, and the compassion which made him unwilling to throw off the yoke that oppressed him. I should certainly have eliminated the children.

An effective story might also have been made by bringing him into contact with some old painter whom the pressure of want or the desire for commercial success had made false to the genius of his youth, and who, seeing in Strickland the possibilities which himself had wasted, influenced him to forsake all and follow the divine tyranny of art. I think there would have been something ironic in the picture of the successful old man, rich and honoured, living in another the life which he, though knowing it was the better part, had not had the strength to pursue.

The facts are much duller. Strickland, a boy fresh from school, went into a broker's office without any feeling of distaste. Until he married he led the ordinary life of his fellows, gambling mildly on the Exchange, interested to the extent of a sovereign or two on the result of the Derby or the Oxford and Cambridge Race. I think he boxed a little in his spare time. On his chimney-piece he had photographs of Mrs Langtry and Mary Anderson. He read *Punch* and the *Sporting Times*. He went to dances in Hampstead.

It matters less that for so long I should have lost sight of him. The years during which he was struggling to acquire proficiency in a difficult art were monotonous, and I do not know that there was anything significant in the shifts to which he was put to earn enough money to keep him. An account of them would be an account of the things he had seen happen to other people. I do not think they had any effect on his own character. He must have acquired experiences which would form abundant material for a picaresque novel of modern Paris, but he remained aloof, and judging from his conversation there was nothing in those years that had made a particular impression on him. Perhaps when he went to Paris he was too old to fall a victim to the glamour of his environment. Strange as it may seem, he always appeared to me not only practical, but immensely matter-of-fact. I suppose his life during this period was romantic, but he certainly saw no romance in it. It may be that in order to realize the romance of life you must have something of the actor in you; and, capable of standing outside yourself, you must be able to watch your actions with an interest at once detached and absorbed. But no one was more single-minded than

Strickland. I never knew anyone who was less self-conscious. But it is unfortunate that I can give no description of the arduous steps by which he reached such mastery over his art as he ever acquired; for if I could show him undaunted by failure, by an unceasing effort of courage holding despair at bay, doggedly persistent in the face of self-doubt, which is the artist's bitterest enemy, I might excite some sympathy for a personality which, I am all too conscious, must appear singularly devoid of charm. But I have nothing to go on. I never once saw Strickland at work, nor do I know that anyone else did. He kept the secret of his struggles to himself. If in the loneliness of his studio he wrestled desperately with the Angel of the Lord he never allowed a soul to divine his anguish.

When I come to his connexion with Blanche Stroeve I am exasperated by the fragmentariness of the facts at my disposal. To give my story coherence I should describe the progress of their tragic union, but I know nothing of the three months during which they lived together. I do not know how they got on or what they talked about. After all, there are twenty-four hours in the day, and the summits of emotion can only be reached at rare intervals. I can only imagine how they passed the rest of the time. While the light lasted and so long as Blanche's strength endured, I suppose that Strickland painted, and it must have irritated her when she saw him absorbed in his work. As a mistress she did not then exist for him, but only as a model; and then there were long hours in which they lived side by side in silence. It must have frightened her. When Strickland suggested that in her surrender to him there was a sense of triumph over Dirk Stroeve, because he had come to her help in her extremity, he opened the door to many a dark conjecture. I hope it was not true. It seems to me rather horrible. But who can fathom the subtleties of the human heart? Certainly not those who expect from it only decorous sentiments and normal emotions. When Blanche saw that, notwithstanding his moments of passion, Strickland remained aloof, she must have been filled with dismay, and even in those moments I surmise that she realized that to him she was not an individual, but an instrument of pleasure; he was a stranger still, and she tried to bind him to herself with pathetic arts. She strove to ensnare him with comfort and would not see that comfort meant nothing to him. She was at pains to get him the things to eat that he liked, and would not see that he was indifferent to food. She was afraid to leave him alone. She pursued him with attentions, and when his passion was dormant sought to excite it, for then at least she had the illusion of holding him. Perhaps she knew with her intelligence that the chains she forged only aroused his instinct of destruction, as the plate-glass window makes your fingers itch for half a brick; but her heart, incapable of reason, made her continue on a course she knew was fatal. She must have been very unhappy. But the blindness of love led her to believe what she wanted to be true, and her love was so great that it seemed impossible to her that it should not in return awake an equal love.

But my study of Strickland's character suffers from a graver defect than my ignorance of many facts. Because they were obvious and striking, I have written of his relations to women; and yet they were but an insignificant part of his life. It is an irony that they should so tragically have affected others. His real life consisted of dreams and of tremendously hard work.

Here lies the unreality of fiction. For in men, as a rule, love is but an episode which takes its place among the other affairs of the day, and the emphasis laid on it in novels gives it an importance which is untrue to life. There are few men to whom it is the most important thing in the world, and they are not very interesting ones; even women, with whom the subject is of paramount interest, have a contempt for them. They are flattered and excited by them, but have an uneasy feeling that they are poor creatures. But even during the brief intervals in which they are in love, men do other things which distract their minds; the trades by which they earn their living engage their attention; they are absorbed in sport; they can interest themselves in art. For the most part, they keep their various activities in various compartments, and they can pursue one to the temporary exclusion of the other. They have a faculty of concentration on that which occupies them at the moment, and it irks them if one encroaches on the other. As lovers, the difference between men and women is that women can love all day long, but men only at times.

With Strickland the sexual appetite took a very small place. It was unimportant. It was irksome. His soul aimed elsewhither. He had violent passions, and on occasion desire seized his body so that he was driven to an orgy of lust, but he hated the instincts that robbed him of his self-possession. I think, even, he hated the inevitable partner in his debauchery. When he had regained command over himself, he shuddered at the sight of the woman he had enjoyed. His thoughts floated then serenely in the empyrean, and he felt towards her the horror that perhaps the painted butterfly, hovering about the flowers, feels for the filthy chrysalis from which it has triumphantly emerged. I suppose that art is a manifestation of the sexual instinct. It is the same emotion which is excited in the human heart by the sight of a lovely woman, the Bay of Naples under the yellow moon, and the *Entombment* of Titian. It is possible that Strickland hated the normal release of sex because it seemed to him brutal by comparison with the satisfaction of artistic creation. It seems strange even to myself when I have described a man who was cruel, selfish, brutal, and sensual, to say that he was a great idealist. The fact remains.

He lived more poorly than an artisan. He worked harder. He cared nothing for those things which with most people make life gracious and beautiful. He was indifferent to money. He cared nothing about fame. You cannot praise him because he resisted the temptation to make any of those compromises with the world which most of us yield to. He had no such temptation. It never entered his head that compromise was possible. He lived in Paris more lonely than an anchorite in the deserts of Thebes. He asked nothing from his fellows except that they should leave him alone. He was single-hearted in his aim, and to pursue it he was willing to sacrifice not only himself—many can do that— but others. He had a vision.

Strickland was an odious man, but I still think he was a great one.

XLIV

A certain importance attaches to the views on art of painters, and this is the natural place for me to set down what I know of Strickland's opinion of the great artists of the past. I am afraid I have very little worth noting. Strickland was not a conversationalist, and he had no gift for putting what he had to say in the striking phrase that the listener remembers. He had no wit. His humour, as will be seen if I have in any way succeeded in reproducing the manner of his conversation, was sardonic. His repartee was rude. He made one laugh sometimes by speaking the truth, but this is a form of humour which gains its force only by its unusualness; it would cease to amuse if it were commonly practised.

Strickland was not, I should say, a man of great intelligence, and his views on painting were by no means out of the ordinary. I never heard him speak of those whose work had a certain analogy with his own—of Cézanne, for instance, or of Van Gogh; and I doubt very much if he had ever seen their pictures. He was not greatly interested in the Impressionists. Their technique impressed him, but I fancy that he thought their attitude commonplace. When Stroeve was holding forth at length on the excellence of Monet, he said: 'I prefer Winterhalter.' But I dare say he said it to annoy, and if he did he certainly succeeded.

I am disappointed that I cannot report any extravagances in his opinions on the old masters. There is so much in his character which is strange that I feel it would complete the picture if his views were outrageous. I feel the need to ascribe to him fantastic theories about his predecessors, and it is with a certain sense of disillusion that I confess he thought about them pretty much as does everybody else. I do not believe he knew El Greco. He had a great but somewhat impatient admiration for Velasquez. Chardin delighted him, and Rembrandt moved him to ecstasy. He described the impression that Rembrandt made on him with a coarseness I cannot repeat. The only painter that interested him who was at all unexpected was Brueghel the Elder. I knew very little about him at that time, and Strickland had no power to explain himself. I remember what he said about him because it was so unsatisfactory.

'He's all right', said Strickland. 'I bet he found it hell to paint.'

When later, in Vienna, I saw several of Peter Brueghel's pictures, I thought I understood why he had attracted Strickland's attention. Here, too, was a man with a vision of the world peculiar to himself. I made somewhat copious notes at the time, intending to write something about him, but I have lost them, and have now only the recollection of an emotion. He seemed to see his fellow-creatures grotesquely, and he was angry with them because they were grotesque; life was a confusion of ridiculous, sordid happenings, a fit subject for laughter, and yet it made him sorrowful to laugh. Brueghel gave me the impression of a man striving to express in one medium feelings more appropriate to expression in another, and it may be that it was the obscure consciousness of this that excited Strickland's sympathy. Perhaps both were trying to put down in paint ideas which were more suitable to literature.

Strickland at this time must have been nearly forty-seven.

XLV

I have said already that but for the hazard of a journey to Tahiti I should doubtless never have written this book. It is thither that after many wanderings Charles Strickland came, and it is there that he painted the pictures on which his fame most securely rests. I suppose no artist achieves completely the realization of the dream that obsesses him, and Strickland, harassed incessantly by his struggle with technique, managed, perhaps, less than others to express the vision that he saw with his mind's eye; but in Tahiti the circumstances were favourable to him; he found in his surroundings the accidents necessary for his inspiration to become effective, and his later pictures give at least a suggestion of what he sought. They offer the imagination something new and strange. It is as though in this far country his spirit, that had wandered disembodied, seeking a tenement, at last was able to clothe itself in flesh. To use the hackneyed phrase, here he found himself.

It would seem natural that my visit to this remote island should immediately revive my interest in Strickland, but the work I was engaged in occupied my attention to the exclusion of whatever was irrelevant, and it was not till I had been there some days that I even remembered his connexion with it. After all, I had not seen him for fifteen years, and it was nine since he died. But I think my arrival at Tahiti would have driven out of my head matters of much more immediate importance to me, and even after a week I found it not easy to order myself soberly. I remember that on my first morning I awoke early, and when I came on to the terrace of the hotel no one was stirring. I wandered round to the kitchen, but it was locked, and on a bench outside it a native boy was sleeping. There seemed no chance of breakfast for some time, so I sauntered down to the waterfront. The Chinamen were already busy in their shops. The sky had still the pallor of dawn, and there was a ghostly silence on the lagoon. Ten miles away the island of Murea, like some high fastness of the Holy Grail, guarded its mystery.

I did not altogether believe my eyes. The days that had passed since I left Wellington seemed extraordinary and unusual. Wellington is trim and neat and English; it reminds you of a seaport town on the South Coast. And for three days afterwards the sea was stormy. Grey clouds chased one another across the sky. Then the wind dropped, and the sea was calm and blue. The Pacific is more desolate than other seas; its spaces seem more vast, and the most ordinary journey upon it has somehow the feeling of an adventure. The air you breathe is an elixir which prepares you for the unexpected. Nor is it vouchsafed to man in the flesh to know aught that more nearly suggests the golden realms of fancy than the approach to Tahiti. Murea, the sister isle, comes into view in rocky splendour, rising from the desert sea mysteriously, like the unsubstantial fabric of a magic wand. With its jagged outline it is like a Montserrat of the Pacific, and you may imagine that there Polynesian knights guard with strange rites mysteries unholy for men to know. The beauty of the island is unveiled as diminishing distance shows you in distincter shape its lovely peaks, but it keeps its secret as you sail by, and, darkly inviolable, seems to fold itself together in a stony, inaccessible grimness. It would not surprise you if, as you came near seeking for an opening in the reef, it vanished suddenly from your view, and nothing met your gaze but the blue loneliness of the Pacific.

Tahiti is a lofty green island, with deep folds of a darker green, in which you divine silent valleys; there is mystery in their sombre depths, down which murmur and plash cool streams, and you feel that in those umbrageous places life from immemorial times has been led according to immemorial ways. Even here is something sad and terrible. But the impression is fleeting, and serves only to give a greater acuteness to the enjoyment of the moment. It is like the sadness which you may see in the jester's eyes when a merry company is laughing at his sallies; his lips smile and his jokes are gayer because in the communion of laughter he finds himself more intolerably alone. For Tahiti is smiling and friendly; it is like a lovely woman graciously prodigal of her charm and beauty; and nothing can be more conciliatory than the entrance into the harbour at Papeete. The schooners moored to the quay are trim and neat, the little town along the bay is white and urbane, and the flamboyants, scarlet against the blue sky, flaunt their colour like a cry of passion. They are sensual with an unashamed violence that leaves you breathless. And the crowd that throngs the wharf as the steamer draws alongside is gay and debonair; it is a noisy, cheerful, gesticulating crowd. It is a sea of brown faces. You have an impression of coloured movement against the flaming blue of the sky. Everything is done with a great deal of bustle, the unloading of the baggage, the examination of the customs; and everyone seems to smile at you. It is very hot. The colour dazzles you.

XLVI

I had not been in Tahiti long before I met Captain Nichols. He came in one morning when I was having breakfast on the terrace of the hotel and introduced himself. He had heard that I was interested in Charles Strickland, and announced that he was come to have a talk about him. They are as fond of gossip in Tahiti as in an English village, and one or two inquiries I had made for pictures by Strickland had been quickly spread. I asked the stranger if he had breakfasted.

'Yes; I have my coffee early,' he answered, 'but I don't mind having a drop of whisky.'

I called the Chinese boy.

'You don't think it's too early?' said the Captain.

'You and your liver must decide that between you', I replied.

'I'm practically a teetotaller', he said, as he poured himself out a good half-tumbler of Canadian Club.

When he smiled he showed broken and discoloured teeth. He was a very lean man, of no more than average height, with grey hair cut short and a stubby grey moustache. He had not shaved for a couple of days. His face was deeply lined, burned brown by long exposure to the sun, and he had a pair of small blue eyes which were astonishingly shifty. They moved quickly, following my smallest gesture, and gave him the look of a very thorough rogue. But at the moment he was all heartiness and good-fellowship. He was dressed in a bedraggled suit of khaki, and his hands would have been all the better for a wash.

'I knew Strickland well', he said, as he leaned back in his chair and lit the cigar I had offered him. 'It's through me he came out to the islands.'

'Where did you meet him?' I asked.

'In Marseilles.'

'What were you doing there?'

He gave me an ingratiating smile.

'Well, I guess I was on the beach.'

My friend's appearance suggested that he was now in the same predicament, and I prepared myself to cultivate an agreeable acquaintance. The society of beach-combers always repays the small pains you need be at to enjoy it. They are easy of approach and affable in conversation. They seldom put on airs, and the offer of a drink is a sure way to their hearts. You need no laborious steps to enter upon familiarity with them, and you can earn not only their confidence, but their gratitude, by turning an attentive ear to their discourse. They look upon conversation as the great pleasure of life, thereby proving the excellence of their civilization, and for the most part they are entertaining talkers. The extent of their experience is pleasantly balanced by the fertility of their imagination. It cannot be said that they are without guile, but they have a tolerant respect for the law, when the law is supported by strength. It is hazardous to play poker with them, but their ingenuity adds a peculiar excitement to the best game in the world. I came to know Captain Nichols very well before I left Tahiti, and I am the richer for his acquaintance. I do not consider that the cigars and whisky he consumed at my expense (he always refused cocktails, since he was practically a teetotaller), and the few dollars, borrowed with a civil air of conferring a favour upon me, that passed from my pocket to his, were in any way equivalent to the entertainment he afforded me. I remained his debtor. I should be sorry if my conscience, insisting on a rigid attention to the matter in hand, forced me to dismiss him in a couple of lines.

I do not know why Captain Nichols first left England. It was a matter upon which he was reticent, and with persons of his kidney a direct question is never very discreet. He hinted at undeserved misfortune, and there is no doubt that he looked upon himself as the victim of injustice. My fancy played with the various forms of fraud and violence, and I agreed with him sympathetically when he remarked that the authorities in the old country were so damned technical. But it was nice to see that any unpleasantness he had endured in his native land had not impaired his ardent patriotism. He frequently declared that England was the finest country in the world, sir, and he felt a lively superiority over Americans, Colonials, Dagos, Dutchmen, and Kanakas.

But I do not think he was a happy man. He suffered from dyspepsia, and he might often be seen sucking a tablet of pepsin; in the morning his appetite was poor; but this affliction alone would hardly have impaired his spirits. He had a greater cause of discontent with life than this. Eight years before he had rashly married a wife. There are men whom a merciful Providence has undoubtedly ordained to a single life, but who from wilfulness or through circumstances they could not cope with

have flown in the face of its decrees. There is no object more
deserving of pity than the married bachelor. Of such was Captain Nichols. I met his wife. She was a woman of twenty-eight,
I should think, though of a type whose age is always doubtful;
for she cannot have looked different when she was twenty, and
at forty would look no older. She gave me an impression of extraordinary tightness. Her plain face with its narrow lips was
tight, her skin was stretched tightly over her bones, her smile
was tight, her hair was tight, her clothes were tight, and the
white drill she wore had all the effect of black bombazine. I
could not imagine why Captain Nichols had married her, and
having married her why he had not deserted her. Perhaps he
had, often, and his melancholy arose from the fact that he
could never succeed. However far he went and in howsoever
secret a place he hid himself, I felt sure that Mrs Nichols, inexorable as fate and remorseless as conscience, would presently
rejoin him. He could as little escape her as the cause can escape
the effect.

The rogue, like the artist and perhaps the gentleman, belongs
to no class. He is not embarrassed by the *sans-gêne* of the hobo,
nor put out of countenance by the etiquette of the prince. But
Mrs Nichols belonged to the well-defined class, of late become
vocal, which is known as the lower-middle. Her father, in fact,
was a policeman. I am certain that he was an efficient one. I do
not know what her hold was on the Captain, but I do not think
it was love. I never heard her speak, but it may be that in private
she had a copious conversation. At any rate Captain Nichols
was frightened to death of her. Sometimes, sitting with me on
the terrace of the hotel, he would become conscious that she
was walking in the road outside. She did not call him; she gave
no sign that she was aware of his existence; she merely walked
up and down composedly. Then a strange uneasiness would
seize the Captain; he would look at his watch and sigh.

'Well, I must be off', he said.

Neither wit nor whisky could detain him then. Yet he was a
man who had faced undaunted hurricane and typhoon, and
would not have hesitated to fight a dozen unarmed niggers with
nothing but a revolver to help him. Sometimes Mrs Nichols

would send her daughter, a pale-faced, sullen child of seven, to the hotel.

'Mother wants you', she said, in a whining tone.

'Very well, my dear', said Captain Nichols.

He rose to his feet at once, and accompanied his daughter along the road. I suppose it was a very pretty example of the triumph of spirit over matter, and so my digression has at least the advantage of a moral.

XLVII

I have tried to put some connexion into the various things Captain Nichols told me about Strickland, and I here set them down in the best order I can. They made one another's acquaintance during the latter part of the winter following my last meeting with Strickland in Paris. How he had passed the intervening months I do not know, but life must have been very hard, for Captain Nichols saw him first in the Asile de Nuit. There was a strike at Marseilles at the time, and Strickland, having come to the end of his resources, had apparently found it impossible to earn the small sum he needed to keep body and soul together.

The Asile de Nuit is a large stone building where pauper and vagabond may get a bed for a week, provided their papers are in order and they can persuade the friars in charge that they are working-men. Captain Nichols noticed Strickland for his size and his singular appearance among the crowd that waited for the doors to open; they waited listlessly, some walking to and fro, some leaning against the wall, and others seated on the kerb with their feet in the gutter; and when they filed into the office he heard the monk who read his papers address him in English. But he did not have a chance to speak to him, since, as he entered the common-room, a monk came in with a huge Bible in his arms, mounted a pulpit which was at the end of the room, and began the service which the wretched outcasts had to endure as the price of their lodging. He and Strickland were assigned to different rooms, and when, thrown out of bed at five in the morning by a stalwart monk, he had made his bed and

washed his face, Strickland had already disappeared. Captain
Nichols wandered about the streets for an hour of bitter cold,
and then made his way to the Place Victor Gélu, where the
sailor-men are wont to congregate. Dozing against the pedestal
of a statue, he saw Strickland again. He gave him a kick to
awaken him.

'Come and have breakfast, mate', he said.

'Go to hell', answered Strickland.

I recognized my friend's limited vocabulary, and I prepared
to regard Captain Nichols as a trustworthy witness.

'Busted?' asked the Captain.

'Blast you', answered Strickland.

'Come along with me. I'll get you some breakfast.'

After a moment's hesitation, Strickland scrambled to his feet,
and together they went to the Bouchée de Pain, where the hungry are given a wedge of bread, which they must eat there and
then, for it is forbidden to take it away; and then to the Cuillère
de Soupe, where for a week, at eleven and four, you may get a
bowl of thin, salt soup. The two buildings are placed far apart,
so that only the starving should be tempted to make use of them.
So they had breakfast, and so began the queer companionship
of Charles Strickland and Captain Nichols.

They must have spent something like four months at Marseilles in one another's society. Their career was devoid of adventure, if by adventure you mean unexpected or thrilling incident,
for their days were occupied in the pursuit of enough money to
get a night's lodging and such food as would stay the pangs of
hunger. But I wish I could give here the pictures, coloured and
racy, which Captain Nichols' vivid narrative offered to the imagination. His account of their discoveries in the low life of a seaport town would have made a charming book, and in the various
characters that came their way the student might easily have
found matter for a very complete dictionary of rogues. But I must
content myself with a few paragraphs. I received the impression
of a life intense and brutal, savage, multi-coloured, and vivacious. It made the Marseilles that I knew, gesticulating and
sunny, with its comfortable hotels and its restaurants crowded
with the well-to-do, tame and commonplace. I envied men who

had seen with their own eyes the sights that Captain Nichols described.

When the doors of the Asile de Nuit were closed to them, Strickland and Captain Nichols sought the hospitality of Tough Bill. This was the master of a sailors' boarding-house, a huge mulatto with a heavy fist, who gave the stranded mariner food and shelter till he found him a berth. They lived with him a month, sleeping with a dozen others, Swedes, Negroes, Brazilians, on the floor of the two bare rooms in his house which he assigned to his charges; and every day they went with him to the Place Victor Gélu, whither came ships' captains in search of a man. He was married to an American woman, obese and slatternly, fallen to this pass by Heaven knows what process of degradation, and every day the boarders took it in turns to help her with the housework. Captain Nichols looked upon it as a smart piece of work on Strickland's part that he had got out of this by painting a portrait of Tough Bill. Tough Bill not only paid for the canvas, colours, and brushes, but gave Strickland a pound of smuggled tobacco into the bargain. For all I know, this picture may still adorn the parlour of the tumble-down little house somewhere near the Quai de la Joliette, and I suppose it could now be sold for fifteen hundred pounds. Strickland's idea was to ship on some vessel bound for Australia or New Zealand, and from there make his way to Samoa or Tahiti. I do not know how he had come upon the notion of going to the South Seas, though I remember that his imagination had long been haunted by an island, all green and sunny, encircled by a sea more blue than is found in Northern latitudes. I suppose that he clung to Captain Nichols because he was acquainted with those parts, and it was Captain Nichols who persuaded him that he would be more comfortable in Tahiti.

'You see, Tahiti's French', he explained to me. 'And the French aren't so damned technical.'

I thought I saw his point.

Strickland had no papers, but that was not a matter to disconcert Tough Bill when he saw a profit (he took the first month's wages of the sailor for whom he found a berth), and he provided Strickland with those of an English stoker who had providentially died on his hands. But both Captain Nichols and Strickland were bound East, and it chanced that the only opportunities for signing on were with ships sailing West. Twice Strickland refused a berth on tramps sailing for the United States, and once on a collier going to Newcastle. Tough Bill had no patience with an obstinacy which could only result in loss to himself, and on the last occasion he flung both Strickland and Captain Nichols out of his house without more ado. They found themselves once more adrift.

Tough Bill's fare was seldom extravagant, and you rose from his table almost as hungry as you sat down, but for some days they had good reason to regret it. They learned what hunger was. The Cuillère de Soupe and the Asile de Nuit were both closed to them, and their only sustenance was the wedge of bread which the Bouchée de Pain provided. They slept where they could, sometimes in an empty truck on a siding near the station, sometimes in a cart behind a warehouse; but it was bitterly cold, and after an hour or two of uneasy dozing they would tramp the streets again. What they felt the lack of most bitterly was tobacco, and Captain Nichols, for his part, could not do without it; he took to hunting the 'Can o' Beer' for cigarette-ends and the butt-ends of cigars which the promenaders of the night before had thrown away.

'I've tasted worse smoking mixtures in a pipe', he added with a philosophic shrug of his shoulders, as he took a couple of cigars from the case I offered him, putting one in his mouth and the other in his pocket.

Now and then they made a bit of money. Sometimes a mail steamer would come in, and Captain Nichols, having scraped acquaintance with the time-keeper, would succeed in getting the pair of them a job as stevedores. When it was an English boat, they would dodge into the forecastle and get a hearty breakfast from the crew. They took the risk of running against one of the ship's officers and being hustled down the gangway with the toe of a boot to speed their going.

'There's no harm in a kick in the hindquarters when your belly's full', said Captain Nichols, 'and personally I never take it in bad part. An officer's got to think about discipline.'

I had a lively picture of Captain Nichols flying headlong down a narrow gangway before the uplifted foot of an angry mate, and, like a true Englishman, rejoicing in the spirit of the Mercantile Marine.

There were often odd jobs to be got about the fish-market. Once they each of them earned a franc by loading trucks with innumerable boxes of oranges that had been dumped down on the quay. One day they had a stroke of luck: one of the boarding-masters got a contract to paint a tramp that had come in from Madagascar round the Cape of Good Hope, and they spent several days on a plank hanging over the side, covering the rusty hull with paint. It was a situation that must have appealed to Strickland's sardonic humour. I asked Captain Nichols how he bore himself during these hardships.

'Never knew him say a cross word', answered the Captain. 'He'd be a bit surly sometimes, but when we hadn't a bite since morning, and we hadn't even got the price of a lie down at the Chink's, he'd be as lively as a cricket.'

I was not surprised at this. Strickland was just the man to rise superior to circumstances, when they were such as to occasion despondency in most; but whether this was due to equanimity of soul or to contradictoriness it would be difficult to say.

The Chink's Head was the name the beach-combers gave to a wretched inn off the Rue Bouterie, kept by a one-eyed China-man, where for six sous you could sleep in a cot and for three on the floor. Here they made friends with others in as desperate condition as themselves, and when they were penniless and the night was bitter cold, they were glad to borrow from anyone who had earned a stray franc during the day the price of a roof over their heads. They were not niggardly, these tramps, and he who had money did not hesitate to share it among the rest. They belonged to all the countries in the world, but this was no bar to good-fellowship; for they felt themselves freemen of a country whose frontiers include them all, the great country of Cockaigne.

'But I guess Strickland was an ugly customer when he was roused', said Captain Nichols, reflectively. 'One day we ran into Tough Bill in the Place, and he asked Charlie for the papers he'd given him.'

' "You'd better come and take them if you want them", says Charlie.

'He was a powerful fellow, Tough Bill, but he didn't quite like the look of Charlie, so he began cursing him. He called him pretty near every name he could lay hands on, and when Tough Bill began cursing it was worth listening to him. Well, Charlie stuck it for a bit, then he stepped forward and he just said: "Get out, you bloody swine." It wasn't so much what he said, but the way he said it. Tough Bill never spoke another word; you could see him go yellow, and he walked away as if he'd remembered he had a date.'

Strickland, according to Captain Nichols, did not use exactly the words I have given, but since this book is meant for family reading I have thought it better, at the expense of truth, to put into his mouth expressions familiar to the domestic circle.

Now, Tough Bill was not the man to put up with humiliation at the hands of a common sailor. His power depended on his prestige, and first one, then another, of the sailors who lived in his house told them that he had sworn to do Strickland in.

One night Captain Nichols and Strickland were sitting in one of the bars of the Rue Bouterie. The Rue Bouterie is a narrow street of one-storeyed houses, each house consisting of but one room; they are like booths in a crowded fair or the cages of animals in a circus. At every door you see a woman. Some lean lazily against the side-posts, humming to themselves or calling to the passer-by in a raucous voice, and some listlessly read. They are French, Italian, Spanish, Japanese, coloured; some are fat and some are thin; and under the thick paint on their faces, the heavy smears on their eyebrows, and the scarlet of their lips, you see the lines of age and the scars of dissipation. Some wear black shifts and flesh-coloured stockings; some with curly hair, dyed yellow, are dressed like little girls in short muslin frocks. Through the open door you see a red-tiled floor, a large wooden bed, and on a deal table a ewer and a basin. A motley crowd saunters along the street—Lascars off a P. and O., blond Northmen from a Swedish barque, Japanese from a man-of-war, English sailors, Spaniards, pleasant-looking fellows from a French cruiser, Negroes off an American tramp. By day it is merely sordid, but at night, lit only by the lamps in the little huts, the street has a sinister beauty. The hideous lust that pervades the air is oppressive and horrible, and yet there is something mysterious in the sight which haunts and troubles you. You feel I know not what primitive force which repels and yet fascinates you. Here all the decencies of civilization are swept away, and you feel that men are face to face with a sombre reality. There is an atmosphere that is at once intense and tragic.

In the bar in which Strickland and Nichols sat a mechanical piano was loudly grinding out dance music. Round the room people were sitting at tables, here half a dozen sailors uproariously drunk, there a group of soldiers; and in the middle, crowded together, couples were dancing. Bearded sailors with brown faces and large horny hands clasped their partners in a tight embrace. The women wore nothing but a shift. Now and then two sailors would get up and dance together. The noise was deafening. People were singing, shouting, laughing; and when a man gave a long kiss to the girl sitting on his knees, catcalls from the English sailors increased the din. The air was heavy with the dust beaten up by the heavy boots of the men, and grey with smoke. It was very hot. Behind the bar was seated a woman nursing her baby. The waiter, an undersized youth with a flat, spotty face, hurried to and fro carrying a tray laden with glasses of beer.

In a little while Tough Bill, accompanied by two huge Negroes, came in, and it was easy to see that he was already three parts drunk. He was looking for trouble. He lurched against a table at which three soldiers were sitting and knocked over a glass of beer. There was an angry altercation, and the owner of the bar stepped forward and ordered Tough Bill to go. He was a hefty fellow, in the habit of standing no nonsense from his customers, and Tough Bill hesitated. The landlord was not a man he cared to tackle, for the police were on his side, and with an oath he turned on his heel. Suddenly he caught sight of Strickland. He rolled up to him. He did not speak. He gathered the spittle in his mouth and spat full in Strickland's face. Strickland seized his glass and flung it at him. The dancers stopped suddenly still. There was an instant of complete silence, but when

Tough Bill threw himself on Strickland the lust of battle seized them all, and in a moment there was a confused scrimmage. Tables were overturned, glasses crashed to the ground. There was a hellish row. The women scattered to the door and behind the bar. Passers-by surged in from the street. You heard curses in every tongue, the sound of blows, cries; and in the middle of the room a dozen men were fighting with all their might. On a sudden the police rushed in, and everyone who could made for the door. When the bar was more or less cleared, Tough Bill was lying insensible on the floor with a great gash in his head. Captain Nichols dragged Strickland, bleeding from a wound in his arm, his clothes in rags, into the street. His own face was covered with blood from a blow on the nose.

'I guess you'd better get out of Marseilles before Tough Bill comes out of hospital', he said to Strickland, when they had got back to the Chink's Head and were cleaning themselves.

'This beats cock-fighting', said Strickland.

I could see his sardonic smile.

Captain Nichols was anxious. He knew Tough Bill's vindictiveness. Strickland had downed the mulatto twice, and the mulatto, sober, was a man to be reckoned with. He would bide his time stealthily. He would be in no hurry, but one night Strickland would get a knife-thrust in his back, and in a day or two the corpse of a nameless beachcomber would be fished out of the dirty water of the harbour. Nichols went next evening to Tough Bill's house and made inquiries. He was in hospital still, but his wife, who had been to see him, said he was swearing hard to kill Strickland when they let him out.

A week passed.

'That's what I always say,' reflected Captain Nichols, 'when you hurt a man, hurt him bad. It gives you a bit of time to look about and think what you'll do next.'

Then Strickland had a bit of luck. A ship bound for Australia had sent to the Sailors' Home for a stoker in place of one who had thrown himself overboard off Gibraltar in an attack of delirium tremens.

'You double down to the harbour, my lad,' said the Captain to Strickland, 'and sign on. You've got your papers.'

Strickland set off at once, and that was the last Captain Nichols saw of him. The ship was only in port for six hours, and in the evening Captain Nichols watched the vanishing smoke from her funnels as she ploughed East through the wintry sea.

I have narrated all this as best I could, because I like the contrast of these episodes with the life that I had seen Strickland live in Ashley Gardens when he was occupied with stocks and shares; but I am aware that Captain Nichols was an outrageous liar, and I dare say there is not a word of truth in anything he told me. I should not be surprised to learn that he had never seen Strickland in his life, and owed his knowledge of Marseilles to the pages of a magazine.

XLVIII

It is here that I purposed to end my book. My first idea was to begin it with the account of Strickland's last years in Tahiti and with his horrible death, and then to go back and relate what I knew of his beginnings. This I meant to do, not from wilfulness, but because I wished to leave Strickland setting out with I know not what fancies in his lonely soul for the unknown islands which fired his imagination. I liked the picture of him, starting at the age of forty-seven, when most men have already settled comfortably in a groove, for a new world. I saw him, the sea grey under the mistral and foam-flecked, watching the vanishing coast of France, which he was destined never to see again; and I thought there was something gallant in his bearing and dauntless in his soul. I wished so to end on a note of hope. It seemed to emphasize the unconquerable spirit of man. But I could not manage it. Somehow I could not get into my story, and after trying once or twice I had to give it up; I started from the beginning in the usual way, and made up my mind I could only tell what I knew of Strickland's life in the order in which I learnt the facts.

Those that I have now are fragmentary. I am in the position of a biologist who from a single bone must reconstruct not only the appearance of an extinct animal, but its habits. Strickland made no particular impression on the people who came in contact with him in Tahiti. To them he was no more than a beachcomber in constant need of money, remarkable only for the peculiarity that he painted pictures which seemed to them absurd; and it was not till he had been dead for some years and agents came from the dealers in Paris and Berlin to look for any pictures which might still remain on the island, that they had any idea that among them had dwelt a man of consequence. They remembered then that they could have bought for a song canvases which now were worth large sums, and they could not forgive themselves for the opportunity which had escaped them. There was a Jewish trader called Cohen, who had come by one of Strickland's pictures in a singular way. He was a little old Frenchman, with soft kind eyes and a pleasant smile, half trader and half seaman, who owned a cutter in which he wandered boldly among the Paumotus and the Marquesas, taking out trade goods and bringing back copra, shell, and pearls. I went to see him because I was told he had a large black pearl which he was willing to sell cheaply, and when I discovered that it was beyond my means I began to talk to him about Strickland. He had known him well.

'You see, I was interested in him because he was a painter', he told me. 'We don't get many painters in the islands, and I was sorry for him because he was such a bad one. I gave him his first job. I had a plantation on the peninsula, and I wanted a white overseer. You never get any work out of the natives unless you have a white man over them. I said to him: "You'll have plenty of time for painting, and you can earn a bit of money." I knew he was starving, but I offered him good wages.'

'I can't imagine that he was a very satisfactory overseer', I said, smiling.

'I made allowances. I have always had a sympathy for artists. It is in our blood, you know. But he only remained a few months. When he had enough money to buy paints and canvases he left me. The place had got hold of him by then, and he wanted to get away into the bush. But I continued to see him now and then. He would turn up in Papeete every few months and stay a little while; he'd get money out of someone or other and then disappear again. It was on one of these visits that he came to me and asked for the loan of two hundred francs. He looked as if he hadn't had a meal for a week, and I hadn't the heart to refuse him. Of course, I never expected to see my money again. Well, a year later he came to see me once more, and he brought a picture with him. He did not mention the money he owed me, but he said: "Here is a picture of your plantation that I've painted for you." 'I looked at it. I did not know what to say, but of course I thanked him, and when he had gone away I showed it to my wife.'

'What was it like?' I asked.

'Do not ask me. I could not make head or tail of it. I never saw such a thing in my life. "What shall we do with it?" I said to my wife. "We can never hang it up", she said. "People would laugh at us," So she took it into an attic and put it away with all sorts of rubbish, for my wife can never throw anything away. It is her mania. Then, imagine to yourself, just before the war my brother wrote to me from Paris, and said: "Do you know anything about an English painter who lived in Tahiti? It appears that he was a genius, and his pictures fetch large prices. See if you can lay your hands on anything and send it to me. There's money to be made." So I said to my wife: "What about that picture that Strickland gave me? Is it possible that it is still in the attic?" "Without doubt", she answered, "for you know that I never throw anything away. It is my mania." We went up to the attic, and there, among I know not what rubbish that had been gathered during the thirty years we have inhabited that house, was the picture. I looked at it again, and I said: "Who would have thought that the overseer of my plantation on the peninsula, to whom I lent two hundred francs, had genius? Do you see anything in the picture?" "No," she said, "it does not resemble the plantation and I have never seen coconuts with blue leaves; but they are mad in Paris, and it may be that your brother will be able to sell it for the two hundred francs you lent Strickland." Well, we packed it up and we sent it to my brother. And at last I received a letter from him. What do you think he said? "I received your picture," he said, "and I confess I thought it was a joke that you had played on me. I would not have given the cost of postage for the picture. I was half afraid to show it to the gentleman who had spoken to me about it. Imagine my surprise when he said it was a masterpiece, and offered me thirty thousand francs. I dare say he would have paid more, but frankly I was so taken aback that I lost my head; I accepted the offer before I was able to collect myself." '

Then Monsieur Cohen said an admirable thing.

'I wish that poor Strickland had been still alive. I wonder what he would have said when I gave him twenty-nine thousand eight hundred francs for his picture.'

XLIX

I lived at the Hôtel de la Fleur, and Mrs Johnson, the proprietress, had a sad story to tell of lost opportunity. After Strickland's death certain of his effects were sold by auction in the market-place at Papeete, and she went to it herself because there was among the truck an American stove she wanted. She paid twenty-seven francs for it.

'There were a dozen pictures,' she told me, 'but they were unframed, and nobody wanted them. Some of them sold for as much ten francs, but mostly they went for five or six. Just think, if I had bought them I should be a rich woman now.'

But Tiaré Johnson would never under any circumstances have been rich. She could not keep money. The daughter of a native and an English sea-captain settled in Tahiti, when I knew her she was a woman of fifty, who looked older, and of enormous proportions. Tall and extremely stout, she would have been of imposing presence if the great good-nature of her face had not made it impossible for her to express anything but kindliness. Her arms were like legs of mutton, her breasts like giant cabbages; her face, broad and fleshy, gave you an impression of almost indecent nakedness, and vast chin succeeded to vast chin. I do not know how many of them there were. They fell away voluminously into the capaciousness of her bosom. She was dressed usually in a pink Mother Hubbard, and she wore all day long a large straw hat. But when she let down her hair, which she did now and then, for she was vain of it, you saw that it was long and dark and curly; and her eyes had remained young and vivacious. Her laughter was the most catching I ever heard; it would begin, a low peal in her throat, and would grow louder and louder till her whole vast body shook. She loved three things—a joke, a glass of wine, and a handsome man. To have known her is a privilege.

She was the best cook on the island, and she adored good food. From morning till night you saw her sitting on a low chair in the kitchen, surrounded by a Chinese cook and two or three native girls, giving her orders, chatting sociably with all and sundry, and tasting the savoury messes she devised. When she wished to do honour to a friend she cooked the dinner with her own hands. Hospitality was a passion with her, and there was no one on the island who need go without a dinner when there was anything to eat at the Hôtel de la Fleur. She never turned her customers out of her house because they did not pay their bills. She always hoped they would pay when they could. There was one man there who had fallen on adversity, and to him she had given board and lodging for several months. When the Chinese laundryman refused to wash for him without payment she had sent his things to be washed with hers. She could not allow the poor fellow to go about in a dirty shirt, she said, and since he was a man, and men must smoke, she gave him a franc a day for cigarettes. She used him with the same affability as those of her clients who paid their bills once a week.

Age and obesity had made her inapt for love, but she took a keen interest in the amatory affairs of the young. She looked upon venery as the natural occupation for men and women, and was ever ready with precept and example from her own wide experience.

'I was not fifteen when my father found that I had a lover,' she said. 'He was third mate on the *Tropic Bird*. A good-looking boy.'

She sighed a little. They say a woman always remembers her first lover with affection; but perhaps she does not always remember him.

'My father was a sensible man.'

'What did he do?' I asked.

'He thrashed me within an inch of my life, and then he made me marry Captain Johnson. I did not mind. He was older, of course, but he was good-looking too.'

Tiaré—her father had called her by the name of the white, scented flower which, they tell you, if you have once smelt, will always draw you back to Tahiti in the end, however far you may have roamed—Tiaré remembered Strickland very well.

'He used to come here sometimes, and I used to see him walking about Papeete. I was sorry for him, he was so thin, and he never had any money. When I heard he was in town, I used to send a boy to find him and make him come to dinner with me. I got him a job once or twice, but he couldn't stick to anything. After a little while he wanted to get back to the bush, and one morning he would be gone.'

Strickland reached Tahiti about six months after he left Marseilles. He worked his passage on a sailing vessel that was making the trip from Auckland to San Francisco, and he arrived with a box of paints, an easel, and a dozen canvases. He had a few pounds in his pocket, for he had found work in Sydney, and he took a small room in a native house outside the town. I think the moment he reached Tahiti he felt himself at home. Tiaré told me that he said to her once:

'I'd been scrubbing the deck, and all at once a chap said to me: "Why, there it is." And I looked up and I saw the outline of the island. I knew right away that there was the place I'd been looking for all my life. Then we came near, and I seemed to recognize it. Sometimes when I walk about it all seems familiar. I could swear I've lived here before.'

'Sometimes it takes them like that', said Tiaré. 'I've known men come on shore for a few hours while their ship was taking in cargo, and never go back. And I've known men who came here to be in an office for a year, and they cursed the place, and when they went away they took their dying oath they'd hang themselves before they came back again, and in six months you'd see them land once more, and they'd tell you they couldn't live anywhere else.'

L

I have an idea that some men are born out of their due place. Accident has cast them amid certain surroundings, but they have always a nostalgia for a home they know not. They are strangers in their birthplace, and the leafy lanes they have known from childhood or the populous streets in which they have played, remain but a place of passage. They may spend their whole lives aliens among their kindred and remain aloof among the only scenes they have ever known. Perhaps it is this sense of strangeness that sends men far and wide in the search for something permanent, to which they may attach themselves. Perhaps some deep-rooted atavism urges the wanderer back to lands which his ancestors left in the dim beginnings of history. Sometimes a man hits upon a place to which he mysteriously feels that he belongs. Here is the home he sought, and he will settle amid scenes that he has never seen before, among men he has never known, as though they were familiar to him from his birth. Here at last he finds rest.

I told Tiaré the story of a man I had known at St Thomas's Hospital. He was a Jew named Abraham, a blond, rather stout young man, shy and very unassuming; but he had remarkable gifts. He entered the hospital with a scholarship, and during the five years of the curriculum gained every prize that was open to him. He was made house-physician and house-surgeon. His brilliance was allowed by all. Finally he was elected to a position on the staff, and his career was assured. So far as human things can be predicted, it was certain that he would rise to the greatest heights of his profession. Honours and wealth awaited him. Before he entered upon his new duties he wished to take a holiday, and, having no private means, he went as surgeon on a tramp steamer to the Levant. It did not generally carry a doctor, but one of the senior surgeons at the hospital knew a director of the line, and Abraham was taken as a favour.

In a few weeks the authorities received his resignation of the coveted position on the staff. It created profound astonishment, and wild rumours were current. Whenever a man does anything unexpected, his fellows ascribe it to the most discreditable motives. But there was a man ready to step into Abraham's shoes, and Abraham was forgotten. Nothing more was heard of him. He vanished.

It was perhaps ten years later that one morning on board ship, about to land at Alexandria, I was bidden to line up with the other passengers for the doctor's examination. The doctor was a stout man in shabby clothes, and when he took off his hat I noticed that he was very bald. I had an idea that I had seen him before. Suddenly I remembered.

'Abraham', I said.

He turned to me with a puzzled look, and then, recognizing me, seized my hand. After expressions of surprise on either side, hearing that I meant to spend the night in Alexandria, he asked me to dine with him at the English Club. When we met again I declared my astonishment at finding him there. It was a very modest position that he occupied, and there was about him an air of straitened circumstance. Then he told me his story. When he set out on his holiday in the Mediterranean he had every intention of returning to London and his appointment at St Thomas's. One morning the tramp docked at Alexandria, and from the deck he looked at the city, white in the sunlight, and the crowd on the wharf; he saw the natives in their shabby gabardines, the blacks from the Sudan, the noisy throng of Greeks and Italians, the grave Turks in tarbooshes, the sunshine and the blue sky; and something happened to him. He could not describe it. It was like a thunder-clap, he said, and then, dissatisfied with this, he said it was like a revelation. Something seemed to twist his heart, and suddenly he felt an exultation, a sense of wonderful freedom. He felt himself at home, and he made up his mind there and then, in a minute, that he would live the rest of his life in Alexandria. He had no great difficulty in leaving the ship, and in twenty-four hours, with all his belongings, he was on shore.

'The Captain must have thought you as mad as a hatter', I smiled.

'I didn't care what anybody thought. It wasn't I that acted, but something stronger within me. I thought I would go to a little Greek hotel, while I looked about, and I felt I knew where to find one. And do you know, I walked straight there, and when I saw it I recognized it at once.'

'Had you been to Alexandria before?'

'No; I'd never been out of England in my life.'

Presently he entered the Government service, and there he had been ever since.

'Have you never regretted it?'

'Never, not for a minute. I earn just enough to live upon, and I'm satisfied. I ask nothing more than to remain as I am till I die. I've had a wonderful life.'

I left Alexandria next day, and I forgot about Abraham till a little while ago, when I was dining with another old friend in the profession, Alec Carmichael, who was in England on short leave. I ran across him in the street and congratulated him on the knighthood with which his eminent services during the war had been rewarded. We arranged to spend an evening together for old time's sake, and when I agreed to dine with him, he proposed that he should ask nobody else, so that we could chat without interruption. He had a beautiful old house in Queen Anne Street, and being a man of taste he had furnished it admirably. On the walls of the dining-room I saw a charming Bellotto, and there was a pair of Zoffanys that I envied. When his wife, a tall, lovely creature in cloth of gold, had left us, I remarked laughingly on the change in his present circumstances from those when we had both been medical students. We had looked upon it then as an extravagance to dine in a shabby Italian restaurant in the Westminster Bridge Road. Now Alec Carmichael was on the staff of half a dozen hospitals. I should think he earned ten thousand a year, and his knighthood was but the first of the honours which must inevitably fall to his lot.

'I've done pretty well,' he said, 'but the strange thing is that I owe it all to one piece of luck.'

'What do you mean by that?'

'Well, do you remember Abraham? He was the man who had the future. When we were students he beat me all along the line. He got the prizes and the scholarships that I went in for. I always played second fiddle to him. If he'd kept on he'd be in the position I'm in now. That man had a genius for surgery. No one had a look in with him. When he was appointed Registrar at St Thomas's I hadn't a chance of getting on the staff. I should have had to become a G.P., and you know what likelihood there is for a G.P. ever to get out of the common rut. But Abraham fell out, and I got the job. That gave me my opportunity.'

'I dare say that's true.'

'It was just luck. I suppose there was some kink in Abraham. Poor devil, he's gone to the dogs altogether. He's got some twopenny-halfpenny job in the medical at Alexandria—sanitary officer or something like that. I'm told he lives with an ugly old Greek woman and has half a dozen scrofulous kids. The fact is, I suppose, that it's not enough to have brains. The thing that counts is character. Abraham hadn't got character.'

Character? I should have thought it needed a good deal of character to throw up a career after half an hour's meditation, because you saw in another way of living a more intense significance. And it required still more character never to regret the sudden step. But I said nothing, and Alec Carmichael proceeded reflectively:

'Of course it would be hypocritical for me to pretend that I regret what Abraham did. After all, I've scored by it.' He puffed luxuriously at the long Corona he was smoking. 'But if I weren't personally concerned I should be sorry at the waste. It seems a rotten thing that a man should make such a hash of life.'

I wondered if Abraham really had made a hash of life. Is to do what you most want, to live under the conditions that please you, in peace with yourself, to make a hash of life; and is it success to be an eminent surgeon with ten thousand a year and a beautiful wife? I suppose it depends on what meaning you attach to life, the claim which you acknowledge to society, and the claim of the individual. But again I held my tongue, for who am I to argue with a knight?

LI

Tiaré, when I told her this story, praised my prudence, and for a few minutes we worked in silence, for we were shelling peas. Then her eyes, always alert for the affairs of her kitchen, fell on some action of the Chinese cook which aroused her violent disapproval. She turned on him with a torrent of abuse. The Chink was not backward to defend himself, and a very lively quarrel ensued. They spoke in the native language, of which I had learnt but half a dozen words, and it sounded as though the world would shortly come to an end; but presently peace was restored and Tiaré gave the cook a cigarette. They both smoked comfortably.

'Do you know, it was I who found him his wife?' said Tiaré suddenly, with a smile spread all over her immense face.

'The cook?'

'No, Strickland.'

'But he had one already.'

'That is what he said, but I told him she was in England, and England is at the other end of the world.'

'True', I replied.

'He would come to Papeete every two or three months, when he wanted paints or tobacco or money, and then he would wander about like a lost dog. I was sorry for him. I had a girl here then called Ata to do the rooms; she was some sort of a relation of mine, and her father and mother were dead, so I had her to live with me. Strickland used to come here now and then to have a square meal or to play chess with one of the boys. I noticed that she looked at him when he came, and I asked her if she liked him. She said she liked him well enough. You know what these girls are; they're always pleased to go with a white man.'

'Was she a native?' I asked.

'Yes; she hadn't a drop of white blood in her. Well, after I'd talked to her I sent for Strickland, and I said to him: "Strickland, it's time for you to settle down. A man of your age shouldn't go playing about with the girls down at the front. They're bad lots, and you'll come to no good with them. You've got no money, and you can never keep a job for more than a month or two. No one will employ you now. You say you can always live in the bush with one or other of the natives, and they're glad to have you because you're a white man, but it's not decent for a white man. Now, listen to me, Strickland." '

Tiaré mingled French with English in her conversation, for she used both languages with equal facility. She spoke them with a singing accent which was not unpleasing. You felt that a bird would speak in these tones if it could speak English.

' "Now, what do you say to marrying Ata? She's a good girl and she's only seventeen. She's never been promiscuous like some of these girls—a captain or a first mate, yes, but she's never been touched by a native. *Elle se respecte, vois-tu.* The purser of the *Oahu* told me last journey that he hadn't met a nicer girl in the islands. It's time she settled down too, and besides, the captains and the first mates like a change now and then. I don't keep my girls too long. She has a bit of property down by Taravao, just before you come to the peninsula, and with copra at the price it is now you could live quite comfortably. There's a house, and you'd have all the time you wanted for your painting. What do you say to it?" '

Tiaré paused to take breath.

'It was then he told me of his wife in England. "My poor Strickland," I said to him, "they've all got a wife somewhere; that is generally why they come to the islands. Ata is a sensible girl, and she doesn't expect any ceremony before the Mayor. She's a Protestant, and you know they don't look upon these things like the Catholics." '

'Then he said: "But what does Ata say to it?" "It appears that she has a *béguin* for you", I said. "She's willing if you are. Shall I call her?" He chuckled in a funny, dry way he had, and I called her. She knew what I was talking about, the hussy, and I saw her out of the corner of my eyes listening with all her ears, while she pretended to iron a blouse that she had been washing for me. She came. She was laughing, but I could see that she was a little shy, and Strickland looked at her without speaking.'

'Was she pretty?' I asked.

'Not bad. But you must have seen pictures of her. He painted her over and over again, sometimes with a *pareo* on and sometimes with nothing at all. Yes, she was pretty enough. And she knew how to cook. I taught her myself. I saw Strickland was thinking of it, so I said to him: "I've given her good wages and she's saved them, and the captains and the first mates she's known have given her a little something now and then. She's saved several hundred francs." '

'He pulled his great red beard and smiled.'

' "Well, Ata," he said, "do you fancy me for a husband?" '

'She did not say anything, but just giggled.'

' "But I tell you, my poor Strickland, the girl has a *béguin* for you", I said.

' "I shall beat you", he said, looking at her.

' "How else should I know you loved me?" she answered.'

Tiaré broke off her narrative and addressed herself to me reflectively.

'My first husband, Captain Johnson, used to thrash me regularly. He was a man. He was handsome, six foot three, and when he was drunk there was no holding him. I would be black and blue all over for days at a time. Oh, I cried when he died. I thought I should never get over it. But it wasn't till I married George Rainey that I knew what I'd lost. You can never tell what a man is like till you live with him. I've never been so deceived in a man as I was in George Rainey. He was a fine, upstanding fellow too. He was nearly as tall as Captain Johnson, and he looked strong enough. But it was all on the surface. He never drank. He never raised his hand to me. He might have been a missionary. I made love with the officers of every ship that touched at the island, and George Rainey never saw anything. At last I was disgusted with him, and I got a divorce. What was the good of a husband like that? It's a terrible thing the way some men treat women.'

I condoled with Tiaré, and remarked feelingly that men were deceivers ever, then asked her to go on with her story of Strickland.

' "Well," I said to him, "there's no hurry about it. Take your time and think it over. Ata has a very nice room in the annexe. Live with her for a month, and see how you like her. You can have your meals here. And at the end of a month, if you decide you want to marry her, you can just go and settle down on her property."

'Well, he agreed to that. Ata continued to do the housework, and I gave him his meals as I said I would. I taught Ata how to make one or two dishes I knew he was fond of. He did not paint much. He wandered about the hills and bathed in the stream. And he sat about the front looking at the lagoon, and at sunset he would go down and look at Murea. He used to go fishing on the reef. He loved to moon about the harbour talking to the natives. He was a nice quiet fellow. And every evening after dinner he would go down to the annexe with Ata. I saw he was longing to get away to the bush, and at the end of the month I asked him what he intended to do. He said if Ata was willing to go, he was willing to go with her. So I gave them a wedding dinner. I cooked it with my own hands. I gave them a pea soup and lobster *à la portugaise,* and a curry, and a coconut salad—you've never had one of my coconut salads, have you? I must make you one before you go—and then I made them an ice. We had all the champagne we could drink and liqueurs to follow. Oh, I'd made up my mind to do things well. And afterwards we danced in the drawing-room. I was not so fat then, and I always loved dancing.'

The drawing-room at the Hôtel de la Fleur was a small room, with a cottage piano, and a suite of mahogany furniture, covered in stamped velvet, neatly arranged round the walls. On round tables were photograph albums, and on the walls enlarged photographs of Tiaré and her first husband, Captain Johnson. Still, though Tiaré was old and fat, on occasion we rolled back the Brussels carpet, brought in the maids and one or two friends of Tiaré's, and danced, though now to the wheezy music of a gramophone. On the veranda the air was scented with the heavy perfume of the tiaré, and overhead the Southern Cross shone in a cloudless sky.

Tiaré smiled indulgently as she remembered the gaiety of a time long passed.

'We kept it up till three, and when we went to bed I don't think anyone was very sober. I had told them they could have my trap to take them as far as the road went, because after that

they had a long walk. Ata's property was right away in a fold
of the mountain. They started at dawn, and the boy I sent with
them didn't come back till next day.

'Yes, that's how Strickland was married.'

LII

I suppose the next three years were the happiest of Strickland's
life. Ata's house stood about eight kilometres from the road that
runs round the island, and you went to it along a winding pathway shaded by the luxuriant trees of the tropics. It was a bun-
galow of unpainted wood, consisting of two small rooms, and
outside was a small shed that served as a kitchen. There was no
furniture except the mats they used as beds and a rocking-chair,
which stood on the veranda. Bananas with their great ragged
leaves, like the tattered habiliments of an empress in adversity,
grew close up to the house. There was a tree just behind which
bore alligator pears, and all about were the coconuts which
gave the land its revenue. Ata's father had planted crotons
round his property, and they grew in coloured profusion, gay
and brilliant; they fenced the land with flame. A mango grew in
front of the house, and at the edge of the clearing were two
flamboyants, twin trees, that challenged the gold of the coconuts with their scarlet flowers.

Here Strickland lived, coming seldom to Papeete, on the produce of the land. There was a little stream that ran not far away,
in which he bathed, and down this on occasion would come a
shoal of fish. Then the natives would assemble with spears, and
with much shouting would transfix the great startled things
as they hurried down to the sea. Sometimes Strickland would
go down to the reef, and come back with a basket of small,
coloured fish that Ata would fry in coconut oil, or with a lobster; and sometimes she would make a savoury dish of the great
land-crabs that scuttled away under your feet. Up the mountain
were wild-orange trees, and now and then Ata would go with
two or three women from the village and return laden with the
green, sweet, luscious fruit. Then the coconuts would be ripe for

picking, and her cousins (like all the natives, Ata had a host of relatives) would swarm up the trees and throw down the big ripe nuts. They split them open and put them in the sun to dry. Then they cut out the copra and put it into sacks, and the women would carry it down to the trader at the village by the lagoon, and he would give in exchange for it rice and soap and tinned meat and a little money. Sometimes there would be a feast in the neighbourhood, and a pig would be killed. Then they would go and eat themselves sick, and dance, and sing hymns.

But the house was a long way from the village, and the Tahitians are lazy. They love to travel and they love to gossip, but they do not care to walk, and for weeks at a time Strickland and Ata lived alone. He painted and he read, and in the evening, when it was dark, they sat together on the veranda, smoking and looking at the night. Then Ata had a baby, and the old woman who came up to help her through her trouble stayed on. Presently the grand-daughter of the old woman came to stay with her, and then a youth appeared—no one quite knew where from or to whom he belonged—but he settled down with them in a happy-go-lucky way, and they all lived together.

LIII

'Tenez, voilà le Capitaine Brunot', said Tiaré, one day when I was fitting together what she could tell me of Strickland. 'He knew Strickland well; he visited him at his house.'

I saw a middle-aged Frenchman with a big black beard, streaked with grey, a sunburned face, and large, shining eyes. He was dressed in a neat suit of ducks. I had noticed him at luncheon, and Ah Lin, the Chinese boy, told me he had come from the Paumotus on the boat that had that day arrived. Tiaré introduced me to him, and he handed me his card, a large card on which was printed René Brunot, and underneath, Capitaine au Long Cours. We were sitting on a little veranda outside the kitchen, and Tiaré was cutting out a dress that she was making for one of the girls about the house. He sat down with us.

'Yes; I knew Strickland well', he said. 'I am very fond of chess, and he was always glad of a game. I come to Tahiti three or four times a year for my business, and when he was at Papeete he would come here and we would play. When he married'— Captain Brunot smiled and shrugged his shoulders—'*enfin*, when he went to live with the girl that Tiaré gave him, he asked me to go and see him. I was one of the guests at the wedding feast.' He looked at Tiaré, and they both laughed. 'He did not come much to Papeete after that, and about a year later it chanced that I had to go to that part of the island for I forget what business, and when I had finished it I said to myself: "*Voyons*, why should I not go and see that poor Strickland?" I asked one or two natives if they knew anything about him, and I discovered that he lived not more than five kilometres from where I was. So, I went. I shall never forget the impression my visit made on me. I live on an atoll, a low island, it is a strip of land surrounding a lagoon, and its beauty is the beauty of the sea and sky, and the varied colour of the lagoon, and the grace of the coconut trees; but the place where Strickland lived had the beauty of the Garden of Eden. Ah, I wish I could make you see the enchantment of that spot, a cor- ner hidden away from all the world, with the blue sky overhead and the rich, luxuriant trees. It was a feast of colour. And it was fragrant and cool. Words cannot describe that paradise. And here he lived, unmindful of the world and by the world forgotten. I suppose to European eyes it would have seemed astonishingly sordid. The house was dilapidated and none too clean. When I approached I saw three or four natives lying on the veranda. You know how natives love to herd together. There was a young man lying full length, smoking a cigarette, and he wore nothing but a *pareo*.'

The *pareo* is a long strip of trade cotton, red or blue, stamped with a white pattern. It is worn round the waist and hangs to the knees.

'A girl of fifteen, perhaps, was plaiting pandanus-leaf to make a hat, and an old woman was sitting on her haunches smoking a pipe. Then I saw Ata. She was suckling a new-born child, and another child, stark naked, was playing at her feet. When she

saw me, she called out to Strickland, and he came to the door.
He, too, wore nothing but a *pareo*. He was an extraordinary figure, with his red beard and matted hair, and his great hairy
chest. His feet were horny and scarred, so that I knew he went
always barefoot. He had gone native with a vengeance. He
seemed pleased to see me, and told Ata to kill a chicken for our
dinner. He took me into the house to show me the picture he
was at work on when I came in. In one corner of the room was
the bed, and in the middle was an easel with the canvas upon it.
Because I was sorry for him, I had bought a couple of his pictures for small sums, and I had sent others to friends of mine in
France. And though I had bought them out of compassion, after
living with them I began to like them. Indeed, I found a strange
beauty in them. Everyone thought I was mad, but it turns out
that I was right. I was his first admirer in the islands.'

He smiled maliciously at Tiaré, and with lamentations she
told us again the story of how at the sale of Strickland's effects
she had neglected the pictures, but bought an American stove
for twenty-seven francs.

'Have you the pictures still?' I asked.

'Yes; I am keeping them till my daughter is of marriageable
age, and then I shall sell them. They will be her *dot*.'

Then he went on with the account of his visit to Strickland.

'I shall never forget the evening I spent with him. I had not intended to stay more than an hour, but he insisted that I should
spend the night. I hesitated, for I confess I did not much like the
look of the mats on which he proposed that I should sleep; but
I shrugged my shoulders. When I was building my house in the
Paumotus I had slept out for weeks on a harder bed than that,
with nothing to shelter me but wild shrubs; and as for vermin,
my tough skin should be proof against their malice.

'We went down to the stream to bathe while Ata was preparing the dinner, and after we had eaten it we sat on the veranda.
We smoked and chatted. The young man had a concertina, and
he played the tunes popular on the music-halls a dozen years
before. They sounded strangely in the tropical night thousands
of miles from civilization. I asked Strickland if it did not irk
him to live in that promiscuity. No, he said; he liked to have his

models under his hand. Presently, after loud yawning, the natives went away to sleep, and Strickland and I were left alone. I cannot describe to you the intense silence of the night. On my island in the Paumotus there is never at night the complete stillness that there was here. There is the rustle of the myriad animals on the beach, all the little shelled things that crawl about ceaselessly, and there is the noisy scurrying of the land-crabs. Now and then in the lagoon you hear the leaping of a fish, and sometimes a hurried noisy splashing as a brown shark sends all the other fish scampering for their lives. And above all, ceaseless like time, is the dull roar of the breakers on the reef. But here there was not a sound, and the air was scented with the white flowers of the night. It was a night so beautiful that your soul seemed hardly able to bear the prison of the body. You felt that it was ready to be wafted away on the immaterial air, and death bore all the aspect of a beloved friend.'

Tiaré sighed.

'Ah, I wish I were fifteen again.'

Then she caught sight of a cat trying to get at a dish of prawns on the kitchen table, and with a dexterous gesture and a lively volley of abuse flung a book at its scampering tail.

'I asked him if he was happy with Ata.'

' "She leaves me alone", he said. "She cooks my food and looks after her babies. She does what I tell her. She gives me what I want from a woman."

' "And do you never regret Europe? Do you not yearn sometimes for the light of the streets in Paris or London, the companionship of your friends and equals, *que sais-je?* for theatres and newspapers, and the rumble of omnibuses on the cobbled pavements?"

'For a long time he was silent. Then he said:

' "I shall stay here till I die."

' "But are you never bored or lonely?" I asked.

'He chuckled.

' "*Mon pauvre ami*", he said. "It is evident that you do not know what it is to be an artist." '

Capitaine Brunot turned to me with a gentle smile, and there was a wonderful look in his dark, kind eyes.

'He did me an injustice, for I too know what it is to have dreams. I have my visions too. In my way I also am an artist.'

We were all silent for a while, and Tiaré fished out of her capacious pocket a handful of cigarettes. She handed one to each of us, and we all three smoked. At last she said:

'Since *ce monsieur* is interested in Strickland, why do you not take him to see Dr Coutras? He can tell him something about his illness and death.'

'*Volontiers*', said the Captain, looking at me.

I thanked him, and he looked at his watch.

'It is past six o'clock. We should find him at home if you care to come now.'

I got up without further ado, and we walked along the road that led to the doctor's house. He lived out of the town, but the Hôtel de la Fleur was on the edge of it, and we were quickly in the country. The broad road was shaded by peppertrees, and on each side were the plantations, coconut and vanilla. The pirate birds were screeching among the leaves of the palms. We came to a stone bridge over a shallow river, and we stopped for a few minutes to see the native boys bathing. They chased one another with shrill cries and laughter, and their bodies, brown and wet, gleamed in the sunlight.

LIV

As we walked along I reflected on a circumstance which all that I had lately heard about Strickland forced on my attention. Here, on this remote island, he seemed to have aroused none of the detestation with which he was regarded at home, but compassion rather; and his vagaries were accepted with tolerance. To these people, native and European, he was a queer fish, but they were used to queer fish, and they took him for granted; the world was full of odd persons, who did odd things; and perhaps they knew that a man is not what he wants to be, but what he must be. In England and France he was the square peg in the round hole, but here the holes were any sort of shape, and no sort of peg was quite amiss. I do not think he was any gentler here, less selfish or less brutal, but the circumstances were more favourable. If he had spent his life amid these surroundings he might have passed for no worse a man than another. He received here what he neither expected nor wanted among his own people—sympathy.

I tried to tell Captain Brunot something of the astonishment with which this filled me, and for a little while he did not answer.

'It is not strange that I, at all events, should have had sympathy for him,' he said at last, 'for, though perhaps neither of us knew it, we were both aiming at the same thing.'

'What on earth can it be that two people so dissimilar as you and Strickland could aim at?' I asked, smiling.

'Beauty.'

'A large order', I murmured.

'Do you know how men can be so obsessed by love that they are deaf and blind to everything else in the world? They are as little their own masters as the slaves chained to the benches of a galley. The passion that held Strickland in bondage was no less tyrannical than love.'

'How strange that you should say that!' I answered. 'For long ago I had the idea that he was possessed of a devil.'

'And the passion that held Strickland was a passion to create beauty. It gave him no peace. It urged him hither and thither. He was eternally a pilgrim, haunted by a divine nostalgia, and the demon within him was ruthless. There are men whose desire for truth is so great that to attain it they will shatter the very foundation of their world. Of such was Strickland, only beauty with him took the place of truth. I could only feel for him a profound compassion.'

'That is strange also. A man whom he had deeply wronged told me that he felt a great pity for him.' I was silent for a moment. 'I wonder if there you have found the explanation of a character which has always seemed to me inexplicable. How did you hit on it?'

He turned to me with a smile.

'Did I not tell you that I, too, in my way was an artist? I realized in myself the same desire as animated him. But whereas his medium was paint, mine has been life.'

Then Captain Brunot told me a story which I must repeat, since, if only by way of contrast, it adds something to my impression of Strickland. It has also to my mind a beauty of its own.

Captain Brunot was a Breton, and had been in the French Navy. He left it on his marriage, and settled down on a small property he had near Quimper to live for the rest of his days in peace; but the failure of an attorney left him suddenly penniless, and neither he nor his wife was willing to live in penury where they had enjoyed consideration. During his seafaring days he had cruised the South Seas, and he determined now to seek his fortune there. He spent some months in Papeete to make his plans and gain experience; then, on money borrowed from a friend in France, he bought an island in the Paumotus. It was a ring of land round a deep lagoon, uninhabited, and covered only with scrub and wild guava. With the intrepid woman who was his wife, and a few natives, he landed there, and set about building a house, and clearing the scrub so that he could plant coconuts. That was twenty years before, and now what had been a barren island was a garden.

'It was hard and anxious work at first, and we worked strenuously, both of us. Every day I was up at dawn, clearing, planting, working on my house, and at night when I threw myself on my bed it was to sleep like a log till morning. My wife worked as hard as I did. Then children were born to us, first a son and then a daughter. My wife and I have taught them all they know. We had a piano sent out from France, and she has taught them to play and to speak English, and I have taught them Latin and mathematics, and we read history together. They can sail a boat. They can swim as well as the natives. There is nothing about the land of which they are ignorant. Our trees have prospered, and there is shell on my reef. I have come to Tahiti now to buy a schooner. I can get enough shell to make it worth while to fish for it, and, who knows? I may find pearls. I have made something where there was nothing. I too have made beauty. Ah, you do not know what it is to look at those tall, healthy trees and think that every one I planted myself.'

'Let me ask you the question that you asked Strickland. Do you never regret France and your old home in Brittany?'

'Some day, when my daughter is married and my son has a wife and is able to take my place on the island, we shall go back and finish our days in the old house in which I was born.'

'You will look back on a happy life', I said.

'*Évidemment*, it is not exciting on my island, and we are very far from the world—imagine, it takes me four days to come to Tahiti—but we are happy there. It is given to few men to attempt a work and to achieve it. Our life is simple and innocent. We are untouched by ambition, and what pride we have is due only to our contemplation of the work of our hands. Malice cannot touch us, nor envy attack. Ah, *mon cher monsieur*, they talk of the blessedness of labour, and it is a meaningless phrase, but to me it has the most intense significance. I am a happy man.'

'I am sure you deserve to be', I smiled.

'I wish I could think so. I do not know how I have deserved to have a wife who was the perfect friend and helpmate, the perfect mistress and the perfect mother.'

I reflected for a while on the life that the Captain suggested to my imagination.

'It is obvious that to lead such an existence and make so great a success of it, you must both have needed a strong will and determined character.'

'Perhaps; but without one other factor we could have achieved nothing.'

'And what was that?'

He stopped, somewhat dramatically, and stretched out his arm.

'Belief in God. Without that we should have been lost.'

Then we arrived at the house of Dr Coutras.

LV

Dr Coutras was an old Frenchman of great stature and exceeding bulk. His body was shaped like a huge duck's egg; and his eyes, sharp, blue, and good-natured, rested now and then with self-satisfaction on his enormous paunch. His complexion was florid and his hair white. He was a man to attract immediate

sympathy. He received us in a room that might have been in a
house in a provincial town in France, and the one or two Polynesian curios had an odd look. He took my hand in both of
his—they were huge—and he gave me a hearty look, in which,
however, was great shrewdness. When he shook hands with
Capitaine Brunot he inquired politely after *Madame et les en-
fants*. For some minutes there was an exchange of courtesies
and some local gossip about the island, the prospects of copra
and the vanilla crop; then we came to the object of my visit.

I shall not tell what Dr Coutras related to me in his words,
but in my own, for I cannot hope to give at second hand any
impression of his vivacious delivery. He had a deep, resonant
voice, fitted to his massive frame, and a keen sense of the dramatic. To listen to him was, as the phrase goes, as good as a
play; and much better than most.

It appears that Dr Coutras had gone one day to Taravao in
order to see an old chiefess who was ill, and he gave a vivid picture of the obese old lady, lying in a huge bed, smoking cigarettes, and surrounded by a crowd of dark-skinned retainers.
When he had seen her he was taken into another room and
given dinner—raw fish, fried bananas, and chicken—*que sais-
je?* the typical dinner of the *indigène*—and while he was eating
it he saw a young girl being driven away from the door in tears.
He thought nothing of it, but when he went out to get into his
trap and drive home, he saw her again, standing a little way off;
she looked at him with a woebegone air, and tears streamed
down her cheeks. He asked someone what was wrong with her,
and was told that she had come down from the hills to ask him
to visit a white man who was sick. They had told her that the
doctor could not be disturbed. He called her, and himself asked
what she wanted. She told him that Ata had sent her, she who
used to be at the Hôtel de la Fleur, and that the Red One was ill.
She thrust into his hand a crumpled piece of newspaper, and
when he opened it he found in it a hundred-franc note.

'Who is the Red One?' he asked of one of the bystanders.

He was told that that was what they called the Englishman, a
painter, who lived with Ata up in the valley seven kilometres from
where they were. He recognized Strickland by the description.

But it was necessary to walk. It was impossible for him to go; that was why they had sent the girl away.

'I confess,' said the doctor, turning to me, 'that I hesitated. I did not relish fourteen kilometres over a bad pathway, and there was no chance that I could get back to Papeete that night. Besides, Strickland was not sympathetic to me. He was an idle useless scoundrel, who preferred to live with a native woman rather than work for his living like the rest of us. *Mon Dieu,* how was I to know that one day the world would come to the conclusion that he had genius? I asked the girl if he was not well enough to have come down to see me. I asked her what she thought was the matter with him. She would not answer. I pressed her, angrily perhaps, but she looked down on the ground and began to cry. Then I shrugged my shoulders; after all, perhaps it was my duty to go, and in a very bad temper I bade her lead the way.'

His temper was certainly no better when he arrived, perspiring freely and thirsty. Ata was on the look-out for him, and came a little way along the path to meet him.

'Before I see anyone, give me something to drink or I shall die of thirst', he cried out. '*Pour l'amour de Dieu,* get me a coconut.'

She called out, and a boy came running along. He swarmed up a tree, and presently threw down a ripe nut. Ata pierced a hole in it, and the doctor took a long, refreshing draught. Then he rolled himself a cigarette and felt in a better humour.

'Now, where is the Red One?' he asked.

'He is in the house, painting. I have not told him you were coming. Go in and see him.'

'But what does he complain of? If he is well enough to paint, he is well enough to have come down to Taravao and save me this confounded walk. I presume my time is no less valuable than his.'

Ata did not speak, but with the boy followed him to the house. The girl who had brought him was by this time sitting on the veranda, and here was lying an old woman, with her back to the wall, making native cigarettes. Ata pointed to the door. The doctor, wondering irritably why they behaved so strangely, entered, and there found Strickland cleaning his palette. There was a picture on the easel. Strickland, clad only in a *pareo,* was standing with his back to the door, but he turned round when he heard the sound of boots. He gave the doctor a look of vexation. He was surprised to see him, and resented the intrusion. But the doctor gave a gasp, he was rooted to the floor, and he stared with all his eyes. This was not what he expected. He was seized with horror.

'You enter without ceremony', said Strickland. 'What can I do for you?'

The doctor recovered himself, but it required quite an effort for him to find his voice. All his irritation was gone, and he felt— *eh bien, oui, je ne le nie pas*—he felt an overwhelming pity.

'I am Dr Coutras. I was down at Taravao to see the chiefess, and Ata sent for me to see you.'

'She's a damned fool. I have had a few aches and pains lately and a little fever, but that's nothing; it will pass off. Next time anyone went to Papeete I was going to send for some quinine.'

'Look at yourself in the glass.'

Strickland gave him a glance, smiled, and went over to a cheap mirror in a little wooden frame that hung on the wall.

'Well?'

'Do you not see a strange change in your face? Do you not see the thickening of your features and a look—how shall I describe it?—the books call it lion-faced. *Mon pauvre ami,* must I tell you that you have a terrible disease?'

'I?'

'When you look at yourself in the glass you see the typical appearance of the leper.'

'You are jesting', said Strickland.

'I wish to God I were.'

'Do you intend to tell me that I have leprosy?'

'Unfortunately, there can be no doubt about it.'

Dr Coutras had delivered sentence of death on many men, and he could never overcome the horror with which it filled him. He felt always the furious hatred that must seize a man condemned when he compared himself with the doctor, sane and healthy, who had the inestimable privilege of life. Strickland looked at him in silence. Nothing of emotion could be seen on his face, disfigured already by the loathsome disease.

'Do they know?' he asked at last, pointing to the persons on the veranda, now sitting in unusual, unaccountable silence.

'These natives know the signs so well', said the doctor. 'They were afraid to tell you.'

Strickland stepped to the door and looked out. There must have been something terrible in his face, for suddenly they all burst out into loud cries and lamentation. They lifted up their voices and they wept. Strickland did not speak. After looking at them for a moment, he came back into the room.

'How long do you think I can last?'

'Who knows? Sometimes the disease continues for twenty years. It is a mercy when it runs its course quickly.'

Strickland went to his easel and looked reflectively at the picture that stood on it.

'You have had a long journey. It is fitting that the bearer of important tidings should be rewarded. Take this picture. It means nothing to you now, but it may be that one day you will be glad to have it.'

Dr Coutras protested that he needed no payment for his journey; he had already given back to Ata the hundred-franc note, but Strickland insisted that he should take the picture. Then together they went out on the veranda. The natives were sobbing violently.

'Be quiet, woman. Dry thy tears', said Strickland, addressing Ata. 'There is no great harm. I shall leave thee very soon.'

'They are not going to take thee away?' she cried.

At that time there was no rigid sequestration on the islands, and lepers, if they chose, were allowed to go free.

'I shall go up into the mountain', said Strickland.

Then Ata stood up and faced him.

'Let the others go if they choose, but I will not leave thee. Thou art my man and I am thy woman. If thou leavest me I shall hang myself on the tree that is behind the house. I swear it by God.'

There was something immensely forcible in the way she spoke.

She was no longer the meek, soft native girl, but a determined woman. She was extraordinarily transformed.

'Why shouldst thou stay with me? Thou canst go back to Papeete, and thou wilt soon find another white man. The old woman can take care of thy children, and Tiaré will be glad to have thee back.'

'Thou art my man and I am thy woman. Whither thou goest I will go too.'

For a moment Strickland's fortitude was shaken, and a tear filled each of his eyes and trickled slowly down his cheeks. Then he gave the sardonic smile which was usual with him.

'Women are strange little beasts', he said to Dr Coutras. 'You can treat them like dogs, you can beat them till your arm aches, and still they love you.' He shrugged his shoulders. 'Of course, it is one of the most absurd illusions of Christianity that they have souls.'

'What is it that thou art saying to the doctor?' asked Ata suspiciously. 'Thou wilt not go?'

'If it please thee I will stay, poor child.'

Ata flung herself on her knees before him, and clasped his legs with her arms and kissed them. Strickland looked at Dr Coutras with a faint smile.

'In the end they get you, and you are helpless in their hands. White or brown, they are all the same.'

Dr Coutras felt that it was absurd to offer expressions of regret in so terrible a disaster, and he took his leave. Strickland told Tané, the boy, to lead him to the village. Dr Coutras paused for a moment, and then he addressed himself to me.

'I did not like him, I have told you he was not sympathetic to me, but as I walked slowly down to Taravao I could not prevent an unwilling admiration for the stoical courage which enabled him to bear perhaps the most dreadful of human afflictions. When Tané left me I told him I would send some medicine that might be of service; but my hope was small that Strickland would consent to take it, and even smaller that, if he did, it would do him good. I gave the boy a message for Ata that I would come whenever she sent for me. Life is hard, and Nature takes sometimes a terrible delight in torturing her children.

It was with a heavy heart that I drove back to my comfortable home in Papeete.'

For a long time none of us spoke.

'But Ata did not send for me,' the doctor went on, at last, 'and it chanced that I did not go to that part of the island for a long time. I had no news of Strickland. Once or twice I heard that Ata had been to Papeete to buy painting materials, but I did not happen to see her. More than two years passed before I went to Taravao again, and then it was once more to see the old chiefess. I asked them whether they had heard anything of Strickland. By now it was known everywhere that he had leprosy. First Tané, the boy, had left the house, and then, a little time afterwards, the old woman and her grandchild. Strickland and Ata were left alone with their babies. No one went near the plantation, for, as you know, the natives have a very lively horror of the disease, and in the old days when it was discovered the sufferer was killed; but sometimes, when the village boys were scrambling about the hills, they would catch sight of the white man, with his great red beard, wandering about. They fled in terror. Sometimes Ata would come down to the village at night and arouse the trader, so that he might sell her various things of which she stood in need. She knew that the natives looked upon her with the same horrified aversion as they looked upon Strickland, and she kept out of their way. Once some women, venturing nearer than usual to the plantation, saw her washing clothes in the brook, and they threw stones at her. After that the trader was told to give her the message that if she used the brook again men would come and burn down her house.'

'Brutes', I said.

'Mais non, mon cher monsieur, men are always the same. Fear makes them cruel. . . . I decided to see Strickland, and when I had finished with the chiefess asked for a boy to show me the way. But none would accompany me, and I was forced to find it alone.'

When Dr Coutras arrived at the plantation he was seized with a feeling of uneasiness. Though he was hot from walking, he shivered. There was something hostile in the air which made him hesitate, and he felt that invisible forces barred his way.

Unseen hands seemed to draw him back. No one would go near now to gather the coconuts, and they lay rotting on the ground. Everywhere was desolation. The bush was encroaching, and it looked as though very soon the primeval forest would regain possession of that strip of land which had been snatched from it at the cost of so much labour. He had the sensation that here was the abode of pain. As he approached the house he was struck by the unearthly silence, and at first he thought it was deserted. Then he saw Ata. She was sitting on her haunches in the lean-to that served her as kitchen, watching some mess cooking in a pot. Near her a small boy was playing silently in the dirt. She did not smile when she saw him.

'I have come to see Strickland', he said.

'I will go and tell him.'

She went to the house, ascended the few steps that led to the veranda, and entered. Dr Coutras followed her, but waited outside in obedience to her gesture. As she opened the door he smelt the sickly sweet smell which makes the neighbourhood of the leper nauseous. He heard her speak, and then he heard Strickland's answer, but he did not recognize the voice. It had become hoarse and indistinct. Dr Coutras raised his eyebrows. He judged that the disease had already attacked the vocal cords. Then Ata came out again.

'He will not see you. You must go away.'

Dr Coutras insisted, but she would not let him pass. Dr Coutras shrugged his shoulders, and after a moment's reflection turned away. She walked with him. He felt that she too wanted to be rid of him.

'Is there nothing I can do at all?' he asked.

'You can send him some paints', she said. 'There is nothing else he wants.'

'Can he paint still?'

'He is painting the walls of the house.'

'This is a terrible life for you, my poor child.'

Then at last she smiled, and there was in her eyes a look of superhuman love. Dr Coutras was startled by it, and amazed. And he was awed. He found nothing to say.

'He is my man', she said.

'Where is your other child?' he asked. 'When I was here last you had two.'

'Yes; it died. We buried it under the mango.'

When Ata had gone with him a little way she said she must turn back. Dr Coutras surmised she was afraid to go farther in case she met any of the people from the village. He told her again that if she wanted him she had only to send and he would come at once.

LVI

Then two years more went by, or perhaps three, for time passes imperceptibly in Tahiti, and it is hard to keep count of it; but at last a message was brought to Dr Coutras that Strickland was dying. Ata had waylaid the cart that took the mail into Papeete, and besought the man who drove it to go at once to the doctor. But the doctor was out when the summons came, and it was evening when he received it. It was impossible to start at so late an hour, and so it was not till next day soon after dawn that he set out. He arrived at Taravao, and for the last time tramped the seven kilometres that led to Ata's house. The path was over-grown, and it was clear that for years now it had remained all but untrodden. It was not easy to find the way. Sometimes he had to stumble along the bed of the stream, and sometimes he had to push through shrubs, dense and thorny; often he was obliged to climb over rocks in order to avoid the hornet-nests that hung on the trees over his head. The silence was intense.

It was with a sigh of relief that at last he came upon the little unpainted house, extraordinarily bedraggled now, and un-kempt; but here too was the same intolerable silence. He walked up, and a little boy, playing unconcernedly in the sun-shine, started at his approach and fled quickly away: to him the stranger was the enemy. Dr Coutras had a sense that the child was stealthily watching him from behind a tree. The door was wide open. He called out, but no one answered. He stepped in. He knocked at a door, but again there was no answer. He turned the handle and entered. The stench that assailed him

turned him horribly sick. He put his handkerchief to his
nose and forced himself to go in. The light was dim, and after
the brilliant sunshine for a while he could see nothing. Then he
gave a start. He could not make out where he was. He seemed
on a sudden to have entered a magic world. He had a vague impression of a great primeval forest and of naked people walking
beneath the trees. Then he saw that there were paintings on the
walls.

'*Mon Dieu,* I hope the sun hasn't affected me', he muttered.

A slight movement attracted his attention, and he saw that Ata
was lying on the floor, sobbing quietly.

'Ata', he called. 'Ata.'

She took no notice. Again the beastly stench almost made
him faint, and he lit a cheroot. His eyes grew accustomed to the
darkness, and now he was seized by an overwhelming sensation
as he stared at the painted walls. He knew nothing of pictures,
but there was something about these that extraordinarily affected him. From floor to ceiling the walls were covered with a
strange and elaborate composition. It was indescribably wonderful and mysterious. It took his breath away. It filled him with
an emotion which he could not understand or analyse. He felt
the awe and the delight which a man might feel who watched
the beginning of a world. It was tremendous, sensual, passionate; and yet there was something horrible there too, something
which made him afraid. It was the work of a man who had
delved into the hidden depths of nature and had discovered secrets which were beautiful and fearful too. It was the work of a
man who knew things which it is unholy for men to know.
There was something primeval there and terrible. It was not human. It brought to his mind vague recollections of black magic.
It was beautiful and obscene.

'*Mon Dieu,* this is genius.'

The words were wrung from him, and he did not know he
had spoken.

Then his eyes fell on the bed of mats in the corner, and he
went up, and he saw the dreadful, mutilated, ghastly object
which had been Strickland. He was dead. Dr Coutras made
an effort of will and bent over that battered horror. Then he

started violently, and terror blazed in his heart, for he felt that someone was behind him. It was Ata. He had not heard her get up. She was standing at his elbow, looking at what he looked at.

'Good Heavens, my nerves are all distraught', he said, 'You nearly frightened me out of my wits.'

He looked again at the poor dead thing that had been man, and then he started back in dismay.

'But he was blind.'

'Yes; he had been blind for nearly a year.'

LVII

At that moment we were interrupted by the appearance of Madame Coutras, who had been paying visits. She came in, like a ship in full sail, an imposing creature, tall and stout, with an ample bust and an obesity girthed in alarmingly by straight-fronted corsets. She had a bold hooked nose and three chins. She held herself upright. She had not yielded for an instant to the enervating charm of the tropics, but contrariwise was more active, more worldly, more decided than anyone in a temperate clime would have thought it possible to be. She was evidently a copious talker, and now poured forth a breathless stream of anecdote and comment. She made the conversation we had just had seem far away and unreal.

Presently Dr Coutras turned to me.

'I still have in my *bureau* the picture that Strickland gave me', he said. 'Would you like to see it?'

'Willingly.'

We got up, and he led me on to the veranda which surrounded his house. We paused to look at the gay flowers that rioted in his garden.

'For a long time I could not get out of my head the recollection of the extraordinary decoration with which Strickland had covered the walls of his house', he said reflectively.

I had been thinking of it too. It seemed to me that here Strickland had finally put the whole expression of himself. Working silently, knowing that it was his last chance, I fancied that here he must have said all that he knew of life and all that he divined. And I fancied that perhaps here he had at last found peace. The demon which possessed him was exorcized at last, and with the completion of the work, for which all his life had been a painful preparation, rest descended on his remote and tortured soul. He was willing to die, for he had fulfilled his purpose.

'What was the subject?' I asked.

'I scarcely know. It was strange and fantastic. It was a vision of the beginnings of the world, the Garden of Eden, with Adam and Eve—*que sais-je?*—it was a hymn to the beauty of the human form, male and female, and the praise of Nature, sublime, indifferent, lovely, and cruel. It gave you an awful sense of the infinity of space and of the endlessness of time. Because he painted the trees I see about me every day, the coconuts, the banyans, the flamboyants, the alligator pears, I have seen them ever since differently, as though there were in them a spirit and a mystery which I am ever on the point of seizing and which for ever escapes me. The colours were the colours familiar to me, and yet they were different. They had a significance which was all their own. And those nude men and women. They were of the earth, the clay of which they were created, and at the same time something divine. You saw man in the nakedness of his primeval instincts, and you were afraid, for you saw yourself.'

Dr Coutras shrugged his shoulders and smiled.

'You will laugh at me. I am a materialist, and I am a gross, fat man—Falstaff, eh?—the lyrical mode does not become me. I make myself ridiculous. But I have never seen painting which made so deep an impression upon me. *Tenez*, I had just the same feeling as when I went to the Sistine Chapel in Rome. There too I was awed by the greatness of the man who had painted that ceiling. It was genius, and it was stupendous and overwhelming. I felt small and insignificant. But you are prepared for the greatness of Michael Angelo. Nothing had prepared me for the immense surprise of these pictures in a native hut, far away from civilization, in a fold of the mountain above Taravao. And Michael Angelo is sane and healthy. Those great works of his have the calm of the sublime; but here, notwithstanding beauty, was something troubling. I do not know what

it was. It made me uneasy. It gave me the impression you get
when you are sitting next door to a room that you know is
empty, but in which, you know not why, you have a dreadful
consciousness that notwithstanding there is someone. You scold
yourself; you know it is only your nerves—and yet, and yet . . .
In a little while it is impossible to resist the terror that seizes
you, and you are helpless in the clutch of an unseen horror. Yes:
I confess I was not altogether sorry when I heard that those
strange masterpieces had been destroyed.'

'Destroyed?' I cried.

'*Mais oui*; did you not know?'

'How should I know? It is true I had never heard of this
work; but I thought perhaps it had fallen into the hands of a
private owner. Even now there is no certain list of Strickland's
paintings.'

'When he grew blind he would sit hour after hour in those
two rooms that he had painted, looking at his works with sight-
less eyes, and seeing, perhaps, more than he ever had seen in his
life before. Ata told me that he never complained of his fate, he
never lost courage. To the end his mind remained serene and
undisturbed. But he made her promise that when she had
buried him—did I tell you that I dug his grave with my own
hands, for none of the natives would approach the infected
house, and we buried him, she and I, sewn up in three *pareos*
joined together, under the mango-tree—he made her promise
that she would set fire to the house and not leave it till it was
burned to the ground and not a stick remained.'

I did not speak for a while, for I was thinking. Then I said:

'He remained the same to the end, then.'

'Do you understand? I must tell you that I thought it my duty
to dissuade her.'

'Even after what you have just said?'

'Yes; for I knew that here was a work of genius, and I did not
think we had the right to deprive the world of it. But Ata would
not listen to me. She had promised. I would not stay to witness
the barbarous deed, and it was only afterwards that I heard
what she had done. She poured paraffin on the dry floors and
on the pandanus-mats, and then she set fire. In a little while

nothing remained but smouldering embers, and a great master-piece existed no longer.'

'I think Strickland knew it was a masterpiece. He had achieved what he wanted. His life was complete. He had made a world and saw that it was good. Then, in pride and contempt, he destroyed it.'

'But I must show you my picture', said Dr Coutras, moving on.

'What happened to Ata and the child?'

'They went to the Marquesas. She had relations there. I have heard that the boy works on one of Cameron's schooners. They say he is very like his father in appearance.'

At the door that led from the veranda to the doctor's consulting room, he paused and smiled.

'It is a fruit-piece. You would think it not a very suitable picture for a doctor's consulting-room, but my wife will not have it in the drawing-room. She says it is frankly obscene.'

'A fruit-piece!' I exclaimed in surprise.

We entered the room, and my eyes fell at once on the picture. I looked at it for a long time.

It was a pile of mangoes, bananas, oranges, and I know not what; and at first sight it was an innocent picture enough. It would have been passed in an exhibition of the Post-Impressionists by a careless person as an excellent but not very remarkable example of the school; but perhaps afterwards it would come back to his recollection, and he would wonder why. I do not think then he could ever entirely forget it.

The colours were so strange that words can hardly tell what a troubling emotion they gave. There were sombre blues, opaque like a delicately carved bowl in lapis lazuli, and yet with a quivering lustre that suggested the palpitation of mysterious life; there were purples, horrible like raw and putrid flesh, and yet with a glowing, sensual passion that called up vague memories of the Roman Empire of Heliogabalus; there were reds, shrill like the berries of holly—one thought of Christmas in England, and the snow, the good cheer, and the pleasure of children—and yet by some magic softened till they had the swooning tenderness of a dove's breast; there were deep yellows that died with an unnatural passion into a green as fragrant as the spring and as pure as the sparkling water of a mountain brook. Who can tell what anguished fancy made these fruits? They belonged to a Polynesian garden of the Hesperides. There was something strangely alive in them, as though they were created in a stage of the earth's dark history when things were not irrevocably fixed to their forms. They were extravagantly luxurious. They were heavy with tropical odours. They seemed to possess a sombre passion of their own. It was enchanted fruit, to taste which might open the gateway to God knows what secrets of the soul and to mysterious palaces of the imagination. They were sullen with unawaited dangers, and to eat them might turn a man to beast or god. All that was healthy and natural, all that clung to happy relationships and the simple joys of simple men, shrunk from them in dismay; and yet a fearful attraction was in them, and, like the fruit on the Tree of the Knowledge of Good and Evil, they were terrible with the possibilities of the Unknown.

At last I turned away. I felt that Strickland had kept his secret to the grave.

'*Voyons, René, mon ami*', came the loud, cheerful voice of Madame Coutras, 'what are you doing all this time? Here are the *apéritifs*. Ask *Monsieur* if he will not drink a little glass of Quinquina Dubonnet.'

'*Volontiers, Madame*', I said, going out on to the veranda.

The spell was broken.

LVIII

The time came for my departure from Tahiti. According to the gracious custom of the island, presents were given me by the persons with whom I had been thrown in contact—baskets made of the leaves of the coconut tree, mats of pandanus, fans; and Tiaré gave me three little pearls and three jars of guava-jelly made with her own plump hands. When the mail-boat, stopping for twenty-four hours on its way from Wellington to San Francisco, blew the whistle that warned the passengers to get on board, Tiaré clasped me to her vast bosom, so that I seemed to sink into a billowy sea, and pressed her red lips to mine. Tears glistened in her eyes. And when we steamed slowly out of the lagoon, making our way gingerly through the opening in the reef, and then steered for the open sea, a certain melancholy fell upon me. The breeze was laden still with the pleasant odours of the land. Tahiti is very far away, and I knew that I should never see it again. A chapter of my life was closed, and I felt a little nearer to inevitable death.

Not much more than a month later I was in London; and after I had arranged certain matters which claimed my immediate attention, thinking Mrs Strickland might like to hear what I knew of her husband's last years, I wrote to her. I had not seen her since long before the war, and I had to look out her address in the telephone-book. She made an appointment, and I went to the trim little house on Campden Hill which she now inhabited. She was by this time a woman of hard on sixty, but she bore her years well, and no one would have taken her for more than fifty. Her face, thin and not much lined, was of the sort that ages gracefully, so that you thought in youth she must have been a much handsomer woman than in fact she was. Her hair, not yet very grey, was becomingly arranged, and her black gown was modish. I remembered having heard that her sister, Mrs MacAndrew, outliving her husband but a couple of years, had left money to Mrs Strickland; and by the look of the house and the trim maid who opened the door I judged that it was a sum adequate to keep the widow in modest comfort.

When I was ushered into the drawing-room I found that Mrs Strickland had a visitor, and when I discovered who he was, I guessed that I had been asked to come at just that time not without intention. The caller was Mr Van Busche Taylor, an American, and Mrs Strickland gave me particulars with a charming smile of apology to him.

'You know, we English are so dreadfully ignorant. You must forgive me if it's necessary to explain.' Then she turned to me. 'Mr Van Busche Taylor is the distinguished American critic. If you haven't read his book your education has been shamefully neglected, and you must repair the omission at once. He's writing something about dear Charlie, and he's come to ask me if I can help him.'

Mr Van Busche Taylor was a very thin man with a large, bald head, bony and shining; and under the great dome of his skull his face, yellow, with deep lines in it, looked very small. He was quiet and exceedingly polite. He spoke with the accent of New England, and there was about his demeanour a bloodless frigidity which made me ask myself why on earth he was busying himself with Charles Strickland. I had been slightly tickled at the gentleness which Mrs Strickland put into her mention of her husband's name, and while the pair conversed I took stock of the room in which we sat. Mrs Strickland had moved with the times. Gone were the Morris papers and gone the severe cretonnes, gone were the Arundel prints that had adorned the walls of her drawing-room in Ashley Gardens; the room blazed with fantastic colour, and I wondered if she knew that those varied hues, which fashion had imposed upon her, were due to the dreams of a poor painter in a South Sea island. She gave me the answer herself.

'What wonderful cushions you have', said Mr Van Busche Taylor.

'Do you like them?' she said, smiling. 'Bakst, you know.'

And yet on the walls were coloured reproductions of several of Strickland's best pictures, due to the enterprise of a publisher in Berlin.

'You're looking at my pictures', she said, following my eyes. 'Of course, the originals are out of my reach, but it's a comfort to have these. The publisher sent them to me himself. They're a great consolation to me.'

'They must be very pleasant to live with', said Mr Van Busche Taylor.

'Yes; they're so essentially decorative.'

'That is one of my profoundest convictions', said Mr Van Busche Taylor. 'Great art is always decorative.'

Their eyes rested on a nude woman suckling a baby, while a girl was kneeling by their side holding out a flower to the indifferent child. Looking over them was a wrinkled, scraggy hag. It was Strickland's version of the Holy Family. I suspected that for the figures had sat his household above Taravao, and the woman and the baby were Ata and his first son. I asked myself if Mrs Strickland had any inkling of the facts.

The conversation proceeded, and I marvelled at the tact with which Mr Van Busche Taylor avoided all subjects that might have been in the least embarrassing, and at the ingenuity with which Mrs Strickland, without saying a word that was untrue, insinuated that her relations with her husband had always been perfect. At last Mr Van Busche Taylor rose to go. Holding his hostess's hand, he made her a graceful, though perhaps too elaborate, speech of thanks, and left us.

'I hope he didn't bore you', she said, when the door closed behind him. 'Of course it's a nuisance sometimes, but I feel it's only right to give people any information I can about Charlie. There's a certain responsibility about having been the wife of a genius.'

She looked at me with those pleasant eyes of hers, which had remained as candid and as sympathetic as they had been more than twenty years before. I wondered if she was making a fool of me.

'Of course you've given up your business?' I said.

'Oh yes', she answered airily. 'I ran it more by way of a hobby than for any other reason, and my children persuaded me to sell it. They thought I was overtaxing my strength.'

I saw that Mrs Strickland had forgotten that she had ever done anything so disgraceful as to work for her living. She had the true instinct of the nice woman that it is only really decent for her to live on other people's money.

'They're here now', she said. 'I thought they'd like to hear what you had to say about their father. You remember Robert, don't you? I'm glad to say he's been recommended for the Military Cross.'

She went to the door and called them. There entered a tall man in khaki, with the parson's collar, handsome in a somewhat heavy fashion, but with the frank eyes that I remembered in him as a boy. He was followed by his sister. She must have been the same age as was her mother when first I knew her, and she was very like her. She too gave one the impression that as a girl she must have been prettier than indeed she was.

'I suppose you don't remember them in the least', said Mrs Strickland, proud and smiling. 'My daughter is now Mrs Ronaldson. Her husband's a Major in the Gunners.'

'He's by way of being a pukka soldier, you know', said Mrs Ronaldson gaily. 'That's why he's only a Major.'

I remembered my anticipation long ago that she would marry a soldier. It was inevitable. She had all the graces of the soldier's wife. She was civil and affable, but she could hardly conceal her intimate conviction that she was not quite as others were. Robert was breezy.

'It's a bit of luck that I should be in London when you turned up', he said. 'I've only got three days' leave.'

'He's dying to get back', said his mother.

'Well, I don't mind confessing it, I have a rattling good time at the front. I've made a lot of good pals. It's a first-rate life. Of course war's terrible, and all that sort of thing; but it does bring out the best qualities in a man, there's no denying that.'

Then I told them what I had learnt about Charles Strickland in Tahiti. I thought it unnecessary to say anything of Ata and her boy, but for the rest I was as accurate as I could be. When I had narrated his lamentable death I ceased. For a minute or two we were all silent. Then Robert Strickland struck a match and lit a cigarette.

'The mills of God grind slowly, but they grind exceeding small', he said, somewhat impressively.

Mrs Strickland and Mrs Ronaldson looked down with a slightly pious expression which indicated, I felt sure, that they thought the quotation was from Holy Writ. Indeed, I was unconvinced that Robert Strickland did not share their illusion. I do not know why I suddenly thought of Strickland's son by Ata. They had told me he was a merry, lighthearted youth. I saw him, with my mind's eye, on the schooner on which he worked, wearing nothing but a pair of dungarees; and at night, when the boat sailed along easily before a light breeze, and the sailors were gathered on the upper deck, while the captain and the supercargo lolled in deck-chairs, smoking their pipes, I saw him dance with another lad, dance wildly, to the wheezy music of the concertina. Above was the blue sky, and the stars, and all about the desert of the Pacific Ocean.

A quotation from the Bible came to my lips, but I held my tongue, for I know that clergymen think it a little blasphemous when the laity poach upon their preserves. My Uncle Henry, for twenty-seven years Vicar of Whitstable, was on these occasions in the habit of saying that the devil could always quote scripture to his purpose. He remembered the days when you could get thirteen Royal Natives for a shilling.

Explanatory Notes

3 Velasquez: Diego Valázquez (1599–1660), major Spanish painter of the seventeenth century, considered one of the greatest of Western artists.

El Greco: Doménikos Theotokópoulus (1541–1614), born in Greece, he became one of the greatest and most unique of Spanish painters.

6 exegesis: exposition of Scripture.

7 Christie's: a well-known London auction house.

Tiberius: (42B.C.–37A.D.), Roman emperor vilified as a vicious tyrant by Roman historians.

8 *auto da fé*: the burning of one's manuscripts.

in extenso: at full length.

10 evangel: doctrine, principle.

Nineveh: ancient capital city (c. 700B.C.–612B.C.) of Assyria on the east bank of the Tigris River.

19 K.C.: King's Counsel.

36 *Bureau au premier*: office on first floor.

"Madame est là?": "Madame is there?"

"Monsieur est seul": "Monsieur is alone."

37 rep: textile fabric with corded surface used in upholstery.

38 Honoré de Balzac: (1799–1850), French novelist famous for his realistic portrayal of human experience.

46 *"Monsieur n'est pas poli"*: "Monsieur is not civil."

52 *Le coeur a ses raisons que la raison ne connait point.*: The heart has its reasons of which reason knows nothing.

59 *Le Maître de la Boîte à Chocolats*: The Master of the Chocolate Box.

62 Chardin: Jean-Baptiste-Siméon Chardin (1699–1779), painter of still lifes and domestic scenes, noted for his feeling for everyday objects and for his simplicity.

"Mon petit chou": "My dear"; literally "My little cabbage."

pantaloon: clown's butt and abettor in pantomine.

65   Manet: Édouard Manet (1832–1883), French painter, important forerunner of the Impressionists.

Corot: Jean-Baptiste-Camille Corot (1796–1875). French painter noted for his landscapes.

68   *feuilleton:* ruled-off portion at foot of French newspapers, devoted to fiction, criticism, and light literature.

73   anchorite: hermit.

75   *Du reste:* besides, moreover.

90   Marsyas: Greek mythological figure who defeated Apollo in a music contest and as punishment was tied to a tree and flayed.

Mallarmé: Stéphane Mallarmé (1842–1898), French poet, a dominant figure in nineteenth-century European literature, and a major influence on the Symbolist movement.

Gaboriau: Émile Gaboriau (1832–1873), French writer known as the father of the detective novel.

103 traps: wheeled vehicles, such as dog carts, though here Maugham may mean Stroeve's possessions.

111 St Galmier: a famous brand of mineral water.

120 Chardin's *Benedicite: The Grace* (1740).

122 Delft: glazed earthenware made at Delft, in Holland.

127 a Roland for my Oliver: in the *Chanson de Roland* (*Song of Roland*) (c. 1100), an epic French poem about the Battle of Roncesvalles in 778, Roland is a recklessly courageous and headstrong warrior while Oliver is his more prudent and cautious friend.

136 Sisley: Alfred Sisley (1839–1899), one of the creators of French Impressionism.

Degas: Edgar Degas (1834–1917), French artist considered one of the greatest draftsmen in the history of Western art.

139 Prometheus: in Greek mythology one of the Titans, the supreme trickster and god of fire. For stealing fire and giving it to the mortals, Zeus had him chained to a rock where an eagle would eat his immortal liver for all of eternity.

140 Mrs Langtry: Lillie Langtry (1853–1927), celebrated English actress and beauty.

Mary Anderson: (1859–1940), American actress widely known for her great beauty.

143 *Entombment* of Titian: Tiziano Vecellio (1488–1576), one of the greatest artists of the Renaissance, painted *Entombment,* a tragic masterpiece about the finality of Christ's death.

144 Cézanne: Paul Cézanne (1839–1906), one of the greatest of post-Impressionist painters, had a strong influence on twentieth-century art.

Van Gogh: Vincent van Gogh (1857–1890), considered the greatest Dutch painter after Rembrandt, and a strong influence on Expressionism in twentieth-century art.

Monet: Claude Monet (1840–1946), French painter who was the inventor and strong advocate of Impressionism.

Winterhalter: Franz Xavier Winterhalter (1805–1873), German painter best known for his royal portraits painted in a romantic style.

Brueghel the Elder: Pieter Brueghel (c. 1525–1569), considered the greatest Flemish painter of the sixteenth century, known especially for his lively scenes of peasant life and landscapes.

146 Monserrat: a mountain in Colombia.

154 collier: coal ship.

156 Lascars: Indian sailors.

162 Mother Hubbard: a kind of cloak.

166 gabardines: cotton raincoats.
tarbooshes: caps like fezzes.

167 Bellotto: Bernardo Bellotto (1720–1780), Italian painter noted for his meticulously drawn paintings of European cities.

Zoffanys: Johann Zoffany (1733–1810), German painter who in the late eighteenth century painted contemporary theater scenes.

170 "Elle se respecte, vois-tu": "She respects herself, you see."
copra: dried coconut.
béguin: infatuation.

172 Southern Cross: constellation of five bright stars visible only south of about 30 degrees north latitude.

173 crotons: native Pacific shrubs, with brilliantly colored leaves.

174 "Tenez, voilà le Capitaine Brunot": "Hold on, there is Captain Brunot."
Capitaine au Long Cours: Captain of Foreign Trade.
"enfin": finally, lastly.

178 "Volontiers": willingly, gladly.

180 guava: tropical tree which produces acrid fruit.

181 "Évidemment": "Evidently."

182 que sais-je?: what do I know?
indigè: indigenous native.

184 pareo: a wraparound skirt usually made from a rectangular piece of printed material and worn by both men and women throughout Polynesia.
Eh bien, oui, je ne le nie pas: Ah well, yes, I do not deny it.

194 lapis lazuli: a bright blue sodium aluminum silicate.

Heliogabalus: corrupted form of Elagabalus (204–222), Roman emperor famous for his eccentricity.

197 Bakst: Léon Bakst (pseudonym of Lev Samoylovich Rosenberg) (1866–1924), Russian artist who revolutionized theatrical design in costume and scenery.

199 pukka: first class and genuine.

200 Royal Natives: high-quality oysters.

FOR THE BEST IN PAPERBACKS, LOOK FOR THE

In every corner of the world, on every subject under the sun, Penguin represents quality and variety—the very best in publishing today.

For complete information about books available from Penguin—including Penguin Classics, Penguin Compass, and Puffins—and how to order them, write to us at the appropriate address below. Please note that for copyright reasons the selection of books varies from country to country.

In the United States: Please write to *Penguin Group (USA), P.O. Box 12289 Dept. B, Newark, New Jersey 07101-5289* or call 1-800-788-6262.

In the United Kingdom: Please write to *Dept. EP, Penguin Books Ltd, Bath Road, Harmondsworth, West Drayton, Middlesex UB7 0DA.*

In Canada: Please write to *Penguin Books Canada Ltd, 90 Eglinton Avenue East, Suite 700, Toronto, Ontario M4P 2Y3.*

In Australia: Please write to *Penguin Books Australia Ltd, P.O. Box 257, Ringwood, Victoria 3134.*

In New Zealand: Please write to *Penguin Books (NZ) Ltd, Private Bag 102902, North Shore Mail Centre, Auckland 10.*

In India: Please write to *Penguin Books India Pvt Ltd, 11 Panchsheel Shopping Centre, Panchsheel Park, New Delhi 110 017.*

In the Netherlands: Please write to *Penguin Books Netherlands bv, Postbus 3507, NL-1001 AH Amsterdam.*

In Germany: Please write to *Penguin Books Deutschland GmbH, Metzlerstrasse 26, 60594 Frankfurt am Main.*

In Spain: Please write to *Penguin Books S. A., Bravo Murillo 19, 1° B, 28015 Madrid.*

In Italy: Please write to *Penguin Italia s.r.l., Via Benedetto Croce 2, 20094 Corsico, Milano.*

In France: Please write to *Penguin France, Le Carré Wilson, 62 rue Benjamin Baillaud, 31500 Toulouse.*

In Japan: Please write to *Penguin Books Japan Ltd, Kaneko Building, 2-3-25 Koraku, Bunkyo-Ku, Tokyo 112.*

In South Africa: Please write to *Penguin Books South Africa (Pty) Ltd, Private Bag X14, Parkview, 2122 Johannesburg.*